I0777642

Latin Legacy

by

LYNNE NICOL

Published by Sun Country Chronicles
501 - 315 St. Paul Street, Kamloops, BC V2C 0J4
stoniernewman@icloud.com
First edition: 2021
Library and Archives Canada Cataloguing in Publication
Stonier-Newman, Lynne, 1941– writing as Lynne Nicol

ISBN 978-1-896736-04-4 ebook
ISBN 978-1-989092-78-1 paper Second Edition

1. Time-shift psychological mystery
2. Family Relationships, Ethics and morals
3. Cultural history: Canada, Mexico
4. Snakes
5. Antique cars: 1937 Packard
6. Photography
7. Computer and electronic history

All contents within and the cover of this publication are solely the property of the author. Her creation of the story is fictional and does not portray an actual person, living or dead, to the best of the author's knowledge.

Writing, photo credits, design and editing:
Lynne Stonier-Newman

Editing, layout, cover design, technical design and electronic publishing:
Carol Creasy

Author portrait: Aggi

First ebook publication: April 2021 KDP
Print publication projected October 2021

ACKNOWLEDGEMENTS

Latin Legacy has been written with so many people cheering me on as its characters and situations evolved. All of your listening and encouragement helped me through its many drafts to The End. Compared to my usual non-fiction writing, fiction has been much more fun. I hope you'll enjoy this book you helped create.

Boundless thanks to my beta readers. To Ulla Behn, Rachel McMillen, Christine Hodgson, Kimberley Lafferty-Stonier and Trudy Montgomery. Your astute advice and suggestions kept enhancing Latin Legacy's characters, plot and settings. This story would not be what it has become without you. Likewise, Garth Stonier's editing is an ongoing gift.

Living with a writer can be challenging as we switch between the world we're creating and the one we live in. Reportedly, we are sometimes distracted. Extra warm thanks to my cherished extended family and to my mate, Brian Newman.

This book is for Carol Creasy, friend and computer guru

CHAPTER ONE
- Sophia

I held the old portrait from decades ago up to the mirror and compared it with my reflection. The resemblances chilled me.

Sure, I'm an old woman and scowling while the guy in the photo is very young and smiling. But we are related.

As I tally the significant factors between us, I reluctantly accept that our sameness can't be coincidental. I know, I'm a photographer. Although now I am known for my wildlife series, I started out doing photographic forensic work for the Vancouver Police Department. My job included identifying the probabilities of genetic connections.

I compared the old photo's image to my face again and we could be cloned. Our oval-shaped faces have the same full lips, same narrow noses and same eyebrow curves. We have similar unruly curls, though his are as dark as a raven's feathers whereas mine now have considerable grey.

Goddamn it, Renee! How come I don't know anything about this man?

Until I opened your posthumous letter, I had no inkling you and I are not sisters, and our parents are, in fact, only your mother and father. I am their grandchild.

I want to disbelieve your confessions! I need to talk with you, ask questions.

Renee, leaving me with this letter of revelations is damn unfair! How could you write,

You're not my sister but my daughter, Sophia, and the portraits I've left you are of your paternal grandparents and Carlos, your father.

And how could you just add the line, *days before we were to be married, he was murdered.*

No explanation.

Is dumping that on me being caring?' I snarled aloud. 'Renee, how dare you die before telling me all this!'

My reflection in the mirror was now a fierce caricature of the one I usually see. I took a deep breath and accepted that Renee has always been able to agitate me. Why would that change just because she's dead?

Six months ago, my grandson Alex and I had organized and attended her funeral. We'd sipped tea and nibbled the usual little sandwiches with seventeen of Renee's fellow churchgoers as we bid her a final farewell.

I had mouthed the platitudes about my ancient sister with them but saying goodbye to her was actually a relief.

The next day, after the reading of Renee's Will by the lawyer and signing all the legal papers necessary for the donation of her estate to the church, I discovered she'd left me four blue, plastic file boxes and one big steamer trunk.

'You didn't know about this bequest, Mrs. Nord?' The young lawyer asked as he'd helped Alex load the boxes and trunk into the pickup box.

'No,' I said tersely.

'Holy hell, Gran, did she leave you a rock collection?' The two of them struggled to lift the big trunk with the curved lid.

After my bequest was loaded and we were on our way, Alex asked me again. 'What do you suspect, Gran? Research for her unfinished autobiography and a request for you to complete it?'

'Better not be!'

I felt nervous about what was in these boxes and trunk. Sorting them would be a tedious and unwanted task.

On our six-hour snowy drive back to Erin Lake, I'd mumbled repeatedly to Alex about the unfairness of this inheritance. 'Why the hell didn't she tell me she was leaving all this stuff to me?'

'Why would she, Gran, she was Renee. We'll stow it in your storage room and when I'm up at Erin Lake sometime, sort it together.'

'Thanks, let's do that.'

The next morning, before I drove Alex to catch his flight back to Vancouver, we'd shoved the trunk and blue boxes down the hall and into the storage room, out of sight.

Almost six months later, I took the lid off the blue box marked, 'Open first.' Alex was coming for a week-long stay, and we'd agree to sort Renee's bequest.

Yesterday, John helped me drag them into the corner in the kitchen and first thing this morning, as my fragrant coffee perked, I sliced off all four boxes' packing tape. After filling my mug, I sat on a footstool beside box one, contemplating.

I drank the whole cup before I opened that box and found a brown envelope with Sophia in big letters written on it. Inside was Renee's letter and three 8 x 10 portraits. I guessed the three people, one young man and two middle-aged people were my unknown father and parents.

I scanned Renee's letter. I was right.

I look like him. I again held up my new father's photo to the mirror and compared it to my face.

'Goddamn!' I swore and turned off the bathroom light, headed into the living room, visualizing Alex's reaction to Renee's confession.

Knew he'd say, 'Renee's done it to us again.'

Alex had phoned a few days ago to suggest we open her boxes and trunk while he was here. 'I'm curious about what's in that trunk. Remember I took a brief look and found old phones, tape recorders and big, archaic data disks?'

'No, I don't. But I was exhausted after the burying Renee saga, so probably wasn't listening. Sure, let's open the damn bequest.

He'd laughed, his deep baritone echoing across the phone line. 'Who knows, some of her old artifacts like the platter discs might add colour to my future PhD dissertation, and those six glass vacuum tubes are worth investigating.'

'Renee left me glass tubes in her trunk? How very strange.'

I was happy Alex was going back to university after all the bumps he's had during the past year. Though I think he's doing okay now, moving forward after his mother's death, only weeks after his divorce was finalized.

My old cat was sleeping on the soft green couch, and I sat beside him to peer at Carlos's portrait in the sunlight.

Somehow, his image fit into this room. Perhaps because he looked like Alex as well as my later son. And me.

All the shades I chose are similar to shades outside the many windows and glass doors my house has. I like the sky's delft blue and the greens of nearby trees. The recliner picks up the rich bronze shades of the oak flooring as well as the darker rocks in the corner fireplace's sandstone.

'My home,' I told the image staring back at me. 'I've been a widow legally for a couple of decades, live in the wilderness above a lake and love my spectacular views of trees, lake and distant hills. And I have John, who's almost my mate, and declares he can see thirteen varieties of trees when he's stretched out on the couch.

I wished I could phone him, tell him about Renee's letter but he and his cowboys are branding this week, and Shannon is away in San Diego for three more days.

Alex will be the next reader of Renee's letter. But not until tomorrow morning. I'll wait until then to give it to him as he's warned me that he will be arriving quite late.

I took the photo over to my library table, laid it down and took Alex's portrait off the wall, placing it beside my apparent father's face.

'Eerie,' I whispered. They could be twins, although Alex is probably five or six years older than Carlos ever was, assuming my father was in his early twenties when he impregnated Renee.

Her letter declared a machete was driven into his back in January 1938, five months before I was born. He was killed days before he and Renee were to marry, and since Carlos lived in the port town of La Paz in the southern part of the Baja peninsula, I would have been Mexican.

'Damn you, Renee, why did you choose to tell me after you'd died?' I felt anger, felt imposed upon. How could she have left me boxes and a trunk instead of telling me?

I grew increasingly furious as I contemplated how not knowing who my birth father was mattered. Mattered more to Alex than me as he'd just finished having a complex genetics profile done. Renee had known about Alex's health issues, understood the complexity of his having an ALS genetic inheritance from his dear mother.

'You selfish old woman, how could have you chosen to not come clean and tell us about who had fathered me?' KitKat wrapped around my ankles, meowing in sympathy as I ranted.

She'd been here with Alex and I shortly after he learned about his mother's diagnosis. Renee and I tried to comfort him when he'd confided how upset his wife Liza was about the ALS diagnosis and what it might mean to their future children.

I took a deep breath and lectured myself. 'Sophia, stop it. There's no point in bellowing at ghosts, is there?'

But I was angrier than I ever had been as I realized that Renee had already written that caring letter to me. It's dated January 2000. Janet's ALS wasn't diagnosed until May 2004.

Maybe Alex will be able to add some perspective? Was this bequest something Renee had been planning to leave me for many years?

Why? Why didn't she tell me about my birth father?

I had calmed down as I could almost hear Alex's reaction. He'll laugh.

During our weekly phone calls, we have been joshing about Renee's stuff because a few weeks after we'd put it into the storage, I announced most of it was going to the dump 'unless, Alex, you find things you want. Those can stay in the cupboard until you inherit this place.'

'Not likely, Gran,' he replied, the phone line echoing with his deep laughter. 'I'm very choosy, as you know.'

Him taking my stuff is a standing joke between us. As I downsize, my grandson thanks me but firmly declines whatever it is I'm offering.

He's very much of his generation, sure about his own tastes and wanting few possessions. For instance, when he and Liza separated last year, she asked to keep the antique furniture he'd inherited from his parents.

'Gran, I pretended I was doing her a favour by agreeing,' Alex confided later, 'but I was so relieved she'd taken it.'

'Well, want it or not, Alex, I will be passing family history and artifacts on to you, but who knows if there will be anything in Renee's leavings that either of us want?'

Shannon will chuckle too, I accepted, and ask, "Can you believe it, Soph? She's done it to you again, even though she's dead!"

My dear friend and neighbour has watched Renee and me over the past dozen years, and used to tell me that the cantankerous old woman did enjoy aggravating me.

Shannon's who helps me regain my perspective, as I do for her, and this mess will amuse her.

When I had pulled out Renee's thick white pages, I had no premonitions I was about to learn my personal history is fabricated lies.

What a strange new reality.

On the other hand, so what?

Even if my dear Dad is my grandfather and I'm no longer the Sophia Eriksen Nord I think I am, I am still me. Nothing changes that.

And what does it actually matter to me and Alex if we do have genetic ties to some Mexican family? Perhaps being fathered by Carlos creates a much more interesting family history than the one we currently have.

'Though, I guess this makes me a bastard.'

I laughed at that because, in 2008, what does that matter? I'm about to turn seventy and not having married parents is irrelevant.

But it sure would have mattered when I was born, especially to my mother-grandmother and her judgmental friends. Most people in that era believed being illegitimate shaded both the child's and mother's position within society.

Is that why Renee didn't raise me herself? Why she let my grandparents pretend I was their daughter?

That makes no sense to me.

Why would my upright, overly moralistic grandparents have agreed to pretend? Especially as, year after year, my grandfather lectured me about the importance of my always being honest?

But even back when I was a child, the rules about honesty often confused me. My mother told me, 'To tell someone an unkind truth was cruel and wrong, so a little white lie was acceptable'. Now I understand that, and also tell little lies – after all, why tell someone her new dress is too tight?

But why the ongoing secrecy, why didn't they tell me once I was an adult, a mother?

Did they fear Carlos' family might want me? Or was it to avoid shaming the family name?

Or, could it be somehow related to Renee?

I remembered the letter I sent when I became pregnant with Scott, asking about the family's health history. I didn't receive a reply to any of my questions, though Mother did write to say she and Dad were looking forward to being grandparents.

Strange. I went out on the deck and leaned against its railing, looked down at the lake below me. A fish jumped for a dragonfly and a duck swam by the wharf with her ducklings as I breathed in the sweet air and relaxed.

I accepted Renee's revelation had come far too late for me to react much to it, though initially, it had been quite a shock.

Now, I probably wouldn't even seek information about Carlos or his family if it weren't for Alex's need to have an accurate genetic profile.

I have so many things I hope to do in my remaining years: exploring my revised heritage has a very low priority. But as it is relevant, I'll be seeking information about my father and suspect Alex will want to investigate his great-grandfather and

La Paz family and be curious about Carlos' murder.

I headed into the kitchen for a peanut butter and marmalade sandwich and a cup of green tea, settled into my usual window seat corner to eat my snack and look down at my backyard garden. Tomorrow, Alex will be here on this bench, across from me in his corner.

Again I thought about our first time on this bench together, one of my favorite memories. At my request, Janet and Scott had trusted their precious three-month-old to me, his supposedly calm and capable grandmother. But as his parents disappeared down the driveway, Alex started screaming.

And kept screaming, despite all my tricks for soothing babies. He continued for so long that I had almost phoned my son to plead, 'Come back.' Instead, I kept rocking and singing lullabies and, what seemed like hours later, my frantic little grandson had fallen asleep.

In the years since, Alex and I have shared this special seat often, sometimes just hanging out, other times sharing laughter. In our sad times, tears.

Who could have forecast that only twenty-eight years after Alex was born, both his parents would be gone? He and I are each other's only relatives, and what is special for me is that he's so like his late father, my only child.

Well, to be more accurate, we were each other's only relatives. Now, who knows how many we actually have? But we'll probably never know, unless Alex wants to investigate.

I would prefer to leave it be.

My schedule is only as full as I want. I'm a photojournalist and I now accept only the nature photography contracts that appeal to me because I value time here in my Erin Lake home and with John, here and at his ranch. Shannon's property is nearby and Thompson City is only a half-hour away while Vancouver's a five-hour drive.

John and I have been together for years. He's ready to have the same address but I'm not yet.

So, we'll continue to have separate addresses, even though

Alex would prefer we didn't around us getting older as we deal with winter roads and frequent isolation. But as I tell my grandson, 'It's currently too complex to have just one home. Visiting each other's working fine.'

John needs to be with his horses, herds of cattle and precious bulls while I like living here with this old cat, the lake and my photography. Sometimes, I like to work most of the night to meet a deadline.

But if I'm honest, I fear a mate's needs might add stress for both of us. Living together still seems too risky to me.

We will, down the way.

Maybe.

Alex knows why, has hinted that when the logging truck hit the Packard and Scott, I became reluctant to risk love, afraid I might lose my thick scar tissue I've developed since my son died.

He's right, and giving him the wrecked Packard increased that reluctance. But when he arrives, I will toast its restoration with Alex and congratulate him on how well it looks tomorrow. And I'm glad he's becoming that ancient car's owner. Rebuilding it took him through the worst times of his and Liza's separation and divorce.

Renee had been visiting me when Alex and I had our big confrontation after he'd asked me to sign over the Packard. She'd been dumb enough to interfere, to support Alex when he'd bellowed, 'It's my father as well as your son that logging truck killed. And I want to restore the car.'

She'd told me the Packard had been a gift to our family, it wasn't just mine. I put her on the bus to Williams Creek the next day, then called Alex, said yes, and signed it over to him.

But now, what's mystifying me is why have I never wondered about where Dad's Packard came from?

What are Alex and I going to be unearthing in your boxes and trunk?

CHAPTER TWO
- Alex

When I hit the gas pedal, my 1937 Packard Coupe bolted forward like a racehorse out of the starting gate.

Yes! My adrenalin surged as I guided the ancient car around the highway's twisting curves, eased on a little more gas and kept increasing her speed.

All the dollars, hours and frustrations I'd put into rebuilding my Dad's car fused into this moment. Tires firm on the road, she glided around the Fraser River canyon's tight corners and I knew I was feeling what my Dad felt when driving the Packard.

We burst out of the last corner, and I anticipated the sunny straight stretch ahead where she'd fly faster.

'Goddamn!'

The brakes squealed as I stomped hard, harder - harder!

Bellowed no, no-o-o-o as pedal hit floor's metal.

And I accepted, 'Holy hell, that's a bull moose!'

The massive animal was struggling to regain his footing in the tumbling rocks and sand, frantic to escape the slide, pushing him across the highway and to the cliff's edge, high above the river.

The Packard surged forward, aiming for the big bull!

Thirty, twenty, ten feet!

'Goddamn,' I whispered, gulped for air and turned the wheel even harder to the left.

I kept the brake pedal tight against the floorboards as the moose shook his massive head, right in front of my face.

My innards roiled. 'Shit, those antlers are wider than the Packard!'

No chance, no chance!'

Car and animal collided as metal shrieked!

Something ripped on the passenger's side and my heavy

vehicle swayed precariously.

'Don't roll, don't roll!' I beseeched the old car as it careened between balancing on its left tires, then on the right ones. Once, twice.

'Stop, stop, for god's sake, please, stop! Don't take us over into the canyon, don't!

Finally, all four tires slammed down, gripped ground.

I sucked in air and saw the moose in the rearview mirror, swinging his huge head, both antlers still attached.

I eased up on the brake and tried to turn the slow-moving Packard towards the centre line. Away from the edge and to safety, to living.

Oh, God, we're not turning.

'No, no!' I lamented as the left tires dug deeper into the loose gravel, pulling us toward the hundred-foot fall. Pulling us over the edge to the bone bashing rocky rapids waiting to mash me and my car.

I mumbled a wordless prayer as I shoved harder on the brake and tried to turn the steering wheel.

Finally!

The tires caught and I sucked in a little air.

After what seemed like forever, the passenger side tires gripped pavement. And held!

I drove the Packard across the highway and parked it by the steep gravel bank, as far from the avalanch debris as possible.

I opened the door and stumbled out, unzipping my fly. My stream of urine cut little canyons in the sand.

I remembered watching similar rivulets a few months ago as the rain had poured into Mom's grave, scoring the earth. Zipping up, I wondered whether I'd have been with her again if I had gone over?

Who knows?

'But, goddamn it, you didn't win this time, Reaper. I'm still alive.

I leaned on the Packard, stroked its sleek hood ornament and found my shaky legs were slowly settling, supporting me again. Other than my pounding pulse, I was fine.

'What the hell's going on in my life?' I shouted.

The canyon echoed back '… my life … my life … my life.'

'Why?' I bellowed and the echo replied, 'Why … why … why?

I wiped my nose on my shirt sleeve and nervously checked about to make sure the moose hadn't returned. 'So much shit! Liza's divorcing me. Mom dying. Bizarre medical reports yesterday. Now, a fucking moose?'

After assuring myself the beast wasn't lurking nearby, I walked around my old car, hearing again that shriek of metal and that ripping sound.

Saw the damaged fender and passenger door and knelt to check for anything dripping or hanging down. Nothing, though I knew that didn't mean the radiator, gas and oil lines wouldn't start leaking when I began driving.

I sniffed deeply and couldn't smell anything other than a rancid odour, not from the Packard.

Oh, I yelped and jumped to avoid stepping in the pile of brown. Big animal. Big shit.

'That fender took the main impact. Thank you for solid metal, Mr. Packard. First that logging truck and now, colliding with a thousand pounds of animal! Do you like hitting cement walls?'

I walked around my car, surveying it, relieved the damaged fender wasn't the left one. If it had been the spare tire mount on the running board damaged, it wouldn't have been drivable, and much more expensive to repair.

I squatted down, gripped hard on the fender's edge and pulled. The metal cracked noisily and the bottom half and broke off as my bum hit the dirt hard.

The break was as clean as a welding torch's cut. I picked up the bottom half, walked around and put it across the back jump seat, though ruefully accepting that the fender would need replacing. The specialty body shop's mechanics were unlikely to agree to patch the fender and door on the Packard they had proudly restored.

What's a few more thousand?' After all, the restoration costs to repair the logging truck's damage was already way more than I had projected. The reality is I have way more money than I've ever forecast.

Droll! I've become rich by being divorced. Liza and her father ended up with my lucrative communication company and I do have my doubts whether they can keep it successful without me. Part of Liza and my marriage ending was the two of them outvoting me, then not fulfilling our clients' needs to my standards. That had affected Liza's and my marriage as much as Mom being diagnosed with ALS.

So, I can fix the Packard again, whatever it costs. It's only money and driving Dad's car is as sweet as I'd hoped.

My most immediate challenge is to secure that passenger door. I got the coil of rope from the trunk and wondered how I could secure it closed as I climbed in, reached across and pulled hard on the right door handle, then the armrest.

To my relief, both seemed firm and I wound the rope through both and around the passenger seat's back, knotting it tightly behind the centre of the driver's seat. That way, if the rope starts slipping, my back would feel it and I could stop before the door flew open.

After I finished that, I crossed back over the highway and looked down. My stomach clenched when I saw how close the Packard's skid had been to the edge.

'What's with you?' I demanded of the Packard. 'Are you jinxed, my ancient treasure?'

I remembered Gran, knew there was no way another close call with this vehicle would not upset her, though she'll say as long as I'm okay, that's what matters to her. I'll call when I get cell service at Merritt. Best let her know I'm running late.

I went back and checked the right tire's air again. It seems to be holding, no sidewall bulges. I'll do a few kilometers at low speed, then check again. If no problems show up with this tire or the undercarriage, I'll continue to Erin Lake, though keeping the Packard's power reined in.

Before leaving, I decided to examine the tire indents, which were deep gouges in the gravel, about three feet from the crumbling edge. I could hear the river crashing against the giant granite rocks below me and knelt, cautiously stretching out on my belly.

We would have been pulverized in those foamy rapids, I accepted, the Packard's and my remains washed away in the canyon's many narrow channels. We'd have disappeared and no matter how many searches Gran organized, there might not even have been a trace.

I lay there mesmerized by the powerful Fraser, hearing the minister's deep voice saying such a short time ago, 'Dust to dust.' And then, the terrible sound of wet shovelfuls of dirt plopping onto Mom's coffin.

A loud whistle roused me and I glanced across to the river's far bank where a snake of train was coming from the south. Three locomotives pulling at least a hundred container cars were on the tracks, halfway up those precarious sandy cliffs. I sat up and, as Mom taught me eons ago, saluted those workers who'd built this railway.

I sighed as I stepped away from the edge, knowing I was lucky to be alive.

A pickup slowed and the driver rolled down his window. 'Need any help?'

'No, thanks, I'm okay. Had a damn close one, though. Hit a moose.'

'No shit! Guess you have horseshoes up your ass, eh?' The guy chuckled before rolling up the window and easing his truck around the slide.

'No shit is right!' I agreed and laughed as I slid in behind the steering wheel. 'Okay, my ancient baby, let's go. Don't want to keep Gran waiting.'

The motor purred and the cassette player blared out the Dirty Dozen's theme song. Pushing eject, I briefly considered heaving Liza's favourite jazz group out the window but I didn't, feeling more okay than I have since our divorce was finalized. Glad to be still alive.

Ten minutes later, I stopped to check and nothing was leaking from the undercarriage. To my relief, the right front tire looked fine, so I climbed back in and slowly took my coupe up to highway speed.

I decided the Packard would be fine and wished I felt the same about me, but the medical reports I received yesterday were unsettling. On the other hand, having some unknown genetics mucking up my profile was trivial compared to that moose coming at me.

I wanted to share all this with Yosh, glad to have time with him and apologize for being an ass when I was with Liza and blew him off. But Shannon assures me Yosh is looking forward to us spending more time together.

I'm free again to be with my friends, especially Yosh, and welcomed that. 'Done is done. Liza and I had two good years of marriage and three grim ones.'

Felt goose bumps when a strange thought hit me. Maybe that moose awakened something in me? Even my sadness after the genetic counselling results yesterday seems to have disappeared.

I may have inheritable risks and have to decide fathering a child could be unwise. Disappointing because I've always wanted to be a father, telling my kids about Mom and Dad, doing the same special things we did. My reality is that's a decision for down the way, if I ever meet the right woman.

But learning I have Latin genes on my paternal side is a mystery. Will Gran know why?

CHAPTER THREE
- Sophia and Alex

I yawned as I opened my grandson's bedroom door, less than five hours after we'd said goodnight. 'Time to get up, Alex,' I called to the lump in the bed.

'Okay, coming!' As he turned over, stuck a leg out and groaned dramatically. 'As soon I get rid of this fuzzy mouth, Gran, I'm ready,'

'Don't dawdle!' I ordered, not feeling even an iota of remorse.

'A good morning to you, too. Have I been imbibing?'

'Perhaps a dram or two.'

Alex hadn't arrived until midnight, apologetic, explaining how two 18-wheelers had collided, and the highway had been closed. I'd been worrying as I waited, of course. Minute by long minute.

'You okay this morning, Gran?'

'Fine,' I lied, knowing that I was far from perky this morning.

'Gran, we don't have to go on our dawn boat ride today. Would you rather we go tomorrow and snuggle back into our beds today?'

'I'm up and dressed so today it is, my laddie, we can nap later. But you best get moving if we're going to catch the sun coming up. I'll be outside by the gate.'

'Okay, Gran. I'm sorry you had that long wait last night.' I paused, knowing I had not heard the whole story yet, because as I took the garbage out this morning, I saw the Packard's smashed fender.

Immediately upset as well as furious, I again cursed that car I used to love. And I was mad. Why hadn't Alex told me about his accident along with the 18-wheelers? What had actually delayed him? Had he been involved?

Trying to regain calm, I perched on the chopping block and contemplated the 1937 Packard, again parked in my big carport as it had been all the years I had owned and enjoyed driving it, as Dad had before me. And then, I speculated, had Carlos been its owner when he fathered me?

Since finding Renee's letter and those portraits yesterday, I've been having memories flashing, rather like watching colour slides projected onto a screen. In one, I see me on a red trike, mystified about why Renee had started sobbing after some man parked it by our white picket fence. And years later, Dad smiling as he presented me with the Packard's keys before I left for university, then recalled how Scott had grinned at me when I put a birthday bow on those same keys and passed it to him.

Now, this ancient car with its damaged fender is Alex's. Makes me wonder if the damn thing is jinxed! I dusted the wood chips off my jeans and stomped up to the house to wake my grandson, but not to ask, what happened? He better tell me that, and soon.

After he was out of bed, I went upstairs for my camera and the boat cooler and headed out into the false dawn to do some deadheading as I waited. I enjoyed how the dew glittered on the lawn's spider cobwebs and yellow rosebuds but wished there was enough light to take photos.

Moments later, Alex jogged across the lawn, and I said, 'Come on, sleepy head, we better move it.'

'A hug first, Gran.' He opened his arms wide, brushed his prickly cheek against mine and we held each other.

'What ungodly hour is it?' he demanded as he grabbed the cooler and opened the gate for me.

'It's almost 5:30. But to cheer you up, I have mocha and croissants.' I zipped up my plaid anorak, hung the binoculars around my neck, camera bag over my left shoulder, and pickedup my walking stick. 'There, I'm ready.'

We followed the winding path down to the lake, our jackets brushing the tree branches' damp leaves, inhaling the air permeated with morning's freshness. High over our heads, a robin burst into song.

'Hear that, Gran? One single bird, just one. Even the robins aren't awake yet.'

Turning to reply, I tripped over a root and Alex grabbed me.

'Thanks, cheeky one,' I laughed as I patted his chest and we continued down the narrow pathway, weaving through the tangle of bushes and cottonwoods.

'I love the smell of wild roses combined with the young poplar trees' tang, Gran,' Alex said. 'Even more, I'm enjoying sucking in this wonderful air. Sure is different from my usual freeway's feast of fumes.'

'This is a treat for me, too, because I seldom head to the lake this early now. Though if John stays over, we do go fishing at dawn and he usually can hook a trout for our breakfast.'

'Well, Gran, it's only you who can get me out of bed this early!' We wound past the trees and down to the wharf. 'Hey, who repaired it? Good to have it all above water again.'

'John.' I climbed into our little aluminum boat, settled myself on the back seat, and remembered I hadn't told Alex our news. 'By the way, John and I have decided his moving in with me isn't going to work, at least, not at the current time.'

'He's not moving in this September? Why? A mutual decision? Or yours?'

'Mine,' I replied. Alex bluntly said he was relieved when I told him John and I were considering living together.

'Ah, well, Gran,' Alex passed me the cooler. 'I'm sure you two will when the time is right.'

Nice that he didn't ask me to explain why I was nervous, but my grandson knows about how being married to his alcoholic grandfather had been much more endurance than pleasure. He'd been only eight when Mike died but Scott and Janet taught him to be cautious around the moody man.

As I watched Alex put the oars in and push us away from the wharf, I patted the copy of Renee's letter in my jean pocket.

Sharing it will be a relief, but not yet, not until after we watch the sun come up.

'Gran, I do understand why John's moving in could be too much togetherness, and you might even see less of him, as he'd be away, working at the ranch with his ranch hand.

'Yup,' I agreed. Alex and John are my two big men, caring and opinionated about me. Luckily, not only do they like each other, they respect each other.

'Plus, I'm not easy to be with when I'm working, Alex, I don't like interruptions and need much solitude. John loves living on his ranch and after about three days away, he's antsy to be heading home. I'm the same, enjoy a few days at the ranch, then long to be back here.'

'Is he okay with changing the plans?'

'When I finally admitted I was hesitant, he agreed with leaving things as they are for now. It was fine with him. I suspect he's equally relieved.'

'You're a wise one, Gran.' Alex began rowing again. 'In retrospect, Liza and I caused each other way too much grief by getting married. By the way, she's already pregnant, expecting in November.'

'How do you feel about that?'

'Relieved I'm not the baby's father. Though I do feel sorry that she's having terrible morning sickness.' He gave the oars one deep pull and we were past the reeds, out on the lake's dark water.

Morning sickness was awful, I remembered from my long-ago pregnancy, and thought about Renee. Had she been throwing up, trapped by having conceived me? La Paz was such a distant world from her parents, and she was only seventeen.

Was it because of her being too young that my grandparents raised me? Or was it that back in 1938, she would have been labeled a fallen woman and have few options? I sighed and crinkled the pages of Renee's letter in my jean pocket. As I drifted off to sleep last night in my scotch haze, I'd felt as if I've tumbled down some rabbit hole and turned into a Sophia in Wonderland.

The little boat lunged forward when Alex pulled hard on the oars and I grabbed for the gunnels, laughing as I pretended to be indignant. 'Trying to dump me overboard, Alex?'

A loon answered. His eerie, undulating cries echoed as he swam back and forth between the boat and the shore, and his red eyes glared at our intrusion. He slapped his massive black and white wings against the water, the staccato cracks accentuating his lamented wailing.

Alex whooped back at him. 'Or what will you do?'

Laughing hard, we peered at the dense cattails by the shore, searching for the female's telltale movement.

'There!' I pointed at where she was fleeing into last year's reeds, a chick balanced on her back.

When Alex turned the boat away and headed across the lake, the male loon swam toward his little family, his cries now celebratory.

'The conqueror,' I decreed.

'Doesn't take much to make us males feel powerful.'

We neared the small bay filled with large lily pads and I watched the promise of daylight reflecting on the lake. Alex pulled hard on the oars and said as we glided into the floating garden, 'We made it before sun-up, Gran.'

'We did, Alex. Now, are you as ready for mocha as I am?' I gave him the thermos, extended the mugs and as he poured, my mouth watered at the tantalizing aroma.

We toasted each other and the morning, then as our Nord traditions demand, we chug-a-lugged, trying to outdo each other with good old-fashioned slurping sounds.

Alex raised his mug to me a second time. 'I declare I'm the slurping winner, Gran, but you're still the mocha-making champion.'

Those words echoed, as they were what Scott used to say. I silently toasted my late son and felt so glad that Alex and I were still using this boat together.

Scott and Janet had given it to their son on his tenth birthday, declaring it was his and my Erin Lake boat. The following year, we had started the annual sharing of summer sunrises in the lily pads. It had been tough for Alex and me to continue the first year after Scott died but I'm glad we did

Alex murmured, as though reading my mind, 'I'm glad you and I still greet the dawn, Gran,'

'Yes, and you're looking more like your dad every year is a bonus, too.'

'I guess our dominant genes are the ones you've passed on, as I also look like you.' He paused and asked, 'Gran, how much do you know about our family's genetic history?'

'Why, Alex?'

'Remember I'm a participant in that ALS screening program I told you about? Yesterday, my doctor gave me the results from my recent blood tests and I have a distinctive marker. But what's bizarre is that only people with a Latin heritage have that component. Aren't our ancestors English, Scot and Scandinavian?'

Holy hell, the realities of genetics! I took a deep breath.

'Funny you should get that report now, Alex. We do have more genes than we know about'. I pulled Renee's letter from my pocket and unfolded the pages.

'I only learned that after I opened the box Renee had marked OPEN FIRST. Found this letter and three old portraits on top of the files.'

'A letter to you from Renee?'

'Yes,' and started reading aloud.

Williams Creek, January 1, 2000

My dear Sophia,
Until yesterday, I planned to go to my grave with my secrets, my lies. My biggest one is that you are my much younger sister because you are not my sibling.
You are my daughter.
And instead of burning all my life's records to start this new century freed from them, I found I couldn't abandon your father and his history, knew I have to pass on all my unknowns about

27

his cruel fate onto you.

You deserve to have them. And to know your real father is my beloved Carlos.

If he hadn't been murdered, you would have been born Mexican.

Our home was to be in Mexico City and I would have given birth at his rich Uncle Rubin's hacienda. Eventually, Carlos and I would have had our own fancy house for you, our first-born, and for all the many children we hoped to have.

We would have regularly brought all our children back to La Paz for visits with Carlos' parents and his sister Marie. She was my dear friend.

But my Carlos died the week we were to marry. As he slept, a machete was driven into his back. It devastated me, and his family.

I then had no options except to return to Vancouver, where you were born. And many months later, my circumstances changed. I agreed my parents would become your mother and father.

I had to, but I never agreed to theirs' and others' firm advice that I forget the past. Forget Carlos? No, never could I have done that. And some of him is still with me and has been over all my many years.

Especially because, Sophia, you are so like him.

Why have I decided to share my secrets, my burdens, with you? Because, my daughter, I do not want my truths buried with me when I die.

They are your truths, too, and I want you and my great-grandson Alex to have this information about your heritage. It is your birthright.

And who knows? Perhaps you may learn who brutally murdered my Carlos. Your father was such a fine man, Sophia.

The four boxes I've left for you have been winnowed down so often, I no longer have a clear perspective of what they contain. The trunk's contents are what I have gathered up over the years as I attempted to investigate Carlos' death.

Your father was an engineer and a talented inventor. Those six tubes in the trunk are his, somehow related to something Carlos had already built while he was a student. I never understood what.

I have added to the trunk two platter discs that had been Professor Morgan's, who was Carlos' teacher and mentor. Perhaps the discs' information somehow is related to the big invention?

Know I regret not having asked Carlos more questions, butI was not yet eighteen and I was often ill as well as scared during my first months of pregnancy. All I know is those tubes somehow relate to your father's invention, which was to be manufactured in his Uncle Rubin's Mexico City factory.

I also want you to know how jubilant Carlos was about you, and he was looking forward to being your father. As well, after his parents' initial anger with Carlos and me lessened, they grew supportive of us, and accepting you would be their first grandchild.

We were to be married within the church by a priest. The Father had only agreed to that because of Carlos' parents' support, and that also enabled us to fulfill the many legal Mexican rules about marriages.

His parents decided a big fiesta celebration was necessary and my fancy wedding dress was finished the day before Carlos died.

There's one more thing I want you to know. Carlos prayed for you to be a girl so you could be named Sophia after his grandmother. She gave us her blessings and permission to name our first daughter after her.

Sophia, accepting all this belated information I'll be leaving to you is not mandatory. You and Alex can discard anything you do not want but I need those decisions to be your choice, not mine.

Renee, your loving mother

CHAPTER FOUR
- Sophia and Alex

'Holy shit, Gran! That judgmental grey wisp of a woman was your mother?'

'And your great-grandmother. If only she wasn't in her grave. I would be asking her many questions.'

Alex grinned at me. 'Very inconvenient of her to be six feet under. And her declaring you have a new father in a letter written eight years ago makes no sense, leaves me stuck for words.'

'It is,' I said and wondered if she'd intended to tell me? When I first read her words, I couldn't get past it being a ridiculous situation, me turning seventy and being told who fathered me? I wished I could ask questions and maybe even bellow at Renee.'

With impeccable timing, the loon surfaced and shrieked. 'I didn't know loons took requests,' Alex chuckled. 'Gran, look up, here comes the sun!'

We watched as the golden rays crested the mountaintop, illuminating the lily pads. They became a palette of verdant greens as the sunlight poured into the boat.

The dark bristles on Alex's cheeks and jaw glimmered and I thought with joy, he's so like Scott. Though, now, the shape of that jaw and those vivid dark eyes also remind me of Carlos' portrait.

Sure that, like it or not, we've genetic connections to the descendants of a family we've never heard of and probably still have many distant relatives down in Mexico.

'Weird, isn't it, Gran? Me learning from Dr. Simo that I've Latin genes, then you opening Renee's letter. Okay if I read it aloud? There's so much to absorb.'

'Please do, Alex.' Maybe hearing it aloud will make it credible?

When he finished her implausible closing, 'Your loving

mother, Renee,' we sipped our mochas, said nothing.

I listened to the lake lapping against the boat's chines and a rooster crowing in the distance. The birds began another morning chorus and Alex pointed to the tiny frog leaping from one lily pad to the next. I murmured, 'Like I've been, since I opened this letter. What else is in Renee's stuff? I'm tempted to just dump all her bequest.'

'Want to, Gran? We can.'

'No, I want to know why my grandparents become my parents.'

'A hell of thing for you to need to know, but we could delay. Since it is your special birthday week, how about we put all Renee's stuff back in the storage room? I'll come back in a month or so to sort with you.'

'No, Alex, if we don't do it now, I'll be left wondering what else awaits me?' Renee's unknown history would haunt me until I know what is in her leavings.

'Renee robbed you, not allowing you to ask her questions.'

'She did do that.' I remembered Renee's and my many dreary conversations and wondered again, why? Why hadn't she told me about being in La Paz, about the realities of her life, and stories about my father?'

Over the years, when I had asked her anything about her-self, she'd switched the conversation to mundane subjects. For instance, she liked to talk about the mold on her climbing roses or repeat her stories like the one about the burnt date squares her friend had the gall to take to the church social. And she never asked me a question unless about something she wanted me to do for her.

Alex rowed us out into the open water into the middle of the lake. 'Gran, thinking about Renee writing you a letter eight years ago, what I find most strange is its tone. It's caring, doesn't sound like her. Maybe she was less whiney back then?'

'I don't know. What I don't understand is her letting our parents raise me, pretending I wasn't her daughter. I never could have pretended Scott wasn't my son.'

Alex rowed for a few minutes before continuing. 'Gran, what's also poking at me is whether her confessions are real? Might they be her fantasies?

'Wait until you see those portraits she left with the letter, Alex. Her revelations are real, we are related to those folks.'

'Plus, there's the issue of my Latin genes,' he said as the loon surfaced near us. Alex slapped the lake and at the sharp crack, the loon reacted as only the big bird can. He came out of the water and began dancing on the water's surface, yodeling his protest at our presence.

We watched the dramatic display, and then Alex said, 'Okay, Gran, we'll sort the four boxes and one trunk this week. What do you hope we'll learn?'

'About my father and his relatives, his murder and, above everything else, Renee's and my history.'

'Do you think it might be worth querying the La Paz police, even though Carlos was killed seventy years ago? He must have died in late January or early February because we know you were born on June 1, 1938.'

'Worth a try but I think it's most unlikely they'll even know about it. Those old reports are probably long gone.'

'What about newspaper stories? With the murder victim being a young engineer at his parents' home, probably there was some press coverage?'

'I've no idea.'

A fish jumped in front of us as we drifted, and my stomach growled noisily.

'Enough about Renee and all that old history. Are you as hungry as I am?'

'Starving! I'm ready for three bacon and tomato sandwiches.' Alex headed for the wharf and the little boat skimmed across the lake.

Rainbows spilled from the oars' slicing in and out of the azure water, and another fish jumped and hovered nearby, reminding me that, eons ago, I used to tell Alex the jumping fish were trying to learn to fly.

'Gran, in the eight years since she wrote the letter, Renee stayed with you often, right? She never said anything about her letter?'

'Not one word! She had to see the eye specialist three times a year and usually came for about a week when I'd be her chauffeur to her various appointments.

'Were those weeks hard? What did you talk about?'

'I was okay with her coming as I scheduled my more difficult photo editing around her visits. She liked my wide selection of tv channels and John and Shannon took turns coming for dinner. That made it easier. And, after I firmly requested Renee stop sharing her opinions about you, Janet and Scott with me, we talked about flowers, her health and her friends.'

'Didn't you and John also visit her in Williams Creek?'

'Once a year, we'd drive up and stay at a motel for two nights. We'd take her to dinner and I would visit her minister and doctor with her so they knew me.'

'What stuns me is Renee writing that letter filled with confessions to you, then pretending she hadn't. How the hell could she not have wanted to discuss it?' Alex guided the boat against the wharf, wound the ropes around the cleats and offered me his hand to climb out.

'Got me,' I said as I took it, climbed out on the wharf, then headed for the path. He followed as I huffed up the hill and as I opened the gate, asked again, 'Gran, are you sure you want to sort today?'

'I do but know either of us can holler 'quitting time. Okay?'

He agreed, turned to cut across the lower-level patio to his room and I headed up the back stairs. 'Back in a minute and I'll slice the tomatoes and cheese, Gran.'

When he joined me in the kitchen, I requested, 'First, let's take a look at the portraits on my desk, the bacon's fine on low. We'll compare your facial features to Carlos'.'

Alex scanned the photos, his disbelief showing. 'Who would have thought? Gran, I feel as if I know these people, they are so like you and Dad.'

'And you.' I picked up Carlos' portrait and led the way to my bathroom's mirror.

'Looks like you two have to be related, doesn't it?' Gran held Carlos' photo next to my face's reflection.

'What am I, three or four generations removed?' I was shocked by the similarities. 'Carlos and I look like brothers and, Gran, you look like him, too.'

'He looks younger than you do. I guess he was about twenty-three when he was killed.'

'So probably about five years younger than me, and looking like someone I don't know anything about, does feel weird,' I said as followed her back to the kitchen.

'And who is my father! I've so many questions with nowhere to get answers.'

'There's bound to be some info in Renee's boxes, Gran, and if we're lucky, there'll be details about why Renee was in La Paz, where they met, where Carlos was educated, what he studied and even what he invented would be helpful.'

'Why, do you think his invention might be why he was murdered?'

'No, unlikely,' I judged and sliced the crumbling old cheddar. 'Gran, this is as thin as I can get it, okay?' She nodded and I continued. 'Driving a machete into a sleeping man's back doesn't seem a logical murder choice around an intellectual property theft. I think how Carlos died has to relate to some-thing emotional. Now, is this enough cheese?

'Do a little more, Alex, I like my tomato slices completely covered. Do you want pickles?'

'Of course! Remember I'm the pickle kid!'

'Right, I remember,' I lied. 'I've been considering Renee's relationship with our folks and how different life was back then.'

'Like how?'

'Well, it's hard for you to understand how much pretense there was. In earlier decades, being stoic and keeping one's emotions hidden was highly valued. According to my mother-grandmother, one was not to expose one's inner feelings. Mind you, she had very many rules.'

'Were you two close?'

'That's a hard question, Alex, and I guess the truth is, not really. Mother could be harsh, gave me more little punishments than hugs. She and her women friends all believed it critical to raise children who knew their boundaries and stayed within the local proprieties.'

I recalled Mother's regular lectures to me about keeping a stiff upper lip - never once told that to Scott.

'Alex, the woman who mothered me conformed to our neighbours' and church's rules and expectations. It was a very judgmental era seventy years ago, especially about how girls and women were to behave, and what was considered appropriate. Even more so in the 1920's era, when Mother had raised Renee.'

'She would have been more horrified than supportive when she learned Renee was pregnant?'

'Oh, yes! Maybe. That during the 1930's Depression, one's personal pride became all many folks had left, including Mother and Dad as he went for two years only getting part-time work at the building supply.'

'Could be, Gran.'

'And something else just occurred to me. Perhaps Renee had a nervous breakdown after I was born. Women often did, and Mother would tell me when someone we knew was 'under the weather', and I was not to visit her daughter for a while.'

'Unless Renee left information in her bequest, there's not a hope in hell we'll ever know about your early years.

Gran sighed and pulled the baking sheet from under the broiler. 'Let's eat. The cheese is perfectly browned, the tomatoes are soft, and smell that bacon.'

We settled on the kitchen counter's stools and I mumbled through my massive first bite, 'Best yet, Gran, thanks!

KitKat meowed behind me and I dropped some bacon pieces.

'Only a tiny bit, she barfs easily now. Cats change too as they age.'

There's the perfect opening, and so I plunged ahead. 'Talking about aging, I didn't know the details of your next photo contract until last night. Won't it be overly physically challenging for you, Gran, maneuvering in caves and treacherous seashores? And avoiding those snakes!'

She sputtered briefly, and then laughed. 'Oh, Alex, you and John are alike, hear the snake word and you shake in your boots. Thanks for your concern but I seem to be remaining physically strong and chugging along easily, despite my many years.'

'Good,' I backtracked, realizing that if the slim woman sitting beside me were a stranger, I wouldn't guess she was seventy.

'I will be with professionals who know how to stay safe. Sammy's a savvy herpetologist, very protective of his photographers, and I'm pleased to be doing another of his and David's projects. But this one isn't finalized yet, around the permissions needed from the Mexican government. I hope it will be soon as I'm glad to be heading for the Baja again.'

'Mexico? I didn't know that. What a coincidence, eh, Gran?'

'It is,' she smiled at me. 'If the contract goes, we'll be on the Sea of Cortez in the Loreto area of Baja South, only a few hours north of La Paz.'

She stood up and opened the dishwasher. 'Mugs before plates, please, and how about we do some sorting next? After lunch, we'll go and toss some hay to Shannon's horses, have naps on our return?'

'You're on, I'll take my computer and check my email over there.' Shannon has an Internet connection while Gran's place is beyond what's being serviced yet. Her address is not going to be hooked up until May, 2009, which is very frustrating for me.

I'm used to being online.

Gran knew what I was thinking. 'Might be good for you to have an electronic sabbatical, Alex. The real world is beyond a computer screen.'

I ignored her gentle jibe, knowing how mixed she felt about the Internet's growing dominance. She used it easily but accessing it on her schedules was fine with her. 'How about when I pick up my emails, I send a query to the La Paz police about Carlos' murder?'

'Worth a try but it seems most unlikely they will know anything. The chances of finding any old information in a Mexico police station's storeroom seems slim, and could be risky. If the boxes have survived La Paz's hurricanes, they're probably housing lizards, spiders and even scorpions.'

'Yuk!' I said, realizing again how little I know about Mexico. 'Do you want to start with Renee's trunk or file boxes, Gran?'

'Let's do the files in the box I opened. And Alex, keep anything you want or it goes into a garbage bag' Gran warned as she hung a big green one over the back of a chair.

'I don't want any more stuff than I already own.'

'Well, I don't either.'

I pulled out a stack of files, passed them to her, and got another big bunch for me. 'Remember, Gran, although I joke around, I'll take any family history you want me to keep.' I am my grandmother's only heir.

That thought reminded me I hadn't admitted to my close call yesterday and decided to show her the fender on our way to Shannon's. Seeing the minimal damage the moose did might make it easier for both of us.

'Damn tedious!' Gran complained about an hour later.

'Why the hell did Renee leave you this?' I held up the stack I was about to put in the garbage bag. 'Okay to heave these articles about political opinions, teaching Spanish and maintaining health?'

'Of course! And put these old phone company's pay records from the 1940's in too, please Alex.'

We had almost filled one garbage bag without finding

anything. 'Do you think Renee had more dementia than we suspected?'

'Could be, especially if she packed up this stuff after she wrote that letter in 2000. But there is one good thing, Alex, about sorting this. I'm motivated to ruthlessly hone down what you'll have to inherit.'

'Gee, thanks,' I laughed, even as I rejected the thought of losing her, too. 'But, Gran, let's keep these garbage bags for a while, might be clues here we don't yet recognize.'

'Good idea.'

I pulled out another stack of folders, passed some to Gran, and settled into my corner of the bench.

Moments later, Gran said, 'Alex, I'm done. Let's finish these folders and go feed the horses. We're not learning a damn thing.'

'We might in this file, it's filled with letters to Rene. Most have a carbon copy of Renee's reply attached.'

'Really? Are they personal or business?'

'Mainly personal,' and passed her some to read.

'Better not find my letters to her. Especially the reply I sent her after she wrote me about my letting you take the wrecked Packard. She'd told me I had been irresponsible because it was jinxed.'

Oh hell! I looked out the window at the white clouds scudding across the blue sky, remembering it was only yesterday when I had asked myself the same thing.

Gran continued. 'I wrote her one sentence back: "Done is done." Never heard another word from her about the Packard.'

'You think she might have kept those letters?'

'Could be, Alex. I'm feeling like a voyeur reading these letters. Do you? Renee's replies are so blunt about what annoyed her. She sounds like Mother, especially in the ones to her fellow church committee members.'

'That tone of hers is what annoyed Mom and me, especially when she'd be talking to you,' Alex confessed. 'Gran, this folder's full of requests and information about vacation places. Yet she didn't travel, did she?'

'No, though she came close to coming with me a couple of times.'

'Didn't Mom and I end up going to Spain with you because Renee backed out at the last minute?' Over the years, we'd joined Gran in extraordinary places, usually for a week or two at the end of one of her photographic shoots.

'You were nine then and we had such fun.' Gran ran her fingers through her short curls. 'Maybe what had happened to Renee in La Paz created a fear of traveling?'

'Who knows what she had to endure. Gran, when we went on that trip to Spain, I remember massive birds, what were they?'

'Lammergeiers.'

'Really? That's a mouthful, what are they? '

'Bearded vultures, Alex. They were easy to photograph. They have black eye patches and short bills, tufted whiskers that look like a full beard. And Big. They often have an eight-foot-wingspan, and because they eat bone easily, they are valuable re-cyclers. I got some ideal shots of them, and those have generated good royalties over the years.'

'Interesting work you do.'

'Do you remember where we stayed? It was an absurdly luxurious resort and as I could only take photos at dawn and dusk. We went on afternoon tours most days.'

'You have had diverse projects.'

'I do, which is probably why the contract for the Sea of Cortez' snakes appeals.'

'Well, Gran, if it goes together, could we connect in La Paz and investigate Carlos' family after? I'm considering driving down the Baja. When does Sam expect to hear about the contract? '

I was amusing myself because I already knew it was a go. What Gran doesn't know is he and David, his business partner and mate, were arriving in two days for her surprise party. What Sammy told me on our last phone call was that they've received their permissions from Mexico and will have Gran sign her contract at the party.

'I'm finished and I didn't keep one letter.' Gran stood up, dumped a batch of stuff into the garbage bag.

'Did you notice the dates?' I asked

'Earliest was 1963 and nothing was to or from Mexico.'

'Do you know if she ever used the Internet? Probably not, because emailing didn't start until the late 1990's for most people.' I got up to let the meowing KitKat in. 'Gran, what I keep wondering about is those phone company pay records from the 1940's. Any ideas about why she kept those?

'Damn if I know. Remember, I was a toddler in the early 1940's, don't know where I lived or who was parenting me.' Gran looked as weary as I felt.

'How about having a snack on the deck before we leave. I need sunshine, fresh air and food. Lemonade, cheese and crackers, okay?'

'Please, though I'll have ice tea.'

As I tied up the full garbage bag, I thought of another question. 'Were people more secretive in earlier decades?'

'Oh yes, Alex. Very much so, and it was considered very rude to pry into another's business. Around that, Mom's left hand could lie to her right hand to protect her proprieties. In fact, thinking about it, once they began pretending I was their daughter, I'm sure she would have almost believed it herself. Which does also help to explain Renee; she was raised to be secretive.'

'Well, I'm glad you didn't learn that. You don't pretend, especially to yourself, and don't expect others to,' I said as I headed down the stairs, 'Back in a moment.'

The front door's cowbell clanged and I heard Shannon call, 'Hi, you two.'

'Shannon, you're home!' Gran replied. 'Thank god!'

'From me, too!' I called, relieved Gran's best buddy's here. Having one's whole history become a lie must be so tough.

CHAPTER SIX
- Sophia

'Hi, Soph.' Shannon opened her arms wide and I stepped into her hug.

'Why aren't you still in San Diego?' I asked, squeezing her back.

'Well, give Cecil a convention and he becomes the famous Dr. Fischer,' she laughed ruefully, 'As do many of my fellow computer engineers who specialize in horn blowing.'

I giggled. Cecil could be challenging.

'But the truth is it's because Yosh and his partner Ana are arriving tonight, bringing the moving truck they bought. It's now full of their precious sculptures and being parked up here for the summer.'

'They're staying for few days?' I confirmed as I headed to the kitchen.

'Yosh's also coming for your birthday,' she reminded me as she followed me, pulling the cooler she'd brought. When she saw the papers stacked along the counter, she asked, 'What is all this?'

'Renee's bequest.' I waved at the boxes, trunk and bulging garbage bag. 'She's dumped a hoarder's trove on me.'

'Hey, Auntie Shannon, do we ever need you!' Alex bounced into the room, lifted her up around the waist and swung her in a wide circle, a tradition he and Yosh had started as teenagers.

'Ya set me down immediately, m'lad!' she ordered in the Irish brogue she does so well. 'Ah, Alex, what a good-lookin' man you are, growing more gorgeous each time I see ya. Why, with that haze of black beard, we could hire ya out to the ad man.'

'Hey, grand lady!' He stopped swinging to hug her. 'With that red hair flowing down yer purple blouse, it's you we'll be renting. Though maybe it's not to the ad man!'

'It's auburn, not red, cheeky. Now, answer me! Have you injured yourself, Alex? I saw the Packard's fender, what happened?'

'Oh, hell!' he sputtered and turned to me. 'Sorry, Gran, I was going to explain what happened before we went to feed the horses and you could see the fender. A moose and I collided.'

'Really?' I said coolly and thought, squirm Alex, it's payback time.

He looked at me as he used to when he was about seven. 'That didn't delay me long, Gran, it was the two eighteen-wheelers' collision that happened about an hour after the moose episode.'

'Really?' I repeated and lost my cool. 'That goddamn car! Are you hurt, Alex?'

'A moose hit the Packard?' Shannon tried not to laugh, knowing how mad I was.

I should have junked that car fifteen years ago, right after Scott died in it. Maybe Renee was right? Have I spoiled Alex?

'What happened was the moose's antler hooked the right fender, quite an impact. But I'm fine. The moose was too, I think.' Alex came and draped an arm around my shoulder. 'I am sorry, Gran, I should have told you sooner.'

'Actually, I've been waiting,' I confessed. 'I saw that fender before we went to the lake. My god, Alex, you hit a bull moose? You could have been killed.'

'But I wasn't at all injured, Gran.'

I sighed and Shannon winked at me, acknowledging she understood. She does because in the years since Scott's death, she's who helped me through my devastating grief and anger. And three years ago, after Alex asked for the Packard, she told me if it had been her in that position, she'd have signed the wrecked car over to Yosh.

Shannon's been my closest friend for fifteen years. She'd left her husband, Hito, in Japan and brought their twelve-year-old son, Yosh, to her childhood home on her family's fifty acres at Erin Lake. He and Alex quickly became close friends as Scott, Janet and my grandson frequently stayed with me during summers.

In the years since, we've become each other's family. For instance, when Janet died this March, it was Shannon who helped Alex and me get through the funeral. Because Alex and I are the last of our family, she, Yosh and John are our mainstays

Well, we were the last until yesterday, before I opened Renee's box.

'So, what's in the cooler Shannon?' Alex asked and told her he'd been about to prepare some snacks.'

'Just bring plates, cutlery, wine glasses and water to the deck,' she directed him. 'I've brought the picnic. Come on, Soph.'

I pulled the yellow and blue plaid tablecloth and napkins from the deck's storage box, covered the round table and then settled into my usual chair looking down at the lake.

'You're feeling okay?' Shannon spread out the food as Alex arrived with the tray of utensils and glasses.

'A little stretched,' I admitted.

Alex scanned the table. 'Hey, two kinds of olives plus artichokes, cheese, meats, buns. Now, Gran, have you told Shannon about Renee's letter?'

When I shook my head, he offered, 'How about if I read it as we eat? After my first bun, that is.'

I agreed, split a flaky butter bun and heaped it up.

'Before I forget, can you come to dinner tonight? John, too, I hope. We'll celebrate Yosh and Ana being here and their recent successes.'

'Of course, for Alex and me, but John's a maybe. He and his crew are finishing up moving the cows and calves.'

Alex asked between bites, 'What was new at the convention, Shannon?'

'There are some fascinating high-speed innovations in digital electronics and programming coming out within the next six months. Including some photographic ones you might like, Soph.'

'What's the most interesting new software?'

'Hmmm, hard to pick, Alex. I guess what's the most startling is the short lifespan of programs. Each new generation of a computer's speed and capacity is making our core software obsolete.'

Alex and Shannon can spend hours talking about technology but it doesn't interest me, except for what I use as a photographer. As they chatted, I munched my cheese, tomato and artichoke bun and watched the crows squabbling over something in my garden. I use many of the new photographic options but as Shannon's a software computer engineer and Alex's former consulting company taught agencies and businesses how to communicate effectively online, they choose what I need and install it for me.

'Did Cecil give a presentation?' asked Alex.

'Yes, an excellent one.' Shannon described Cecil's fellow hardware gurus' reactions to his latest invention, sounding proud of her almost mate.

I was proud of him, too, and glad Cecil's medical manufacturing firm is doing well. He'd had rough years growing up,which I knew about as his needy family had lived at Erin Lake,too.

'Gran, I'm finished eating, want me to read Renee's letter?'

'Please. Ready for some stunning news, Shannon? Renee's not my sister, she's my mother!'
'Holly shit!' she sputtered and choked on her mouthful.

'I agree,' and took the letter from my jean pocket, passing it to Alex.

He unfolded the white pages. 'And Gran's and my history and genetics aren't what we thought. Her father was a young engineer from Mexico.'

'Oh, Soph,' sympathized Shannon. 'Having Renee turn out to be your mother is unbelievable. What are you feeling?'

'Damn if I know. Annoyed, bewildered but more than anything, mistrusting everything I thought I knew about my childhood. And wondering what other lies have she and my grandparents fabricated about who I am? So, to summarize,

I'm overwhelmed, angry, sad - and a little curious.'

'And that's just to start,' Alex laughed. 'There's also the strong possibility that we have Mexican relatives.'

'Right. Why the hell did Renee keep your parentage hidden for seventy years?'

'Who knows, Shannon?' Alex shrugged. 'So far in our sorting, we hadn't found anything to help us understand.'

'It would have been a hell of a lot more convenient if she were alive to answer our many questions,' I complained ruefully. 'The last thing I need or want is a different mother and a different father than I've had for seventy years. But when you see the portraits she left with her letter, Shannon, I have to accept that it's true.'

'I'll get them,' Alex said, and arranged the three photos in front of Shannon when he returned.

She peered at Carlos, his parents and the three of them under the large palm tree. 'You two are Carlos' and his father's clones.'

'Gran and I have noticed that.'

As I looked at my grandparents in the sunlight, I decided his expression looked friendlier than hers, though having one's photo taken in the 1930's could have been a stressful.

What happened to them after their precious son was murdered?

Shannon picked up Renee's letter and skimmed it. 'Soph, these words don't sound like they were written by the Renee I knew.'

'It is her handwriting, Shannon. But Alex and I also recognized it doesn't sound like the Renee we knew either. Perhaps because she was writing about Carlos and that made her happy?'

'Her keeping him secret from you for seventy years is unbelievable,' Shannon paused before asking, 'What else have you two found in her files?'

'Frustratingly little. We've filled a garbage bag with her old financial records, invoices, student marks, teaching papers, personal letters. Nothing so far about her, our parents or about Renee's and my early years.'

'Gran, are you forgetting about those letters in Spanish?'

'I am. We've found five letters needing to be translated from Spanish to English, Shannon. My smattering of Spanish doesn't include reading.'

'They might have valuable information, once we find a translator,' Alex added.

'Ana will do it.'

'Who's Ana?' Alex asked, looking confused.

'You know, though I don't think you've met her? She's Yosh's fellow sculptor and they're exhibition partners,' Shannon reminded him as she picked up the portrait of Carlos. 'Ana's Mexican, a gorgeous woman with dark sable eyes, olive skin and curly black hair. Latin-looking, she looks similar to you two. And by the way, why do you two look like you need naps?'

'Well, I need one. We only had about five hours sleep. Plusfinding out about my revised parentage and that I'm illegitimate has been a little weighty.'

'Okay. A nap now?' Shannon asked.

'No, in about an hour,' I declared. I headed to the kitchen, took a large stack of folders from Box One, and shared some with both Shannon and Alex.

I took my window seat corner, Shannon settled into the other end and Alex perched on a stool by the counter. We sorted silently until I announced, 'Done, and there's not one interesting find. Damn. More, please.'

Alex dumped our rejects into the garbage bag and passed both Shannon and I another stack. 'Gran, did you ever have a feeling that your folks and Renee were hiding something from you? Would they stop talking when you came into a room?'

'Of course, but that was usual back then. They were the adults and I was the kid, Alex. In my era, children had to go play or go study or peel the potatoes, and children obeyed the adults without questions. Asking why was not allowed.'

'Which in this era, is almost unbelievable,' Shannon added. 'Almost as much so as Renee going to Mexico and taking a lover at seventeen.'

'Do you think she might possibly have known Carlos before she went to La Paz?'

'Yes,' Shannon and I agreed, though I hadn't considered whether Renee could have met Carlos before she went to the Baja with Mrs. Morgan.

Shannon stood up and stretched. 'Since I need to leave as soon as Yosh phones from Thompson City, I want to see the trunk's contents. Okay if I spread the stuff on the dining room table?'

'I'll help,' Alex said. 'What interests me is two mainframe platter computer discs from about the 1960's, and six glass tubes,' Alex said.

'My god, why did Renee keep all these old phones?' Shannon sounded astounded as they stared down at the trunk's contents.

Shannon picked up one of the glass tubes. 'These are electronic vacuum tubes, or valves, as they're called in England. Old ones, I suspect, from this glass. There are millions of them worldwide, all different sizes.'

'What would these have been used in?' Alex asked.

'Who knows but Renee having these probably relates to Carlos's being an engineer. Cecil might have more ideas about them than I do, '

'When's he home?'

'I'm unsure, Soph. Any chance Renee was a kleptomaniac? Or a spy?' Shannon added facetiously.

'Who knows? Mysteries abound, which reminds me, Alex, you haven't told Shannon about your medical reports.'

'Right. Just before I left Vancouver, my doctor informed me that my genetic profile has considerable Latin genes.'

'Oh. More proof you were fathered by Carlos,' she said to me.

'Yes, which gives Alex a Latin great-grandfather.

Shannon considered that. 'And friggs up the ALS studies about your genetic history.'

'Yes, creates many unknowns,' he agreed.

'So you start again,' she said pragmatically. 'Sophie, I

know these black phones were used in the mid-1940's, and that raises another question. Do you know where you started school?'

'Thompson City, Mother kept all my report cards, grade one to twelve. And I went to Vancouver for college.'

'Do you know if Renee ever lived with you?'

'I don't think so, I just remember her coming for visits.'

'Did she bring you gifts? And was it winter or summer?'

'Books,' I said, surprised I did remember that. 'And she'd read them to me. We'd sit beside each other on the flowered chesterfield, each holding one side of a picture book. It was summertime, because after dinner, Dad always took us for the ice cream in the park.'

'What else can you remember? Maybe a special dinner?'

'Yes, Mother made roasted chicken with dressing and gravy, and used the good china. Renee slept in my room and I slept on a mattress in Mom's tiny sewing room downstairs.'

'What about Christmas, Soph?'

I thought about it and shook my head. 'I don't think so. Can't remember Renee coming to the carol singing or the nativity play, just that I was squished between Mom and Dad in a pew and unable to see.'

'Gran, a professor once told me that recalling memories is like seeding a garden. So, as we dig through this stuff, how about writing down any random flashes you have after we find something?'

'I will, Alex. What I'm hoping we find is answers. Like, did Renee ever mother me and why did my grandparents take me, and when? And, Shannon, do you think Cecil might have some ideas about these artifacts?'

Alex added, 'And do you think these discs might have data?'

'That's another question for Cecil, as are these tubes.' She picked up one again.

I did, too. 'Looks like an elongated glass saltshaker with thin wires inside.'

'So many millions were manufactured, Soph, exactly like

these electronic tubes, though from much smaller to much larger. Even after the 1950's when transistors started being much more commonly used, vacuum tubes remain the core of many electronic applications.'

I sighed and looked out the window, saw a squirrel scampering along the back railing. I remembered reading that squirrels hide twice the quantity of nuts they will need for winter because they don't remember well. Could it have been Renee was like that, literally couldn't sort her stuff so just passed it onto me?

Shannon asked what else I remembered from my childhood. 'Think of the fun things. Did you go to movies with your folks?'

'Never,' I laughed. 'Don't forget, you two, it was very different when I was a kid. There wasn't television until I was about fifteen and we certainly didn't have a set.'

'What can you remember, Gran?

'School, playing outside, usually riding my trike, and then on my tenth birthday, a used two-wheeler Dad had painted blue. We had supper as soon as Dad came home from work and washed up. Then homework, and we'd listen to some radio shows before bed. We went to church on Wednesday nights and Sunday mornings, though if it was a holiday, we would go back to the church after dinner too, for Evensong and sing hymns.

'Gran, let's try something. Close your eyes and pretend you're in a vehicle between your folks. See or feel anything?

I let myself drift back ... and wished I could get my legs down straight but the truck's gearshift was there, no room. My legs were sore when we arrived in Vancouver where all the streetlights were fuzzy in the fog. I hadn't seen that before.

The next afternoon, we're at a party in a park with her and many other students wearing black robes but what I remember is a very long table covered by many plates of cakes and cookies and everyone could have two, or even three. I told that to at Alex and Shannon, both now perched on stools by the kitchen counter, and they looked mystified.

'Hey, you two, what that means is it must have been after

the war if sugar was available for baking. So, I was at least
eight or nine.'

'What else can you recall, Soph?' Shannon asked.

'I kept stroking Renee's blue soft dress.'

'Can you see where you are, Gran?'

'At a park with many big trees and chairs lined up in rows
on green grass, and at the front of the chairs, there was a long
stage.'

I suddenly remembered the stage and speculated, 'it must
have been Renee's graduation because she went up the stairs
and onto the long stage twice. We all kept clapping for each
person wearing the black gown and a flat hat.'

'Gran, what were you wearing?'

I remembered and felt as if I was looking at a faded photo.
'A summer green, new plaid dress which itched my neck, but
the skirt twirled. And I remember Mother talked often to the
strangers sitting beside us. That was very strange because she
had a rule about talking to strangers.'

'What about your father?'

'Dad's hair was all white, Alex, and he smiled more than he
talked because he couldn't hear very well.'

'Do you know if Renee returned to Thompson City?' asked
Shannon.

'There wouldn't have been room in the truck. But I don't
know, everything is blurry after being in the park. How much
can either of you remember from when you were eight?'

'Only fuzzy scenes, like me pushing the big pram with my
baby brother in it,' Shannon said.

'What I can recall best are smells, Gran. You would smell
of apples and cinnamon when we'd arrive, and you'd hug
me. And I remember you always had a big red hat on when
we were outside.'

'Alex, I lost that sun hat when you were about four.' I
suddenly had a lump in my throat and sounded hoarse as I said,
'Scott loved sticky cinnamon buns with chunks of apple and I
always made them for him.'

Alex patted my shoulder. 'I guess my memories are clearer

after I was about ten, like us putting my new boat in the lake. Do you remember Dad holding that long rope? I was learning to row. You and Mom watched, sitting on the wharf and dangling your feet.'

'Maybe our memories don't become sequential until we're in our teens?' Shannon said. 'Soph, what can you remember about Renee when you were in high school? Did she teach you anything? Like maybe some Spanish? After all, she was a Spanish teacher.'

'No. In fact, when I took a Spanish course when I was doing my two-year photography one, Renee wasn't encouraging. Of course, as she spoke and taught classical Spanish, my taking a colloquial one probably offended her.' I didn't add that she also wouldn't answer when I'd tried a few phrases on her.

'I didn't know you've studied Spanish, Gran. Can you converse easily?'

'No, I've a poor accent and a minimal vocabulary, mainly have the courtesies.'

We went back to sorting files until the phone rang and Alex answered.

'Hi, Yosh.' After they visited briefly, he passed the phone to Shannon and told me, 'I'm ready to quit, Gran, done for the day.'

'Me, too,' I agreed.

'They will be here in about an hour,' Shannon announced. 'I'm out of here, need to wash my hair and get the roast in. See you about six, okay?' She blew us kisses and rang the cowbell twice as she left.

Alex and I wandered out on to the deck and he said, 'Before I go for a run, will you tell me about Ana?'

'I only met her at their Seattle Exhibition but Shannon really likes her. And wait until you see her work. Ana's an amazing sculptor. She's been exhibiting in art museums with Yosh for a couple of years now. Do you know they met when she was studying in Paris and she was Beth's roommate there?'

'Paris? Isn't Ana Mexican?'

'Sculptors often go to Paris to study, Alex, just as doctors do. Since Beth was studying contagious medicine there then, she and Ana lived together. They've been close friends since their school days in Boston, though Yosh hadn't met Ana before going to Paris for a holiday with Beth.'

'What area of Mexico is she from?'

'Her family has a ranch at the south end of the Baja, though she considers Boston is also her home. That's where her grandmother lives. Glad she's coming and can read those Spanish letters for us.'

'Hope we learn more from them, Gran, than we have from this first box.'

'I know, I'm finding this sorting tedious, too. Want to take the other three off to the dump, unsorted?' I asked, only partly facetiously.

Alex pretended to ponder, and then said, 'No, all the unknown contents would haunt us.'

CHAPTER SEVEN
- Alex

After changing into my running gear, I pounded down the dirt driveway, pushing myself hard.

What a twenty-four hours.

I was unsettled for Gran, angry with Renee and aware searching for Gran's father's family could become a nightmare for us. But I do want to know about these strangers who are suddenly part of my genetic profile. In fact, if there's ALS in that family, I need to know.

The reality is neither Gran nor I have the time or inclination for endless researching.

And unless we discover some clues in those letters written in Spanish, I think we're spitting in the wind. Renee's bequest so far seems as if she put all her records in blue boxes rather than disposing of them.

After my run and shower, I glanced into Gran's bedroom, saw she was sound asleep, and took the last ten folders out of box one.

The very last file folder was thick, and I let it fall open on my lap and celebrated. Finally, some promising pay dirt.

The little bulletins were from Renee's and Gran's family's church. I divided them into years on the kitchen counter and found they went from 1934 to 1936. I began reading the earliest four-page folder, scanning all the announcements and activities for the Eriksen name.

'Is it morning?' Gran asked as she walked into the kitchen. She looked at the bulletins, picked one up and started reading.

'Lots of info in these, Gran.

A few moments later, she whooped. 'Here we go, Alex, these are facts.'

'Read it, Gran.'

'Okay, this is in the October 24, 1935 Bulletin under 'Missionary Society's News: *Mrs. R.G. Morgan is arriving from Vancouver to discuss future missionary projects and will give a talk on November 17th, 1935. Join us. The potluck dinner starts at 5 p.m.*

'That's the woman who took Renee to La Paz, right?'
'Yes. Do you know that when I was a kid, Alex, the weekly church bulletins were like my family's calendar? Both my parents were involved in the church's activities, though Mom more so because of her belonging to the Missionary Society. And Dad had to work ten hours, six days a week at the building supply.'

'Is it feasible Renee met Carlos though Mrs. Morgan?
'Who knows?'
We kept scanning the bulletins until I said, 'Found it.'
'What?'
'This is in the October 25, 1936 Missionary Report, Gran:
NOTE 1: The Missionary Society meeting scheduled for Feb. 26 is cancelled, as Mrs. R.M.G. Morgan is no longer able to attend.

NOTE 2: Miss Renee Eriksen will be away for an extended stay in Vancouver with Professor and Mrs. Morgan. She will be assisting Mrs. Morgan as she recovers from her broken leg.

Gran gave me thumbs-up. 'Mrs. Morgan must have been Mom's friend, if Renee was taken down to Vancouver to help her. Alex, that might mean she did meet Carlos there.'

'Yes,' I agreed. 'Maybe Carlos had followed Professor Morgan to the University of British Columbia? I know it expanded rapidly in the later 1930's, built big additions and added numerous staff. Around the looming war, students from North America probably stopped going to Britain and Europe.'

'It's possible,' Gran agreed as she read aloud another bulletin: 'This is May 26, 1937: *Mrs. R.M. Morgan and Miss Renee Eriksen will be departing in late June for missionary work in the Mexican Baja.*'

I opened the last bulletin I had to scan. 'There's more in this one: *June 22, 1937: Mrs. R.M. Morgan of the International Revival Missionary Society has announced she and Miss Renee Eriksen, her interpreter and companion for the upcoming mission, will depart on June 28th for La Paz, Mexico. Mrs. Morgan's purpose will be to assess the feasibility of establishing a mission home for unwed mothers.'*

'Incredibly, they're off to La Paz, Alex. Why the hell there?'

'It's a peculiar destination for sure. How would they have travelled, Gran?'

'Probably took a train from Vancouver to San Francisco, Alex, then a passenger ship to a major port on Mexico's Pacific coast, perhaps to Mazatlán, and from there, crossed the Sea of Cortez to the Port of La Paz.'

'What a long trip.'

'And a pleasant one, Alex. Travel by rail or ocean was leisurely', Gran told me. 'Can't you just imagine the two of them? One corseted matron in a patterned silk dress and Renee in a navy dress with a little white lace collar.'

'Proper missionary attire, Gran?'

'Don't know if it's that but Mother was very opinionated about how young women dressed. Modesty mattered, which meant navy or gingham checks or stripes.'

'How horrified Mrs. Morgan must have been with her assistant's pregnancy!'

'Our parents would have been disgraced, Alex, if it became known.'

'Would they have been supportive?'

Gran paused for quite a while. 'Not necessarily. Having a pregnant, unmarried daughter would have been very hard for Mother. Yet, they did end up raising me.'

She stacked the church bulletins and put them into a plastic bread bag. 'I'm going to change, you go on ahead, if you like. John's coming to pick me up.'

'I'll wait for him.'

When she joined me on the deck a few minutes later, she was wearing a multicoloured skirt and a coral top. I told her she looked Mexican and she laughed.

'Seems I partially am, Alex.'

'How many days will you be on that snake project?'

'Sammy has requested a ten-day permit to be in the preserve. We'll be hunting snakes along the Sea of Cortez's shoreline and caves below Loreto while living aboard a 50.ft. cruiser. It has a large zodiac.'

'What happens after you finish shooting?'

'We'll do the primary editing stage at the Loreto hotel. Sammy and David will decide which photos work for their herpetologist articles, and I'll be assessing which photos meet media reproduction standards, weighing whether any could be cover shots.'

'Gran, how risky is it?'

'A little, but Sammy and David have never lost or injured a photographer yet. They are so experienced at working around snakes and being on slippery and unstable rocks. I'm more hesitant about maybe having to crawl through tunnels connecting a series of caves than the snakes.'

'Isn't it tough to take photos inside caves?'

'Lighting is a big issue and I'm planning to buy some new portable narrow light bars. I've heard big snakes are fascinating to shoot but getting quality is a challenge.'

'Fascinating? I sure wouldn't choose to be in caves with snakes! So, Gran, when could you meet me in La Paz?'

'Early August, though that's a very hot time for you to be driving down the Baja.'

I heard a truck door slam. 'John's here.'

'We're on the deck,' Gran called.

John came up the stairs, bent and hugged her before giving me one. Although I'm a couple of inches over six feet, his bulk makes me feel like I'm being squeezed by the friendly giant.

John cut to the quick, as usual. 'You okay, Alex? I saw you've already mashed up the Packard's fender.'

'I'm fine and so is the moose.'

'Holy moley, you hit a moose?

I filled him in on my collision in the Fraser Canyon.

'You've a campfire yarn for years,' John chuckled. 'That fender doesn't look too bad, could be Yosh will be able to weld it for you?'

'I'm hoping. Everything go well with the round-up?'

'Inoculated and ear marked 178 fine calves, and I'm relieved we're finished. My back doesn't like being in the saddle day after day.'

'Now, Soph, tell me about Renee's bequest. What have you found?'

I watched the disbelief grow on John's face as she filled him in on Renee's letter, Carlos' murder and our changed heritage.

'So, to summarize, my dear,' Gran said, 'I've gone from being born in wedlock to being a bastard - though my parents almost were joined in holy wedlock.'

John laughed until tears ran down his cheeks. 'Oh, my poor Sophie, how bizarre! That Renee has even managed to twist your tail from her grave. But, isn't it nice that once upon a time, her life was sweet?'

'John, trust you to come up with a new slant.' She hugged him and started down the stairs. 'Come on, you two, time to get the show on the road.'

CHAPTER EIGHT
- Sophia

'You riding with us, Alex, or taking the Packard?' John asked as his size thirteen cowboy boots clumped after me.

'Taking it, need to show Yosh the fender.'

Fifteen minutes later, John turned into Shannon's driveway and I opened the truck's window, wanting to smell the poplar trees and wild roses. Erin's Lake has four distinct seasons, and I like how each one has a distinct scent.

Though to be honest, I could do without winters. When John's ready to let his foreman run the ranch for a couple of months, we'll go somewhere warm, and I've already told him, probably the Baja.

Strange one of my favorite places is where I was conceived.

Over the years, I've been there often. First time was after I finished my photographic diploma and was a restless forty-year-old, considering divorce. For five months, I camped a few miles out of La Paz in my old van on the shores of the Sea of Cortez. Those days and nights of bucolic heat and salty moisture revitalized me. In most of the thirty years since, I've returned to the Baja for at least a week.

To be with Alex in La Paz will be special,

As soon as John parked beside Shannon's patio, Yosh opened the passenger door to help me down from the high truck and give me his gentle hug. 'Hello, Auntie Soph.'

'Hi, Yosh.'

He stepped back so Ana could move forward. 'Here's someone else happy to see you again.'

'Hello. Ana, this is John.'

He doffed his cowboy hat, gave the gorgeous pixie his slow smile and a full bow.

Ana curtsied with an innate grace and poise, then stuck out her tiny hand which John engulfed in his.

'I've heard stories about you,' she said. 'Yosh tells me them because my father's a rancher too, and I'm always a little homesick for our ranch.'

Although Ana looked slight next to John, I knew her apparent fragility is an illusion. When we met in Seattle, I had asked about the work involved in creating large three statues and she'd replied it built up her muscles.

Now, I could see that tone rippling under her long turquoise dress as she turned to me and said, 'Sophia, thank you again for those photos of Yosh and my Seattle exhibit.'

He snickered. 'Hey, Aunt Soph, be aware Ana needs photos for her retrospective and I've told her you're who can capture her work's nuances. Wait until you see what she has in our moving van.'

I replied that maybe we could trade as I'm hoping she'll translate some Spanish letters.

'Shannon gave them to me. I've already scanned them, Sophia, and can paraphrase them for you tonight, if you like. Doing the actual translations will take me a day or two. They're written in formal Spanish, a style that's seldom used in Mexico now.' She paused before asking, 'Do you know Marie's letters are sad and very personal? Renee and you mattered to her very much.'

Alex drove up, parked the Packard coupe beside John's crew cab and eased out of the driver's seat. He and Yosh slapped each other's backs before Yosh turned him towards Ana.

'Finally, I can introduce you to this guy. Ana, meet Alex,' and winked at Alex, aware he was startled. 'This is Ana.'

I watched with amusement as my grandson took her hand, smiled warmly and murmured, 'A pleasure.'

John had also picked up that Ana was not what Alex had expected Yosh's sculpting associate to be and winked at me.

As we walked into the dining area through the patio door, Shannon ordered, 'Okay, everyone into the living room. Before I go back to kitchen duty, we're going to toast our sculptors.'

She passed the champagne to Alex to pull the cork and held up a flute for him to fill. I distributed the glasses and raised mine to her, silently acknowledging how special this salute to Alex was for her as well as for her son.

Though both she and Hito had been mystified by Yosh's choice originally, they have been supportive of his career. And now, their son was winning awards

Shannon raised her glass and toasted Ana and Yosh, then announced, 'We're celebrating their latest achievement. They just signed a contract for a major exhibition tour over the next twelve months. The first opening is in Portland in October.'

I raised my flute and added, 'Wow! To our sculptors.'

We settled into Shannon's living room, one of my favourite places with its peaceful shades of cream and soft molten blue. I was in my usual curved chair and John was on the love seat beside it. Alex and Yosh took the matching tub chairs on each side of Ana's stool.

'Will you pass the appy plate, Yosh?' Shannon requested, 'and tell us the rest of your and Ana's news.'

'It's only speculative at this stage but even that's exciting. We might be invited to the National Art Gallery in Ottawa next year and maybe to Boston the following one.'

'Impressive! Ana, isn't Boston where your grandmother lives?' I asked.

'Yes, and if this all comes together, how about coming to our exhibition's opening and meeting her? I would enjoy taking you and Shannon to my special places in Boston, I've a lot of them.'

'May I come, too?' Alex asked.

'Of course, and Shannon was telling me about you going back to school to study how our body language communicates. I want to hear more about that as I've studied some about how the same word and the same body language's meaning differs between cultures.'

Chuckling to myself about their immediate compatibility, I

followed Shannon into the kitchen and sniffed appreciatively. 'Roast beef studded with garlic?'

'Especially for you and John, my friend, and I'm assuming you'll make the gravy?'

I agreed and asked,' Have you heard from Cecil?'

Before she could reply, Alex joined us and asked, 'Ana wants to know whether in the time before dinner, you would like her to paraphrase some of the letters, Gran?'

'Fine with me, Soph, we've about thirty minutes,' Shannon judged. 'Once I get this cornbread into the oven, I can listen, too.'

I agreed and returned to my chair. Ana was on the long hassock in front of the fireplace and Yosh was pushing a floor lamp closer to her.

'Enough light, Ana? More wine?'

'Water, please,' she said and shuffled the blue pages on her lap. 'Sophia, although I'm short-talking here, Marie's actual words will be in the written translation.'

'Thanks. Alex and I are hoping we'll learn much more about my father's family from these letters'

'First, a bit of a summary. I'm assuming this is the Marie who was Carlos' younger sister and Renee's friend, so, she is Sophia's aunt, which, by the way, she spells the Mexican way, with an f. And although my excerpting will make Marie's words sound choppy, her formal writing is very gracious:

December 20, 1938

Dear Renee, my little sister,

I miss you so, as much as I miss Carlos. How I wish you were still in La Paz, sitting with me on a rug under our special tree and we were playing with Sofia.

How good of you to let us know she is thriving. Sofia is beautiful in the photograph you kindly sent, and I laughed at the big bow you managed to tie in her small amount of hair. Do you expect it is going to curl like Carlos'? I am happy she looks like her father.

'Marie's letter goes on to ask many, many questions about the baby. Okay if I read just a few?'

I nodded, moved to be hearing about myself as an infant.

'Does Sofia have any teeth yet? Is she sleeping most nights? What toys does she like? How do you find being a mother, is it very hard?

I have good news, Renee. When this very sad year of the mourning for Carlos ends on January 20, Papa has agreed Juan and I may have our banns of marriage read by the priest.

How I wish you and your darling daughter could be my attendants when Juan and I are married on April 15, 1939.

I'm relieved Papa has decreed our fiesta will be much smaller than what your and Carlos' wedding festivities would have been because of two sad reasons.

Madre is unwell, she mourns and prays for Carlos for many hours each day. All of us try to cheer her but she stays secluded.

The second reason is because our family has to be frugal now. Uncle Hector is no longer Papa's business partner. They believe differently about the war coming between England and Germany.

My dear aunt and uncle no longer come to our home, and we don't go to theirs. It is very strange, a little worrisome for me as Juan agrees with Uncle Hector more than Papa.

Uncle Hector is joining a Mexico City business that manufacturers for a German company. Papa will stay connected with Great-Uncle Rubin's businesses that only sell to the English. And he and Uncle Hector will not be able to make as much money as they did working together.

'That finished the first letter, except for Marie's many wishes for you and your mother.'

'You were a welcomed child, Soph,' John said, 'And I find it moving to hear how the animosities of pre-WWII even influenced events in Mexico. It was a tough time for so many.'

'Yes, and in all the next letters, Marie mentions the

troubles in the extended family. Now, this second letter is from March 5, 1940. It's six pages on tiny writing so my summarizing is going to sound jumpy:'

I have been Juan's wife for almost a year now, Renee. Most of the time, I like being married, especially around our sweet private time together. But we are sad not to have started a baby yet. Juan expects us to have many children.

La Paz is a less happy place now, the men argue much more than they laugh. Three months ago, Uncle Hector and his family left on a ship for Mexico City with all their furniture and belongings.

Madre's crying often again, missing Carlos as well as older sister, and doesn't expect to see her again.

Papa has the priest come often to comfort Madre and to pray with her.

Renee, I am fearful for her mind. If only I soon could give her a grandchild, that might help, and I pray to start a baby three times a day.

The answer to your last letter's questions is nothing has been discovered about Carlos' murderer. Papa's furious with the police and they are with him. Please know I will write you immediately when we have any news about Carlos.

I am very worried for my parents because my father isn't making much money without Uncle Hector. Juan tells me that although Papa is a clever inventor, Hector was the company's businessman.

'That's interesting, tells us Carlos' father was an inventor, too. If only we knew more about the family and their businesses. Electrical or maybe something related to communication?' Alex said as Ana stopped to sip her water.

'Most likely,' Shannon agreed. 'But it doesn't mean Carlos' murder is related to his invention. Using a machete seems revenge to me.'

'Though pretending it was a passion killing, Mom, would be a clever cover for a contract killing, wouldn't it?' Yosh asked. 'Ana, what do you think?'

Ana speculated whether his death had been thoroughly investigated, considering how isolated La Paz was back then. 'Alex, do you realize you'll need to be cautious as you ask questions about Carlos? People might be defensive about where their family's wealth came from. Now, here's the last page of Marie's second letter:'

Next month, I have to move from the casa beside my family's home. Juan's parents have given us a dark little house that needs much repair and I do not like it. It is beside their big one. We will be so far away from Madre and Papa, but my husband insists we move.

'Juan sounds as if he had far too much control. I'll be back, checking the oven,' Shannon said as she headed for the kitchen.

'We have about another twenty minutes.'

'Want me to keep reading?' Ana asked.

'Yes,' we all said.

'Okay, the third letter is dated June 3, 1941. Marie starts by apologizing for not writing sooner because she's having a baby in the middle of summer. She's lonely, scared about giving birth, but so very happy to be having a child.'

'I wish I could ask you many questions because Mama is too unwell and I do not like my mother-in-law, or Juan's sister. They enjoy being unkind to me. I've written for advice to my older sister, Luisa-Grace, but she may not get the letter and can't come home. She and many other nuns are helping to nurse the wounded in Italy.

'Poor Marie, having a baby under those circumstances,' I sympathized. 'Similar to what Renee must have endured when I was born. I wonder if she ever considered going back to La Paz to help Marie and Carlos' mother? I would have been old enough to make the long trip by then and Marie's letters seem to confirm I was still living with her.'

'Probably it wasn't even an option in wartime,' Alex said. John agreed.

'As well, remember mail services in the Baja were very slow, even today,' Ana added. 'Now, Sophia, Renee's and Marie's lives become even sadder in these last letters. On September 6, 1942, Marie wrote:

'My dearest Renee, I am devastated to hear you have been in a sanatorium for almost six months and so sad that your chest hurts you terribly.

How I wish I could come on one of Uncle Rubin's ships to visit and bring you my wee Juan. I asked the priest, but he says civilian travel is almost impossible but, more, even if I could reach you, I would not be allowed to visit with you. That no one will be able to be visiting you, including your precious Sofia. Tuberculosis is too contagious.

Know I am very sad, my almost sister, and I say prayers twice a day for you to become well again soon.'

I gasped. Renee had tuberculosis.

'No wonder your grandparents took you!' Shannon said.

We looked at each other as I struggled to comprehend what that meant.

Ana blew her nose, continued. 'Okay, this is from the last letter, then enough of all this poignant history.'

I agreed as my mind wrapped around the reason why Renee had not raised me. Tuberculosis! If my grandparents hadn't taken me, I could have ended up as a ward of the province.

'Oh, Sophia, that's a dreadful disease,' John said. 'Our neighbours' oldest son got it, then his mother. I wasn't allowed to go over or play with any of their children.'

Alex stood up and put a hand around my shoulder. 'God, Gran, Renee had no choice. Lucky your grandparents were able to pretend you were theirs. Wish we could find out that story, but we probably will never know how they managed that.'

'I don't know much about tuberculosis,' Ana said. 'But

when I was little, a cowboy I liked started coughing blood and Dad took him away somewhere and he never returned.'

'T.B.'s a life sentence,' John said, aware the rest of us probably didn't know as much about the disease as he did. 'Thankfully, it's mainly been eradicated in Canada. But in the 1940's, once she was diagnosed, Renee's life would have become controlled by public health.'

Shannon added, 'Yes, even after she was allowed to leave the sanatorium, probably a couple of years later, she would have been tracked medically, with annual tests forever.'

'You must have been tested, Soph,' John added. 'Do you have any memory of going to many doctors?'

'No, only our old doctor, twice a year.'

'Would Renee have been very ill?' Ana asked.

'There were few drugs then. I think the main treatment for TB meant months of isolation, bed rest in fresh air. Even when TB patients were medically cleared, many people who knew that somebody had been in a TB sanatorium shunned that person. And Renee would have not been allowed to be with you, Soph.'

'Beth deals with TB patients in Africa, and she's told me that isolating them from their families is so hard,' Yosh said. 'But if they don't, a village can be wiped out.'

'How the hell did they keep that from you for decades?' John puzzled. 'And why the hell did Renee and your grandparents keep it secret from you?'

'I'll never know that,' I took a tissue from my pocket and had a good blow. 'But knowing what she went through does explain much about Renee and why she was strange. So many losses, including me. '

'For sure, Sophia, for her to lose Carlos, then become so ill she couldn't mother you would have been devastating,' Ana sympathized. 'Shall I stop now, or do you want me to read the last two pages?'

'Read,' I said and blew my nose again. 'But after, everyone, when Ana finishes, let's park Renee and her history until tomorrow. I want to hear about your summer plans, Ana, and details about where you and Beth are going, Yosh.'

Ana said, 'Good idea,' and told us Marie's last letter was dated November 23, 1942:

I received your short letter, telling me you are startingto heal, Renee, and that Sofia is doing fine with your parents. I was happy to hear that.

My sad news is Madre passed away on November 13th. The church was filled when we said goodbye to her, full of friends and flowers, as many loved her. Her grave is right beside Carlos' and I am sure they are now somewhere together.

Luisa-Grace was still in Italy, very sad she was unable to even contact Madre. She'd only received my letter in late March and I'm glad I fibbed in it, wrote her that I am fine now.

But I'm still a little unwell, praying daily that after the war is over, the Church will allow her to visit me and my children. I do need her to help me understand why all these terrible things are happening to you and me, and our family.

Juan is often angry. He says my crying has been bad for our wonderful little Juan. My son is ten months old now and he's trying to walk. Like your Sophia, he looks more like our Carlos than his papa. Sadly, since his birth, he does cry often.

I am having another child in four months, and my good news is that Juan has already agreed that if we have a daughter, we will name her Sofia for my grandmother. And, although I will never tell my husband this, also after my dear niece, your and Carlos' precious child.

My dear, dear Renee, I pray twice daily for you to become healed and feeling very well soon, able to be with your and Carlos' daughter.

'There!' Ana stood up and put the stack of blue sheets back into the brown envelope as the buzzer started in the kitchen.

'Whew!' I gave her a hug and added, 'Thank you! We've gained so much new knowledge but such sad words to read and hear.'

'Thanks, Ana. A little more wine?' asked Alex.

'No wonder Renee became a negative person is what Beth

would say and add, *The poor dear had too many losses, too fast.*' Yosh said softly.

John stood up and followed Shannon to the kitchen, asking, 'Shannon, may I cut the roast?'

'Of course, Soph's making the gravy.' She held the kitchen door for us and told the young ones, 'Prepare to head to the dining room in five.'

I heard Alex thank Ana again, and her reply.

'My privilege, and I'll have the actual translations done soon. I'm glad I could do something for your grandmother as I'm honoured she's agreed to take the photos I need for my retrospective.'

The three of them moved into the dining room where the long teak table and chairs were separated from the kitchen by open shelving and a pass-through countertop.

'One more thing before we stop talking about Renee, okay?' Yosh said. 'When Mom told me about Carlos being killed by a machete, I recalled something. I once took lessons about how to use a katana. Wasn't that the same year we moved to Erin Lake, Mom, that Father bought me a katana sword and enrolled me in lessons?'

'Yes, it was, Yosh,' Shannon agreed. 'And in fact, that was actually like the last straw because Hito had done that without conferring. We were disagreeing often over you.'

'Really? I didn't know that. Well, back to what I've been thinking about. A katana is somewhat like a machete, though the action to use it differs. But one thing to be considered when you're trying to investigate Carlos' murder, Alex, is it would have to be a tall man to drive a machete straight into Carlos' back. Considering a bed's height and looking at the physics of it, a short man or woman couldn't have done so.'

'Thanks, that might help with my investigating. If I can find a very old person who lived with, or visited with Carlos' family, I can ask, do you remember anyone very tall?'

'It's good question,' Ana agreed. 'In Mexico, large or tall men are unusual, and very few women are tall, though that's changing now. So a man - and do you think Carlos' murder was made to look like a crime of passion around stealing his invention?'

'Not to be a pessimist,' I sighed, 'but I don't think we'll ever know that either.'

John set a platter of roast beef into the center of the table while Shannon put a heaping bowl of mashed potatoes down and said, 'The sabbatical from murder and Renee's what if's starts now.'

'Good,' I agreed, carefully balancing the gravy boat as I passed it to Alex. 'My mouth's watering for that roast beef and my brain's wanting pleasant subjects.'

CHAPTER NINE
- Sophia

By 8 a.m. the next morning, I was debating whether to pull weeds or to continue with Renee's folders. Alex had gone to Thompson City to have the Packard inspected and John and his crew are moving the cows up to summer pasture.

The folders won. I poured myself the last of the coffee and reluctantly took a stack over to the window seat. Though listening to Marie's letters had ended my simmering anger with Renee, I was still impatient with her. I wanted our story, not her invoices and mundane trivia.

By the time I'd almost filled a new garbage bag, I was bribing myself. Five more folders and time to water the deck's flower pots, I decided, as I opened an envelope. And found two pages in Renee's tiny writing:

February 23, 1938 - Aboard The Carolina with Professor and Mrs. Morgan.

Dear Mother and Dad,

I know I cannot come home but will you please visit me at the Home in Vancouver before my baby comes? I pray you will.

I am also praying so hard for your forgiveness. Even though I know how very disappointed you are with me, please don't shun your future grandchild, Mother. Even if you cannot forgive me, he or she needs you, and Dad.

I will be the best mother for my precious child who no longer has a father. Carlos would have loved our child and was so happy we were having a baby.

Being February, the ocean is rough. I usually stay in my cabin beside the Morgan's large one but when the weather's not too windy and the waves somewhat calm, I walk the ship's deck, trying not to cry for Carlos. Mrs. Morgan told me it's

71

very unhealthy for my baby, and it is bothering Professor Morgan and our fellow passengers.

I don't know how to stop my awful nightmares about Carlos' being murdered. The Morgan's become very angry when my screams awaken them.

Three more days, and we will be in Vancouver. I will stay only one night at the Morgan's home, and then she will take me to the Home. They are leaving Vancouver, moving to Mexico City, so I won't know anyone. The Professor leaves as soon as Carlos' uncle's ship arrives in Vancouver. Mrs. Morgan has to sell their house before she can go.

Mother and Dad, I pray you will forgive me. Please, please, visit me at the Home. I love you both very much,

Your daughter, Renee

Ana came up the back stairs and stuck her head in the open top half of my Dutch door, said, 'Hi, Sophia,' before noticing I was crying.

'What's happened?' She rushed in and sat down beside me on the window seat.

'A poignant Renee letter, read it. I need a tissue and am going to make more coffee, want some?' I asked as I slid off the window seat.

'I never say no to coffee.'

I had a big blow, told her I can't remember ever crying for Renee before, and changed the subject. 'Ana, you look about fifteen with your pigtails. Where's Shannon?'

'Off to the airport, Cecil's on an earlier flight. She hopes to bring him here before going home but will phone and let us know. May I read this aloud?'

'Yes, please,' I said taking down two blue china mugs and put cranberry oatmeal cookies on a plate.

Ana paused after murmuring, 'Your daughter, Renee. '

'Oh, Sophia, how poignant for Renee! And your folks. And you.'

I agreed as we took our coffee and cookies out to the deck. A thunderstorm was building behind the mountains and the air was as muggy as I felt. All this ancient history was depressing. 'Ana, what do you think the chances are of us finding any of Carlos' relatives in La Paz?'

She sipped slowly before answering. 'I guess relatively good, despite it being so many decades since he died. Although some Mexican people like me travel extensively, many young adults usually marry and raise their children fairly nearby their parents and grandparents. Families are connected to each other, come home for holidays together.

I settled onto the chaise lounge as Ana chose the swinging rattan swing. 'Alex hopes old people might recognize the Packard.'

'That's a possibility. What about Renee's artifacts, is there anything maybe connected to Carlos there?'

'Not that we've figured out yet, Ana, though what Renee kept is so strange, especially the platter discs and those glass tubes. Cecil is the most likely to come up with a theory around why she kept them.'

'I'm looking forward to meeting him. Yosh likes him, though has shared that he sometimes wishes his mother had chosen a less complex man.'

I laughed, having often wished the same thing for Shannon. 'Cecil's definitely complex,' I agreed.

'How?'

I paused, unsure what to say. 'I've known Cecil since he was an intense teenager. Since my late husband and I moved to Erin Lake when Scott was a toddler - he was Alex's father, of course. Cecil came to sell me eggs and I began inviting he and his little sister Lily to come for lemonade and cookies. Both began coming because they loved being with Scott, but they were very wary of me. Their parents were very anti-neighbours and shunned visitors.'

'Do you know why?'

'The father was apparently abusive to the children and mother. But as Shannon's father pointed out to me when I wanted to do something about it, Cecil and Lily would probably be worse off in a foster home in town. I regularly visited with those old folks and Shannon babysat Scott a couple of times before she left for university. Lily ran away when she was fifteen, never has come back to this area.'

'And Cecil?'

'He got a large scholarship for a university in California. When Cecil said goodbye to me, he said he wasn't ever coming back. And although Lily used to phone me very intermittently, it was almost forty years before I saw him again. When Cecil moved back here, almost a dozen years ago now, he startled me, just rang the cowbell.'

'For lemonade and cookies?' laughed Ana.

'To invite me out to dinner after telling me he'd bought Lily out of their joint inheritance and would be building a home on his parents' fifty acres as well as a factory in Thompson City.'

'Did you recognize him?'

'Yes, though there's little of the boy in the elegant man Cecil's become. Shannon was living here by then and was disturbed by his arrival, avoided him for years. Do you know they were previously engaged?'

'I think Beth told me they had been at university. She's looking forward to Shannon being her mother-in-law, seems to know more about her than Yosh.'

'Well, she would, being female and a doctor,' I winked at Ana. 'Long time ago as Cecil's fifty-six now, four years older than Shannon, and they are a couple again, most of the time. I'm sure Shannon's why he came back to Erin Lake and chose Thompson City for his medical manufacturing facility.'

'The secrets we carefully hide from each other,' Ana summarized pragmatically, sounding much older than she is.

I'd asked Yosh last night whether she was in a relationship and he'd shrugged. 'Broke off her engagement to a Mexico City lawyer a couple of years ago. Told me that she couldn't have married him and been a sculptor. She's an amazing and dedicated one, Aunt Soph.'

We watched a squirrel jump from the bird feeder near the

deck, scurry along the railing and down the one beside the stairs.

'I like where you live, Sophia. Having this home is probably like my family's ranch is for me. Always there for me to return to, no matter how many months I'm away.

'Exactly, this is where my roots are. So will tomorrow morning work for me taking your photos?'

'Yes. Yosh and I are setting up my sculpture later this afternoon and I'm to ask you where along Cecil's wall.'

'Right at the same place we photographed his work. I checked the weather forecast and it's ideal so will you be at Cecil's about seven?'

'Of course, I'm so grateful you're doing this. Now, want to start sorting again? She took my empty mug and lead the way to the kitchen.

Not really, I thought, as we each took a pile of folders and headed to the window seat. But I want those blue containers empty.

'Sophia, I keep thinking about Marie's letters, and the fact you never knew Renee had TB. So strange. Weren't your medical records transferred when you went to university?'

'No, the winter before I left for university, our old doctor's house and office were destroyed in a fire, all his medical records burnt. No electronic back-ups in those days. Thinking about it now, I was checked every September and April while my friends only had to go to the doctor once a year. I used to complain to Mother about that.'

'Do you remember those exams?'

'Always the same, deep breathing in and out while the doctor listened to my chest. And then he took a blood sample, prodded and weighed me. In retrospect, I hope the kindly old man was going to tell me when I was adult.'

'Good chance he would have?'

'A maybe, Ana. He and my father were good friends, both church elders, and back then, the men decided what was best for women and children. It seems very patriarchal but they usually did what their women told them to do and I'm sure Mother would have not wanted me told.'

'Do you think you were expected to develop T.B.?'

'Possibly, because Renee would have nursed me but I'm sure I am not a latent carrier. Since I go to third world countries on shoots, I've had so many examinations for visas and travel insurances, been well-prodded and poked since I was forty. And Alex is regularly checked medically because of Janet's having ALS.

'Me too, because Beth lectures both Yosh and me that working with stone can be hard on the lungs. Which reminds me, I better book to get the annual check-up done while I'm staying with my grandmother. Although my folks' main medical place is La Paz, Boston's most convenient for me.'

'Would La Paz havehad a hospital in Carlos' era? What Alex and I were wondering yesterday is whether there might be old medical records for the Hernández family, Ana?

She jumped up and her folders slid off her lap onto the floor. 'Hernández? Is that Carlos' last name?'

'Yes. Why?'

'It's mine, too. My father is a Hernández.'

'What!'

'Yes. I'm only Ana Avila when I exhibit, that's more memorable for a sculptor. And Avila is my mother's surname. Hernández is too common, like Jones or Brown is here.'

'Do you know whether there are Hernández' living in La Paz?'

'I'll ask Madre. She keeps track of the extended family in both Baja sur and norte.'

She thought for a minute. 'But who knows about the Hernández family history in Carlos' and Renee's era is my Boston grandmother. I know she researched it when she came to the Baja as a bride.'

'Where did she come from?'

'Spain, her extended family is in the Barcelona area, and that's where she met and married my grandfather. When she moved to his isolated Baja ranch, by then pregnant with Papa, it was like arriving on the moon. She was stunned to learn he didn't keep in touch with his relatives and began contacting them, made the ranch a welcoming place for the geographically scattered Hernandez clan. Madre has continued doing that.'

'Could we be related?'

'Maybe.'

'Do the Hernández in the Baja have a large family tree?'

'I don't actually know,' Ana admitted with a grin. 'Other than Dad's family gatherings at our casita up at El Triunfo, I know Madre's relatives in Mexico City much better than my Hernández ones. Madre usually took my brother and me to her family on holidays. Oh, and we did go to Spain twice with my Boston grandmother to meet her elderly relatives.

'Does your family still go to El Triunfo? I like that old mining town and stayed up there for a couple of nights, many years ago.'

'Did you go down in the mines?'

'No, though we walked around the old administration area.' 'My folks and brother's family usually go up for a couple of weeks around all the families' gathering, we have a big old place. I haven't been for years, but I'll be going this summer, then continue on to the cabin I've inherited up in the mountains above El Triunfo.'

'Alex is going to be surprised you're a Hernández, Ana.'

'You are?' he said, startling us as he came in from the living room. He came and pecked my cheek, announced that the Packard is in good shape, and then turned to Ana and pointed out he'd been introduced to Ana Avila.

She explained again and said, 'who knows, Alex? We might be distant cousins. And I'll definitely be able to help with finding out about Carlos' family.'

I asked him to pass me more folders and put my discards in the garbage bag.

'How's finding out our family secrets going, Gran?'

'Found a sad letter Renee wrote on the ship returning to Vancouver with the Morgan's.'

'I've never thought about how many secrets there are

within families,' he said. 'Have you, Ana?'

'Only since seeing this bequest.'

'Me, too,' I agreed, though as soon as I said that, I knew it wasn't true.

Sorting our family's truths from Mother's white lies was always challenging. She taught me that a gentle white lie and embellishing the truth was being kind, just as she must have taught Renee, eighteen years earlier. I didn't agree from quite a young age but perhaps that was why Renee needed to be secretive.

'Don't you two find it strange that there is nothing in here about health? Do you think she had reoccurrences of tuberculosis?'

'Perhaps, Ana. I don't know much about T.B. except that it used to be horribly contagious before antibiotics were invented. After, people were cured.

'When I was working on the written translations of Marie's letters this morning, I realized we can probably research she and Carlos' older sister, Luisa-Grace. She'll be in Catholic Church records. Want me to ask Madre how to go about doing that?'

'Yes,' Alex and I said together.

'Look!' Ana jumped up and spread four tiny black and white photos along the counter.

Alex peered at them as I got my magnifying glass from beside the phone and joined them.

'Can you make out the two people by the Packard? I'm sure it's my coupe?'

I passed him the magnifier. 'Look at the woman's hair climbing into the passenger seat in the third photo.'

'Blond, long and curly, it has to be Renee, Gran. Can you enhance these faded images digitally?'

'Maybe. It does look like your Packard with that spare tire on the driver's running board.

'And that palm tree must be in La Paz,' Ana said. 'I just noticed it's almost three, I'm off. Just to confirm, you want my sculpture positioned where you photographed Yosh's work?'

'Yes, keep it four feet from the wall. Is your sculpture more round than square?'

'She's roughly this size, quite a big woman, Sophia.' Ana held her arms stretched above her head, then out wide.

'Do you and Yosh need help?'

'Thanks, Alex, we're good with just the two of us. You can keep sorting,' she said as she went down the hall to the door.

He snorted and I laughed. 'Well, I'm taking fifteen and then am going to do another hour. I think Shannon and Cecil might be coming so he can look at the stuff from the trunk.'

'Good. And, Gran, I talked with your mechanics about driving the Packard to the Baja and they agreed it will handle long trips easily. I am going to drive it down.'

'Well, Ana and I agree that both the Packard and you looking like Carlos might twig some old people's memories.'

'I might have her as my translator going down. Do you know she's riding her motorcycle to her family's ranch this summer?'

'I didn't but that would be great for you, back-up on the trip.'

'You don't think anyone will understand my Spanish, Gran?'

'It's a long, often isolated road and the Packard's old, despite being rebuilt. And although I've found Mexicans often more helpful than we Canadians or the Americans usually are to travelers, very few backyard mechanics will speak English. 'Want some ice tea?' I offered and headed for the fridge

'Yes, and cookies.'

Once we were settled on the deck's swing, he continued. 'John sends his warm wishes and a reminder it's time for you to bring the Jeep in. And after I told him about what we're finding in Renee's bequest, he lectured me about poking into old murders, especially in Mexico.'

I laughed. John's five years older than me and been looking after our vehicles since I was a teenager. 'He's always been opinionated about my travels, Alex, especially when I was heading to the Baja in my old camper van all those years ago. I had many John warnings and an equal amount of spare parts.'

'Do you think Carlos' murder will be well-remembered if I do find people who lived in La Paz then?'

I thought about that before answering. 'Probably not accurately, it's been seventy years. Older people are the same every-where, Alex. As we age, details become fuzzy. And those who claim they remember everything usually jumble up what they think they remember, and how they were involved. Makes the story much more interesting.'

'Not just old people,' Alex chuckled ruefully.

I didn't acknowledge I knew we were both thinking about how his former wife Liza could exaggerate. 'More tea? I want some and am going to get the letter Renee wrote aboard ship in February 1938. She was with the Morgan's.'

'No, thanks, Gran.'

When I passed him the letter Renee wrote on her way home from La Paz, I watched his expression change. 'Damn. Doesn't Rubin's ship picking up Professor Morgan in Vancouver seem suspicious to you? He must have been taking over Carlos' invention.'

I agreed.

'And poor Renee, going from almost being a pampered wife in Mexico City to fearing she would be shunned by her parents. Do you think your folks visited her?'

'I wish I could say yes for sure, Alex, but Dad did what Mother decided. Perhaps she sent him for a visit? Although she was a keen fund raiser for unwed mothers' shelters, I suspect she didn't go.'

'Which makes them deciding to claim you as their adopted daughter even stranger, doesn't it?'

CHAPTER TEN
- Alex

I was glad to see Shannon's van drive up as Gran and I had gone back to sorting, trying to finish the second container before quitting.

'Come on, Alex, we'll meet them on the deck.'

Shannon came rushing up the steps and as she hugged Gran, I overheard my grandmother whisper, 'Shannon, you're glowing. The rift's over about you leaving the convention early?'

She replied, 'that it is. Sorry we're so late, Cecil had to go to his office. But he's curious about Renee's stuff, thinks there might be some prewar and WWII era items. Apparently, that would make tracing them easier.'

'You may have treasures, Sophia,' he said as he put an arm around her shoulder and brushed her cheek before turning to me and offering his big hand.

As we shook, I caught a whiff of his citrus cologne and thought again what an elegant man he is, and found myself wondering about where he found a sable leather blazer? Cecil enjoys dressing dramatically. We're friends, though not intimate ones as I find him interesting, but he can be a little too arrogant.

'Come on, Cecil,' I offered. 'First, let's look at Renee's artifacts, then how about an ice tea or a beer? Gran and I are hoping you'll be able to tell us more about the six glass tubes.'

'Probably not, Alex,' he said, examining one. 'These are just electronic tubes, mass manufactured, and narrowing down their usage is most unlikely. But those old platter discs are interesting, probably from the fifties and might still have data on them. I know a hacker who could check for us.'

Gran said, 'Cecil, please do have them checked. And know you're welcome to take anything.'

He picked up various things and shook his head. 'Not much of value here, Sophia, it's a weird combination of stuff. Renee was a peculiar person, even though it's turned out she's your mother. You are certainly nothing like her, must have taken after your father,' he speculated as he examined the wall phone, then the tiny tape recorder.

'Discovering I have different parents has definitely been a shock to me, though I like learning my birth father was Mexican. The Baja has always felt like my home away from home.'

Shannon picked up one of the six tubes and held it up to the dining room window. 'I think this glass is very old, Cecil.'

He stood close to her while she turned the little tube in the sunlight. 'Might be European but I'm not an appraiser of glass. Could be these are early radio vacuum tubes?'

'I don't know either, how can we find out?' Both of them had wide connections as established computer engineers, Cecil a hardware specialist known for his medical inventions and Shannon a software guru who's also a professor.

She and I can go on for hours about what's feasible in future communication technology because I'm the guy who utilizes that to help people clarify their business communications with each other.

I had hoped the tubes would lead us to answers, and clues about Carlos' invention, but knew finding out anything from what Renee had put in here was iffy.

'Cecil, who could compare these electronic tubes to what's used in an antique radio?' Shannon asked. 'Communication devices seem most likely to me, and Renee's hoard relates mainly to that'

'Could be, because when transistors replaced the majority of electronic tubes, electronic communications devices continued to use tubes.' Cecil picked up a tube again and had another look. 'To me, it's just another electronic tube. But I've an engineer who's a collector, very knowledgeable about how WWII inventions and innovations happened and, basically, took us into the computer era. Sergi might have some ideas. Okay if I take a couple of these with me, too, as well as those platter discs?'

'Of course.'

'But chances are slim, Sophia. Electronic tubes were manufactured in the millions and identifying what these were used in is like searching for a needle in a haystack. What Renee packed in her trunk mystifies me, yet I agree it probably relates somehow to Carlos.'

'And what he was working on? What was his and Morgan's area of expertise? Oh, and what Rubin manufactured? '

'That, too, would be helpful, Alex. But this maze of gadgets sure doesn't tell us. Now, I'll take you up on a beer, dark, preferably.'

'And I would love an ice tea,' Shannon added, heading to the kitchen. 'How did it go with the sorting today, Soph?'

'Slow, those four snapshots on the counter and another Renee letter.'

Shannon glanced at the tiny images as she perched on a kitchen school. 'The Packard looks like Alex's and that must be Renee. Can you enlarge these?'

'Only a little, they'll blur,' I said and passed her Renee's letter.

She read it and sighed. 'Poignant. And you suspect your mother didn't go and visit Renee, don't you?'

I smiled, glad Shannon knew me so well. 'Yes. But it's what she wrote about the Morgans that interests me most. Rubin's ship picking him up must mean he was continuing with the development of Carlos' invention immediately. And whatever it was had value to Rubin. Makes me suspicious.'

'If only we knew.'

'Shannon, I've had a wild idea that it might have been the core of all this. What if the whole missionary story was a ruse, created as the reason the Morgans had to stay in La Paz?'

'Gran, that's a stretch,' I protested as I took two bottles of beer from the fridge. 'That missionary trip was planned over many months.'

'It is going way far out, Soph. Yet on the other hand, if the professor wanted ownership of Carlos' invention, it would have given him an excuse to live in La Paz.'

'Which also means you think Professor Morgan hired someone to murder Carlos?' I asked, knowing I sounded as doubtful as I was. A professor authorizing use of a machete didn't seem at all likely to me. 'Didn't having him alive until they were in Mexico City make more sense?' I added as I headed back to the dining room.

Cecil had the bottom plate off an old phone. 'This is effective and so simplistic, Alex. Makes me wonder if we engineers aren't becoming overly complex? These phones are a series of small sequential upgrades. Maybe that's why she kept them?'

'We know from her files, Cecil, that she worked for a phone company in the forties. What Gran and I assumed was she was an operator, but maybe she was an assembler?'

'That makes sense, after she got out of the sanitorium, assembling phones could have been her first job. She could do it at whatever speed her health allowed,' he pointed out.

'I haven't thought about what she did on her release. Assembling phones makes sense, would have also given her time to study because she did become a Spanish instructor. And Renee probably wasn't allowed to have Gran back living with her. It seems so inconceivable Gran wasn't told about all this.'

'Not to me, Alex, because as you know, I was a battered kid. I understand secrets,' he said and headed for the kitchen. 'Sophia, how old do you think you were when Renee became ill?'

'Must have been two or three when she was hospitalized, Cecil. I don't remember anything before my grandparents took over as my parents.'

Shannon offered Cecil a cookie from the jar and he took two. 'Eating cookies with beer means I am hungry.'

'Dinner's leftovers at my place, my dear, and Soph and Alex are joining us.'

'Sounds good, but before we head out, I've another question about that invention. Do you think it was finished, ready to be manufactured?'

Gran and I looked at each other and nodded.

'That's why I was going to be born in Mexico City,' she said. 'I suspect before Renee became pregnant, Carlos was moving to his Uncle Rubin's and starting work in his manufacturing facilities after the holidays. Rubin owning ships means he was a powerful man, so my pending arrival didn't change his and Carlos' plans, just delayed them a few weeks.

I added that I thought Rubin probably funded and organized his nephew's education and was who'd bought him a Packard when he finished his first degree. 'Cecil, what are the chances of finding out what Mexican inventions were made in 1938?'

'Highly unlikely, unless Rubin's factory is still functioning?'

'We don't know that yet, but Ana is asking her uncle, a Mexico City lawyer, to find out,' I said.

'Good, because tracing inventions is complex. Although each country has patent registries, those are often incomplete as patent pending delays are usual. And that prewar and WWII world was a secretive era. Do you realize we are only learning some details about what actually happened with the scientific evolution now? Those records are finally being unsealed.

'We can speculate endlessly but there are no facts,' Shannon summarized, sounding like the pragmatic scientist she is.'See you about seven, Soph?

'Sure, Alex and I'll be there. By the way, tomorrow night, let's dress up for our dinner in town, okay?'

'Of course, it's your big birthday,' Shannon leaned down and brushed Gran's cheek, and gave me a surreptitious nudge as she raised her eyebrows.

I nodded slightly, acknowledging that as far as I knew, we were managing to keep what was actually happening tomorrow night a surprise. John, Shannon and I had been scheming for months, planning Gran's 70th birthday celebration.

'Come on, Shannon,' Cecil said and told us getting the old platter discs examined would take a while but his engineer would probably have an opinion about the electronic tubes soon.

'Great,' Gran said. 'Oh, and Cecil, I'm using your wall and

patio again, taking photos of Ana's sculpture tomorrow morning about seven.'

'You know any time, Sophia. I'll be gone, early meeting.'

After they left, I offered, 'I'm off for a row, Gran. Want to come?

'No, thanks. A fast walk is what I need, and a nap. First, a question - do you know what Cecil was referring to about WWII records?

'I've read a bit about archival records being found that are being shared with the worldwide scientific community.'

'They cooperate with each other?'

'A little, Gran, but I don't think it actually does or ever did. The competition to be first remains ruthless and secrecy is the reality. I'm speculating Carlos' invention was some innovative communication device, but I don't think we'll ever know what it was.'

She laughed. 'I agreed. And my second question is whether you suspect he was murdered because of it because I don't.'

'Me either, my gut feeling is his death didn't relate to his invention.'

We'd gone out on the deck and were leaning on the railing, watching a stellar jay in the nearby bird feeder. He fluffed out his sapphire blue feathers and scratched through the seeds as though he was performing for us.

'Alex, his scratching is like what we're doing, sorting this damn bequest. I want to know whether you have any inclination to holler 'let's quit now', because, I would be easy with that.'

'Well, it's a long way from how we planned to spend your birthday week. But I'm looking forward to driving to and digging around in La Paz. Maybe we'll find some relatives, which is partly around my medical history but more because I'm curious. After we do that, let's dispose of her leavings, donate what we can of the artifacts neither of us want and dispose of the rest.'

'Gone will be good,' Gran agreed immediately. 'Certainly, I've had unexpected gifts from her bequest, like our going to

be together in La Paz and my being able to feel compassion for
Renee. But that's quite enough.'

CHAPTER ELEVEN
- Sophia

I parked in Cecil's circular driveway the next morning beside Ana's slinky red sports car. She jumped out, wearing a swirling black shirt and white culottes.

'Hi, Sophia, how are you? I'm so excited. Now, what can I carry?'

'A grand day it is, a clear sky and no wind are ideal.' I passed her the tripod and my bulky attachment bag before shrugging on my camera knapsack. 'I've brought two digital cameras and my ancient manual one for black and whites, all well with you?'

'I'm fine, though have a drippy nose. What's blossoming?'

'The sage, tangy, isn't it? Makes me sneeze, too. Now, what are you visualizing for your retrospective's photos? I need to understand that very clearly before we start.'

Ana and I stopped to look at Cecil's magnificent fountain, which was ten feet tall with seven waterspouts.

'This makes me a little homesick, my great-uncle's fountain in Mexico City is similar to this, a miniature mountain of waterfalls.'

'Tell Cecil that, he's very proud of this one.' I remembered the summer when Yosh and Alex help him build it. The three of them had a good time, hauling rock, gravel and cement, and I took the photo of the boys holding their shovels high, which won second prize in an international black and white photo competition. 'Ana, describe where photos will go in your booklet. All are black and white?'

'Yes. I would like a very dramatic cover photo that wraps around to cover about half the back one, and various sizes for inside. I do have a few already of my earlier work. And, Sophia, please invoice me at your professional rate.'

'No, remember? We're trading. You're Alex's and my

official translator. You interpreting Marie's letters was invaluable. And, my dear woman, do you realize what a relief it is for me that you'll be overseeing who Alex hires to help him communicate in La Paz? I'm honoured to be photographing your work.

'Okay,' she smiled and waved her arm at Cecil's vast patio. 'When Yosh brought me here yesterday, maneuvering the forklift with my sculpture through this amazing oasis was somewhat challenging. He's proud of it, told me those two summers working here with Alex were special.'

'Cecil paid them generously and it was an ideal change from university. He's been generous with me, offering me full use. I regularly take photos here and am welcomed to float in his exercise creek anytime. It's heated, seven feet deep, a stretched-out swimming pool.'

We walked past the chaise lounges, glass tables and many potted trees and flowering bushes. 'His curved tower wall is an ideal backdrop, Ana, as its stucco turns a velvety green in this early morning light.'

'What's in the big tower room? The views must be wonderful.'

'Shannon and I call it Cecil's Citadel. It's his library and office, has amazing views. I especially like it on a starry night or in a turbulent storm, but my favorite feature is the varying views from the eight elongated windows that follow the curve of the tower's stairwell.'

Ana asked whether Cecil had created the house's design himself or had an architect.

'Both, but it's all Cecil's creativity. I think Yosh is as proud of the end result as Cecil is. They spent many hours pouring over its architectural drawings together.'

I stopped so abruptly she walked into me and murmured, 'Sorry.'

'Ana, she's magnificent!'

Her towering sculpture took my breath away, just as a spectacular sunset, a smiling baby or a hummingbird can.

'She's a celebration of light and magic.'

'Thanks, Sophia.'

As I contemplated the huge bronze sculpture, the glimmering wires crisscrossing her torso and upper half mesmerized me. The sun's rays played on them and she looked as if she were dancing with joy.

I recalled I needed to take her photos before this light disappears. 'Ana, she awes me.'

'Do you think she'll photograph well? I know capturing her wires is not an easy challenge.'

Sympathizing with her artist's angst, I nodded slowly as I pondered. Capturing this vision was definitely a challenge, how can I capture that fluidity of light?

In all my years as a photographer, I've never shot anything similar, and it's strange to find myself feeling nervous. What I finally realized was that because of the wires, this massive sculpture appears alive, similar to a moving bird or snake slithering up a leafy tree.

I recognized the techniques required are those I teach in one of my photography workshops. Its wordy title, 'How To Focus On Negative Space To Capture Movement' summarizes my challenges here.

I felt like a neophyte as I breathed slow breaths, fastened my digital camera to the tripod and adjusted the focus. I closed my eyes, counted five seconds before slowly opening them, then took shot after shot. Then, as each of my cameras have different features, I switched to my other digital and repeated the process. Some of the shots elated me and I hoped that the camera was capturing the wires' light and movement I was seeing through the lenses.

'Can I do anything?' Ana asked me when I stopped to unscrew the second digital and attached my manual onto the tripod. Since the photographs were for print, I would also use old techniques, develop black and whites in my dark room where I had maximum control.

'Yes, stand beside her and look up, it will give size perspective. Ana, what are her dimensions? Though I guess that's confusing to judge around her wires. Have you named her?'

She beamed at me as she stepped near her sculpture. 'I call her Phoenix, which is a little pretentious but seems right for her. She's just over seven feet tall and about four feet wide including her wires. Weight, almost a ton.

'Phoenix is perfect, Ana, she is powerful and luminous.'

My knowledge of Greek mythology is slight but this combination of wires and bronze somehow reminds me of the poem a friend gave me after Scott died. It's about a phoenix going forward, finding her light again, and in the fourteen years since I lost my precious son, I still read it every July 21st.

This Phoenix reminded me of those words and I'm awed by how gifted Ana is. So young to be able to hone stone into this, I mused as I switched again to my other digital camera.

I need fast, clean shots to capture how the wires weave in and out of the bronze nymph's curvy core. Each one is angled slightly differently to create the illusion that Phoenix's dancing. It's like trying to record the little rainbows on drifting snow or the sun on blowing autumn leaves.

'Ana, do you realize you've created magic?'

'Thank you,' she grinned at me, her chocolate eyes glowing. 'Thanks, Sophia.'

I hid my myriad of emotions with pragmatism. 'When we check these photos, you are to be honest, Ana, blunt. If today's takes of Phoenix are not quite right, I'll take more tomorrow, perhaps half an hour earlier for a softer light. Although I'm the technical judge of each photo's quality, you decide what is right for your retrospective.'

'Okay,' Ana agreed, and then changed her mind. 'No, Sophia, I need your recommendations, opinions, about which photos will reproduce best.'

'Okay,' I agreed, appreciative she understood that. 'Eliminating the ones that won't print well is critical. Now, tell me about creating Phoenix and how you welded those fine wires. Oh, and do you want close-ups of any specific areas or only full view photos?'

She considered. 'Both, please, because I give welding workshops as well as sculpting ones. Enlargements of where the wires appear to pierce her core would be helpful. I had so many failures at first, Sophia, welding became my biggest challenge. But worth it now as it's her wires that makes her interesting.'

'How many welds are there?'

'Thirty-six as there are eighteen wires. It was complex welding.'

'Where did you learn to weld like that?'

'I grew up watching Uncle, he was our blacksmith, and almost a family member. He'd apprenticed with a master craftsman in Italy when he was a teenager, came to Mexico after that and, somehow, my grandmother met him, hired him.'

She paused and I sensed she was editing what to tell me.

'They became very good friends. So, when I turned ten, Madre allowed me to go into Uncle's welding shop and he started teaching me. I did my first weld on my eleventh birthday and he continued giving me lessons when I returned from my grandmother's every summer. Do you know that after elementary grades, I went to school in Boston?' She dug out a tissue and blew her nose. 'Uncle died a few months ago.'

'I'm sorry, Ana.'

'Yes, it's hard, even though he'd told me it was nearing his time when I was home last Christmas.'

'Your mentor as well as a dear friend?'

'He taught me so much. In all my training since, I've had wonderful teachers but no one who could weld like Uncle.

Once I turned fifteen, he let me weld whatever I wanted, taught me how the various metals react to welds,' she sniffled. 'He's who taught me how to make the finest of cuts with the fire nozzles'.

'So, Phoenix with all her multitude of welds is your tribute to him?'

She blew one more time, then grinned at me. 'That's a lovely thought, thanks. Phoenix does honour everything Uncle taught me.'

'Did he also create with metals?'

'Miniatures only, did intricate work to create a tiny horse and cowboy, a child looking at a flower or a cactus in bloom. He never sold anything he made, gifted what he made to the many people he loved or to museums.' She perched on a chaise and looked at Phoenix. 'But Uncle told me I am not to follow his example, advised me to charge lots.'

'Good policy,' I laughed and recognized she'd been as lucky with her mentor as I'd been. Using negative space techniques today had reminded me of that crusty proud Scottish woman who had taught me both techniques and the value of my work. 'Mentors are gifts.'

'Yes. Uncle left me his tiny mountain studio and all his belongings and when I'm home this summer, I'll go up, stay there for a few days, and collect his tools. I plan to use those as his torch heads are amazing. They'll enable me to do cuts and welds that have become very uncommon.'

Ana pulled a stool over and sat down, looking up at Phoenix.

As I moved my tripod to get another perspective, I remembered more about Fiona MacKendrick. She'd hired me to help carry her equipment while she photographed Rocky Mountain sheep, but I should have been paying her. She taught me so much about light, balance and negative space. Fiona was probably the most creative person I'll ever meet, and I still judge my work critically by thinking, what would she say? I knew Fiona would have loved Phoenix, and her creator.

And I had a random thought; did my need to create come from Carlos, the inventor?

I'm sure those genes didn't come from Renee or my maternal grandparents, and again considered what a different life Renee and I would have had if Carlos had lived.

I snapped three photos of Ana contemplating her accomplishment. She looked such a tiny person to have carved Phoenix out of a block of stone.

'Is Uncle's place far from your family's ranch?'

'About one hundred kilometers, up in the mountains, not

far from El Triunfo. It can be slow going as some of the old mining roads are in rough shape. And as Uncle always did, I'll be hiking very carefully up the last two kilometers. That whole area is a network of underground mines and many hidden shafts.'

'Sounds both intriguing and challenging,' I said as I stretched out on a chaise, needing a brief break.

'Our branch of the Hernández family has an old house there, and my grandmother knows about the earlier Hernández family who were silver miners and built it. As well as the annual gatherings, Madre and my sister-in-law take the children up there to escape the summer heat, hurricanes and summer fevers, just as my grandmother used to take Papa and my late aunt, and a decade later, sometimes went with Madre and us.'

'Is there any mining now?'

'Not for many decades but they apparently had been rich mines, utilizing very modern technology. Even Gustave Eiffel was there, Sophia, oversaw the construction of El Triunfo's smokestack. I assume before he built Paris' famous Eiffel Tower.'

'I look forward to seeing that. I loved climbing the Eiffel tower, though now use the elevator but do go up, everytime I'm in Paris. '

'Me, too.'

'One of the stories Uncle would tell around campfires was about how his father helped install the underground rails in those mines and riding on a runaway ore cart. Said it beat bull riding as a thrill. Apparently those rails were what enabled deep mining, getting the silver ore and tunnelling debris out.'

'Will you use his cabin often?'

'Infrequently for the next few years, then who knows?

'Are other residents living nearby?'

'Not to my knowledge, used to be a couple of hermits and one eccentric old lady whom Uncle loved dearly, and I suspect, had considerable history with in earlier years. I liked the wild abstracts she painted.'

'Have you stayed alone up at the cabin before?'

'Only a few times, went up for three days after I had been to Mexico City to tell my fiancé I couldn't marry him. That was two years ago.'

I knew not to ask more … Ana's like me, private. Instead, I said, 'Ready to head home and see the photos we've got? Shannon's probably already there, sorting.'

'Yes, but first, Sophia, if I'm not being intrusive, I want to ask you whether it's hard, Renee leaving you all this information about your father and his family? Are you okay with it?'

'Basically, I am, though sad she didn't just tell me, let me help her sort her stuff together.'

I passed her the tripod and shrugged on my camera pack. 'What matters most to me is Alex and how our new family tree affects him. Hope we'll find more leads for him to research in La Paz before he leaves.'

'Why don't you come to Boston with me next week? It would be a treat for my grandmother to meet you and tell you about the Hernández history she knows.'

'Why not? I like that idea, and John's taking me somewhere as my birthday gift. We could come to Boston and go onto New York, he likes Broadway plays as much as I do.'

As we approached the fountain, we startled about fifty yellow and black grosbeaks bathing. A few flew but most ignored us.

Ana laughed, 'I know leaving Phoenix here is safe, but she might become a roosting place.'

'As soon as we check these photos, she can go back in her summer storage. We'll sort for awhile, then download them this afternoon.' I always leave a little time between shooting and editing.

CHAPTER TWELVE
- Ana

When we arrived at Sophia's, Shannon told us she'd been sorting for an hour and was so hungry. 'I was about to eat the muffins and fruit alone. How did the photo session go?'

'Phoenix is enchanting. The big question now is whether I've captured her magic? We'll download this afternoon,' Sophia said.

'Tell your butterflies they'll be wonderful.'

Shannon picked up the carafe and mugs, passed Sophia the muffins, the fruit bowl to me and led the way down the back steps to the picnic table there. I hadn't actually noticed this garden oasis before and looked at the rows of vegetables bordered with poppies and marigolds before I sat down.

Sophia turned on the water sprinklers and the birds flew in immediately to dig in the soil and play in the water. Watching them reminded me of home as, at the ranch, we always have wrens and sparrows scavenging under the veranda's picnic tables. Here, it was like an aviary with camp robbers, robins, blue jays and variegated thrushes competing for fat worms.

'This is my usual breakfast place, Ana. I come down, weed for a while and put on the water while I eat.'

The birds' chattered, and watching them as I ate my first muffin relaxed my tight stomach and chased away my slight fears. I was a little nervous about Phoenix's photos too.

I mumbled through my mouthful of muffin, 'Thanks, Shannon. Will you pass me an orange?

'And me another muffin, please. Did you find anything good this morning in Renee's stuff?'

'Church bulletins from Williams Creek. I scanned them. Nothing other than Renee usually took apple crisp to potlucks. I put them in the garbage as I did her power bills for the last six years, but if you two have had enough, let's get back to it. I have to leave in an hour.'

The two of them settled on the window seat and I perched on a kitchen stool and put my stack of folders on the kitchen counter.

'Ana's invited me to go to Boston with her and meet her grandmother,' Sophia told Shannon. 'I think John and I will.'

'Good, he's hoping you would choose New York over San Diego. Makes going to Boston first easy.' She asked me, 'Ana, do you have other relatives there? And how many relatives do you have on your father's side?'

'Got me. Madre or my Boston grandmother could tell us. I don't know. It used to be a large extended family but many are gone or very old now. Some of those folks might be able tell us snippets about Carlos and his family.'

'Well, I'm delighted I will be able to ask your grandmother,' Sophia said as I passed her more folders.

'Were these from box four? Because once we get it done, I'll be free again. Sorting has become both compulsive, and wearisome.'

'Yes, but it's packed tight. If you had a magic wand, what answers would you most like to find?'

'More about my father, what he'd invented, why he was murdered and what Renee learned about the investigation. That's my first wish but I know chances are slight.'

'Of course,' Shannon said saluting Soph with her coffee mug.

'And I wish I could travel back in time, be part of that family, before Carlos' death, of course. I think their way of living would have suited me better than the childhood I had.'

'Really, why?'

'From my many visits to the Baja, I've noticed how Mexican people seem to nurture their children without being up-tight. There's more laughter and music there, way more than in Canada. Though my grandparents were probably more uptight than most.

'Interesting,' Shannon mentioned, adding each culture does differ in raising children.

'Like it's subtle how much the Japanese differ too. Very high expectations put on a child there. Yosh gained many freedoms when we moved back to Canada.'

'What I want to know from Renee's stuff is who benefitted from Carlos' death?' I interjected.

'Maybe the Morgans? I've been wondering again why the hell did Mrs. Morgan travel to La Paz to build a Home for Unwed Mothers? Canada needed those, too. It's so coincidental on top of his being Carlos' professor and, apparently, mentor.'

'And that they rented a place next to his parents,' I reminded them before Sophia's words hit me. 'What? Mrs. Morgan went to La Paz to build a home for single pregnant women? That's ludicrous. I thought she was just another missionary seeking converts, maybe wanted to start a church. The Baja attracts lots of those.'

'No, Ana, guess you haven't seen the old church bulletins? I'll get them for you later as what they record details why Mrs. Morgan took Renee as her translator. She was funded to build a home for unwed mothers,' Sophia said.

'Why in La Paz? Even more, why did she and her missionary society think there was a need?' I watched as Sophia ran her hand through her short curls, in exactly the same way that Alex does.

'I've no idea. Guess it sounds normal to me because when I was young, Mother was always involved with the Mission Society fundraising for 'The unfortunate young women,' as she called them. Building a facility in La Paz does seem most peculiar.'

'It isn't credible, especially in 1937,' I told them. 'The whole La Paz area had only about five thousand people then. Besides, Mexico is a very Catholic country, and a pregnant girl would not have been sent to strangers. She would have had options, and most in the Baja still would have now. Families are tightly connected, look after their own.'

'What happens?' Shannon asked as she got up to fill her mug with water.

'The local priest still might become involved and the girl married off. Either to the child's father, if he doesn't already have a wife, or to a widower who needs a new wife to look after his children. Or she might be sent to help older relatives in another village. And she and her child might live with them.'
'The pregnant girl has choices?'

'Well, her mother and the priest probably decide which one's best for her. So, whereas a shelter home makes sense for somewhere like Mazatlán or Mexico City, it doesn't at all in smaller places. Certainly not in La Paz in 1937.'

'We need to find out more about those Morgan's,' Shannon declared.

'Yes, that would be most helpful. And we don't know much about Carlos's history, could his murder have been a payback? Perhaps Carlos had impregnated someone else earlier?' I asked, looking over at Sophia.

'What, my father was a tom cat?' She laughed ruefully. 'Or perceived to be one?'

'Well, I guess it's possible, except, Ana, before his two years in Vancouver he was studying in England for many years.'

'Renee's gestation time fits in with Carlos' return to La Paz so what I suspect, is they resumed a relationship they had started in Vancouver, Shannon speculated. 'Seems unlikely that he'd had time to start or rekindle another relationship, impregnate someone else?'

Sophia agreed and we went back to sorting thick folders, full of page after page of irrelevant information.

'Look at this!' Sophia spread a sheath of papers beside my stuff on the counter. 'It's my preschool art scribbles and Renee had them, kept them. Maybe my folks mailed them to her when she was in the sanatorium? And now, they're gone,' She dumped them into the green bag and said she'd be back in five.

Shannon waited for her to be a distance away before asking, 'Do you think Soph suspects anything about tonight?'
'I'm sure she doesn't know about the party. Yosh has been

telling some of what was happening and it's going to be a fun evening. Just ask if I can help with anything.'

'Another forty minutes, then that's it for the day.

'Sounds good,' Ana and I said, sounding relieved. Both of us wanted time with the photos of Phoenix. And I had promised John that around our late evening in town, I would nap today.

'Look at that ancient man's arrogant expression. His chair suits him,' Shannon laughed. He was seated in an elaborately carved master's chair and eight headshots surrounded him. 'Bet he could've given lessons in being a judgmental old man.'

I was looking at his deeply-wrinkled face and decided he'd been born in mid-1850's. Arrogant isn't the right word. Maybe worn?

'This is my father's family, Carlos is top row center, his father's to the left of the old man, who is probably my great-great-grandfather. The man on his right side must be Hector, Carlos' uncle. And that's Carlos' mother on the left in the middle row, with her sister-in-law and niece. Isn't Marie gorgeous?'

'She looks much like I had visualized her,' I said, feeling connected to her since I'd translated her words. She had a maze of dark curls and classic Latin features and I thought Sophia must have looked similar in her youth.

'Looking at these two with their dark hair wound high and in matching lacy high-necked dresses, the rift between Hector and Gabriel seems doubly sad, they're sisters as well as related by marriage. And, Soph, you look like Marie. Eerie how genes carry forward, isn't it?' Shannon said, and then noticed the time. 'Whoops, I'll be late. I'm out of here, you two. See you tonight.'

I kept staring at the photo and read out the faded names I was distantly related to, too. 'It's Juan Carlos Hernández Garcia in the magnificent chair and Carlos's father's full name was Gabriel Juan Lopez Hernández.

'Who's the lad to the right of Carlos? He looks English, Ana.' We studied the thin pale face with little round glasses.

'That name is too faded, I can only make out part of the surname. -wers. Sophia, your father's face shows strength and character, he was a special man.'

She began gathering up the unsorted folders on the counter. 'That pleases me because I've learned you sculptors are as adept at reading faces as we photographers are. I've had enough of Renee's stuff, let's pack it up, Ana, and download Phoenix's images.'

I agreed and added, 'But, first, a question I've been speculating about this morning. Do you think Renee might have initiated the relationship with Carlos? She must been pleased to suddenly have him chauffeuring her to purchase the Morgan's groceries, she'd probably had never met a similar young man.'

Sophia laughed. 'No, she probably hadn't.'

'Do you think there's a possibility her accompanying Mrs. Morgan to La Paz was at her initiation? Renee was probably as manipulative as a teenager as she was an old woman.'

'That's quite a suggestion. And, yes, it's feasible. According to those church bulletins, Mrs. Morgan's mission was in the works before she broke her leg, and before Renee was sent to Vancouver to help her. Where she probably quite quickly met Carlos.'

'And, perhaps, got to know him very well?'

'Ana, that makes sense. What doesn't to me was Renee being pregnant by September, having been seduced after only arriving in La Paz in August. That just isn't credible for me. We were raised by the same woman who was overly strict about boys,' Sophia assured me. 'But if Renee and Carlos became intimate in Vancouver, her scheming about how to have Mrs. Morgan take her to La Paz is credible.

Sophia picked up the stack of folders Shannon had been working on and a tattered school scribbler fell onto the window seat.

'What's in that? You might have found gold.'

Sophia gently flipped through the pages. 'This is Renee's writing. Listen to this first page, *I threw up again this morning.*

'Are there dates?'

'Yes, the second page says Wednesday, November 29th, I'll read it.' Sophia took a big gulp of water before beginning.

'As soon as I woke up today, I again threw up into my wash-basin. Mrs. Morgan must have heard me because she told me later that the doctor will be coming for his week in La Paz soon and she's taking me to him. I know she suspects why I keep throwing up. So do I. Should I tell Carlos yet? I am frightened about what he will say.

Sophia sat down on a kitchen stool. 'I was born on June 1, 1938, so Renee would have been almost three months pregnant by later November. Ana, will you read this so I can listen?' and passed the scribbler to me.

'Of course.'

Renee's writing was faded and quite small but I could read it easily.

Wednesday December 1st: Carlos' parents were very angry when he told them about our baby. His father shouted as we just stood there and held hands, though Carlos' was holding mine too tight as his father asked how could his only son be that stupid? He said how disappointed he was in Carlos, and how unfair he was to his mother.

Carlos became very white as she sobbed loudly, her face hidden in her hankie. I was sobbing, too, but neither of his parents even looked at me, though Marie, Carlos' younger sister came and gave me her hankie.

Marie stayed standing very close to me and patted my

shoulder as I cried. I felt Carlos shaking more, but he told them he was going to marry me and his voice was calm, firm.

It's been three days since then, very awful ones.

Mrs. Morgan lectures me frequently and orders me to go to my room, get down on my knees and pray for forgiveness. Professor Morgan glares at me whenever I'm not able to avoid him.

Carlos is trying to be brave but when we managed to meet in the garden, tears were running down his cheeks, even as he lectured me I have to stop crying because it's bad for our baby.

Every time we can sneak a little visit together, he tells me he's going to be my husband and a good father to our baby. He says we will be married soon somewhere, even if his parents do not agree.

When I first told him about me having our baby, Carlos hugged me for a long time before we went to talk with Mrs. Morgan. She'd been very angry after the doctor said I was pregnant. She told me that I would be returning to Vancouver on the next ship.

Carlos told Mrs. Morgan, "No," very firmly, his arm around my shoulder. Then we went next door to tell his parents, which was even harder than going to the doctor. I was so terrified.

But Carlos held my hand tight and kept saying as his father shouted, 'Papa, I intend to be Renee's husband and our child's father.'

Until this morning, we've had to wait for three days since Carlos' father sent us away, said he would let us know what he and Carlos' mother have decided after they talked with each other and the priest. Now, he's told Carlos we are to come to the parlour at 4 p.m. tomorrow.

I pray and pray we will be allowed to marry. I know how Carlos loves his parents, sister and home. That means he can't run away to be with me, he would be too unhappy.

I don't know what I'll do if they say no.

Mrs. Morgan is still yelling at me now about Carlos being a Catholic. She says she can't allow me to marry him because

*my parents would not approve. And the Morgan's are shunning
me, I have to take a tray to my bedroom. They do not want to
eat or talk with me.'*

I got off my stool to refill my water and offered more to
Sophia, who was scrunched up in her corner. 'Want me to keep
reading?'

'Let's do one more entry, and then, I want to download
your photos. '

*Saturday December 4th: When we entered the parlour, I
was glad it was Father Morales there with Carlos' parents.
He is the priest whom I like more than the one who smells and
scowls all the time. The Father had his hands clasped behind
his long black robes as usual and was standing near the sofa
where Carlos' Madre and Papa were sitting. He waved at us to
sit on the two chairs set up about seven feet in front of them.*

*No one smiled or said anything. Carlos' mother's face was
all red and puffy. My knees were knocking so loudly, I
wondered if they could hear them.*

*Carlos spoke first. 'Renee and I appreciate your talking
with us and we will listen carefully, but please accept that we
will be married and Renee will become my wife.'*

*He sounded very grown up but as they discussed something,
I couldn't follow their rapid Spanish. My mind wandered as
they talked on and on, and I decided that the dark room seemed
unfriendly. Its big windows were hidden behind thick lace
curtains and the heavy burgundy velvet side curtains were
partially pulled. Although it was a sunny day outside, that room
felt as cold as I was.*

*I could understand a little of what Father Morales was
saying, as he talked slower to Carlos and me, sounded like he
was giving a sermon. He lectured us for our improprieties over
and over.*

*But then, when he told Carlos he was going to have to do
many penances, I started feeling hopeful.*

The priest next stepped closer to me and asked in very

slow Spanish, 'Do you want to be accepted into the Catholic Church, Señorita? It will mean much studying for you. And you must agree all your and Carlos' children will be raised to be Catholic.' I tried not to sob with my relief, suddenly understanding these questions meant we were going to be allowed to marry.

'I agree, Father,' and sobbed so loudly that Carlos asked Marie to get me some juice.

I know Mother will be very angry with me. Maybe as Mrs. Morgan says, as much as about my agreeing to become Catholic than as about my being pregnant. I don't know, but what I'm praying is she'll let Dad continue to talk with me and, someday, with his grandchild, even if she shuns me.

I stopped reading.

'Well, nice to know I came damn close to not being a bastard,' Sophia chuckled. 'I'm sympathetic for Carlos' parents. What a massive compromise for them to give their permission and blessings to their only son's marriage to an immature, naive and pregnant Canadian girl.'

'Yes, his mother must have been especially devastated as she'd have understood what it meant that Carlos' wife wasn't going to be a gracious Mexican woman. She'd have contemplated how Renee not having been trained to run a complex household as she nurtured Carlos' and her children, and enjoyed being a matriarch, would change her son's life.'

'Renee had been raised to keep her stew fork to use for her pie.' That image said so much, we both laughed until the tears ran and Sophia got up to blow her nose and pass me the tissue box.

'Okay, Ana, I've had enough with Renee's world. Let's go download Phoenix's photos and decide whether we need another shoot.'

We watched the photos come up on her large monitor, mounted above her wide work counter. Photo after perfect photo took my breath away.

'Sophia, they're perfect.'

I kept murmuring in my voice husky, 'Look at that one. And that one! Thank you, thank you.'

'It's my pleasure and I'm pleased with the quality. These give you choices for your retrospective.'

'They're incredible photos. 'Now I can see Phoenix as others see her, Sophia. I haven't been able to do that because I was still looking at all the parts of her, wondering if I should have attached a wire a few inches higher.

'I feel that way about some of my photos, until I'll see it framed and on someone's wall.'

We began sorting, grouping similar ones and mulling what might work best for my retrospective until I admitted, 'I have to stop, I'm so overwhelmed by my choices. What are you going to do next?'

Sophia thought about it. 'I think read more of Renee's scribbler.'

'Do you want to be alone or shall I read the rest of it aloud? I'm curious, too, and don't need to leave for half an hour.'

'Then, Ana, will you read the story of my genesis, please?'

CHAPTER THIRTEEN
- Sophia

We went to the deck's shady area, Ana stretched out on a cushioned chaise and I chose the padded swing. She opened the ancient scribbler: 'Date's December 8th, 1937, Sophia, and two pages long.'

Carlos' mother has decided January 21st is when Carlos and I will marry. It's a special Saint's Day, celebrating the one who will protect me and my baby, if I pray enough.

Marie told me later it will also suit Uncle Rubin as he's arriving January 20 on his ship. We will probably be aboard and leaving three days later. We are taking some furniture for our rooms in Mexico City, including the family's bassinette, crib and English pram. And, of course, Carlos' lab things and the Packard will be going.

I am very nervous about meeting Uncle Rubin. What will he say about our baby coming too soon? I am afraid he will be very angry, though Carlos says no, he will not. He says Uncle Rubin is his friend as well as his uncle, and he will like me, and I will like him very much. I hope so.

But I'm worried about what if Carlos' uncle thinks I am not the right woman for his nephew? Carlos is to eventually be the manager of Rubin's factories and is Rubin's heir.

I do intend to be whatever kind of wife Carlos needs but Marie says that is very complex. She told me I must start formal Spanish lessons right away, not to wait. And to not talk much, to listen to how people speak as well as what they say.

When Marie was drawing me a diagram of Uncle Rubin's twenty-room house, Carlos' mother saw it. She sat down with us and talked for a very long time about my responsibilities. Told me that I must learn about how to manage a house and its staff. Then she had us look at her housekeeping records and

*lists. Marie and I were surprised at how much work there is.
Now I am nervous about housekeeping, too.*

*Carlos is unsure about where he and I will live. I hope it
will be somewhere with a little kitchen so I can cook for him
when we don't have to eat with Uncle Rubin.*

*More than anything, where will my baby be born? I don't
know anything about all that yet, and I am very scared.*

*I wish I could talk to my girlfriend in Thompson City who
had a baby last year. And I long to be with Dad and Mother.
But Carlos told me yesterday we might be able to go there the
following year, not this one.*

*Father Morales gave Carlos many penances and one is
a very big punishment for me, too. We are not allowed to be
alone together until after our wedding and we can only talk
with each other when we are with the family.*

'Poor Renee.' Ana closed the scribbler and stood up to
stretch. 'Rubin's home sounds much like my Mexico City
grandparent's one. It's like a little hotel. My brother and I used
to play hide-and-seek for hours there.'

'Poor Renee is right, Ana. Are you close to that
grandmother, too?'

'She died last year but we've always been closer to
Grandpapa. He likes Papa and comes to the ranch often while
my grandmother only did once. She was probably still angry
with me. Last time I saw her, she'd told me that I had
disappointed her as much as my mother had when she
married Papa.'

'Really?'

'Well, I had,' Ana spread her hands wide and settled on the
chaise again. 'I'd just told her I had broken off my engagement
to her dear friend's grandson. But as Madre says, 'Isn't it lucky
she had three daughters? Both her sisters have large families
and they all enjoy the prestige and many social obligations
Grandmother's heritage gives them within Mexico City.'

I laughed at her summary and thought of Renee. I had
survived her many opinions by being equally pragmatic.

Ana sighed and picked up the scribbler again. 'Interesting how reading Renee's words gives me a deeper understanding of why I couldn't be a lawyer's wife and a sculptor.'

'Good, though do you want to keep reading?'

I assured her I did and resumed.

December 14th:

I moved over to the Hernández hacienda today and am to sleep on the small bed in an alcove in Aunt Guadalupe's massive bedroom. Professor and Mrs. Morgan are as glad as I am.

But I will miss having my own room and don't like this dear old lady's smells. Those are very noticeable, and she's often noisy. Not to be able to be hugged by Carlos is very hard. He is too methodical about obeying the priest's orders! That can make me angry and sad, especially as I'm already having his baby and would like my back rubbed.

Ana flipped through the next pages and asked, 'Okay if I skip through these next entries, Sophia? They are quite trite and Renee's listed who she's meeting only by first name and relationship, untraceable.'

'A summary would be much preferred.'

'Well, family and close friends were dropping in frequently, as it was Christmas season. Although she liked holding the babies and playing with little children, Renee's weary, and feels everyone is judging her. She's decided most are not pleased that she's going to be 'their' Carlos's wife. As well, she found it exhausting to try and follow their Spanish.'

'It would be. I find the folks on the Baja speak considerably faster than those on the mainland.'

'We do. Now Soph, here's an interesting bit she wrote on December 26th.

Because it's Christmastime, I was allowed to ride with Carlos to go to his aunt and uncle's hacienda today. We blew each other many little kisses as he drove.

Carlos told me much more about Mexico City and how he

hoped his invention works well, and that he will see we have our own kitchen. Best of all, he gave me a special Christmas present.

After our baby is born, and when we can afford to buy another car for him, the Packard will become my car. Although I had liked learning how to drive it when we used to get the Morgan's groceries, I never expected it might be mine.

I've never even dreamed of having my own car. Or that I would be having a baby and husband so soon!

How strange my life is now but I mainly like it, around being so lonely for Dad and Mother. Even though I was angry with her for making me go live with Mrs. Morgan, I am now very grateful she did. Because that is why and how I met Carlos.

Likewise, I only got to come to La Paz with Mrs. Morgan because she heard how well I could speak Spanish. Every Sunday, Carlos was invited over to the Morgan's for dinner and, as Professor Morgan speaks Spanish well and she's trying to learn, we spoke in Spanish.

'So now we know. And, Ana, guess what? I'm surprised at how my parents knowing each other quite well before conceiving me pleases me.'

'This tells us that Carlos was more than just Professor Morgan's student. Do you also suspect some personal connection there?'

We heard a diesel truck come to a stop in the driveway, a door slam just before the cowbell rang three times. 'Where are you, Soph?' John called

'We're on the deck,' I slid out of the swing as he strode in, gathered me into his arms.

He said over my head, 'Hi, Ana.'

'Aren't you about three hours early?'

'Yes, Soph, but I'm finished, Tom's supervising moving the cows to the summer pasture. And I'm hoping you'll feed a starving man? Then how about a hot tub and nap, because if

I'm to stay awake late tonight, I need one.'

Ana passed the scribbler to me. 'And I need to check my emails and have a nap, too, see you tonight. Sophia, I can't thank you enough for Phoenix's photos. Don't forget to ask John about Boston.'

'I will, and my many thanks to you for all you keep doing for me.'

Ana headed down the stairs as I offered, 'How about a couple of western sandwiches? And want to take me to Boston, then New York?'

'Why not? And western sandwiches are ideal, maybe three? Obviously, the photo session went well, what about Renee's stuff?'

'We found her journal of when she was first pregnant and it's loaded with info. Reading it is a little tedious, John, she writes like the teenager she was.'

John raised his thick eyebrows and grinned. 'Well, quite a jump for a naive young woman raised in Thompson City by parochial parents to become a Mexico City senora.'

I visualized how I would have been expanding her belly and asked myself, would I have been able to manage all that?

As I lounged in the hot tub and watched the fluffy white clouds, I wished again that she'd told me I was her child.

Although I am a creative who needs variety and adventures whereas Renee liked sameness, and wasn't very interested in books, art or my work, she was my mother. I would have honoured her, not often ignored her as my frustrating older sister.

Again, I wondered why. Maybe she'd found me impossible to talk with, especially about my father? Or maybe Renee wanted him to herself, her precious secret?

Well, done is done, and I am very relieved there's less than half a box of her archives to go.

John flipped water at my face. 'Has the weight of Renee's bequest caught up with you or are you trying to decide what to wear tonight?'

'Renee. I'm wearing that grand swirly teal dress you

bought me for Christmas.'

'Well, to be honest, Alex chose that, he's my secret shopper. What I've brought over is my black silk shirt and, my love, also a blazer to go over it for your special birthday.'

CHAPTER FOURTEEN
- Alex

'Alex, thank you.'

I helped Gran down from John's truck, having been waiting in the Six Mile Lodge parking lot for them.

'And for finding me this special dress.'

I grinned at John as he winked and gave me a thumbs up.

As I tucked her hand under my elbow, she swirled the skirt and I gave a wolf whistle. 'I'm glad you two decided to switch our dinner here instead of going all the way into town, John. But it's strange there's so many cars here.'

'I think there's a gathering down in the convention room,' I lied and cheered silently, we've done it! Gran doesn't suspect she's about to be surprised.

As we walked towards the log lodge, Ana came down the steps and took John's arm.

'You're looking like a Latin señorita with your hair piled high and that wonderful Aztec necklace,' Gran told her as the four of us went up the lodge's wide steps and through the carved cedar double doors.

'Oh my god,' Gran gasped as she saw the green sign strung across the dining room's wide entrance. Rainbow coloured letters proclaimed *Happy Birthday, Sophia.*

She tightened her grip on my arm as we all started singing, *For she's a jolly good friend,* as I escorted Gran to head of the U-shaped table.

The thirty people there moved on to chanting as they sat down, 'Happy Birthday, Sophia, Happy Birthday!'

'I'm overwhelmed! Thank you,' she called and waved to the guests, beamed at me as she began to absorb who was there.

Sammy and David from Australia were on Gran's left and blew her a kiss.

To her right were her dear friends, Penelope, her fellow photographer, Albert, her scientist husband, and beside him was Clyde. During my initial phone call with Penelope in London, she'd suggested he be invited, as he was the son of Gran's venerated mentor.

I hadn't expected the now famous photographer to fly from Inverness to Thompson City but had called him. He'd accepted immediately, said he would be pleased to come because Sophia had been so generous to him when he was starting out and it also somehow honoured his mother.

The waiter brought Gran her usual three olive martini as the lights dimmed and a spotlight illuminated Shannon at the tables' far end. She was wearing a top hat, waving a flashing wizard's stick, and on her signal, everyone raised their glasses and again launched into *Happy Birthday, Sophia*.

Gran stood and toasted everyone, and requested, 'Now, please join in toasting Shannon, Alex and John. I don't know how they managed to gather all you grand people here, but I am so grateful they did.' She raised her glass. 'Thanks for being here for my 70th birthday, and, yes, I am surprised and delighted!'

John reached behind Gran's back to jab my shoulder, as pleased as I was.

Five months ago, when I proposed my idea, he and Shannon had agreed immediately. And making the film for Gran, helping Shannon script her play and contacting the international guests had helped me get past my grief about losing Mom.

When we finished the prime rib dinners, Yosh and I headed to our temporary props room. Cecil was there, swearing quietly as he tried to fasten the saddle to the sawhorse.

Yosh and I offered to take over and he said peevishly, 'Certainly. I am here as a guest, not a stagehand.'

'Thanks, Alex,' Shannon laughed as she pulled herself into the saddle to test it. 'Cecil said we were inept engineers.'

Once we knew the saddle was stable for her, I rolled the large white screen out to where each guest would have a good view and put my computer and stool in place. It was the opening act for the floorshow we'd put together and when Shannon gave me the nod, I dimmed the lights, focused the spotlight and our vaudeville show began.

She walked into the bright circle in her top hat, waving her flashing microphone, and began amusing our guests with stories about how, along with Gran, Yosh and me, she'd become an adventurer. After a few anecdotes from the many outdoor trips we'd shared, she announced in a dramatic voice, 'Now, Alex's film for Sophia, his grandmother.

The lights came up and I focused my computer on the screen. These seven minutes had taken John, Shannon and me many hours to agree on what to include but as I watched, Gran's photographs slowly rolled across the screen, and heard the guests' ooh's and ah's, I knew we'd got it right.

We had captured Gran's amazing talent as an internationally respected photographer.

As each photo filled the screen, followed by its details and where Gran had been shooting, my film created a visual biography of her impressive career. From those massive buzzards I had watched her record as a kid, to tiny hummingbirds, alligators, otters, scorpions, arctic wolves and many more, we saw what her photography had captured in exquisite detail.

My favourite photo is the vertical black and white she is very proud of, an astounding shot of the Fraser River's rapids boiling below the stark sand cliffs. I chose it to end and fade into a full screen Happy Birthday, Gran, and The End.

When the clapping quieted, Shannon directed, 'Sophia, will you please come and join us?' as Sammy pushed a rolling podium out into the spotlight.

He escorted Gran to it and up onto a stool by the high podium, opened the round hatbox on it and removed a white safety helmet. With much ado, he placed it on her head and read its bold red lettering, SNAKE PHOTOGRAPHER.

Next, he passed her a long pen topped with a feather and

requested, 'Sophia Nord, will you please sign this contract? It gives you the Mexican government's official permission to be a photographer within the Parque Nacional Bahia de Loreto.'

Gran signed and waved the contract at the guests.

'Our team has received all the necessary permissions to go snake hunting along the Sea of Cortez' shores,' the herpetologist explained, then added, 'And as my partner David and I are gratified to be doing another contract with you, Sophia Nord, please accept your appointment as the expedition's Honorary Leader.

The guests cheered until Shannon stepped into the spotlight, waved her wand and announced there would be a ten-minute intermission before the grand finale.

When she joined Yosh and me in the storeroom to change and inspect how we looked in our cowboy hats and western shirts, I asked, 'Ready for Broadway, Shannon?' before heading out with the gaudy microphone.

'Howdy, folks! Welcome to the very first performance of *Sophia's Flight To The Future*, a one act play created and produced by Shannon Saito, Yosh Saito, Ana Avila and me, Alex Nord.'

The second spotlight swung onto Shannon, sitting tall in the saddle atop a big carpenter's sawhorse in a ruffled red shirt, jeans and a black cowboy hat.

'Hey, son!' she drawled as Yosh galloped up on a big kid's hobby horse, its long green mane down to his knees.

'Hi ya, Ma. Y'all ready to go ridin'?

'Sure am, I'm a-good to go. But ya know, what I'm wishin' is we was headin' off on a campout because I was just a'rememberin' when we used to go with Sophia and Alex to the mountains. Thinkin' bout how we'd head up to da high pasturelands in that big old wheezin' truck loaded up with our horses and campin' gear.

'I sure do remember that, Ma. Them was fine times,' Yosh drawled back. 'Ya got any special memories from dem days?'

'Ah, there's so many fine ones I have, son. Like dem stars always being so bright at night I could've plucked them from the sky. And all da special hours that Soph and I spent sippin' scotch by the fire. And our early mornin' races to skinny dippin' in an icy mountain stream while our lads were still snug in your sleepin' bags.

'Yeah, da fun we had. Well, most of the time. What I kin also remember is how m'feet froze despite two layers of socks! T'weren't all cozy, Ma. But most of them were terrific times, weren't they?'

Shannon flicked her reins at the sawhorse and drawled, 'Da ya ken how prideful Soph and I were to be watchin' ya two sprout up, becomin' men? Tryin' to do fancier rodeo tricks each summer? All dem memories is pritty sweet.'

'Like me and Alex burning da beans so bad that we had to move the horses out of the smoke?' Yosh guffawed loudly and galloped the hobby horse in a circle.

'Hey, Ma, ya just reminded of my very favourite time. Re member when Aunt Sophie Learned To Fly?'

'Ah, Yosh, never could I forget that grand day!' Shannon pulled herself tall in her saddle and proclaimed, 'Look over thar, boys! Har comes our Sophie down that dusty logging road … Jumpin' Jehosaphats, she be a-standin' in her saddle! And listen to her a-hollerin', 'Gid-di-up, Blackie, gid-di-up!'

Yosh yelled, 'Hey, Ma, ain't that a fine sight! Dat's our Sophie, a-standin' on that horse's back. She's a-lookin' like a ballerina in blue jeans wit her long hair a-streamin' behind her, jus like dat black horse's tail.'

The lights went down as our cheering guests rose to their feet. Ana and I helped Shannon dismount from the sawhorse's saddle, then we all crowded into the spotlight as it came up again, arms high and loudly declaring, 'We watched agape as our Sophie galloped by on that mighty horse of hers, a-flying into her future.'

CHAPTER FIFTEEN
- Sophia

Hours later, I was still flying as I snuggled beside John, chatting about the guests, the play, the fun.

He snored. Not ready to sleep, I slipped out of bed, grabbed a quilt and headed for the swing to gaze at the stars and keep enjoying the grand celebration. I remembered in my earlier years, I've projected I would be retiring and feeling old by seventy. But what I feel is energetic and balanced.

Two great horned owls hoo, hoo-ed to each other and I hoo'ed back as I snuggled under the fluffy quilt. 'Yup, owls, once upon a time, I did stand up on my horse.' Done that, no inclination to do it again.

This new decade of mine is going to be full of sorting what I want to do and what I don't as meaningful time is what matters. Sure, sorting Renee's bequest is an unwanted task, though it might have unknown benefits, like expanding Alex and my family, learning about our Mexican heritage.'

All that laughter is still echoing, as are all the moments we shared. Sammy putting the Snake Photographer safety helmet on my head does summarize my next gig for the guests, and in a funny way, for me. Penelope and Clyde amused themselves by wanting the technical details of just how I intend to shoot snakes in caves and why the hell doing so appeals to me?'

I got them by claiming I like dark and scary places but was bluffing as I'm a little unsure about what I've bitten off this time.

The swing rocked gently as I wrapped more quilt around me and mulled why. I guess mainly because the three earlier projects I've done with Sammy and David were fun and the photos I ended up with have been rewarding. During my thirty years as a photographer, probably what I've enjoyed most is its diversity.

Diverse in not only the species I've recorded but in all the people I've worked with in such different geographies. Some have been more satisfying or challenging than others but as Alex's wonderful film reminded me, I have traveled as a photographer and managed to get some fine shots.

Strange that Renee hadn't enjoyed looking at my work, but she didn't and I'll never know why.

'Droll, isn't it?' I murmured to KitKat who'd joined me under the quilt. 'My wondering about a mother-daughter relationship that never happened as I turn seventy.'

A shooting star flamed across the night sky's horizon and as it disappeared, I thought, tonight is the beginning of my new decade, and yawned deeply as I headed back to my bed and John's warmth.

A few hours later, I awoke, pulled the quilt off my throbbing head and returned to the swing. John and Alex were at the patio table, devouring bacon and eggs, and my grandson kindly offered coffee.

'Yes,' I whispered. 'Talk quietly, please, and I'll have a pot of it.'

'More for me, too,' John agreed. 'Some breakfast, Sophia?'

His morning voice is too loud, getting croakier all the time, sounds like those damn crows squawking far too loudly overhead. Well, he is seventy-five this fall, considerably older thanme. 'Yes, will you be kind enough to get me some soda crackers?'

'Bring your grandmother some crackers,' he bellowed and I buried my face into the cushion, pretended I was floating in the lake.

I rolled over and stood up when Alex banged the tray on the picnic table. 'Remember, Gran? We are the hosts at the brunch buffet for your guests.

'Right, I'm looking forward to that,' I lied before remembering, I would have only one more visit with all those special people before most of them boarded planes or drove away.

I ordered myself, Shape up, Now!

Two muffin halves and two cups of coffee and I gave Alex a hug. 'Thanks! Why do you smell lemony?'

'My new shampoo's a bit strong. Okay if I take the jeep? The Packard won't work for airport shuttles.'

'Of course, and we'll be at the hotel in less than an hour. Want to race?'

Ana had just parked as John drove into the hotel's lot and waited so the three of us could go in together. As we walked down the long hall to the banquet room where our lunch was being served, I heard the lobby's old grandfather clock bong 11:30 and wondered, why hasn't Shannon phoned me this morning? She said she would call when she picked up Cecil after Yosh's plane left. He was off to Germany, then Johannesburg, where Beth would be meeting him.

As I slid into my chair in the dining room, nodding and waving to my dear friends, I took out my cell to call her when it rang.

CHAPTER SIXTEEN
- Alex

I watched Gran as she sat down on the chair John had pulled out and answered her cell. Ana and I were at one end of the long banquet table and they were at the other, but I could see her angst as she talked on her cell. I watched her stand and rush from the dining room.

I caught up with her in the hall as she sank onto a love seat, heard her lamenting, 'Oh, Shannon!'

'What's happened, Gran?' I murmured, kneeling in front of her.

She held her phone out so I could hear, too.

My god! Was that loud sobbing Shannon? My heart raced as I thought, something's happened to Yosh's plane.

'Oh, Shannon!' Gran sympathized into the phone. 'Tell me more. Why is Cecil dead? Was it a stroke or a heart attack?'

'Someone murdered him. Strangled him, Soph!' Shannon's sobbing turned into broken hiccups.

Gran and I stared at each other in disbelief.

'Murdered Cecil? Oh, my poor dear! I'm coming. Shannon, where are you?' Gran leaned against the love seat's leather upholstery and swiped her nose against her silk blouses' sleeve. When I offered a tissue from my pocket, she grabbed it and blew softly.

Shannon sobbed as she tried to explain and we looked at each other, neither of us getting what she was saying.

'Who's with you now, Shannon? And where are you again? John and I are coming, we'll be there soon.' She passed the cell to me. 'Ask where?'

'It's Alex, Shannon. Where can Gran find you?'

We heard her blow her nose but when she didn't reply, Gran grabbed the phone back. 'Are you okay, Shannon, or hurt? Please tell me where you are.'

'I'm a little hurt, Sophie. I fainted and hit my head. But it's almost okay now. Where we are is in the lab's first aid room, the three of us. Me, a constable and a detective.'

'Okay, we're coming.' Gran stuck out a hand and I helped her up as she continued talking. 'The drive will take John and I about fifteen minutes, Shannon. Will you be staying where you are?'

She asked someone whether she needed to go back to Cecil's office or anywhere else.

'No, Dr. Saito,' that person said loudly, as though hoping we could hear him, too. 'Have your friend come here.'

'I'm to stay here in the medical room at Cecil's lab. Okay? Goodbye now.'

'We'll find you.' Gran looked as stunned as I felt. Cecil had been strangled?

By then, Ana and John were standing beside us and he put his arm around Gran's shoulders.

'You're very pale, Soph, let's sit for a moment and tell me what's happened?' as he sat her down, keeping his arm around her.

'Yes, perhaps for a moment as I'm wobbly. But I never faint. Shannon did after she found Cecil. He's dead, John! Someone strangled him and Shannon found him. Fainted, hit her head when she fell. She needs us, let's go.' Gran stood up suddenly and headed toward the exit.

John started after her, then turned and nodded towards the dining room, raising his eyebrows at Ana and me. Gran stopped and came back, remembering her guests.

'Alex, Ana, will you please say thank you and goodbye to everyone for me? Explain Shannon's had an emergency and needs me. Don't say Cecil's dead, we'll tell them that later, okay?'

'Of course, Gran, phone me as soon as you can.'

'Thanks, you two.' She turned and sprinted down the hall, John striding behind her.

Ana and I returned to the dining room where I passed on

Gran's goodbye and her thanks. 'Shannon, John and myself add our warmest thanks to each of you for coming and helping to give her a fine birthday celebration. Now, one more thing for those folks I was chauffeuring to the airport, I'm about to have the front desk arrange your transportation.'

After I finished doing that and returned, many people had already left and Ana was with Penelope, Albert and Sammy near the desert table. She hadn't told them, having decided I should.

I explained the little I knew.

'Strangled?' whispered Penelope.

Ana nodded and added, 'Once John and Sophia get to the lab, she'll phone Alex but that will probably be awhile. Shannon fainted when she found Cecil and injured her head.'

We kept saying good-bye as the guests left and I tried to figure out what I should be doing next. One thing for sure was Yosh couldn't be here for his mother.

'Alex, under these circumstances,' Sammy said, 'David and I won't come up to Erin Lake. I think what we'll do is rent a car and head back down to Vancouver for the three days before our flight to Australia.' They had been going to stay with Gran, both for a visit and to organize the Loreto shoot.'

Penelope and Albert were coming up to Gran's, too, though continuing to stay at the hotel. 'Alex, I have to fly back to London tomorrow but Albert's plans were staying in Thompson City to work with Cecil for a few days.'

'I have a device currently being manufactured here,' he explained. 'Please tell Shannon I'm available for whatever as Cecil's dying is also a massive loss at the lab. Do you know his assistant, who was his right hand, died in a kite flying accident a month ago?'

'I didn't. And trying to begin to contemplate the consequences of Cecil's death is unreal. What I know is it will load so much onto Shannon, as she's on his company's board of directors.

When I looked at my watch again, Ana pointed out, 'It's

too soon, Alex, probably be an hour or so before Sophia has time to phone us.'

Penelope took charge. 'Come along, let's wait in our suite.'

CHAPTER SEVENTEEN
- Sophia

'Soph, do you know where the medical room is when we get to Cecil's complex?' John asked as he wove the truck in and out on the freeway.

'I'm not sure. If we can turn left as soon as we go through the gates, then I think I know.'

Arriving at the complex with its multi-buildings and manicured lawns, I felt overwhelmingly sad as John drove past the custom metal gates that Yosh had designed for Cecil.

He'll never drive through them again, I accepted.

'Who the hell could have strangled Cecil? He's taller than me and although he's not nearly as thick, he's probably stronger. How could someone have killed him?' John asked, then demanded, 'Soph, where do I turn? I don't have a clue of where anything is in this maze.'

There was a street to the left and I pointed to it.

'I've only been here twice,' John continued. 'With you to the grand opening of Cecil's big expansion, which was maybe three years ago, and remember, I was here this spring? Cecil brought me to see his fancy chair before we met you and Shannon at that riverfront restaurant. He'd been insistent I had to come and try it. He was so sure I needed to buy one like it for my back.'

'Turn at the next corner, John, the medical room is in that far wing.'

A police car was parked about halfway down the short street and John pulled in beside it, near the door with a large red cross. 'Soph, the truck sticks out too much here. I'll go park by the front entrance. See you in a few minutes.'

'Okay.' I took a deep breath, slid out of the seat, pulled my tight skirt down, went to the door and knocked firmly. When the uniformed female constable opened it, I could see Shannon.

She saw me and jumped off the cot, the blanket wrapped around her falling to the floor as she rushed into my arms.

'Sophie!' she sobbed as we clung to each other.

Shannon looked terrible, her face as white as flour and her eyes red, swollen. We rocked for a bit and I stroked her back before pulling away slightly to examine her more. My stomach clenched when I saw her left pupil was almost a third larger than the right one.

Damn, she's got a severe concussion and is in shock, I realized, as I felt her body shaking. 'Come, let's sit,' and guided her back to the cot.

We sat close together and the young constable helped me tuck the blanket around her again. 'Shannon, where is your head hurting?'

'Cecil's dead, Soph. And I wish I hadn't seen his tongue. I can't stop seeing it, now. Looks horrible! Who did that to him? Who could have done … '

'Shhhh, breathe slowly, Shannon. There, there, my dear,' I pulled her closer to me, trying to comfort her.

John knocked, the constable unlocked the door and he strode across the small room, knelt and wrapped both of us in his big arms.

I finally noticed a very large man who'd been sitting in the eye-wash station nook. As he stood and adjusted his vivid green-striped tie, he said to John and me, 'I'm Detective Sergeant Moffatt.'

John stood up, stuck out a hand and they shook as he introduced me, and himself. 'Sophia Nord is Shannon's close friend and I'm John MacNeacall.'

'Glad you're here,' the detective repeated as the young constable pushed Moffatt the examination stool. He carefully balanced himself on it and rolled nearer the cot.

'Dr. Saito has had a profound shock plus she hit her head on Dr. Fischer's credenza.'

'Is a doctor coming?' John asked as he slid toward the eye-wash corner. Having five of us in this room made it feel very small.

'Shannon, can you show me where your head hit?' I asked and passed her the tissue box.

'It does hurt here, from my left ear to up here.' She wiped her nose and cupped her hand around the back top of her head.

The detective and I exchanged a look and he said that Detective Inspector Woiden had called the Emergency and was now waiting for a call from the doctor.

'Maybe I should try and reach her own doctor?' On top of her shock from finding Cecil, she definitely had a concussion and would need x-rays.

'Let's wait for the ER doctor's call,' Moffatt said, explaining that if Shannon went to the hospital's emergency waiting room now, she might not remember what she'd seen in Cecil's office.

'Emergency might not be the ideal place for her,' I acknowledged.

He nodded, took a glass of water from the constable and passed it to me.

'Sip a little, Shannon. Is your head hurting more or less, or the same?'

'I think about the same as long as I stay sitting up. I tried to lie down but that made it pound more and I became very dizzy, almost barfed. I can't get these tears to stop. Because,' Shannon sniffled and wiped her cheeks impatiently, 'because, Soph, Cecil is dead. It isn't real but I know that. I saw him. But how I wish I hadn't.'

'That was very awful for you and I'm so sorry and sad we've lost him. I patted her shoulder and passed her the cup. 'Drink a little more, okay?'

Moffatt waited while she finished the water before asking in a quiet voice, 'Dr. Saito, do you feel up to my asking you a couple of questions?'

'Yes, I know you have to find who murdered him. Who could have someone done that to Cecil and why? However I can help, I will.' She blew her nose again, hiccupped a sob and repeated to me, 'Why would anyone do that to Cecil?'

The detective answered. 'We don't know yet, Dr. Saito, and I appreciate your help as we go forward with the investigation. My first question is about the time before you went into Cecil's office and fainted. Can you tell me what you did after you parked your car?' The detective sounded as though he had all the time in the world.

'I walked down the hall and opened his door.' Her voice became a whisper, 'saw Cecil with his tongue lolling out, so very large. And so awful! That's all I remember.' Shannon dropped her face into her hands and sobbed softly.

I wrapped the blanket more tightly around her shoulders and took a deep breath. After she'd described Cecil, my stomach turned over.

She sat up and turned to me. 'He was stretched almost flat out in his damn chair, Soph, just like he was twice daily. His head was angled strangely but all I looked at was his swollen tongue.'

Detective Moffat rolled a little closer and asked, 'Dr. Saito, will you help me, I've more questions, though I know remembering hurts. I am very sorry about Dr. Fischer's death,' he acknowledged. 'As you looked across his desk at him, is there anything else you can recall?'

'That man in Cecil's chair didn't look at all like him!'

'Was the chair where you expected?'

'It only fits one way when it's stretched open. I only remember seeing Cecil, don't know what happened next.' Shannon now sounded a little irate and placed my hand on the back of her head. 'Soph, feel this big bump.'

The detective nodded at me, and I stood up to feel her head. 'Shannon, look at me, please, I want to see your eyes again,' I ordered, trying to get her past finding Cecil, and also feeling concerned about her injury.

'My head's sore but okay, it's throbbing a little less. May I have some more water?'

The constable refilled the cup and Shannon drank the whole thing before shaking off the blanket again. 'I'm too hot. Detective, what is happening to Cecil?'

I looked over at John, who was now crunched into the eye-wash chair, then at the detective, and knew they were as unsure about what she was asking as I was. Does Shannon want to know about his body now or about what would happen with Cecil?

Detective Moffatt paused before answering both questions. 'Well, by now, Dr. Fischer's body will be on the way to the coroner's office. It will be examined and eventually released as directed. And around what has happened, you know as much as we do, currently. Someone killed Dr. Fischer when he was stretched out in his reclining office chair. Now, you said he opened it up like that twice a day? Why, Dr. Saito?'

'Yes, everyone knew he did that, probably including whoever killed him.' I realized Shannon sounded abrupt, unlike her usual self and worried about how deep her concussion is, yet knowing there isn't a magic pill.

John interjected. 'I know about Cecil's chair since he recently demonstrated it for me. And I had actually tried it out, felt like I was upside down on a jungle gym - or a horse. He had done considerable research into brain health and firmly believed that lowering one's head below one's body does get oxygen to the brain, keeps it healthy and delays ageing. That's why he bought the tilting recliner.'

'Interesting,' Moffatt raised his thick eyebrows and I took his one word as skeptical, as did Shannon.

'To my surprise,' she said, 'I think it was working for him, his face looked less tense.'

'Do you know if Dr. Fischer tilted his chair at a specific time each day?'

'I think so but not for sure. Cecil does like scheduling so probably about mid-morning and mid-afternoon.'

'That's what he told me,' John recalled.

'How long did it take him?'

Shannon shrugged. 'To be honest, I didn't listen well to Cecil's chair details. He likes buying gimmicky things whereas I don't. He kept wanting to buy me that chair, and I kept saying no.'

Oh, Shannon. Her explaining about what Cecil liked reminded me of how different they were. And as people go, how complex he was, many layers.

'Detective,' she sniffed, trying to sound calm, 'Is there a typical time it takes to find a murderer?'

'I wish. It varies widely and can take a very long time. Dr. Saito, are you okay for me to keep asking you questions?'

'Yes, okay.'

'Do you remember whether Dr. Fischer's office door was open or closed?'

'It was open about six inches and I pushed it wider as I called hello and walked in. Cecil's chair was below the window, fully opened up and tipped downward. That's how Cecil had to angle it or there wasn't enough room?'

Moffatt's eyebrows shot up. 'It had to be in the same place? Is there much room behind him when it's down?'

'Hardly any but Cecil had measured it carefully before he bought the chair. Last week, he asked me whether his colour was better?' Shannon added sadly. 'I lied and said yes to make him feel good.'

'Was he having health problems?'

I noticed Moffatt's face was increasingly red, his shirt's top button too tight as he rolled his stool back a bit. Shannon's looked even whiter.

'You okay? 'I interrupted the detective's next question.

'Maybe. Soph, will you tell the detective about Cecil's deciding to buy the chair?'

'Just before last Christmas, he showed all of us the miracle chair's promotional pamphlet and said he was buying himself a gift. We had been stunned that the mechanical recliner cost over eight thousand dollars.'

'We knew Cecil was a bit of a mark about his health but that had seemed overly pricey,' John added. 'And why I had come to admire his chair. He'd done the same for me when I've splurged on a horse.'

'Cecil had no known health issues, he was just zealous

about maintaining it,' Shannon said bluntly.

Moffatt nodded appreciatively and continued. 'Do you remember, Dr. Saito, if the chair looked completely flat?'

'I don't know. Once I saw his tongue, I only saw that,' she whispered as her tears overflowed again.

'Do you usually park by his windows?'

'Yes, I always park there, sometimes honk and Cecil came out if we were going somewhere. I have a key. Don't have to go through security when I'm going to his office.'

'Do many people have keys to that door?'

'I don't know. I didn't honk today because I came in and used the washroom right by the door before going down the hall to his office.'

Shannon was gaining a little colour. 'Detective, do you think it has to be someone at the lab who killed him?'

'We'll have to find that out, Dr. Saito, and we need your help.'

'It doesn't make any sense, does it? Cecil wouldn't have just let someone go behind him, strangle him.'

'No but that is what has happened. Now after using the washroom, tell me about going down the hall. Did you see anyone?'

'No one I don't know.'

'Who did you see?' Moffatt gingerly adjusted himself on the stool again.

'Peter, I saw him. Dr. Peter James, one of Cecil's assistants. His office is right across from the outside door, but his back was to the door and he was wearing his earphones. I don't think he saw me and I didn't say hi, not wanting to interrupt.'

As she talked, I touched my head and raised my eyebrows at John, unsure about her head injury, worried it was more than a concussion. I wondered if the emergency room doctor had called?

He raised his, signaling he was equally unsure.

'Dr. Saito, when you parked and got out of your car,' the detective continued in a chatty voice, 'was there another vehicle there? Or did you see anyone?'

'Only Peter's motorcycle and Cecil's SUV.'

'So you unlocked the door and saw Dr. James. What about in the hall, did you see anyone in the distance?'

'No, it was empty both ways. But I could hear the big vacuum, somewhere nearby in the other wing.'

'What did you do while you were in the hall?'

'Only walked to Cecil's office, pushed his door open and called 'Cecil.' She sighed and turned to me. 'I won't ever be able to do that again, Soph. He's dead.'

'He is,' John agreed, and asked, 'Shannon, how's that head of yours feel now?'

'Still has a big bump that hurts,' she reported, after raising her hand and running her fingers across the top of her head, then checking them for blood. 'The bleeding's stopped. I'll be okay except - except I can't believe Cecil's dead.'

Which is so damned unfair. After such tough early years, I knew how Cecil reveled in his successes and knew he would have hated the infamy of being a victim of murder. The inevitable publicity and investigators prying into his personal and professional history would have horrified him.

Damn! Now he'll become known as that rich scientist who was strangled. If he had to die, I wish he could have died in an accident.

As Detective Moffatt wrote in his notebook, the petite and silent constable offered water to John and me after she refilled Shannon's cup. While I sipped mine, I contemplated the investigation. We all knew it was a premeditated murder, planned in minute detail.

But the question is why? Why the viciousness? Strangling seems so malicious, an act of vengeance causing the victim's death. I thought again of the similarity to Carlos' murderer, Cecil's killer had been intimately involved in ending his life.

'Is there anything we can do to help, Detective Moffatt?' John stood up and stretched out his back as someone knocked firmly on the door to the hall.

A lithe man of about fifty entered, and came forward, hand out. 'Hello, I'm Inspector Woiden.' I shook his hand and felt myself relax some. He was more compact and a little shorter than John but equally muscular and had spectacular eyes, similar to a mountain lion's yellow-green.

His intensity dominated his face, made him appear to be crisply efficient. A hunk of auburn hair slipped onto his forehead and he impatiently flicked it back as he asked, 'How are you feeling now, Dr. Saito?'

'Better, thanks, Detective, since my friends arrived,' and waved at us. 'This is Sophia Nord and John MacNeacall - Cecil's friends, too, of course.'

'Well, I just talked with the doctor and she says you need to come to Emergency if you have more headache than earlier or feel nauseous. If not, then you must go to your own doctor tomorrow. Meanwhile, you need quiet, though you must not go to sleep for at least twelve hours. You need someone with you overnight and if your condition changes, you are to be taken toEmergency immediately.

'My head is aching less, I would like to go home.'

'I will be staying with Shannon.' I said.

'Good, then you can go now.' Woiden said and offered Shannon a hand up. 'We will come to you later, after we've been to Dr. Fischer's home, which I understand is close to yours. Probably in about three hours, okay?'

'Yes, that's fine. Cecil and my properties adjoin. And know whatever I can do to help identify his murderer, I will.'

'I have one question now, having seen the photo on Dr. Fischer's desk. Is it correct that you and he had a close relationship?'

'Yes, we do - we did. Sophie took that photo about four years ago, Cecil's Christmas gift from her. He and I were intimate life companions, though lived separately.'

The detective considered that for a moment. 'How long have the four of you been close friends?

'Shannon and Sophie have known Cecil for many years,'

answered John, 'I met him through Sophie and we are a couple. Also one with two residences.'

'Okay.' Woiden looked as if he would like to ask more about that topic but didn't. 'How many years ago did Dr. Fischer return to this region?'

'Almost twelve?' and asked, 'Shannon, do you know? He first opened his medical manufacturing laboratory, which was very small compared to this one. The next year, he started building his home on his late parent's fifty acres at Erin Lake.'

Shannon took over. 'That took him four years, then he built on a significant addition to the lab. My son, Yosh, and Sophie's grandson, Alex, spent all their university summers doing construction jobs for Cecil.'

'Where is Yosh now?' Detective Moffatt asked from where he was leaning against the built-in medical cabinet.'

'On a plane, heading for Africa,' Shannon stopped to blow her nose. 'He and his fiancée, a medical doctor who works there, are going to Greece.'

'Yosh will return to Erin Lake in about a month or so,' John added.

'So you all know each other and Dr. Fischer well?'

'Yes, though I'm the only one who has known Cecil since he was a teenager.'

He nodded and looked down at Shannon, bent some to see her eyes better. 'Now, Dr. Saito, be honest, how are you feeling, better or worse?'

'A little shaky but better,' she assured him. He pulled cards out of his pocket and passed one to Shannon, me and John. 'Okay, call me anytime, including if you remember something that might help us, even if it seems small to you.
We'll see you in a few hours.' With that, he turned towards the hall door.

'Just a minute, Detective Woiden,' Shannon announced. 'I've a question before you leave. Please tell us what you've found out so far?'

He nodded before pragmatically summarizing. 'Dr. Fischer was strangled in his office while lying prone in a mechanical office chair. You arrived at the lab he owned at about 11 a.m., found him deceased, fainted and injured your head. A cleaner called 911 and Detective Moffatt and I arrived at 11:28 am.'

'I don't remember that.'

'The cleaner is an older man, has worked for the lab for eight years. He told us he found you leaning on the credenza and wanted to take you to the first aid room, but you declined his assistance and told him you couldn't leave yet, you were staying with Cecil. We have not yet located anyone within the lab building who saw or heard anything, including your arrival.'

'Okay,' Shannon's voice was shaky, and John took her elbow.

DI Woiden noticed. 'I'll finish later at your home, Dr. Saito. Alright'

'No, now's better, please continue.'

I hid my amusement. Shannon's much more used to giving direction than taking them. Similar to me, I guess.

Woiden smiled slightly. 'Alright; upon your finding Dr. Fischer's body, we assume you fainted and hit your head, apparently on the corner of a credenza.'

'I don't remember that.'

'Okay. When Detective Moffatt and I arrived, we found you semi-conscious, confused and lying on the floor. When I checked your head for blood, I found a small oozing wound. On talking with you, I talked with the hospital Emergency nurse who decided you could go to the lab's medical room and the Emergency doctor would call me. The constable attending you contacted Mrs. Nord. Our crime scene investigators arrived to examine Dr. Fischer and the crime site.'

'Thank you, we'll leave now,' Shannon said, still clutching John's arm.

'I'll be back with the truck in five,' John said and followed Woiden and Moffatt out the hall door.

The constable, Shannon and I went outside to wait, and when John pulled up, she helped Shannon and me into the truck, then walked over to the police car.

'Where are Ana and Alex?'

'I'm unsure, Shannon, but waiting to hear from me. Do you want to talk with them or should I?'

'You, I'll see them at home. And Soph, tell them not to email or phone Yosh!'

Alex picked up on the first ring. 'Gran? Is Shannon doing okay?'

'She's right here, sitting between John and me, and heading for Erin Lake. She's managing okay but she took a big bump on her head. All that's known so far is Cecil was strangled in his office chair.' I told him that the detectives would be coming to Shannon's in a few hours. 'All the guests get away okay?'

'Yes, fine, everyone sent their warmest wishes, Gran, and I told them we'll send details soon. Ana and I are with Penelope and Albert in their hotel suite. What's the doctor said about Shannon's injury?'

I explained what was happening with that and passed on Shannon's order not to contact Yosh.

'No, we wouldn't unless she's with us. Yosh told Ana he'd check in with her from Johannesburg.'

'Sammy and David are headed to Vancouver. When I told them about Cecil, they said not to worry about arranging trip details, there's lots of time and I'm to tell you they want a rain check for a visit to Erin Lake.' Alex paused until my cell's crackling stopped. 'Gran, can you tell me anymore about what's actually happened?'

'Someone walked into Cecil's office and strangled him while he was flat out in his chair. Shannon found him, fainted and hit her head on the credenza. Her head has a large bump and a small cut, and her eyes reveal a significant concussion. The emergency doctor said she has to stay awake for twelve hours, and go to hospital if anything changes. Tell Ana I'll be staying overnight.'

'Seems so impossible, Gran. We'll see you up there, though Penelope and Albert aren't. They asked you to give hugs to Shannon from them and to make sure she knows Albert's staying here for a week and can stay longer, do anything needed to help.'

Shannon had been listening and when I closed the cell,

she murmured, 'I had forgotten that though Cecil told me. Albert's latest medical invention is about to be manufactured.

'Will it help, having Albert here?' John asked Shannon.

'Yes, he's probably the only one who's informed about Cecil's overall plans. In the month since Cecil's assistant died, Albert's been helping find a replacement and had recommended one of his own employees, but that man's wife won't leave London. Also, Albert knows most of the engineers well.' She leaned back and closed her eyes.

I wiped my sniffle on my sleeve as the reality of Cecil being gone sunk in. We'd first met when he was a skinny and forlorn thirteen-year-old. Shortly after we moved into our new Erin Lake home, he'd knocked on our door

When I answered it with Scott in my arms, Cecil had muttered, 'Missus, I'm your neighbour, do chores for $1 an hour.'

He'd stretched out a gangly finger, stoked Scott's cheek. 'I like babies.'

I had passed him Scott and he clutched my baby, smiled crookedly at me and his eyes weren't flat anymore. I will miss Cecil.

CHAPTER EIGHTEEN
- Sophia

When we reached Shannon's, she and John settled on the couch while I put the coffee on and started cooking bacon. The smell might make Shannon hungry, I hoped, aware her not having eaten today could be contributing to her headache. Her pupil sizes remained considerately different, and I wasn't comfortable she was okay.

'Remember, Shannon, no napping,' I called from the kitchen.

John called out, 'Shannon, would you like a fire? Takes the chill off.'

'Yes, John, there's kindling and some chopped wood in the box. I am very cold and tired but if I wrap up in a quilt, I'll go to sleep. Can you believe Cecil is dead? I can't.'

'None of us can, Shannon.' After quite a pause when I knew he was searching for subjects to keep her awake, he asked, 'Tell me about Albert and Cecil, were they close friends?'

I was glad he was going to make her talk.

Shannon took a while to answer. 'I haven't even thought about Cecil's company yet but Albert's being here is a big relief, he'll help build the bridges needed. Some of Cecil's engineers have worked for him previously plus the two of them have had regular and very long phone calls about technical developments. Albert's an amazing hardware guru, probably knows what's about to happen in electronics development better than anyone else I know. He'll understand what needs to happen at the lab. He's kind of like a ship's captain, able to manage whatever the weather.'

'Have you worked with him?'

'No, British software isn't my expertise.'

'And Albert's my good friend because he's married to

Penelope and the four of us holiday together annually, but we've never really understood each other's work worlds. Is it going to be tough going at the lab, Shannon?'

I sliced tomatoes and toasted bread, listening to them chat, aware the hole Cecil leaves within his company is huge. He liked being secretive and, I suspect, didn't delegate easily.

'Chaotic, John. It's less than a month since his trusted kite-flying assistant collided with a mountain. He'd been with Cecil almost five years. Replacing him wasn't going to be easy.'

Shannon thought about it awhile before continuing. 'He's like you, John, easygoing. Albert doesn't get his shirt in a knot about anything.'

I put the platter of sandwiches on the wheeled kitchen cart, added plates, mugs, carafe of coffee, cream and sugar, pushed it through the swinging door and announced, 'Self- serve.'

Once we each had a full plate and a mug, I added to John's earlier question. 'I've been listening in, and do you know, Shannon, I've never quite understood why Albert had Cecil's lab doing his prototypes and manufacturing. Do you know?'

'They're both very creative inventors but Albert's never been a manufacturer, picks his manufacturers for their reputation and ongoing quality. Cecil's company grew quickly after Albert started using it. Before that, the lab mainly manufactured Cecil's own inventions.

As I nibbled at my sandwich, I considered the complexities that Cecil's death creates for Shannon.

Last year, he talked her into being on the Board of Directors for two years because he needed a director who's a software expert.

Even more complex is that last November, after his sister Lily insisted on being replaced as his named executor and recipient of his wealth, Shannon agreed to be his personal executor.

She hadn't been happy and had mulled with me whether to agree, since she liked being his mate but hadn't committed to marrying him. When I'd asked the odds for five years from now, she'd laughed and said they were high.

Cecil had assured her all the estate's details would be handled by lawyers and pointed out there wasn't really anyone else. Shannon agreed to be named but was adamant she could not be his personal beneficiary. I've no idea who is.

John refilled our mugs as Shannon asked, 'What do you two think about the chances of them finding the murderer?'

Her plaintive voice immediately reminded me of Renee, and of all her decades of living with Carlos' unsolved murder. Cecil's murder immediately seemed similar to me, equally gory and without any warning. Renee had awakened, probably thinking of their wedding being only a week away, only to discover her future husband had been executed.

I took a deep breath and, as finding the killer didn't seem likely, lied. 'I think the detectives will eventually, but it will probably be slow-going.'

John hesitated, aware I was fibbing and did the same. 'I agree it'll be slow going, Shannon, but those detectives know what they're doing.'

The phone rang. 'Hi Gran, we're at Cecil's place, about to pack up Phoenix. Ana decided it's best to get her in the moving truck and at Shannon's. Probably take us a while. I don't have Yosh's skills to assist her.'

'Do you want John to come and help?'

'No, Ana says we'll manage easily. Hey, a grey car's just parked, must be the detectives. See you when we get there.'

Shannon was nibbling at a sandwich, but she looked as weary as I felt. We've all had so little sleep, John about six hours, me less as I had watched the stars for quite a while, still on such a high from my surprise party. I knew Shannon and Cecil had been together but didn't know at which house, probably here.

But around Shannon's concussion, she and I weren't napping today. Being in fresh air would be second best to a nap for me, and would probably work for Shannon, too. And there's something comforting about rubbing a horse's nose and ears. 'Want to go talk with the horses before the detectives arrive?'

'I'd like that, Soph, and I'll take a shower after our walk. It will be a while before Woiden and Moffat arrive, if they just got to Cecil's.'

'Are you feeling a little better?'

'Not really, but it isn't because of my head. It's throbbing less, Soph, but I keep seeing Cecil. Do you think he would have died fast?'

'Very quickly, Shannon,' I said firmly, though I didn't have a clue.

'I hope so,' she murmured. 'We came here after your party, and we were so content with each other this morning, peaceful. We weren't always as you know - and as you and John appear to be.'

'I do understand.' Ongoing mixed emotions was what I'd shared about my late husband after he'd become an alcoholic, but I've never felt similar about John. I knew Shannon had at times about Cecil. 'I'm sure ready for some fresh air. You?'

'Yes.'

When Shannon's mare saw us, she came galloping over to the corral's fence, stretched out her long neck across it and whinnied. Shannon rubbed her ears and muzzle while I stroked Yosh's gelding. We strolled for almost an hour and then went back into the living room where we found John asleep on the long couch.

Shannon beckoned me into her office area at the far end of the kitchen, filled two glasses with lemon water and, as usual, we settled on her cushioned window seat. She'd had a duplicate of mine made, though hers is covered with a fascinating fabric from Japan, a collage of language symbols and I latched onto those as a topic, asking, 'Shannon, was it very hard to learn to speak and write Japanese?'

'Impossible at first to understand the written language and although I learned to speak a small number of words quite quickly and became fluent by the time Yosh was a toddler, my pronunciation was always off.' She paused and added pensively, 'Such a long time ago.'

We kept talking about her time in Japan until she said, 'Listen, that's the moving truck's motor and another vehicle. The detectives, you think?'

'No, probably my jeep, Alex is driving it.'

When he and Ana came in a few moments later, they told us the detectives were about ten minutes behind them as they went over to Shannon and took turns hugging her.

'I'm so sad about Cecil,' Ana said and Alex added, 'Whatever I can do, just ask, okay, Shannon?'

She agreed she would, assured them her head was improving and asked, 'Are you two hungry?'

Alex peered at her eyes and said, 'Well, your pupils are not okay yet. I'm starving but I will make us something, you rest.'

'I can smell bacon and would like a BLT,' Ana agreed. 'But after I shower. Wrapping and moving Phoenix is grubby work.'

I offered to make them sandwiches as I headed to the living room. 'I best wake John, he'll want a few minutes to himself before the detectives arrive.'

I gently grabbed John's sock on the couch's wide arm.

He awoke and rumbled, 'That you, Soph? What's happening?'

'You look like a bear coming out of hibernation,' I laughed and he pretended to kick me before he stood up and gathered me into his arms.

'How are you doing, my dear? Any word from Woiden? I've got to feed tonight.'

'They'll be here soon,' I told him and headed back to the kitchen as he went down the hall.

'Want help, Gran?' Alex offered

Shannon stood up. 'No, Alex, I need to move, I'll help Soph. How about you restocking the wood box and keeping the fire burning? Late afternoons do cool off.'

As he left, I guided Shannon under the fluorescent light and peered at her pupils. 'It's coming along, certainly not equal yet but improved from this morning. Can you leave a message with your doctor's answering service about seeing you first thing tomorrow?

'Yes, I want to go first thing, I've so much to do tomorrow.' She walked over to the phone on her desk, chatted with someone, then said, 'There.'

Alex came in and asked, 'How about I make a big pot of coffee, Shannon? I'm ready for about three cups, and those detectives probably will be, too.'

'Use the big pot,' she told him. 'And, Soph, will you cook all the bacon? They might want sandwiches, too.

CHAPTER NINETEEN
- Alex

I filled and put the tall blue coffee pot onto boil and sat beside Shannon. She'd turned a kitchen chair and was staring out at the pasture and cloudy sky, her feet on the low windowsill. 'How are you doing?'

'I'm numb, Alex. Wish I hadn't been who found Cecil and wish I could block seeing him.'

'I wish you hadn't', I agreed.

'Bizarrely, I'm angry at him. But he would understand, tell me it's okay to be.'

'Cecil did enjoy satire, didn't he?' and didn't add it could also aggravate me. I found myself thinking, he could be a little cruel as Liza's humour often was.

I realized in some ways, Shannon's and Cecil's relationship was similar to what Liza's and mine had been. Like her, Cecil was always sure of his needs, though not always of hers.

Gran came up behind Shannon and mimed to me to keep her talking.

'Tell me about the detectives, Shannon. Ana and I only met them briefly as we had Phoenix on the forklift when they arrived. I had to keep moving and then went into the house and called we were leaving. Don't even remember their names.'

'Detective Sergeant Moffatt and Detective Inspector Woiden; they've been kind and considerate, but I don't know anything about them.'

'Ana thought the older big guy probably plays at being not too bright, because of his lime green tie, said it was his prop.'

'She could be right. I like him. He's who took me to the medical room and wrapped the blanket around me when I was shaking so. Then the female constable arrived and she took the facecloth from him to clean up the blood.'

'Blood? From what, Shannon?'

'It was on my cheek and hair from this.' She parted her auburn hair and I saw the inch-long cut high behind her left ear. 'Head wounds bleed, Alex, and this one did.'

'It's congealed well now. How much is you head aching?

'Some. Less than at first, it did hurt badly after I fell against the corner of the credenza. Staying awakes hard. I'm longing to go to sleep.'

'Only five hours to go,' Gran said, her voice betraying her weariness. 'The emergency doctor Woiden talked with directed that and she has go to her doctor tomorrow and be closely monitored overnight. I'm going to sleep on the chaise in her room.'

I'll bunk into Yosh's room, I decided. Better than Ana having to drive to the hospital, if necessary.

The front doorbell chimed and Shannon said, 'Get that, Alex? Take them to the living room, I need to wash my face.'

When I ushered the detectives in, they stopped and stared, like most visitors to Shannon's do as her decor is as unique as Cecil's. Her spacious room has a high ceiling, indirect lighting, and a multitude of ferns and tall plants. Its cream and teal shades appeal as does all her comfortable loveseats and chairs. Across from the fireplace is a long chesterfield and behind it on the wall hiding the stairs are three massive misty Japanese paintings.

Those mesmerize me, as do Yosh's abstract sculptures. Two are as tall as I am and I named them the spaceships, which amuses Yosh. His third piece is a burnished bronze and sits on a long low table in front of the floor length window. It shimmers in the light to various shades of bronze and reminds me of a big swan spreading its wings, about to fly.

'Hello, again,' Shannon greeted the detectives. 'We've coffee brewing, if you would like a cup?'

'Of course, Dr. Saito, thanks. I'm enthralled with your unique room,' Detective Woiden said as he stepped close to her and peered down into her eyes. 'Are you doing a little better now?'

Shannon nodded as Gran arrived. 'Detectives, would you like a sandwich with your coffee? I'm making BLT's for Ana and Alex.'

Both readily agreed.

'Does us gathering in the living room work okay or would you prefer us sitting around the table?' I asked

'I am ready for a little comfort and want to stay in this special room,' Moffatt said and settled into the couch near Woiden in a grey tub chair.

'Hi,' John said as he came down the hall from Shannon's library-guest room. 'Glad you've arrived as I need to go soon. It's my stockman's night off and I've got animals to feed.'

'You can leave now, as long as all of you can come to Headquarters tomorrow afternoon, say at 3 pm? We'll discuss Dr. Fischer's history then and having all of you there will be helpful.' Woiden glanced around the room and each person nodded.

'Okay then, I'll head out now and see you then.' John gave Gran and Shannon hugs and gently punched my shoulder. 'Detectives, know I'll help however I can, but I do have a question now. Sophia and I are booked to be away for a short holiday. Is that still feasible or do you need us to stay in this area?'

'And I return to Vancouver Sunday,' I added. I've appointments next week in Vancouver to have the Packard repaired and repainted as I start organizing for my trip to La Paz. And suddenly remembered, I don't know what's happening with Cecil. Would the funeral service for him be soon or would it be a memorial service down the way?

Ana, arriving in jeans and a navy sweater, her hair in two pigtails, listened as Woiden answered John's and my questions, then added, 'I'm leaving, too.'

'Continue with your plans, though we'll need ongoing contact information, preferably a phone number. Asking questions by email isn't as efficient. After our session tomorrow, Dr.Saito is who will be with us quite often.

Do you have plans to be away in the next ten days?

'A symposium in Edmonton but I'll probably cancel that.'

John said goodbye and headed out the front door as Ana and I went into the kitchen. We made more sandwiches, loaded the cart, and Ana passed out plates while I filled mugs with coffee.

'Thanks, and as we don't want to intrude on you for too long, we'll keep asking questions as we eat.'

Woiden stirred cream and sugar into his mug before asking Shannon if she could summarize the genesis of Cecil's obvious wealth.

'From his own inventions at first. His first one, a monitor used by diabetics to measure blood sugar did well and continues to earn substantial royalties. As does just about everything else Cecil developed. The lab adds substantially to his and his investors' wealth. And there's his personal property and home, and a considerable art collection.'

'His estate is valuable, Dr. Saito,' Moffatt commented dryly.

'Yes. And he enjoyed using the options his wealth brought him. His home is too big for my liking, though the combination office and library upstairs is a special place, as is the patio. He spent a lot of time outside, liked looking after his plants and was diligent about exercising. Do you know the patio's creek is actually an eight feet deep swimming pool?'

'Creative,' Moffatt grinned and added, 'And I would steal his fountain, if it was feasible. Do you know if Dr. Fischer kept company records in his home office?

'I'm unsure. What he did was almost always carry two thick briefcases with the information he might require immediately. Do you know where those are?'

The detectives looked startled. 'No, though I'm sure they were not in his home office. Where might they be?'

'Probably in his SUV I saw parked outside the lab,' Her voice dropped and she sniffled.

Moffatt asked softly, 'Was it usual for him to leave

his briefcases in a vehicle?'

'Yes, they're heavy, back-up materials for whatever he was working on, and he liked working and making calls in a vehicle. He would sometimes sit outside here for a couple of hours.'

Woiden and Moffatt digested that as I passed the sandwiches. They each took another one, murmured thanks.'

Gran asked as Ana refilled the coffees, 'What did you think of Cecil's home?'

'Well, Mrs. Nord, it told me considerable about Dr. Fischer,' Woiden replied dryly.

We relaxed some with these men who will be questioning everything we think we know about Cecil. Two professionals doing their job, starting on what might become one of their most challenging murder investigations. Who killed him, and why?

How the hell will they investigate this maze of possibilities? As I wondered that, I was also aware of the pressure the detectives are under. Finding Cecil's murderer matters to all of us, particularly Shannon and the lab's employees. There, until the killer is exposed, suspicions about who did it will multiply.

My investigating Carlos' death won't be at all similar as it only matters to Gran and me. And if I discover those old La Paz police records have been discarded, or destroyed in the many hurricanes La Paz has had since 1938, the search is over almost before I start. But watching Woiden and Moffatt might teach me more about how to go about investigating because I also know I am a novice, and naive.

When I told Ana about having written to the La Paz police, requesting their assistance, she laughed. 'Alex, you don't understand, Mexico's mail can be slow. You'll probably get to the station before your letter does.'

For about the hundredth time, I asked myself, what the hell am I taking on in a country I know so little about? And Woiden and Moffatt would probably roll their eyes at me if I asked for tips.

When I returned to the present, Woiden was asking Shannon about the lab, after acknowledging he knew Cecil's assistant had died a month ago.

'Unknown, as Andre was his Chief Operating Officer and right hand for five years and replacing him was going to be a difficult challenge for Cecil. That's why I appreciate Albert's being here. He's liked as well as respected and can probably help you sort out who's who best. He's offered to help and knows details about Cecil's projects and the staff engineers' responsibilities.'

Shannon's one of the most pragmatic people I know, as well as one of the kindest, I thought, impressed she'd pass the lab's complexity over to Albert to explain. A very good move, and I was relieved to hear her sounding better.

She gave them Albert's cell number and added, 'Albert doesn't know what I'm requesting yet, but I meet him in the morning as soon as I see my doctor. How about we call you when we're together and you can give him the list of what you'll need?'

'That will work,' Woiden agreed and stood up. 'That's it for tonight, Dr. Saito. My sympathies to you, and before we leave, have you any questions for me?'

'Yes, Detective. What happens with Cecil next?'

He paused, recognized he was talking with a scientist and gave the long version. 'The medical investigative procedures and processes usually take about a week, though because of Dr. Fischer's complex condition, possibly longer. After those are completed, his remains will be released according to your directions. Which reminds me, tomorrow, please let us know which funeral parlour is to be notified. Are you projecting services for Dr. Fischer fairly soon?'

Shannon shook her head. 'No, perhaps it'll be in later September. Although I'm Cecil's executor, his sister will pick the date for his memorial in Thompson City.'

'Lily?' Gran sounded startled.

'Well, she's his only legal relative,' Shannon sighed deeply. 'What Cecil asked of Lily was when he died, she would come

to his memorial in Thompson City. She could choose the date
but it had to be within six months.'

'Oh?' Moffatt asked, raising his eyebrows.

'She'd keep delaying otherwise. Lily's somewhat childlike,
three years younger than Cecil. They exchanged Christmas
presents and very occasional phone calls. We did go to her
third wedding a couple of years ago. She lives in rural Ontario
with her wealthy husband, whose English we found
challenging to understand, though she does easily. Even
contacting Lily could take me some time as they often travel to
eastern Europe.'

'Okay, so Dr. Fischer's service isn't an issue,' Woiden said
briskly. 'What's your next question, Dr. Saito?'

I watched him sit up in his soft chair and he reminded me
of a cat waiting to pounce, though appreciated how gentle he
was with Shannon.

'I've no experience with police investigations, let alone a
murder one. What do we need to understand about the process,
Detective Woiden?'

He nodded at Moffatt.

'An investigation is as complex as a crossword puzzle.
If the A-down answer is wrong, many others will be as
well. It changes everything. Which is why you'll find we
ask the same question in different ways, over and over.
Although none of you are suspects, and neither of us expect
that to change, there are no guarantees,' the older detective
warned. 'Investigations can be intrusive and aggravating,
particularly for you, Dr. Saito. You are Dr. Fischer's mate
and we need to investigate all his current and former
friends, acquaintances, employees, and business contacts.
That will be slow going and sometimes it will appear we
are very inept. Know we'll answer your questions when we
can, but investigating can be very secretive.'

I thought, damn it, we don't need a lecture tonight and was
debating whether to say so.

Woiden smiled at me and took the lead. 'Cutting to the
quick here, it is the small pieces, as DS Moffatt says, that we
eventually fit together. We need to understand Dr. Fischer's

social involvements, hobbies, sports, etc. Our questions will often be repetitious. We find answers through persistence.'

'Do you anticipate being able to identify Cecil's murder?' Gran asked bluntly, and I knew she was thinking about Renee and Carlos.

'Of course, Mrs. Nord, but to be honest, I suspect it will be challenging. You're all thinking, how the hell will they do that?' Moffatt put his mug down and leaned his bulk forward. 'Well, there's a glass vacuum tube on Dr. Fischer's credenza. Right now, all we know is it's there and we have to find out why.'

I didn't know that and felt annoyed Renee's bequest had become involved. 'It's probably one of the two tubes Cecil took from an inheritance Gran recently received.'

'Why?' Woiden demanded.

'He offered to assist Gran and I research a relative's invention. He took two tubes from it possibly to show his engineers. But, Detectives, it's most unlikely those tubes were not pertinent to Cecil's death, because he only took them two days ago. Wouldn't have planning Cecil's complex murder taken considerable time?'

'Yes,' Woiden agreed. 'Two tubes? Where's the other one?

We all looked at each other.

My god, if one of Cecil's engineers doesn't have it, did the murderer take it?

'Possibly with the engineer, I'll find out tomorrow,' Shannon said.

'Thanks. Now, before we leave, Dr. Saito, some requests. Will you and Albert call me tomorrow morning and I'll have a list of what we need from the lab. And will start writing down anything you remember about Dr. Fischer or his activities? So, is there anything else before we leave?'

Shannon's voice was firm. 'Detective, of course. We will think on that. I'm realizing is there's so damn much I don't know about Cecil.'

'Fair enough, Dr. Saito. Nothing is black and white during

an investigation and the possibilities are grey, a faint suspicion.
I'll be honest as I can be within our changing parameters,'
Woiden replied. 'We are not magicians, though often wish we
were.'

'You're hunting a very shrewd and dangerous person,' Gran
interjected, 'and we all appreciate having your expertise.'

'Thanks,' Woiden smiled at her. 'Dr. Saito, sorry, but I do
one more question. How long have you and Dr. Fischer been a
couple?'

Shannon paused and sighed deeply. 'Hard to explain, but I
guess we've been a couple for approximately five years, though
taken a few sabbaticals around reconnecting. As well, Cecil and
I have some earlier history. During our last year at university,
we were engaged for seven months.'

Smooth summary, Shannon, your son would be impressed.
She'd been equally so when Yosh and I were young teenagers.
When Shannon wouldn't go out with Cecil, Yosh had asked her
why. She'd told him about their former relationship and that
it was okay to tell me as she's told Sophia. What ended their
engagement and made her unsure whether she wanted to be
Cecil's friend at Erin Lake was that he had impregnated
another woman while engaged to Shannon.

For many years, Yosh and I had weighed that when
discussing whether Cecil was right for Shannon. We haven't
lately, probably because both Yosh and I now understand the
intricacy of relationships much better than we did when we
started judging Cecil.

'Cecil and I mutually broke the engagement off, Detective,'
Shannon lied, sounding dismissive. 'Shortly after, I went to
Japan and married Hito Saito, Yosh's father. Until Cecil moved
back to Erin Lake, we didn't stay in touch or follow each
other's careers except through alumni bulletins.'

Personally, I don't believe that was true for Cecil. Yosh
and I think Cecil chose Thompson City more because of
Shannon being here than having inherited his family's acreage,

and that Cecil was following Shannon's career ever since she divorced Hito.

'Shannon, may I add something?' Gran interjected. 'That you didn't welcome Cecil to Erin Lake and had no contact with him for years after his return.'

'That's true, I wasn't delighted when Cecil decided to make Erin Lake and Thompson City his home.'

'Okay - now, please tell me more about your son.'

'Yosh is 28, a professional sculptor as his professional partner, Ana, is,' nodding at her. 'Our son is close to both of us. His father, Hito Saito, is a professor in Tokyo. When we divorced amicably fifteen years ago, he gave me full custody and as much financial support as we wanted.'

'Where is he currently?'

'En route to Africa where he'll be with his fiancée, Dr. Beth Walsh. They will be leaving for a holiday in Greece next week, then Yosh will return to Erin Lake for a week or two before returning to his studio in Vancouver.'

'Your son's work?' Moffatt waved at Yosh's tallest piece. 'I like it very much.'

Woiden added he did, too, and noticed Shannon try to stifle a yawn.

'Okay, sorry, we're done,' he stood up and waved his hand slightly. 'Thanks for your assistance and the sandwiches and coffee. Before we go, how's your head feel, Dr. Saito?'

'It's improving, only a dull ache now, though I'm very tired. I'll see the doctor early and will call when I'm with Albert, be at Headquarters for 3 pm. Do you know that I am Cecil's personal executor and I sit as a director on his corporation's board?'

'No, we didn't,' Moffat answered from the entry. 'Around that, may I ask one more question?'

'A short one,' Shannon ordered.

'Does Dr. Fischer have any current or previous partners in the company? And was he the majority shareholder and CEO?'

Wow, Moffatt looks like he's hanging on until he can retire

but he asks astute questions.

'It's all Cecil's, he owns 100% of the corporation's shares. Next year, he was going to add a share option for board members, the engineers and senior administrative staff. Everyone at the lab knows that and as far as I know, they are a good team who liked and respected Cecil.'

Gran stood up. 'Cecil has achieved so much and I'm probably the only one who fully understands that. He was thirteen when my late husband and I moved to Erin Lake, and his and Lily's family became our challenging neighbours. Their father was an angry man, a miserable miser and their mother was downtrodden, unable to protect them. Cecil spent considerable time at our home.'

'Thanks, knowing that helps, Mrs. Nord. So, Dr. Fischer earned his own wealth and enjoyed it fully.'

'Wonder who will inherit?' Moffatt speculated.

Shannon smiled and, remembering she's the executor, I raised my eyebrows at her.

Ana asked what we all were wondering. 'Could that be related to Cecil's death?'

'Of course, Miss Avila, though that motive seems unlikely,' said Woiden as he nodded at the door and Moffatt opened it. 'Good night.'

CHAPTER TWENTY
- Alex

When we heard the tires crunch the driveway gravel, I said, 'Alone at last!'

Gran laughed and agreed. 'How are you doing, Shannon? I feel very sad we've lost Cecil but, right now, I'm concerned for you.'

She sighed ruefully, pulled a footstool closer to her high back chair. 'More than anything, I want to go to bed, have this day over.'

'How about another slow stroll, then a snack? After that, it will be okay for you to go to bed, though with an extra pillow,' Gran announced. 'Don't sleep flat, okay?'

'You two are amazing and I'm ready for a walk. I love the smell of this air and the stars appeal, in such a different location than at our ranch.'

'How about I make cocoa and toast as you three walk?' I volunteered, aware of how exhausted Shannon and Gran were. Seemed unbelievable that it was only last night I was watching Cecil, alive and vibrant, pulling Shannon into a tight hug.

'Sounds ideal, Alex, but before we go, may I check your eyes, Shannon?'

She angled her head so Gran could see.

'Still uneven, I can tell from your expression. Okay, I'll be ready in five minutes,' and headed to her bedroom.

'Are you very concerned about her concussion, Sophia?' Ana asked.

'John is, and that matters as he's more knowledgeable about concussions. He's had a few himself, as have most cowboys who break-in horses.'

'Papa has, too, he trains his own horses, though my brother and Madre are becoming quite firm about what he can do, including not riding bucking broncos.

Gran laughed. 'Funny, I ordered John to do the same. I do hope to meet your parents this summer and am looking forward to being with your grandmother next week.'

'She's collecting Hernández history for you and is thinking about who she knows in Mexico who could assist Alex find the official records about Carlos. I haven't told her about Cecil yet, I'll wait until I get there.'

'Understandable,' I agreed. 'What I'm finding eerie is us trying to research Carlos' brutal murder and having Cecil be murdered even more cruelly today. I think both were executions.'

'Yes, but why?' Gran agreed as Shannon came down the hall and I switched subjects.

'May I be your chauffeur tomorrow?' I asked her and she agreed immediately.

'Thanks, Alex, I do have a full day. First the doctor, the meeting with Albert, then Cecil's personal lawyer before that 3 pm conference with the detectives. Though, remember, my SUV is at the lab and the Packard is not ideal.'

'John's picking me up so I don't need the jeep,' Gran said and passed out the fleeces that hang by Shannon's backdoor. 'It's cool outside. I've put cocoa on low, it'll be ready in about twenty minutes.'

As I followed the women down the driveway, I was thinking about how violent Cecil's death was and worrying about what if Woiden's team can't find the murderer? Although Shannon's in no way similar to Renee, not knowing will haunt her.

But there's so little known about his earlier history, how can the detectives begin to identify who is a suspect? Strangling's personal. Someone hated Cecil, I thought, and then questioned that. Or is it? Maybe his murder is supposed to appear to be a personal vendetta but maybe it wasn't? Some inventors are apparently quite demented. 'Shannon, do you know if Cecil had any crazy unhappy inventors threatening him in the last couple of years?'

'No but he probably wouldn't have told me. What I've been considering is how few intimate friends of Cecil's I've met or know about. There are very few and I find that sad. Alex, remember how we had to hone down Soph's list of special people to invite to her birthday? Yours and my list would be similar, we have a number of close friends. But as far as I know, Cecil had us, Lily, Albert and Penelope. Certainly he had reams of employees and many professional friends, mainly engineers or fellow business owners. They will all come to Cecil's memorial but might they be suspects?'

'And other than us, who will grieve his loss?'

'Probably not many,' Ana agreed. 'Death seems more final here or formalized or something as compared to in our culture. Most Mexicans do not believe death is an end but a part of the continuum of life.'

We all digested that until Gran said, 'I partly understand that Ana, having once had a special year-long relationship with a Mexican man. I went with him to his hometown, Patzcuaro on Janitzio Island and went to the Graveyard for Dia de los Muertos after midnight with his family. Many, many families were there, keeping vigils and lighting the multitude of candles. Their light illuminated all the marigolds covering each altar, quite magical.' Gran's voice was soft.

'For a year?' I queried, not curbing my curiosity about a man I've never heard of before but who obviously had mattered to my grandmother.

'A not-to-be relationship, though we'd hoped it might work out. But, mainly around each of our need for our home geographies, it couldn't. We still exchange notes on Christmas cards and he's now grandpa to five teenagers.'

'Ah, Soph, all our untold stories,' Shannon laughed softly. 'Ana, what about at your folks' ranch when someone dies. What happens to mark the passing? I want Cecil's service to be special.'

She thought as we strolled and I listened to the nearby male nightingale's declaring his availability, briefly amused about how a bird bluntly declares his need.

'Shannon, it's hard to summarize. I wish I had the letter Madre wrote me about Uncle's burial, it's full of details. So many came from far away, they almost outnumbered the locals, and there was a very long parade of mourners.'

'Parade?' Shannon asked.

'Yes, when it's feasible, we walk the departed person home to his or her resting place. Whereas funerals in cities are probably similar worldwide, villages develop special customs. Our tradition at the ranch is everyone carries a palm frond or flowers and we're like an escort, walk up the long hill to our little chapel and fenced graveyard. Madre told me Uncle's wooden coffin was in the back of his old pick-up and completely covered with palms and flowers, and everyone following it sang Dios Nunca Muere over and over. It was Uncle's favorite song.'

'Very special,' Sophia murmured.

Ana nodded and continued, 'Our family and Uncle's closest friends would have squeezed into the chapel, and everyone else circled it while the priest prayed between the hymns. Usually six, I think. When the service ended, Uncle's coffin would have then been put into his grave and each person including the children would have put a handful of dirt on it. After that, there would have been the stories and toasting, much food and cerveza, and the many guitars would have played the sad songs far into the night.'

'You cared for him very much,' Shannon murmured.

'Yes. I'll be saying my own goodbyes up at Uncle's cabin in the mountains later this summer.'

'Shannon, what about perhaps playing a song Cecil liked at various times during his service? It would act like a theme, make it unique to him.'

'That might work, Alex. He used to stretch out on a chaise and play one of Debussy's Preludes over and over.'

'Shannon, how about us going in now?' Gran added, 'that hot chocolate will be ready and I'm surprisingly hungry.

We ate without talking until Shannon pushed her unfinished toast away. 'I keep wishing Cecil had died from a heart attack or even in a road accident. What's so unreal is that we sat here this morning, had two glasses of orange juice each and talked about what fun the party was.' Her voice dropped to a whisper. 'I can't believe he's not coming back. Soph, how long before I can go to bed?'

'Another hour.'

'Damn! Okay, to help me stay awake let's talk about what we're all wondering. Who murdered him?'

'Oh, Shannon, I have no idea,' Ana sighed.

'Me, either,' Gran and I said in unison.

'But Cecil was brutally killed by someone. If we talk about it together, maybe we'll remember something that could help the detectives.'

'Okay, Shannon,' Ana agreed. 'Let's start with Cecil's office, what shape and size is it?'

'It's rectangular, quite long, not very wide,' I replied. 'I've only been in it a few times, the last being after New Year's. Remember Shannon, Cecil demonstrated his new chair for Yosh, you and me. Didn't it almost fill the space behind his desk when it was open?'

She shuddered and whispered, 'Yes,' obviously envisaging what she'd seen this morning.

'Where's the credenza on that long wall, closer to the desk or the door?' Gran asked and patted her shoulder.

'The door.'

'Did you notice it when you came in?' I asked, recognizing how weird it is that Renee's mysterious electronic tubes have become a factor in Cecil's murder investigation.

Gran stood up. 'It's time, we can go to bed and, Shannon, may I bunk on your bedroom chaise lounge? Are you using Yosh's room, Alex?'

I agreed I was and Ana ordered, 'I am to be awakened if anything's going on during the night.

At 6 am, I found Shannon at the kitchen table. 'How are you?'

'Watching the sun's rays dance on the dark pasture, thinking about Cecil. Sad, sore, but look, my pupils have improved some. And I know I disturbed your sleep. Sorry.'

I looked at her pupils and felt relieved. 'There is a little improvement. That coffee smells delicious, ready for another cup? I sure am. How are you doing?'

'Numb describes me best, I guess.'

'Hey, you two,' Ana said, joining us. 'I just checked the weather, it's going to be sunny today. Did you sleep?'

'Not much,' Shannon and I said together as Ana opened the bread cupboard and checked the contents.

'How about some toasted muffins? There's a whole package of lemon and raspberry ones.

Before either of us answered, the back door opened and Alex said in a surprised voice, 'Hey, I didn't expect all three of you to be up.' He came and put his hand on Shannon's shoulder. 'You okay?'

'To be honest, no, how could I be? Cecil is dead.'

'How come you're already dressed for the day?' I asked him, smelling his aftershave as he gave me a peck on the cheek.

'I was awake so did the farm chores here, then went home to get town clothes. I have to be dressed properly to be Shannon's driver and assistant. I've put the horses out into the back pasture.'

'Thanks, Alex, they're good there for days. That creek's running full. Shannon said and shook her head when Ana offered her a muffin.

'No, thanks, my stomach's queasy. Which does make me

even more relieved you're my chauffeur.'

'Which reminds me, Ana, since your car's at the hotel, okay if you ride into town with Soph and John? Or you can use the Packard?'

'If it works for you,' Gran added, 'ride in with us. And if you come over with me now, we can finish sorting your photos this morning.'

Ana asked Shannon if there was anything she could do for her before agreeing. 'Good idea, I would like to do that, and I can pick up my car after meeting Woiden and Moffatt.'

'What I am realizing is I know so much about Cecil in some areas and so little in others. Have any of you suggestions for the list Woiden requested?'

We looked at each other and I imagined I could almost see Cecil standing behind Shannon, his hands on the back of her chair, waiting and watching. Over the last few years, I've noticed he usually never suggested an outing together, then when someone else did, he might subtlety shape it to suit him better. Cecil was a complex man and I occasionally saw the shadows created by his childhood.

Shannon put her mug into the dishwasher and asked, 'Soph, would you try to connect with Lily? We need to tell her about Cecil and with the three-hour time change, you might catch her.'

She passed me an address book and the phone and as I punched in the Ontario number, I tried to figure out what to say. A breathy voice whispered, 'Hello?'

I pushed the speaker-phone button so Shannon, Alex and Ana could hear.

'Hello, Lily, it's Sophia Nord from Erin Lake.'

'Yes? I know it's you because of your voice, even though it has been a long time. Remember, we talked when you phoned me to say Merry Christmas?'

'Lily, I'm calling now because I have some very sad news.'

'What sad news?' Her voice sounded like a child's.

'I'm so sorry to have to tell you this, Cecil died yesterday.'

There was a long silence. 'Cecil is dead? Sophia, how very

odd, my brother isn't old. My husband is eight years older than him. Was it a heart attack? That's what took our father. And you know what I said then, "Thank god!"'

'No, not heart. Sadly, Cecil died a violent death, Lily. The police detectives are investigating who killed him.'

'Killed him? Detectives? Was Cecil murdered?'

'Yes, Lily.'

'Good gracias! Cecil would be upset about dying like that. So very public.' She paused for quite a while before asking in a quivering voice, 'Sophia, do you think there will be much publicity? He would hate that.'

'There'll be some, Lily, and so many of us are going to miss Cecil very much.' I hesitated again, deciding she still sounded okay, and plunged ahead. 'Shannon's asked me to call you.'

'That's the woman who won't marry him yet, isn't it? My brother brought her to our wedding and I liked her. She's smart, a professor, you know? And she has such lovely curly auburn hair.' She gave a long sigh and I heard her sniffle. 'I am very sad about Cecil being dead.'

'I am, too, Lily. Would you like to go and tell your husband and I'll phone back in fifteen minutes?'

'No, he's gone, had another early meeting. I will tell him later this afternoon, after I get my hair done. And I need to hang up soon or I will be late.'

I was struggling with what to say next when she added, 'Do you know what's very strange, Sophia? I have often been thinking about Cecil, much more than I usually do. May I ask, how was he killed?'

'Lily, it's very tragic. Cecil was strangled at his office.'

'What? Do you mean by a rope around his neck? Or hands? Do they think it was a business killing? '

Her voice was a whisper now and I wished I could hug her, knew how processing my actual words was difficult for her.

'Yes, a rope was involved.'

Another long silence, 'Sophia, no one else I know has died like that.'

'Are you all right, Lily?'

'Thank you for asking, I am very sad. Would Cecil have suffered?'

'No, he died very quickly,' I said firmly, even though I didn't know.

Shannon whispered, 'The memorial service?'

I nodded. 'Lily, I have a question about Cecil's memorial service. Remember you agreed he would go to yours or you would come to his, when you resigned from being his executor.' I knew it was unlikely because Lily's childhood head injury had affected her memory. 'When can you come to Thompson City?

'No, I do not remember that. But I believe you and if you say so, I will come. But returning to Thompson City will be hard for me, Sophia.'

By the time we said goodbye, Lily had agreed to Cecil's memorial being on Saturday, October 2nd, and announced she would come alone by train. She wanted to see Cecil's home and fountain but definitely could not stay with me.

'I never want to sleep at Erin Lake, Sophia.'

'Is there anything you would like?'

'Yes,' she said firmly. 'I would like to do the flowers for my brother's funeral. Do you know what colours would he like? Will you promise me that I do not have to stand up and talk?'

'Of course, Shannon and I both promise that. What about the fall shades, bronzes, deep reds and yellows? Cecil planted those shades for fall.'

'Yes, our mother loved those ones, too. But she stopped planting flowers after the man stomped through her wonderful gardens with his boots.'

'He was a cruel man, wasn't he, Lily? Now, I have one more thing to tell you before we hang up.'

'What is that?'

'A detective will be calling you because he needs your help. Do you want him to call in the morning or afternoon?

'Oh, no, Sophia, please tell them about my memory and to not phone me. Asking me questions gives me a bad headache and I do not know many answers. And I do not want to try and answer questions about Cecil and my family.'

'Well, Lily, the detective who has to phone you is kind,' I reassured her, and suddenly recalled something myself. 'Remember that accident Cecil had in California? You phoned me when he was in hospital, close to where you lived in Los Angeles. He can ask you questions about that.'

'I do remember it a little because I visited him many times in hospital. He was so scared he might have to go to jail, Sophia. But he didn't.'

I almost dropped the phone. 'Jail?'

Ana, Shannon and Alex looked as startled as I probably did.

'Do you remember what I told you? Karen died after a while, though their baby didn't. She was in the incubator, I got a look at her. Then after Cecil got out of hospital, he told me Karen's mother took the baby to her house far away. She never let him go and see the baby girl. Before he left for England, a letter came about the baby dying.'

'Do you know where the grandmother lived?'

'I do not remember, maybe Wyoming. Or was it Kansas? I really must go now or I'll be late, Sophia, and my hairdresser becomes annoyed with me.'

'All right, phone me any time you want.'

'I will, Sophia, and thank you for telling me the very sad news about my brother. I will miss Cecil very much. Will you say hello to Shannon from me? She will miss him, too.'

I offered the phone to Shannon and she shook her head. 'Lily, please help the detective and I will call you again soon.'

'Thanks, Soph.'

As we went back to the kitchen table, she added, 'She's beautiful but Cecil worried about her vulnerability.'

'Beautiful? I still think of her as waif-like.'

'Oh, she's gorgeous, tawny blond hair like Cecil's and vivid green eyes. She's about my height but so fine-boned, I felt hefty next to her. Cecil had liked Severino at the wedding and told me comparing him to Lily's first two husbands was like trying to compare a BMW to a rusty jalopy. Though he was suspicious about all his noticeable wealth and huge home, hoped that it didn't have mafia ties. Neither of us could understand his broken English much, though Lily seemed to easily.'

'Well, good you reached her,' Ana said, standing up. 'I need to get ready and call Boston, back in about twenty minutes.

'Time for me to get moving, too.' Shannon stood up quickly and then grabbed onto the table to stay balanced.

'You okay?'

'Not quite, but if I'm at the doctor's office as it opens, I'm sure he'll see me. What I'm feeling stunned about is that baby. But no wonder I didn't know about Cecil's daughter, I wouldn't let him talk at all about our university years after we got back together. All I've known about was Karen dying and Cecil being badly injured in that car accident.'

'Shannon, it's okay because he probably didn't want to rehash the past either.'

'Maybe, Alex,' she said impatiently. 'Or maybe not.'

'Who knows?' Alex turned to me, 'Gran, I never knew what you meant about Lily being a little slow but it shows in her speech. What are her memory issues?'

'I suspect an early injury but I haven't seen her since she was fourteen. In the decades since she fled Erin Lake, we've had irregular and often confusing phone conversations. Similar to what Cecil received, he told me she called him at Easter to tell him she likes her husband very much. He'd joked she'd said that about the previous two shortly before announcing she was divorcing. He hoped she would keep her current husband.'

'How are you going to summarize this conversation for the detectives?'

'Briefly, Alex. I'll say I notified his sister of Cecil's death, tell him the date of the memorial and told her a detective would be calling.'

'They need to know that Cecil had a child. Please tell them that, too,' Shannon ordered.

'Okay but it probably isn't relevant. In recent years, have you or Cecil met with anyone from your university years?

'Both of us regularly bump into the occasional person at the scientific symposiums or conventions but Albert's our only friend.'

'Albert?' I knew his doctorate was from a California university because Penelope sometimes teases him about his American perspective but didn't know it was the same one.

'Albert was Cecil's fourth year mentor in our first year there, but I barely knew him. Or Cecil. We started dating in third year. But enough of this old history, I'm off for a long shower. And Soph, I've decided even though my dear and very proper mother would have demanded I wear black, I'm not going to, okay?'

'Of course okay Shannon, black for mourning is as archaic as dial phones. Now, as soon as Ana's ready, we'll head out, so meet you at the station at three. But I want to know what the doctor says. Phone me.'

CHAPTER TWENTY-TWO
- Ana

Alex squeezed onto the Packard's narrow backseat and Sophia drove when we headed to their place where Alex would pick up the jeep.

'Good to be behind the old lady's wheel again, Gran?'

'Yes, she feels fine despite been battered by a moose.'

'Do you know this was Gran's car for over thirty years, Ana? And, Gran, it's been eons since I've been scrunched in here.'

'I suspect you've probably grown considerably since then.'

I laughed, enjoying their banter. 'Alex, when you drive this in La Paz, you'll be noticed, some old people might even remember seeing Carlos driving a car like it.'

'Ana, what about the summer heat? Do you think the Packard will manage that?' Sophia asked me.

'Previous to my motorcycle, I used to drive a 1953 Jeep up and down the Baja highway often, had to top up the radiator more often in summer. This car will be fine, though best not to drive in the midday. Are you able to do some minor repairs yourself?'

'After working on her rebuild for so many months, I know how but the tools are specialized. I'll have the mechanic figure out what extra parts to take and some detailed maintenance instructions. But, Ana, if I do have a breakdown, I expect you to keep going.'

'Don't be silly, I'm not on a schedule either. I want to help you find an interpreter in La Paz and to meet my friends there. And it's unlikely breakdowns will be an issue.'

Once we said goodbye to Alex, we went in and she filled KitKat's bowl, then led me to her large office off her bedroom.

When she turned on its lighting, I gasped when I saw the long digital display board was covered with shots of Phoenix.

'Sophia, you even captured her dancing,' I scanned the many photos displayed. 'Thank you, to have these photos and to see my work displayed like this is such a gift.'

Sculpting Phoenix had taken me almost two years of intense work and I now could see what I managed to achieve. Yosh has told me I'll have an epiphany when I know I am a professional sculptor and all those hard moments are worth it - and this is it.

'These photos will all print well technically,' Sophia said. 'Now, I'm going to leave you to choose which ones you want and go sort the rest of Renee's stuff. Box four is close to being empty and I hope to finish before John arrives.'

'I'll help after I figure out which ones to use. Saying thank you is so inadequate but know I'll be saying it to you every time I pass out my retrospective.'

As I sorted, I was trying to view everything through Yosh's perspective. He understands more than I currently do what the museum and gallery curators want. And then wondered again about Yosh and Beth's reaction to Cecil's death? It might change where they decide to settle. I understand why Shannon doesn't want to tell them and shade their early honeymoon. But I know why they do need to know soon as while they're together, Beth's deciding where in BC she wants to establish her medical practice. Her Africa contract ends in December.

Shannon doesn't know that but I'm going to tell her before I leave for Boston. As I chose the last two photos, I thought about how much she has to endure in the next while. On top of losing Cecil, the investigation will intrude on her life as his history is probed.

When I returned to the kitchen, I saw the empty blue box and cheered.

'Not quite yet,' Sophia said and pointed at the stack of folders on her lap, then at the green garbage bag. 'That stuff is all the duplicates of our parents' history I sent her, and I guess she didn't recall I have the originals. But flipping through our Mother's and Dad's history again was a benefit as I kept comparing their narrow life to the one Renee and Carlos would have shared. Even before she got TB, Renee must have found it tough. Though, Ana, I'm not sure whether they would have let her come home to Thompson City, even after I was born.'

'That's sad. Now, how can I help?'

'I'm hungry, how about you making us some sandwiches while I finish these folders? Choice is tuna or tomato and cheese.'

'Tuna.'

'Okay, fresh buns are in the upper cupboard by the sink and the tuna's in the bottom drawer below that. I like mayo, lettuce and lots of pickles, please. Let's eat on the deck and, after, are you okay with reading the rest of Renee's scribbler?

'Of course.'

While we ate, I asked her whether the parallels between Cecil's and Carlos' deaths seemed as odd to her as they do to me. 'The violence, the possibility of having been killed because of having invented something?'

'I find it an eerie coincidence, Sophia.'

'Certainly has me thinking about Carlos' actual death, about how everyone would have reacted after he was found and hoping it wasn't Renee who found him.'

'Shannon's not ever going to be able to stop seeing Cecil, is she?'

'No, and of course she is also wondering if he was the person she thought he was and worrying about the investigation, as well as grieving for him and for the loss of all they planned to do together. But, whatever, she will be okay. She's like you, Ana, lots of inner resources. Different from Renee, she's an established professional. Her going forward isn't changed by Cecil's loss, though her personal life sure is.'

'Yes, so very different from Renee's loss.'

'One thing about her damn bequest is it's had me remembering my own life, and how when I had to get married, my core world became as narrow as my folks, focused on being a good mother and wife. But after we bought this place at Erin Lake, I built up a market gardening business and am so glad I had those years of raising Scott. Then when I turned forty-five,I decided to go to photography school, which has turned out even better than I hoped. And I met John.'

I munched and looked down at the kayakers on the lake and thought, funny how I'm gaining understanding about why I had returned Titus' ring, two years ago. Although I loved him, and always will a little, it would have smothered me to be what he needed; be his wife, supportive of his law career and mother of our children. My sculpting would have been secondary.

Not at all feasible for me. I am a sculptor, I celebrated, thinking about all Sophia's shots of Phoenix.

She interrupted my reverie. 'Ana, what's going to be hard for Shannon is the waiting, the not knowing. All the questions she'll be asked will be exhausting and create even more uncertainties about Cecil.'

'For sure.'

'I asked her this morning whether she wanted me to stay with her, told her delaying John and my weekend away wasn't a big deal and she became annoyed, told me to carry on because of course she can manage whatever. But she did agree to come with us on the overnight trip we're making on our return, when John's delivering horses. So we're off to Boston and New York, and meeting your grandmother is going to be a highlight for me. Isn't it amazing she was with Renee and Carlos for Christmas in 1937?'

I was relieved Sophia was still coming. My 88-year old grandmother is excited about her being Carlos' daughter and related to the La Paz Hernández family. Daily emails have been coming from my grandmother's helper, telling me about the history she was remembering and that she's found her journal, which has good info for Sophia.

'I'm glad I can be with your grandmother before Alex and I are in La Paz,' Sophia said as she returned from taking the dishes to kitchen and getting Renee's scribbler. 'When I duplicated all the photos Renee left for Alex to take with him, I made copies for her.'

'She'll be delighted, and they might help her remember. Grandmother's request this morning is she meet John and has invited you out for an early dinner on your second night in Boston.'

'Sounds lovely,' she agreed, 'and John will insist on being the host.'

'Okay, ready?' and I picked up Renee's old scribbler.

'As much as I'll ever be,' Sophia admitted, 'though I would much rather you and I were heading down to the lake. I'm weary of Renee's revelations.'

I skimmed the next entries and summarized how she was helping with all the work over many guests staying at Carlos' parents for the Christmas holidays and for the preliminary preparations underway for the wedding fiesta. 'Renee and Marie were sewing lace whenever they sat down or making decorations around assisting with their daily chores of preparing many vegetables and making tortillas.'

Sophia sighed, 'I think Renee would have enjoyed that.

'Not always, listen to this from December 27th.'

There are so many rules to learn and I am so very tired! But I'm not throwing up anymore, and I do like most of the people here. The women are always teaching me what is proper and what isn't, telling me about how Mexican ladies must sit and stand, how I am to learn to manage the household and be a good cook myself, even though Uncle Rubin has a cook. All day long, every day, someone's telling me something I am supposed to remember.

Sophia laughed, 'My being in her belly probably helped her be completely cooperative with whatever.'

I nodded and wondered if I would ever know what that was like. 'On January 3, 1938, Renee wrote that Carlos' mother had made her stand sideways and decided she will have to wear a heavy lace veil over her wedding dress. Now, the next entry, January 5th, is confusing. Have we heard about someone called

171

Matias before? Listen to this:

Carlos is upset because Matias was punished, and I so wish I hadn't screamed. Everyone kept yelling and I was sent to bed as I couldn't stop crying.
'Who the hell is Matias?'
'No idea, but this gets even stranger.'

If only I hadn't screamed when the poor giant snuck up behind me and pulled my hair up into his big hands, Carlos would not have shouted at Matias. But it was very scary and when I did, everyone rushed out of the house and yelled at each other.'

'Screamed? Renee? Mother never raised her voice, she hissed in whispers when she was mad at me or at Dad so I'm sure Renee was raised to never scream,' Sophia said. 'Any more about Matias?'

Ana scanned ahead. 'Nothing. On January 8th, she's back to her future mother-in-law's dictates:

I am to wear my wedding dress for two days, first for the private marriage ceremonies in Father Morales' office on January 21st, then for Carlos and my fiesta starting at noon the next day.

Marie told me yesterday that Carlos and I are being marriedin the priest's office only because of the large amount being donated to the church. Father Morales will be marrying us at 9am with Carlos' parents, his two aunts, Uncle Rubin and Marie there as our witnesses.

Carlos says the blessings and prayers will take a very long time but the family feast at the hacienda will be fun. Family members also give us blessings and tell stories. And then, when everyone leaves, we can go to bed together and Carlos can feel our baby.

The next day at our fiesta we are supposed to talk to each person, a very big job as there will be so many guests. I get

*weary trying to talk Spanish so Carlos says I can just keep
smiling and nodding. We'll eat, visit and his Madre has told us
we cannot leave until 11 p.m.*

*Right now, I'm watching the window in my bedroom alcove
because the rain and wind are blowing so hard. It's frightening
and very noisy. I wonder if the windows ever break? I pray there
won't be a storm like this on our fiesta day.*

Sophia said ruefully, 'It's hard for me to visualize Renee
being the center of a grand fiesta.'

'And what I'm giggling at is bribing the priest, which I
suspect wouldn't be cheap.'

'Would have that been usual?

'I don't know, though it does mean that Carlos' family were
comfortably well-off and perhaps powerful. Perhaps because of
being affiliated with Rubin and his manufacturing companies
and at least one ocean-going ship. What I do know is Renee
would be taught to become a gracious Mexican matriarch and
directed how to raise you and your siblings to conform to the
cultural do's and don'ts.'

Sophia chuckled. 'That doesn't appeal at all, Ana. Were you
raised that way?'

'Oh, my grandmothers' influence about rights and wrong
is engrained but Madre's humour balanced it nicely', I said
as I skimmed ahead. 'Okay, in this entry, Renee's again
showing some backbone.'

*January 12: We are to live in Uncle Rubin's great house
in Mexico City for at least a year and Carlos' mother says my
work will be to supervise the maids and nanny.*

*I did not tell her, but I will be looking after our baby myself.
The nanny can help me learn how to because I don't know
anything about looking after babies yet.*

*Or about having one. I wish I could talk with my friend who
had a baby. Or with Mother, I guess.*

*I have not had a letter from home since I wrote to them
about Carlos and me getting married, and our having a baby. I
know they must be very angry, and I pray often that a letter*

will come soon.'

'Sophia, would Renee have had some sex education or know about birthing a baby?'

'Probably none about birthing, token about sex.'

'Well, the older Mexican women would have been whispering wisdoms to her and she would be coached and celebrated before and during birthing. One of the things I've learned is discussing body functions in Mexico seems to have way fewer taboos than in the US and Canada?'

'Really? I wasn't aware of that.'

'Just my perception,' I added. 'Soph, there's one more entry, then many pages are ripped out. And has Renee ever used the work angry before?'

January 16: It's a sad day and I feel very angry. Carlos just told me the Morgan's are coming to Mexico City with us and he will be working at the lab. But two good things are they will not be living next door and she will have to be much nicer to me because I will be Carlos' wife.

Sophia and I laughed, then she asked, 'Ana, can you tell how many pages are ripped out? I wonder if Renee did that or someone else.'

I felt the edges at the scribbler's spine and slowly flipped forward. 'Hard to tell, maybe six or more, and all the remaining ones are blank.'

'How frustrating!'

'Yes, and as her last entry was five days before the wedding. Carlos must have been murdered on either January 17th, 18th, 19th or 20th.'

'Poor Renee,' Sophia murmured. 'But enough, time to return to being ready to talk about Cecil, it's twenty minutes to two. I'm going to get ready for town.'

We were waiting by the driveway when John arrived and I helped Sophia up, climbed into the backseat and listened in as she summarized the questions the detectives had asked last night and the phone call with Lily

'What did the doctor say?' John asked.

'Shannon's booked for x-rays and tests tomorrow. And she told me that although Albert's stepped into Cecil's shoes at the lab, she could feel the aura of nervousness and suspicion there.'

'Of course, Soph,' John said.

'Right now, she and Alex are with Cecil's personal lawyer. He's having her sign a number of authorities and his firm will look after things.'

'Authorities for what?'

'Handling the actual aftermath of Cecil's death, John. They'll do the arranging for the transfer of Cecil's remains from the police morgue to the funeral home and look after the many notifications of his death that are needed.'

'Good, that takes some of the pressure off Shannon.'

'And we're helping with doing Cecil's obit tonight, going to her place for a deli dinner after we're done with the detectives. You okay with that?'

'I'm planning to stay and overnight with you, okay?'

'Of course.' Sophia turned to look at me, 'On her last call, Shannon asked me to share something with you two.'

'What?' John asked.

'Who inherits Cecil's personal estate as she's decided to tell the detectives.'

'So who, Soph?'

'Yosh.'

'Yeah, that makes sense because who else did Cecil have?' John said and added, 'Yosh liked all the stages building Cecil's home took, went over all the architectural plans and the many, many revisions. Remember how the rest of us would roll our eyes and disappear when Cecil brought out the architectural drawings.'

Sophia chuckled with him. 'And it was Yosh who designed those circular stairs and the fountain's metal foundation but what I'm happy about is Cecil's grand place will not be going to strangers. Though it is droll that Shannon will end up helping to manage the property she firmly refused to inherit.'

'Ana, what do you think Yosh's reaction will be?' his deep blue eyes reflected in the rearview mirror.

'Mixed, I suspect. Honoured to be Cecil's heir but the timing's so wrong. He needs the next four months for uninterrupted work before our next exhibit opens. Plus, I don't know if he and Beth would consider moving to Erin Lake. He loves his studio in Vancouver with its views of the ocean and all the gatherings with fellow artisans, and Beth was considering the smaller towns nearby for her practice and their home.'

'Inheriting is inconvenient?' John sounded disbelieving while Sophia added the timing of receiving bequests mattered.

'Yosh is like me,' Ana tried to explain. 'Money doesn't matter much. Each of us was lucky to be financially supported by generous parents as we became sculptors. Now that we are selling our work, we each make a comfortable living but it's that increasing recognition as artists we value. It's way more important than mere money.'

John chuckled, and that deep sound reminded me of Papa's laugh. 'Sophie's similar. She judges her photos by awards more than the considerable loot each one earns.'

Sophia sputtered and poked him in the ribs. 'And you?'

'Well, I guess I'm sort of like that too, m'darlin'. Except I judge the value of a bull's sale around how many more horses it will enable me to buy. Now, another question, what's going to happen at the lab in the long term?'

'I think it's pretty cut and dried because all the shares are still held by Cecil but there are plans in place to go public next year,' I told them. 'Shannon told me Albert's willing to stay for six months because his company has a prototype currently being manufactured by the lab. She'll recommend him to the Board of Directors as the temporary administrator, and Albert will find Cecil's replacement.'

'Did Cecil and Albert ever invent anything jointly?' John asked.

'Not that I know of, though Cecil did work for Albert in his family's internationally respected business in London. It contracts out manufacturing, which somehow related to why Cecil could build a lab here.'

'Ah, that makes sense,' Ana said. 'Cecil had his major client before he built.'

'Yes. Personally, I'm hoping Albert's taking on the lab might mean Penelope will often be in Thompson City.'

'That would be good,' John agreed.

'It's a strange little world, isn't it, Ana? Phoebe and I had been colleagues for years and I never knew Albert, Cecil and Shannon had gone to the same university until this morning. Now, I'm going to turn on the local news to see if anything is on about Cecil's murder.'

I settled back against the truck's soft leather back seat and thought about the coincidences I've had in my life. Starting with Uncle choosing to be the ranch's blacksmith as well as a sculptor. Without having him as my mentor, I wouldn't be one now. Same with Yosh becoming my business partner. I only met him because Beth and I were roomies in grade twelve at the Boston boarding school and, years later, shared Paris.

John interrupted my daydreaming when he asked, 'Sophie, do you know what lighting you need for those damn cave snakes yet?'

'Damn cave snakes?' Sophia laughed at John.

'Those ones - and when do you fly to Loreto?'

I felt rather like a kid listening in to the adults talking and their ease with each other reminds me of my parents.

'Sammy's still organizing dates, it will be mid-July. But I haven't talked with him since Cecil died.'

'What about the variety of snakes in that area, do you know that yet, Soph?' John sounded surprisingly uptight for him.

Sophia's voice was gentle as she replied. 'No and we won't know.' The project's purpose is to investigate and record what species are in the caves and along the Sea of Cortez shore. But be assured, John, herpetologists are very careful with their photographers.'

John said over his shoulder, 'Ana, when I first met this dear woman, she travelled everywhere to photograph birds. I liked that better than her now seeking snakes.'

I leaned forward. 'John, my father dreads some snakes, too. Lost a young wrangler to a rattler bite about four years ago - he and all his cowboys now wear double leather boots.'

'We do, too,' John agreed. 'Surviving a rattler's bite can be dreadful. 'Soph, what footwear will you be wearing in those caves?'

She described the reinforced rubber foot safety gear from a specialty manufacturer in Australia. 'John, your concerns about snakes are like those I have when you move a massive and dangerous bull on your own.'

'Yeah, living is about choosing what risks to manage well,' John agreed and paused. 'Reminds me about Cecil and what I keep wondering, how the hell did his murderer manage to kill him in that chair?

'He or she had to have known him. I keep thinking, why?' Sophia admitted.

'Tell me more about Cecil,' I said, leaning forward. 'He was different than I had expected from all Yosh's stories.'

'How?' Sophia asked.

I wished I had kept my mouth shut. 'Well, I guess I found him edgy. Not as relaxed as I expected for Shannon's mate and someone as successful as he was. What am I trying to say? Compared to you, John, or my father or uncles, Cecil seemed young, still having to measure up somehow? Though he actually was younger, too, than most of you. Does it make any sense?'

'Yes,' John agreed it did while Sophia sighed. 'Ah, Ana, you're perceptive. My opinion is Cecil was typical of an abused kid, trusting others is hard. His father was a very angry and cruel man.'

'It does make sense because I have a dear friend in Mexico whose father was a similar destroyer. Even though she's now a successful lawyer, she can't easily trust anyone. She projects being antsy, which I though Cecil was.'

'Finding out who maliciously strangled him will be tough

but what I sure the hell hope, is that murderer doesn't get off on a criminally insane defence!' John turned into the old Justice building's parking lot and added, 'Now, we're ten minutes early. Do you two want to walk down and wait by the fountain?'

The smell of sweet flowers mixed with tangy pine was like stepping into a peaceful sanctuary, far away from contemplating Cecil's murder. When I heard the fountain, I thought how glad I'll be to be back home with all Mexico's gracious court-yards and fountains, and the people I love.

In these last two days, I've begun to understand why my grandmother says a murderer is an evil thief who does not deserve compassion.

CHAPTER TWENTY-THREE
- Alex

As I parked Gran's jeep at the Court House, Shannon noticed John, Gran and Ana down by the Court House's ancient fountain. 'Alex, they're sitting on the bench where Cecil and I spent many hours. He contemplated this one as he designed his.'

'I didn't know that. Take my elbow, Shannon, this cobblestone path is uneven for your high heels.'

Gran and Ana hugged her while I jazzed John about being in his suit again. 'Wow, you're looking good, man. Twice in one week?'

I know how much he dislikes suits but here he was, only two days after Gran's birthday, wearing it again.

'I don't have much experience with police interviews, Alex,' he rumbled. 'But I always wear a suit to a banker's so decided doing the same for detectives is probably in my best interests.'

He turned to Shannon. 'And my friend, you look wonderful but how are you under all that make-up?'

'Not great, John, hanging on, very tired. But I could get used to Alex chauffeuring me, I've been catnapping some.'

'Though you have turned me down for chauffeuring tomorrow.

'Well, I think best when driving and I'm only going to the x-ray department and lab tomorrow.'

Today, we'd talked more about Renee than Cecil. On the way into town, Shannon asked me whether Gran had found anything about her months after Carlos' death? And I gained some empathy for the annoying old woman today, but it was shaded by what I found in her unfair secrecy.

I stood on the far side of John as he made room on the park bench for Shannon by sliding closer to Gran and said to her,

'So Yosh inherits?'

'Well, who else did Cecil have, after Lily and I refused to inherit? And I've decided to meet them in London and tell them. They need to know about Cecil and his inheritance.'

'Yes,' John said, 'they do. Inheritances and bequests abruptly change status quo.'

'Cecil dying now instead of in forty years makes it's all too complex,' she sighed.

'Almost three o'clock, we best head up to the station,' I interrupted and led the way up the worn steps to the old Courthouse.

Shannon had told me over the phone this morning that she and Albert had met with Woiden briefly and he'd agreed later with her take that the detective was a savvy professional. Woiden had been blunt, told them what was unusual about Cecil's death was the sheer number of potential suspects without anyone to start investigating first.

I asked her more about that meeting after we reached the wide road.

'Albert said Cecil liked being a secretive person and told him that fit well with his work as manufacturing new medical devices is highly confidential.'

'Do you think Cecil was secretive, Shannon?' Alex asked

'Always has been. He used initials in his journal back in our university days, probably has continued to do that. Only Andre knew most of those codes and could have interpreted Cecil's daily agendas and notes if he wasn't dead?'

'Dead?' Alex asked.

'Flew kites, hit a mountain only last month, which adds to the difficulties ahead. Woiden said they're having a hard time understanding what Cecil actually did.'

'Could you explain that?' Alex asked.

'Albert did, said Cecil's lab is like a consortium of little businesses, sharing services and facilities but an independent entity. Explained that on his own project, only he, Cecil, two engineers and their three technicians knew all the actual details.'

John pulled the heavy glass security door to the police headquarters open and held it for us as we filed in. 'Makes it heavy going for the investigators.'

Shannon went up to the desk constable who notified Woiden, then directed us to sit. John settled his big frame beside me, muttered, 'If you did it, Soph, please confess now and save us from this gong show.'

I poked him in the ribs.

CHAPTER TWENTY-FOUR
- Sophia

I looked at the others waiting on the long, padded bench and wished for a camera.

We looked like birds on a wire, huddled close to each other in little groups. On the other side of me was a man with a terrified-looking young teenage girl, then a skimpily clothed blowsy woman sitting a distance from him and beyond Ana and Alex were a group of three boys.

I glanced at Shannon, feeling concerned about her. She looked ready for anything in her navy suit and peach blouse, though she was unusually pale and I knew how bone weary she was.

Detective Moffatt arrived, ushered us in through the security and directed, 'We're going straight down to the last room on the left.'

I scanned the chairs as we walked into the big room with its long brown table. What I choose to sit on matters, and I was relieved to see that although six chairs around the table were the stacking bum-numbing beige vinyl, the other seven were upholstered in a blue tweed cloth over what looked like thick padding.

I sat down on the nearest one. Ah, the foam was still soft I judged with pleasure and inspected my surroundings in this old courthouse.

The end wall's three long windows let in only a little sunlight as the grime was winning, while the high ceiling had painted-over tubes concealing the wires to the three big light bulbs. Six scrubbed white boards dominated the wall space and at the far end, beside the semi-open door to the toilet, a coffeemaker sat atop a green fridge beside the microwave on a spindly utility table.

I watched everyone settle themselves around the table,

knowing they were all hoping this wouldn't take long.

Across from me, Alex slid into the chair beside Ana while Shannon chose the blue chair to my right and John took the vinyl one on her other side as Alex announced, 'Now that we're gathered here on these uncomfortable chairs and our apprehensions, let the action begin.'

We chuckled and the tension eased some.

To me, and I know I have an overactive imagination, Cecil was hovering, and his murderer felt like a malevolent ghostly presence, wondering what might we learn about him that he didn't want known?

And, I thought, what do each of us not want to know?

When the detectives arrived a few minutes later, Moffatt was carrying a jug of ice water and a stack of plastic glasses.

'Glad our interrogation includes being allowed water,' Shannon said.

Woiden gave her a grin. 'You seem feisty today, Dr. Saito. How's your head?'

'It's okay, thanks, Detective. How are things progressing?'

'Slow going so far but, hopefully, this session will help us speed it up.'

He glanced around the table and came back to Shannon. 'First question is to Dr. Saito. Would you please tell us more about Dr. Fischer's personal history, beginning with his university years? Mrs. Nord's overview yesterday covered his child-hood adequately.'

Shannon paused for almost a minute. 'First, I need to explain Cecil and my early history. Although our homes are on adjoining acreages, we didn't know each other during our childhood. For two reasons, the first being my mother did not approve of the Fischer family and secondly, I was younger than them. Lily's four years older than me and Cecil was six. He and I became somewhat acquainted during our first year at Thompson City's college but were not friends until our university years. Computers were just coming into public use and many scholarships were offered around that technology.

Both Cecil and I had high science marks and a savvy college counsellor who got both of us a scholarship at the University of Southern California.'

'Six years is quite an age difference,' Detective Moffatt noted. 'Which makes me wonder, why was Cecil in his first year of college when you were?'

'His uncle left him an inheritance which specified for educational use only, which freed him from being his father's slave.'

'Slave?' Woiden queried.

'That was Cecil's description. And the university was where we met Albert. He was a fourth-year student and assigned to mentor Cecil.'

'Albert was studying in the United States even though he's British?' Moffatt asked. 'The same Albert who's going to fill in as the lab's administrator?'

'Yes, he came to South-Cal because it was one of the most progressive universities in the new digital age.'

'Did Albert and Cecil become friends then?' Moffatt asked as he passed down glasses of water.

'I don't know more than Albert was Cecil's mentor, probably just junior and senior computer hardware colleagues at first but they must have become friends. A couple of years after Cecil graduated, he began working for Albert's family's company in London,' Shannon looked toward the detectives.

'Were you engaged to marry Dr. Fischer while at university?' Woiden probed.

'Yes, for seven months during our fourth year.'

'And your former husband was also at the university during that time?'

'Only for six months. That's where I met Dr. Hito Saito. He was a visiting professor who invited all fourth-year software students to contact him if we wanted a practicum in Japan. After I graduated and with Dr. Saito's assistance, I moved to Tokyo for a computer software engineer practicum. And that's when I started going out with him and we eventually married.

Then when our son Yosh arrived, I took a three-year sabbatical.'

'Was Dr. Saito why yours and Dr. Fischer's engagement ended?' Woiden asked softly.

'No, it ended because Cecil had impregnated another woman, who was his lab partner and fellow hardware computer student.' Shannon sounded terse.

'Okay,' the senior detective nodded.

I wished Shannon had mentioned the pregnant woman was also her closest friend and wondered how much they already knew about Cecil's accident as the details might still be in easily accessible records.

'Now, Dr. Saito, switching subjects, can you summarize for Detective Moffatt and me what Dr. Fischer's main successes as an inventor are? And give us an overview about the products being manufactured in his lab's facilities?'

Shannon spread her hands. 'Only if you narrow that extensive subject down to specific questions, Detective Woiden. My describing and rating Cecil's inventions, or the lab's diverse and numerous medical products, is just not feasible.

Woiden flicked his hair off his forehead as he considered. 'Okay, let me try again. First, what invention did Dr. Fischer make that benefitted him financially.'

'When he was working for Albert, he privately continued with his own inventing. That's when he designed a measuring device that is still used by some diabetics. With Albert's help in producing it, that tool made him a fortune, and continues to pay him royalties.'

'So his wealth started from that?' Moffatt raised his unruly and thick eyebrows.

'Yes, and that is a usual start-up for successful inventors,' Shannon added. 'Their first success allows them to fund more complex projects.'

Moffatt asked, 'Dr. Saito, would Dr. Fischer be considered a famous inventor?

'By whom?' Shannon inquired a little sharply. 'For the past twenty years or so, his successes have been recognized by his professional colleagues and his diverse medical devices are publicized and widely respected internationally but he isn't famous.'

'Other than financially, how has he benefitted?'

She thought about that before replying to Moffatt. 'I guess the main benefit is an increasing number of inventors approach Cecil with their own inventions. He does - he did assist a few annually to take their inventions to the next step. Or, if the inventor preferred, bought the rights to the concept as it might prove out.'

Woiden took over. 'Can you give me an example?'

When Shannon shook her head, Alex leaned forward. 'I can, one Cecil told me about. A private inventor who was turning eighty brought him a prototype and wanted to sell Cecil all rights. As the device had potential and he knew the man needed funds, he bought the rights outright, though unsure about its feasibility; usually it would be a joint venture with the inventor. Now, three years later and after considerable lab development and testing expenditures, the device has recently been released to market.'

Shannon started nodding and smiled at Alex as he continued.

'It enables a fetus' growth to be assessed more accurately and it has received kudos from the medical communities. But it also has received considerable negative publicity from pro-life activists, as its old inventor told Cecil it would.'

Moffatt asked, 'What negative publicity, Mr. Nord?'

'I happened to hear Cecil on the CKV Science Open Line about a month ago. He was their expert guest, explaining how the new tool helps a doctor to identify and treat potential medical problems in a fetus. The call-ins' anger on that open line show startled me. Although the interview had been about how it enabled earlier medical repairs for a fetus with difficulties, the callers were mainly anti-abortionists. One woman was even cut off as she started ranting maliciously, implying threats to Cecil.'

Woiden scribbled some notes before turning to Shannon again. 'Dr. Saito, would you find that reaction to a new device usual or unusual?'

'Most unusual, and Cecil told me he and his marketing team hadn't projected the amount of anger widely generated.'

Moffatt asked a perceptive question. 'Are inventors almost always scientists with academic degrees in engineering fields?'

Shannon thought about that before replying. 'I'm unsure. But Cecil did mention recently that he was receiving more proposals from scientists who were mining old inventions.'

'Mining?' Woiden asked before sipping some water. 'Why?'

'Some inventors sift archival records for patents or intellectual properties that have expired. Those 'miners' find ideas that didn't make it to manufacturing decades ago but might now be viable. It's rather like reworking an old gold or silver mine.'

That caught Alex and my attention and we looked at each other, both thinking of Carlos.

Could his invention have been an unsuccessful one from earlier years?

But what we were learning around Cecil's murder investigation was that our tracing what Carlos and the professor were working on was most unlikely.

'Why there are records of inventions for inventors to mine is, much of the scientific documentation sealed after WWII have started being declassified.'

'Rich pickings, and probably made Cecil even more willing to meet confidentially with inventors,' Woiden said before nodding at Moffatt.

He cleared his throat and looked at me. 'Mrs. Nord, the cleaner has confirmed there were two vacuum tubes on Dr. Fischer's credenza. Assuming they came from the bequest your older sister left you, could you explain why he had them?'

'I gave them to Cecil to investigate their use with his engineers. By the way, that bequest informed me Renee was my mother, not my older sister, and my father was Mexican, an electrical engineer.'

Damn, I'm saying too much. Alex and I had agreed it was

best to say as little as possible about the bequest.

He took over, to my relief. 'Detectives, if I may interject, if the tubes are from the bequest, the timing's off. Cecil only took them a couple of days ago.' Alex sounded relaxed, as communication consultants do when they are trying to redirect.

'We are aware of that and are also checking whether the missing one is elsewhere within the lab,' Woiden said. 'I do recognize it's unlikely there are any ties between bequest and this investigation.'

John glanced past Shannon at me, and I knew he was thinking what he, Ana and I had decided on our trip into town. Cecil's killer has to somehow be connected with the lab. 'Any theories yet about why the murderer cut the rope and took most of it?'

'Not yet,' Moffatt said.

Woiden looked at Shannon. 'This is a subjective question, a gray one. In your opinion, if an invention developed at the lab failed testing, would its inventor have blamed Dr. Fischer? Perhaps sought revenge?'

'In all my years within the scientific community, I've never heard of that happening. Failures are usual during testing, Detective, you have to understand that inventors expect to keep revising. Sometimes it's hazy about why something keeps failing which can create animosities between partners and delays progress, but revenge? Not to my knowledge.'

Hazy! The word describes what we know about Carlos' and Professor Morgan's relationship. Ever since I learned the Morgan's were going to Mexico City with Carlos and Renee, I've doubted that the professor was only my father's mentor. Was he a partner in the invention? Which meant he might have benefited from Carlos' death.

'Help us understand Dr. Fischer better,' Moffatt requested, leaning forward on his thick forearms. 'Did he usually work as part of a team, Dr. Saito?'

'No, Cecil was a loner with a few intimate relations with people he trusted. Me, his assistant Andre, Albert and everyone here, though his kindred person was Yosh. Cecil efficiently directed a team and incorporated their opinions and results before deciding what's next, but valued his own conclusions highly. He could be quite imperious without even noticing he was upsetting someone,' Shannon said and turned to me.

I nodded. 'He wasn't always emotionally perceptive.'

Woiden laughed. 'Sounds like me but, so far, I don't think being too arrogant has motivated anyone to murder.'

'Yet,' chuckled Moffatt.

'Must be challenging to figure out what does motivate someone to take that horrendous step,' Ana commented drily, flashing her pixie grin. 'I've heard of sculptors going at each other with chisels but that's rage, not planning. Is there a profile for a strangler?'

'A good question but not one we've found to date.'

'May I add something?' John said. 'I always thought Cecil was like a hunter when he talked about having met someone and perhaps having discovered a new doodad. Could he have been encroaching in someone else's territory?'

Astute, I thought, suddenly aware of how he and Cecil had been alike in that. John's taciturn about finding the right bull or stallion until he owns it, and he enjoys outbidding most of his fellow competitors.

'Yes, John, Cecil liked finding a neophyte inventor first,' Shannon agreed. 'He never discussed what he was doing butI could sense when his searching was going well. But he also liked being generous when buying rights or sharing royalties and my perception is inventors liked working with or for him.'

'Would anyone know what inventions he wasn't interested in, and had immediately rejected over the years?' Moffatt asked.

'Andre would have.' Shannon stopped and thought before explaining, 'Cecil respected how much trust it took for a first time inventor to share his idea and he was cautious about not raising false hopes. I know he checked out an inventor's credibility before meeting with him or her, and provided the would-be inventor with a package of information about how uncertain the process is.

But weeding out the crazies isn't always possible.'

'Tried to eliminate the flakes, did he? Would there be a list of who has received those packages over the years?'

'I would be surprised, Detective Woiden. Cecil offered and gave confidentiality. I think he liked secrecy, though in our relationship, I thought and hope, he wasn't secretive with me.'

I ached when Shannon said 'hope' because why Cecil was murdered is as unknown as an unexpected precipice.

Woiden studied his notes and asked about the lab's history. 'Are the two engineers who first worked with Dr. Fischer still involved? Do you know if either have financially invested yes in the lab?'

'Neither are involved now. Sam Abrahams, a brilliant inventor and Cecil's university friend, died last year from lung cancer. He'd also worked at Albert's lab in London after graduation and told me quite often that he'd only benefitted financially from his own inventions because of Cecil's business acumen. Sam was totally disinterested in the business end of developing and manufacturing devices.'

'Was he an investor in the lab?'

'No, both the first engineers were salaried employees. Cecil didn't need money because his royalties for his digital testers for diabetics funded his start-up. And continues to generate good returns as does most of the devices Cecil develops.'

'Who was the other engineer?' Moffatt asked.

'Padrig Khan, and I never met him. Khan only stayed with Cecil a couple of years, decided both computer hardware engineering and Thompson City weren't for him, and returned to racing his sailboat internationally.'

'Okay,' Woiden sighed. 'What about the lab's current engineers, eight men and two women? Do you know their professional history?'

Shannon tried to hide her amusement. 'Why would I know that, Detective? I am a software professor, Cecil's engineers are hardware specialists.

'You don't know as a director of the corporation?'

'No. Employees aren't what board directors know much about unless he or she wins an award. What the board discusses and evaluates is the corporation's current and long-term projections. We're like the sounding board. In actuality, Cecil still owned all shares and had full control. Now, what I do know about is how Cecil chose his engineering team.'

'Please tell us,' Woiden invited, spreading out his palm. Noticing his long fingers, I wondered if he was a piano player as I stifled a yawn.

Shannon explained that Cecil always chose his engineers for diversity of experience and education. 'He took pride in hiring internationally, said the lab's team gave it a worldwide network of information and expertise. It actually does as most engineers do keep in touch with former colleagues and our fellow alumni.'

'He hired from around the world?' Woiden groaned and flipped his right hand at Moffat.

He complained, 'There goes the detailed background checks on each engineer.'

Woiden grinned at his sergeant and asked, 'Dr. Saito, this is way out, but do you suspect the most likely murderer is a lab employee?'

Shannon considered before answering. 'Yes. And no. Which translates to I don't know.' She sounded weary and I hoped Woiden noticed.

'Time to wrap up,' Woiden decided. 'Before we go, do any of you have any suspicions about someone? Or can you, Dr. Saito, remember feeling uncomfortable with someone in the lab or a person Cecil introduced you to as a new colleague? This is important because it might mean someone dangerous is watching you.'

'No one comes to mind.'

Woiden slowly looked around the table and then stopped at Ana, 'I've missed the question we planned to ask you, Miss Hernández. Since you met Dr. Fischer for the first time last week, would you share your impressions with us?'

Ana flushed, paused and repeated what she'd shared with

John and me on our drive into town. 'I found Cecil a gracious and interesting person but also a surprisingly young soul. To me, that means someone who continually weighs how he's measuring up to his own expectations.'

She looked uncertainly at Shannon, who smiled warmly and nodded.

'Do you recall what you and Dr. Fischer talked about?' Woiden continued.

'My being a sculptor, and about the intricacies of welding which was also one of his skills. He and I had quite a bit in common, although Cecil's work was micro and most of mine is macro, both of us attach various metals and other materials to create something.'

Woiden said thanks as he scanned his list. 'Damn, we've also missed discussing the chair. The coroner's office has requested more details about Dr. Fischer's office chair. Who's most knowledgeable about its workings?'

'Me, I guess,' Alex said. 'Cecil demonstrated it to me when he was helping edit Gran's birthday film. The chair's upholstered in some high-end material over memory foam, adjusts from being an upright chair into a recliner which becomes almost a bed. The head rest goes lower than the foot.'

'Mr. Nord, could someone not in the chair have operated it?' Moffatt asked. 'Or a better question is could the murderer have put the chair in that prone position when Dr. Fischer was in it?'

'No, I don't think so, even if Cecil allowed that. Accessing the controls would have been a problem.'

As Alex spoke, those Latin genes from Carlos showed in his dark five-o'clock shadow and proud profile, and after I admired my grandson, I shivered. Was his poking into that ancient La Paz murder wise? Safe?

'Almost done,' Woiden looked directly to me and I knew I looked as tired as I felt. 'We need to borrow another electronic tube from your bequest, if we may? The one we've got is being analyzed. What's mystifying us is if Dr. Fischer took two, where's the other one?

Albert has checked all the possibilities within the lab.'

That thunderbolt reflected in all our faces. Where the hell was that second tube?

'Now, and the last question, do any of you know what kinds of rope Dr. Fischer used?'

'Rope? What kind of rope?' John rumbled.

'That's the question,' Moffatt sounded matter of fact. 'As only a small amount was left behind, identifying the rope is challenging.'

Shannon took a deep breath. 'Cecil used rope like the rest of us, to tie something up. Every tall plant in his patio is tied to a support but he was fussy about tying and only used a special cotton cording. It's probably in his garden shed. But his main activities were swimming, bike riding and downhill skiing, which didn't require rope.'

'Apparently the rope's fibers are unusual,' Woiden said as he again reviewed his list and flicked the hunk of auburn hair off his forehead. 'We're done. Detective Moffatt and I thank you for your assistance and please keep your guard hairs up. The murderer knows he's being hunted. If any person or any situation feels off to you, call either of our cells immediately, 24/7. Okay? This person we're hunting is a dangerous and ruthless person.'

Moffatt stood up and stretched. 'But we'll find him or her, it's our team's job and we're good at it.'

CHAPTER TWENTY-FIVE
- Alex

After that long session with the detectives, we decided
to delay writing Cecil's obituary until tomorrow's brunch at
Gran's and go to our homes. Ana drove Shannon in the jeep
and I climbed in the back seat of John's pickup, who was
dropping us off and going on to the ranch.

I was glad to have the evening with just Gran as I was
leaving for Vancouver tomorrow afternoon. Wouldn't see her
again until she arrived in La Paz after she'd finished
photographing snakes. Guess our concerns about each other
are real. We'd both be in new and unknown territories in the
interval between visits.

Once the Packard was ready, I was leaving for San Diego
where I would rendezvous with Ana, and then we were heading
down the Baja.

'So, you two, what odds do you give the detectives?' John
asked as he turned off the freeway and onto the highway north.'

Gran turned to look at me. 'Not quite as long as I the ones
I had before the meeting, but there are so few facts, I am not
hopeful they'll find the murderer. And you, Alex?'

'Like you, the range of their questions, how technical some
were and their ability to integrate answers impressed me. I'm
sure they will unbury Cecil's past, but will that help? There's
somany diverse possibilities without any leads.'

'Yet,' John said. 'I think they will find the murderer, but it
might be blind hope, for Shannon's sake.'

The next morning, I came up to make coffee and get an
apple before heading out on a long run and found Gran had left
a pile of stuff in the hall. My immediate reaction was to groan
like a kid being over-equipped for summer camp but knew I'll

be taking it. She's experienced driving in the Baja and I'm not.

In fact, I'm only beginning to comprehend the courage she had, driving it alone in her old van thirty years ago. The Baja highway was mainly dirt and gravel and there weren't many services back then.

I took her gifts out and stowed them in the Packard, appreciating her astute caring and recognizing I needed the compact first aid kit with the usual stuff plus potent antihistamines, antibiotic pills and cream, two bug sprays, a shovel, a bulky coil of rope, a heavy rain poncho that converts into a tent and mosquito netting. I appreciated the extras, a large tin of dark chocolate with a spoon and my ancient copy of Jules Verne's Twenty Thousand Leagues Under The Sea.

I was now as personally equipped as I could be for driving fourteen hundred kilometers of hot and treacherous highway.

Ana was also giving me bits of advice about preparing to be in Mexico. Yesterday morning on the way to Gran's, she'd added that the Baja has scorpions so don't leave your shoes on the floor. And it's dengue season. That means wearing longshirts and pants.

Gran had added, 'That also garners you more respect from most Mexicans who dress conservatively.'

'Though our young like the international weird fashion trends, you're right, Sophia,' Ana added. 'Most Mexican men do not wear shorts except at the beach.'

After my run, I found John frying bacon and preparing to make blueberry waffles, once Shannon and Ana arrived.

'Good morning, laddie. Chores are done at the ranch and Slim's back so I came over early. Your Gran's in her studio and coffee's ready. Will you pour me one?'

His damp-dry white hair was a halo of light in the sunlight streaming in through the kitchen window. I gave him a gentle punch and took out two mugs. 'I'll have a mug before I shower.'

'I was just thinking about your trip and want to remind you that I have a whole network of ranchers I'm acquainted with in the northern Baja, can get someone to help you quickly, if you

need it. And I might able to come down if something went
awry and you need me.'

'Thanks, John, I appreciate that.'

'Oh, and another thing, Alex, about you being the
foreigner and not knowing the local or cultural codes. Don't
assume anything and ask permission. Being overly polite is
best, and watch your back and your gear.' He turned from the
stove and gave me an unexpected bear hug.

'Thanks, John,' and gave him a big squeeze back. 'I didn't
know you bought and sold in Mexico, too. Is Ana's father on
that database?'

'He is, though I haven't sold a bull into the South Baja yet.
But I sold three in the last couple of years and delivered one
bull myself as we traded animals. I got a fine stallion from him
and thoroughly enjoyed the road trip. You'll like that area
below Tijuana, spiky mountains, cacti and massive spreading
trees

Gran had enlargements of Rene's photos hanging on her
light board and was holding up the one with the nine people.

'Hey, Gran, that great-grandfather of yours sure looks old
and grumpy'

'Hi Alex - yes, he does. But he's probably younger than I
am. I'm making another set of the photos you're taking to La
Paz to give to Ana's grandmother.'

The cowbell clanged and we went out to greet Ana, Shan
non and to our surprise, Albert.

'Albert came up early - well, I enticed him with an
invitation to join us here for brunch. We've been going
through at Cecil's office,' Shannon said.

She didn't look as though she'd slept much, and Gran
peered at her pupils. 'Almost equal but you need much rest.'

'I'm okay but it was hard to be in his office and home,
knowing how much he enjoyed what he had. Including me, and
I'm missing him so much.' She blew her nose firmly and asked,
'Are you the cook, John? I also need food.'

'Come along and sample my test waffle.

Albert brushed Gran's cheek and thumped my back. 'So

you're both heading out on adventures, good for you.'

'Tell them what we've decided,' Shannon ordered over her shoulder.

'Yes, my dear friend,' he said, exaggerating his rounded British accent. 'I'll be moving into Cecil's, and as Phoebe likes gardening, I hope to entice her to come and look after Cecil's. We can stay during the probate period, if Yosh agrees.'

'Wonderful, Albert,' Gran laughed. 'Tell Penelope I expect her to be here by the time I get back from the Baja.'

'Living near you is the main reason I expect her to come,' he jested and sniffed deeply. 'Come along, the bacon awaits.'

We filled mugs with coffee and headed to the deck where John had the long picnic table set up with plates, cutlery, a massive dish of butter and wide variety of syrups.

John arrived with a platter of waffles and Gran followed with her hot blueberry sauce. Other than requests for passing, and the sounds of a jay and squirrel squabbling, we ate in silence until Ana said, 'John, thanks, and Sophia, I'm grateful to be at this table with all of you, though so wishing Cecil was with us.'

We raised our coffee mugs and agreed.

After the table was cleared, Shannon passed me a yellow pad and pen and asked, 'Okay?'

'Sure,' I agreed. 'So, first, how to begin? Do you want it business style? Like starting with Cecil being the CEO and Chairman of Fischer Medical Manufacturing Ltd., and the esteemed inventor, graduated from, awards, etc.'

'Yes, Alex, let's do that. His lawyer told me to combine professional and personal, and his staff will look after distributing to both business and personal friends.'

It took us almost two hours to finalize the words, then as we stood up, Gran asked, 'Is it time for you to get going, Alex?'

'Yes, I want to be home before nine.' My apartment is out by the university, and I have to drive through downtown Vancouver before being able to climb into my own bed. These last few days have been such a mix of ups and downs that we're all exhausted.

'A call, please, when you arrive home tonight,' Gran requested as I hugged her, and then John. He winked at me and refrained from saying 'watch out for moose.'

Shannon followed me out the door. 'I've left your old mandolin you sold to Cecil on the Packard, Alex. Maybe you should take it south?

'Good idea, thanks,' thinking how tight room in the Packard was. 'Did he ever play it?'

'Sometimes but never got around to taking more lessons after the ones you gave him. Remember how he'd get that funny half smile, trying to play along with your guitar? Those were sweet times, Alex.' 'She gave me a hug, 'And I'm glad I have those memories.'

'They were. Please pass on hugs from me to Beth and Yosh. I'm glad you're meeting them in London. Oh, and Auntie, take very good care of yourself.'

'I will,' she said, and gave me another hug. 'And you, too. Have an interesting and safe trip and I'm glad you're travelling the Baja with Ana.'

CHAPTER TWENTY-SIX
- Sophia

After Alex left, John said he was off, too, and would be back Tuesday morning at 5 am. Ana, he and I were on the first flight to Calgary from Thompson City, then onto Toronto and Boston.

Shannon yawned and looked at Albert who'd stretched out on the porch swing. 'Do you want to do anymore sorting at Cecil's today?'

'No, I'm ready for my hotel room and a nap. Show me Renee's artifacts and photos, Sophia, then my lovely chauffeur can take me to my rented wheels.'

'Come along,' Shannon said and led the way to the dining room.

'Did you two find anything at Cecil's that might help with the investigation?' I asked, thinking about his long wall of built-in filing cabinets.

'Many addresses and names I don't recognize, three files full of his correspondence back to 2000. And an overflowing folder labeled 'Cecil: notes.'

Albert looked up from examining Renee's little tape recorder to add, 'All those business and research records are being moved back to the lab where the detectives will have easy access. Eventually, they'll be sorted and will become the core of the founder's library and Cecil's professional archives.'

I sighed and wondered if Rubin's factory history was available. If so, we could narrow down Carlos' area of expertise. All we know so far is his degrees were in electrical engineering.

'Interesting, certainly an overview of phone technology but I don't see anything helpful. Now, Sophie, may I see the photographs Renee left you?

He chuckled after I got them from my studio and passed

them to him with Carlos' and his parents' portrait on top.

'My word, the seed holds true, Sophie. Both you and Alex are alike with your father and grandfather. Isn't it lamentable that Renee didn't share all this heritage with you two when she was alive? Mind you, that probably wasn't feasible for her. The only time we met, I did find her a shattered person.'

'Shattered, Albert?'

'Yes, Soph, she seemed like a trauma survivor to me. I asked Penelope later if she knew what had happened to your oldersister.'

'Ah, you are a perceptive man,' I said and passed him the photo of the nine faces around the old man in his chair.

'The patriarch without a whip,' Albert commented dryly. He studied the faces, then asked, 'What do you know about Carlos' schooling?'

'Many years in London, although his doctorate is from the University of British Columbia. Why?'

'This lad in the upper corner has to be part of the Tommy Flowers' family.'

'Who's Tommy Flowers?' I asked.

Both Albert and Shannon started to reply but she nodded for him to continue.

'Tommy Flowers is famous as the mechanical engineer who finally made the British phone system operational, some-time about 1930. Then during WWII, it was Flowers who helped engineer the code-breaking Colossus, the very first programmable electronic computer.'

'I've heard of Colossus but what was it?'

'A massive machine that had 1800 thermionic valves - or in North American lingo, vacuum tubes,' Albert explained. 'Colossus and all the many human operators it required to run could decode encrypted German messages. Colossus is credited with helping to end the war.'

'How does that relate to this photo?' Ana asked as she came in from the living room where she'd been stroking KitKat.

'That lad in the corner looks as much like Tommy Flowers as Sophia looks like Carlos, could be related. Strange to find his image in an Hernández family portrait. Perhaps they met during their schooling, became friends.'

He took a valve from the box of the four remaining and went out into the deck's sunshine.

I followed and sat down in the swinging chair, weary of all the questions whirling in my head. Why all those phones and who used that tiny recorder? And where was the missing valve Cecil had taken?

A bald eagle screeched repeatedly as he appeared out of the high clouds and circled overhead. I watched his graceful flight, amused again by how an eagle's shrill voice doesn't match its might. Rather like Albert, I thought to myself, whose high voice and small stature masks his power.

I had been startled when I first met Phoebe's husband. They seemed mismatched, but I soon discovered how wrong I was. Their intellects blend and their droll humour amuses John and I. We do have fine holidays together.

'These are unexceptional,' Albert judged after examining the small glass cylinder in the sunlight. 'It's good quality glass, perhaps British? Just one of the millions of connective vacuum tubes used, but this size was used extensively in the early sound industry.

He paused to watch the eagle circling before continuing. 'And around the Flowers and Hernández connection, what I'm wondering is if it's Rubin having an electronic manufacturing factory in Mexico City and Carlos being educated in London. Back in the 1930's, Rubin probably took his nephew to his first year of school, perhaps introduced him to the Flowers family. That lad beside Carlos in the photo is the clone of his famous relative. Makes me wonder if your father's invention was in the communications field rather than the computer one?'

'Albert, are you speculating?'

'Shannon probably can explain this better than me. There's two strands of development related to what electronic tubes were and are used within; computer technology and communications technology - phones, radios, tv's, etc.'

Shannon agreed and added the communications technology

continued to use tubes more than the computer technology.

'But why did Renee keep six electronic tubes?'

'No idea, Soph, quite peculiar.' Albert shook his head. 'The phones must relate to something, but they have no relationship to these tubes.'

'Any guesses about why Renee would have kept the tubes?' Albert shook his head. 'Other than I know during those pre-war and World War II years, governments started dumping billions into research. Engineers and scientists went from being obscure men in back rooms to becoming the golden boys in the scientific circle because of receiving funding.'

'So, if it's a Flowers in this photo, it might be significant?'

'Indubitably, Sophie. Mexico has traded for eons by the shipping routes across the Atlantic. As Europe disintegrated into war, what happened internationally was electrical manufacturers worldwide switched to producing weapons and warproducts and often stopped manufacturing their regular products.'

'And that might explain why Professor Morgan and Carlos moved to Vancouver,' I suggested.

'Definitely,' Shannon said. 'Though that sure doesn't explain why Mrs. Morgan's missionary scheme targeted La Paz.

Albert yawned deeply. 'Too many if's and but's. And on that note, I want my nap. May we leave now, Shannon?'

CHAPTER TWENTY-SEVEN
- Ana

Dawn was lightening the indigo sky when we heard John's diesel coming up the driveway and we went down the back steps, setting off the automatic lights in Sophia's vegetable garden. Two deer outside its high fence leapt away as John's pickup pulled up beside us. Sophia opened the passenger door.

'Good morning, m'dear, all well with you and at the ranch.'

'As good as I can set it up. Are you two ready for our bum-numbing day?'

We stacked our carry-ons onto the back seat and I gave Sophia a gentle push up and then went around to climb in beside the luggage behind John. I wasn't feeling as cheerful as Soph, much more of a late night person than early morning.

'You look about as perky as I feel, Ana,' John teased me as I yawned. 'And I might be too old for all this rushing from one side of the continent to the other. Plane seats are an endurance for me.'

I didn't share that I find them comfortable and like jumping from one place to the next, fly often. But I haven't visited my grandmother for four months because of Yosh's and my Seattle exhibit and am glad to be going to Boston.

'Watch for deer,' John requested as he drove around the curving highway through the forest. When we came into the misty pasturelands, the morning light increased and I watched the cattle grazing on the spring grass. Thought of home.

'Are you comfortable with leaving the animals to your new stockman?' Sophia asked John, putting a hand on his knee.

'I am. Slim seems very methodical and talked with each animal as we fed. Do you know he worked for Winston for quite a while? Only left as he married, and his wife doesn't want to be that isolated. So, Winston told me 'time to slow down, you need another hand, hire Slim.'

I chuckled to myself as it sounded like how Uncle used to manage Papa.

Soph turned toward me. 'Winston's been John's friend for eons and it's his Fraser plateau ranch that we're delivering horses to next week. John, I invited Shannon.'

'I'm glad, it'll give her a break.'

'What do you think about telling Woiden that Winston is a specialty rope distributor and rope historian?'

'Good idea, I'll call and tell him. Identifying that rope could be critical to identifying Cecil's murderer. The more I consider who that could be, the more I realize how complicated the plans were and that he or she watched him die. Ruthless and Malicious.'

'I suspect Cecil had history with his killer.'

'Why, Soph?'

'In recent years, I haven't sensed anything was out of sync or worrying him. He was content. But when he first came back, I thought he was leery around people. He's not now, his empire's in balance and he had Shannon. Are you following what I'm trying to say?'

'Yes, it's almost ten years since I met Cecil - and you're right. When he came back and started building his first manufacturing facility, then his mansion, he could be grating to be with, though I wasn't often. He was edgy, too self-centered or something.'

'Yosh thought he was brilliant,' I added, 'though he'd mentioned a couple of times he was glad his mother wasn't about to marry Cecil soon. He told me that shortly after I broke off my engagement and was pondering marriage and whether I would ever want to marry.'

'Goddamn, this is so unfair to Cecil. If he'd died from an accident or illness, we wouldn't be picking him apart and searching for his flaws.' Sophia turned her head toward the truck's side window and blew her nose.

'I agree, my dear,' John said softly. 'We'd be celebrating his life, not trying to figure out why he was murdered.'

The traffic became heavier as John turned on to the freeway and we stopped talking. Whoever strangled Cecil had minutely studied him, could identify when and where he was vulnerable. I decided it had to be someone within the lab.

Once we'd gone through airport security and were in the waiting area munching on cinnamon buns and drinking awful coffee, John continued, 'What you said, Soph, about not celebrating Cecil is sad because he did achieve so much.'

'For sure, and his medical inventions help so many people. I was remembering Cecil's first opening celebration, when he renovated that old car dealership into his first manufacturing plant. It was either 1999 or 2000. Shannon came with you and I, coolly congratulated Cecil, then ignored Cecil. It's only about five years since she started going out with him.'

'Did Cecil go out with other women here in Thompson City before Shannon?'

'I don't know,' Sophia said slowly, as though that was a new thought. 'I only saw Cecil occasionally before they became a couple. When I analyzed how little I actually know about him, I realized how complex those detectives' jobs are.'

Once we were settled into our seats, John by the window, Sophia in the middle and me on the aisle, he added quietly, 'Cecil had many layers and he wasn't forthcoming about himself or where he'd been, what he'd done. Whereas I shared my stories about teaching animal husbandry in India or why I ended up selling prize bulls at my horse ranch, Cecil never responded by telling me anything about his earlier years.'

'Do you know much, like where he'd actually lived over his years away, Sophia?' I asked.

'Vaguely, I think he was in England for quite a number of years, then perhaps North Carolina. Cecil was at McGill in Montreal for the three years before returning to Erin Lake. Lily is who knows, if she remembers.

'You care for her,' I said.

'Yes,' Sophia agreed as she adjusted the seat's back. 'Woiden's attempted to phone her' and told Shannon her cautions about Lily had been inadequate.

'Didn't go well?'

'No, Woiden hoped to get more details about Cecil's baby but she said she was sorry, that she didn't want to talk with him and hung up.'

'And?' John raised his thick white eyebrows.

'Woiden has decided Moffatt can try next but told Shannon that Lily would not be a credible witness in court. When he'd asked what Cecil had told her around his baby having died, Lily did tell him Cecil received a postcard when he was in London and it made him sad.'

'I think of Lily as about an eight-year old,' Sophia added. 'I suspected she has a brain injury when I first met her. And once, when he had a badly bruised cheek, I asked Cecil whether I could get them help around his father's smacking them. He burst into tears and explained they couldn't become foster kids because not being with their mother would be worse than their father being stopped. He stopped visiting Scott and me for a few months, but I didn't notice as that was around the time my husband broke his leg and lost his job.' I didn't add I was transcribing legal reports about fifteen hours a day to keep us financially afloat.

We all dozed for a bit but when I sat upright to drink from my water bottle, Sophia said she'd been thinking about Mrs. Morgan. 'It's so peculiar she was concerned about unwanted babies in La Paz, Ana. I know the missionary society gave her money for that, it's in Mother's copy of the church bulletin.'

'Most peculiar,' I agreed. 'Yesterday, I did some web history research about single mothers' assistance in the Baja. The only entry I found was one grant for 300 pesos, and it was a budget line in the financial records for the Catholic diocese there. Sophia, I suspect we'll never know why she went there and took Renee with her.'

'I agree, Ana,' and leaned back into her sleep pillow.

I also slept between Calgary and Toronto but once we cleared customs and settled in for the short trip to Boston, Sophia and I resumed chatting about my grandmother.

I told her I was unsure what we both might learn about the extended Hernández family as it was so many decades ago and she's hadsuch a full life since she passed on the ranch to Papa.

John leaned over Sophia and asked, 'Ana, is your grandmother okay with us going out to dinner?'

'She's looking forward to it.'

In fact, being with John will be a treat for her. Over the years, Madre and I like to get her talking about marrying a cowboy instead of finishing her art degree in Spain. She's wonderfully humorous about how stunned she was when she arrived at my grandfather's isolated Baja ranch. And she tells me to remember I have her pluck, so I can do anything. Then my mother adds, "From both sides of your genes" because she too married a rancher after being raised to be a Mexico City matriarch.'

She laughed and asked, 'Will me staying for two hours of talking weary her?

'Soph, although she's 88, she can wear me out. Best tell her the time you have to leave when you arrive or she'll want you to stay all day. She's seen many of your photo-journalism spreads in magazines and is excited about meeting a fellow creative as well as to be sharing Hernández history.'

CHAPTER TWENTY-EIGHT
- Ana

When Grandmother's ancient entry bell chinged-chinged, I opened the door. 'Welcome, and wow, Sophia!'

Her purple and mauve skirt swirled around her knees above purple high-heeled sandal straps, and her copper earrings dangled delicately.

'Hi, Ana,' she grinned. 'That shade of yellow is perfect on you. Fun to play dress-up sometimes, isn't it?

My grandmother stepped forward, equally elegant with her patterned cane matching the soft greens of her silk suit. I took her elbow and used the Mexican honorific she prefers over grandmother. 'Sophia Nord, this is my Abuela, Iona Hernández Dalla Santa.'

Sophia gently shook the brown-spotted hand and thanked her for the privilege of visiting.

'Welcome, the pleasure is all mine.' Abuela pulled herself to her full height, about six inches above Soph and me, and slowly led us down the hall into the library. Before settling into her raspberry wing chair, she waved Sophia into the matching one.

But Sophia was walking across the room, having noticed Grandmother's massive abstracts on the white brick fireplace wall. She examined the three long canvases on the white brick.

'Each is magnificent,' she said as she came and sat down.

My grandmother smiled. 'Thank you, I particularly enjoyed painting these three. I've seen your extraordinary photographs and you also are blessed to be an artist.'

I watched Sophia glance around Grandmother's room as I sank into the very soft burgundy sofa in front of the fireplace. Grandmother's sanctuary is as unique as she is.

The two wing chairs are across from the sofa, each with an oval side table and tri-lamp, and in front of Grandmother's chair is her circular leather hassock. It melds all the colours of the rainbow and is a treasure she had shipped from Turkey.

From her chair, Grandmother can see her paintings, the fireplace, the walled courtyard beyond the window and patio door, and some of her bookcases. They cover another wall, floor to ceiling. She relishes her prized collection of dictionaries, rare art books and diverse library of fiction and non-fiction books.

I looked out at the patio's cushioned lounge, which is where I've been snuggling in summers since I was a kid and Abuela painted at the tall wooden easel. Sadly, her hands have become too arthritic to paint now, but on sunny days, she's often out on the cobblestone patio. She sits at the scrolled-iron table under the sumac's spreading branches, having tea or a gin and tonic and reading a book.

'Mrs. Dalla Santa, your room and patio are so inviting.'

'For heaven sakes, girl, do call me Iona. After all, we are Related. You are my grandniece since Carlos was my husband Guillermo's nephew. I'm startled by how much you resemble your father.'

Sophia laughed. 'Do you realize how long it's been since anyone called me girl? And will Aunt Iona be okay with you?'

'Fine. Though as I watch you, you are also like Carlos' younger sister Marie. Probably similar to his older one, too, though I never met her until she retired from being a nursing sister and Mother Superior.'

'My grandson, Alex, also looks so much like Carlos' portrait, as did his father, my late son.' Sophia added, 'Carlos' portrait was what confirmed Renee's letter about my being his daughter.'

She reached down and pulled an envelope from her flat purple handbag. 'I've brought duplicates of the photos we found in Renee's bequest for you.'

I suggested, 'Abuela, before you look at the photos, perhaps we should have our coffee?'

'Good idea. While you get it, I'll tell Sophia about my 1937/38 journal entry about meeting Renee that Christmas.

As I left, my grandmother asked, 'Do you know your mother was like an angel with her long golden curls, even though her situation belied that. I did like Renee. But I'm angry she hid your history from you, abdicated her responsibilities.'

I nodded my agreement.

'Any idea why?'

'She had devastating years after I was born, Aunt Iona, developed tuberculosis, probably when I was a toddler. That seems to be when my grandparents started pretending I'm their daughter.'

'That does explain considerable.'

When I returned with the coffee and muffins my grandmother's helper had ready, Abuela was reminiscing about theHernández family.

'Carlos's family was close, and all were missing the older sister, the nun. Sophia, do you know when you and Alex are in La Paz, you'll be close to the little abbey where she's lived since retiring? If the Mother-Superior is back from her eye surgery in Mexico City, you could visit her.'

'I hope we can.' Sophia stood up to help me put the coffee tray on the library table as Abuela directed, 'Ana, I'm down to two spoons of sugar now but not skimpy ones.'

She leaned back in her chair, put one long leg up on the hassock and murmured, 'so glad you're here.'

I agreed, put her coffee and thickly buttered blueberry muffin on her end table and spread a large white napkin on her lap.

She devoured the muffin before continuing. 'Do you two understand Renee contacting tuberculosis explains the secrecy around your grandparents taking you? Though perhaps you are too young.'

I knew Sophia was trying not to laugh aloud at being told she was too young. We picked up our fragile cups and toasted each other with the fragrant coffee before I asked, 'Why?'

'In that era, many people didn't admit to having a relative with that contagious disease. Why, if your grandparents had revealed they'd taken you because Renee had tuberculosis, they might have been shunned by neighbours, even by long-term friends.'

'Shunned?' Sophia looked as startled as she sounded. 'I haven't heard that before.'

'Yes, so many people were dying of 'The TB', as everyone called it. Finding blood in one's handkerchief was devastating, considered a possible death sentence. Before I married Guillermo, one of my fellow art students in Spain developed tuberculosis and all of us in her class had to have our throats swabbed at three different times. Sadly, she died within weeks.' She stopped to sip her coffee and told me another muffin would be appreciated.

'That diagnosis would have been ominous for your mother and grandparents in three ways. First, would she live? Second, how many years would it take her to recover? But the biggest one was keeping you in the family. The government authorities had broad powers back then and Renee and your grandparents would have feared the social workers would seize you, especially without a father to claim you. Once Renee was sent to the TB Sanatorium, you could have easily been made a ward of the province as your grandparents might not have deemed it acceptable to raise you, judged to be too old.'

Sophia absorbed what that meant as I refilled our coffee cups.

'So, my grandparents probably claimed they were my parents to protect me?' she said slowly. 'Thank you for telling me that as it explains much, sweetens their ongoing lying considerably. Any idea why neither they or my mother told me as an adult?'

Abuela put her cup back on its saucer and sighed. 'No, though I suspect Renee became numb, stopped caring to survive. She'd lost Carlos and had no longer been acceptable within her society as an unwed mother. Then, tuberculosis?'

I finally understood and felt a wave of sadness as I stood up and pulled the window's soft drapery over some to get the sun out of Abuela's eyes.'

'Devastating,' Sophia said pensively.

'But if she's shared her and your history, Sophia, I think it would have been freeing for her, don't you?'

She agreed. 'But leaving me this most convoluted bequest probably wasn't satisfying for her. As I've sorted, I've felt sad for her rather than found bits of happiness. Her trunkful of stuff confuses everyone whose seen it.'

I told Abuela a little about the artifacts Renee had left.

'She left you many phones? How peculiar, though I think Carlos was working on some new communication thing but I'm sure it wasn't a phone. There weren't many of those in the Baja back then.'

'What can you tell me about my parents, Aunt Iona?' Sophia asked, though first, may I tell you I'm surprised and curious about how unalike you two are?'

I laughed and agreed. 'I'm all Hernández, having inherited Madre and Papa's dark Latin colouring. Who looks like Abuela is my brother, another Guillermo. He has the red wavy hair Abuela had and startling blue eyes, as does their six-year old daughter. Genetics.'

Abuela chuckled with me. 'Though of all our family, Ana is much like me and thinks similarly.'

I agreed and asked whether she wanted me to read from her journal now.'

'I best mention Professor and Mrs. Morgan first, while I re-member. They lived right next door and as he was with Carlos most days, she came over frequently. We all liked him, not her. Carlos' mother, Fatima, said it was lucky the English woman didn't know Spanish, as the women did poke fun at her. She was one of those British women who are sure they know everything, had been a head nurse in London before their move to Vancouver.' Abuela leaned forward and confided, 'She even tried telling me how I should be mothering. Ha! I straightened her out fast.

Sophia choked on her coffee as she laughed, then asked, 'Aunt Iona, do you know anything about what the Professor and Carlos were working on? Apparently Rubin would be manufacturing it?'

'No, Sophia, I wasn't interested. They would be in the lab most of the day but wandered out and visited two or three times a day. Professor Morgan was such a big teddy bear of a man with a curly grey beard, and my baby girl would always smile for him. His jacket pockets always bulged and he would pull things like glass tubes out and make a pretend train for Guillermo.'

'Tubes?' Sophia and I demanded together.

'Yes, you know? Tubes like those glass oblong things used in radios.'

'Do you know what he used those tubes for?' Sophia asked.

Abuela pondered that before shaking her head.

'Did Carlos' father spend time in the lab with them?'

'No, he went to his office most days. Do you know the professor was somehow related to Carlos' mother?

'No.' Sophia pondered that. 'Any idea how?'

'No. Meeting so many of Guillermo's relatives totally confused me, especially as they were delighted with our children. It was a blur then and more so now, Sophia.

'How many brothers did he have and did they have sister?'

'Four boys, and the Hernández brothers were very spread out in age. Rubin was much older than his two brothers in La Paz, Hector and Carlos Senior, who were in business together and had married sisters. My Guillermo was ten years younger than his Uncle Carlos and twelve years younger than Uncle Hector. Later, when Guillermo and I learned about them ending their partnership, we were sad for them.'

'Why did they?'

'Carlos' papa and Uncle Rubin were very strong supporters of England while Hector wanted to do business with Germany.' Abuela yawned and put her feet back up on the hassock. 'Ana, I've remembered the journal.'

I opened the little book covered in stained leather, glanced at the page. 'Abuela, really? You watched Carlos' Packard being off-loaded from Rubin's ship? Alex will be blown away when he reads this.'

'Well, we'd also come to La Paz to deliver horses to the port. We took that arrogant and beautiful black stallion and two fine palomino mares directly to the port where they were to be loaded onto Rubin's ship. He'd kindly arranged our first sale into Mexico City. After they were offloaded, we saw a burgundy sports car dangling in the crane's transfer net and Guillermo drove us close to watch, noticed Carlos standing there. It was his Packard.'

'Aunt Iona, that car eventually became my Packard. Then Scott's, and now, is Alex's precious car. We're unsure who arranged to have it delivered to Renee after the war ended. Perhaps Marie, but Renee refused to even ride in it and Carlos' car became Dad's. He gave it to me as I started college.'

'Guess you were the only girl arriving in one?' Abuela asked.

She has owned many sporty vehicles, taught me that one's vehicle is more than just transportation. In fact, she gave me my first Fiat, a little black convertible.'

Sophia chuckled, 'I evolved from being a small-minded, shy, little church-going girl to being the girl with the Packard very quickly.'

'Now, Ana, might as well miss the unloading details and start with us arriving at the hacienda.'

'December 8, 1937: We left the ranch yesterday for the tedious trip up to La Paz, where we will spend Christmas. Travelling with our two little ones in a stock truck with three precious horses is not a delight ...

By the time we arrived at his brother's massive hacienda, our baby and son were crying, worn out with travelling. Guillermo dropped us at the wide brick steps before going to park the stock truck and I started up them. A girl in a whitedress came out of the doors, smiled at me, knelt down and offered our sobbing son her hand. As he took it, she looked up at me and said, 'I'm Renee.'

I understood why Carlos loved her.

He'd told Guillermo and me at the port about he and Renee

having a baby and were to be married soon, and that it had been hard for his parents ...

When my grandmother tried to hide a yawn, I said, 'Okay if I paraphrase, Abuela?'

'Fine, a good idea.'

Sophia reminded us John would be arriving in about fifteen minutes to pick her up.

'Okay, I'll summarize,' and read the rest of the long entry, then said, 'You and Guillermo liked Renee, found her good humour and spunk impressive, particularly with how she kowtowed to her future mother-in-law. She and Carlos were happy together and both helped with the dying grandmother and your children. And you both thought that despite Renee's youth and naivety, their marriage would work out fine.'

'It would have, Sophia,' Abuela assured her. 'And of course, that dying old woman was your great-grandmother. She gave her blessings to Renee and Carlos and requested if you were a girl, you be named Sophia after her.'

'And I was.'

'Yes,' Abuela agreed telling Sophia the journal was now hers. 'Will you read it tonight and ask me questions tomorrow. I'm off for my nap now and I am so glad you came to meet me, my niece. Family matters.'

CHAPTER TWENTY-NINE
- Sophia

Ana came with me as I cautiously went down the brownstone's stairs in my high heels and opened our rented Audi convertible's passenger door for me.

'Good morning, Ana, good visit?' John asked us.

We told him a very special one.

I continued after we were into the flow of traffic. 'John, Iona's a wonderful storyteller and a grand lady. Told me I am to call her Aunt.'

'So you and Alex do have more relatives?'

'Many,' I tried to keep my voice light but was again feeling annoyed with Renee. If only she had been able to share our history with me, we could have connected with them years ago, perhaps become part of this welcoming family decades ago. 'Wish I had met them much earlier.'

'Might have made a vast difference for Renee, too,' he sympathized.

'Iona's stories have made Carlos' and Renee's relationship real for me, John. She told me that once Carlos' penances ended, Renee would pull him into a corner and meld her tiny body against his stocky one. She remembers watching them see each other across a room and smiling.'

'She liked Renee?'

'Very much and her husband was sure she'd make his nephew happy.'

'How different my childhood would have been if they had been my parents. And Scott's grandparents. Why the hell didn't Renee at least tell me about my father and his family?' My vehemence stunned me and startled John.

'Pissed right off at her again, aren't you?

'Yep,' I laughed, embarrassed. 'And changing subjects, are

you hungry? I'm starving.'

'The wharf for fish and chips good?'

'Of course.'

'Soph, one more question. Tell me why you are now angrier with Renee.'

'And with Mother because Iona attempted to stay in touch, got Renee's home address from the priest and wrote her a couple of times. Both letters asked how we were, whether we needed anything and invited us to the ranch when travel was feasible again after the war. She never received an answer.'

'You're assuming they arrived?'

'Yes, and I can see Mother heaving any mail with a Mexicanaddress without opening it,' I admitted. 'Ah, well, done is done.Although I wish I had known about my father's family decades ago, I didn't. And I suspect Renee chose not to reconnect.

I patted his knee as he wove through the traffic, enjoyed the wind in my face, though was unsure if I could smell the Atlantic's salty air through the traffic fumes and missed Erin Lake's air.

'Soph, in my opinion, Renee was a very selfish woman. I do feel compassion for her losses, but I feel more for you.'

She was selfish, I accepted, thinking about her writing that confessional letter in 2000, eight years before she died. Did she start filling those four boxes after that?

Am I at all like her? I've learned considerable about genes around Janet's ALS and I do have half of Renee's. Yet we were so different, I can't think of many similarities. She and Mother were quite alike, both in appearance and personality. Opinionated and reserved whereas Dad and I were much more affectionate, liked chatting, exchanged hugs. Mother didn't.

I remember thinking about that when I had Scott and had so much joy to share with him. That continued to grow throughout his too-short life. Now, I realize I didn't know what being cherished meant until I met John. Though I think I would have, if Carlos had lived.

As we walked from the massive waterfront parking lot and suggested, 'Let's walk past all the cafes before we chose.

'Sure. Ana says that after La Paz prawns, Boston's blue crab is her favorite meal, so I want to have crab.'

We picked an old cafe across from the wharfs and sat outside at a slab wood table where we could watch the people and boats go by as we ate. As we strolled, we tried to identify the smells, but frying onions combined with smoky diesel fueldominated. The colours and variety of vessels appealed and I decided I wanted time here and with a better camera than my purse one. 'John, let's come back again tomorrow?'

'Suits me, I like wandering working wharfs, considering whether I should buy a tug.'

'I didn't know that but if you want to, I'm half in and I have a friend in Victoria who would find us moorage.'

'Oh, Soph, you're scary. Let me see how Slim manages the ranch, then we'll think about it.'

After we'd devoured our first crabs and ordered more, he said, 'Describe Iona, she sounds feisty for 88.'

'Yes, she's dynamic, kind and oozes graciousness. She and Ana are kindred, though they are physically so different. Iona is six inches taller than Ana with white curly hair that used to be red. We're meeting at the restaurant tomorrow night, so you won't see her special room and abstract paintings this visit. They're mesmerizing and it's sad her hands are too arthritic to paint now.'

'Does she remember considerable about Renee?'

'Yes, and she's good at relating it. She also has her 1937/38journal, which she's given to me. Ana read what she wrote after meeting Renee when she's helped calm Iona's children. They became friends immediately.'

'What about Carlos' parents' home?'

'It was large and within their compound of thirty acres of fruit trees, additional housing for servants and employees. The house itself was long with two wings off it. She said the covered porches were as long as the house and bordering the back courtyard. She and Guillermo were in the big bedroom in Carlos's wing where his lab and bedroom were.'

I paused and John asked, 'What else?'

'Iona said Renee fit in and was part of the fun and furor of preparing for the Christmas holidays and the wedding. She was wonderful with her children, told Iona how excited she was to be going to be a mother.'

We watched a trawler maneuver into its moorage as we ate our second helpings. After the waiter refilled our coffee mugs and removed the paper plates, John asked, 'What else did you learn about the house?'

'Iona described it as a Mexican-style mansion, looked like a fortress from the front and the whole property was wrapped in high fencing because of the valuable fruit crops.'

'So secure, hard to access for Carlos' murderer, if he didn't live there?'

'I asked that and Iona pointed out the living room, dining room and kitchen had big folding hurricane doors, open all day, only closed at bedtime. By Carlos' rooms was an outside door the servants used as it was shortest route to their homes.'

'What did you learn about them?'

'The nearest casita to the main house was the head gardener's and his wife. Beside it was the cook's place which housed a large family; included her sister, who cared for Matias and helped in the kitchen, three teenagers, the cook's elderly mother and an uncle.'

'Who's Matias?' John asked.

'Iona told Ana and me that he was related to Carlos' mother and after he'd been kicked by a horse as a child, had lived with the family. He'd turned eighteen and was a very large man but was like an eight-year-old. She said everyone kept an eye on him as he didn't realize his own strength.'

John finished his key lime pie before asking, 'Soph, what about Carlos' invention and his relationship with Professor Morgan? Did Iona know anything about that?'

'I asked but she doesn't recall anything other than he and the professor worked for hours in the lab. She is a delight, had

Ana and me giggling about how Carlos' aunt and the other matrons snickered together about Renee being pregnant behind his mother's back as she'd had been overly smug in earlier years about her perfect son.'

I want more time with Iona and said to John, 'I'm going to come back this fall to visit with her again.

'Good, I'll come if you invite me because I want to explore Boston. Fascinating place, haven't been here before. But back to speculating about Carlos, it sounds as if the murderer could have easily entered his bedroom from outside.'

'Yes, and probably there was as many possible suspects as there are in trying to locate Cecil's murder, unless Alex discovers more information about the killer being identified.'

'What did she say about the photos you took her?'

I started laughing. 'She was shocked that we'd decided the old grandfather in the chair was a curmudgeon. Turns out he wasn't at all but disliked being photographed. And the lad with the round glasses had been Carlos' roommate in England and was working for Rubin in Mexico City, but often in La Paz because he was courting Marie.'

John beckoned to the waiter for the bill. 'Last question, Soph. Does Iona know anything about the investigations after Carlos was murdered?'

'No, she and Guillermo didn't even know Carlos had been killed until weeks later. Because their baby became ill, they left La Paz in mid-January and didn't return until they came up for Maria's wedding, over a year later. By then, Fatima was frail and ill, grieving for Carlos, and Iona didn't care for Marie's groom. They didn't stay long as Guillermo became angry and frustrated with his older brothers' disagreements.

Later, John and I stacked up the pillows on the big bed in our hotel room and stretched out. I passed him Iona's journal before I called Shannon.

She'd told me at Woiden's suggestion, she'd been going through their university grad book, trying to recall who Cecil had met at computer hardware conventions. And she'd just talked with Albert who told her the detectives interviewing every employee at the lab was causing havoc with production. We didn't talk long as she admitted she was exhausted, and very glad she'd decided to come with us to Winston's ranch.

After I hung up, John said, 'Soph, listen to Iona's entry for December 21, 1937.'

A lovely day. La Paz is special, reminds me of Spain somehow. And I love how the palms along the massive bay are always waving in the sea breezes to the sound of the waves rolling in. The town is actually a long string of little settlements, each a unique village with a mixture of homes and businesses.

Mid-afternoon, I took the children down to the beach and spread a blanket for Catherine and me. I enjoyed watching her sleep while our little Guillermo picked up shells and played with the waves. Tonight, Renee stayed with our sleeping children and Guil and I walked for miles along the shore as the Cortez's deep aqua deepened into a midnight blue and a full moon rose.

'Sounds idyllic, John.'
'There's a little more.'

We ate as we walked, barbecued prawns on sticks with pineapple and double-decker ice cream cones. Visited with the folks also strolling by the sea, their children chasing the seagulls and pelicans along the beaches' shallow water.'

'Reminds me of my months there the year I turned forty. Walking the white sands often with friends or alone, eating ice cream, watching the fishermen bring their panga-boats in loaded with seafood and the sailboats and cruisers heading to the marina. The big freighters anchored way offshore. As the day's heat cools, many people come, some with their extended families or friends, to visit and laugh together and eat the street vendors' tacos and fruit, to visit and laugh,' I reminisced and giggle softly. The young hot-blooded ones lay under a palm,

often close together on a blanket but under the watchful eyes of
someone's grandmother. There's always the sounds of children
playing, dogs barking, roosters crowing, laughter and
arguments, as well as that damn repetitive mariachi music, day
and night. I feel vibrant, alive when I'm there.'

John put Iona's journal down and stretched out,
murmuring in his deep voice, 'hey, Soph, my vibrant mate,
how about coming a little closer?'

CHAPTER THIRTY
- Alex

Gran and I had pre-booked her calling me Sunday noon my time, which was mid-afternoon in Boston. I made a latte, settled in my Euro-fusion leather recliner, sucked in the latte's rich smell and contemplated the stuff on the couch across from me.

Decision-making time as I head south at dawn and there's no way this is all going to fit in the Packard. When Sara, the neighbour down the hall, dropped in for the keys as she's picking up my mail and watering my three plants, she'd looked at the full couch and wished me happy discarding.

The phone rang and after Gran and I exchanged greetings, she asked, 'All packed?'

'Almost,' I lied.

'Then you're a better organizer than me. Usually, an hour before I have to be out the door, I'm still swapping out what to take, what to leave. Of course, my having to pay overweight and all the mandatory photography stuff makes me ruthless, unless I'm going somewhere isolated without shopping options. Then I go in fully equipped and pay whatever the charges. Don't count on what you need being available in the Mexican villages.'

'Right, how's your holidaying?

'Fabulous. We saw Mama Mia last night, then John took me to the Rooftop for a late supper and, Alex, we actually danced. Tonight is the Phantom of the Opera.'

Gran's voice revealed how special John's birthday gift was, and I felt envious, longing for similar to whatever it was those two had. I sure the hell hadn't ever had that with Liza.

'Have you heard from Ana?'

'Last night to set up our meet in San Diego and she told me about you and Iona becoming immediate friends. And her declaring she's your Aunt Iona now'

'Meeting her felt as if I had known I her for many years. You have a warm invitation to visit her soon.'

'I will,' but didn't add her being Ana's cherished grandmother motivated me even more. My resolution to take at least a year or two to recover emotionally from Liza isn't as firm as it was. Sure didn't project meeting someone like Ana.

We chatted about Shannon as she and I had a long phone chat last night and I shared that Woiden and she had spent a few hours at Cecil's house. He'd found everything revealing, including Cecil's choice of artwork and the books in his extensive library. He'd explained how creating a profile helped with the search.

'Gran, what was bothering Shannon was he'd labeled Cecil's home, other than his unique upstairs room, patio and staircase, as typical of a rich single man. She'd asked him to explain that and he tried to by comparing Cecil's to her home, how his was without much warmth while hers was welcoming, inviting, reflected her warm personality. She said she found his comments illuminating and disturbing as that was somehow similar to Cecil. She's so weary of the investigation, not sleeping without nightmares and considering staying in London for a couple weeks when she meets Beth and Yosh.'

Gran agreed that was a good idea and switched subjects. 'Alex, as members of the Hernández clan, we have quite a heritage, according to Iona. So I'm glad we're going to La Paz, even if you don't learn anything more about Carlos' invention or murder.'

'How well did Iona know Carlos, Gran?'

'He was her friend, only a couple of years younger than her, though eight years younger than his uncle. Carlos had spent some summers at the ranch and told Iona when they first met he was relieved - she was the right wife for Guillermo.

'So Iona knew him better than she knew the rest of his family?'

'Yes, and told her that Christmas after she'd said she liked

Renee, he was so glad. Iona recollected that he'd added he could certainly understand why accepting Renee was damn hard for his parents.'

'What did Iona say about Renne?'

'That she had spunk and would have learned to be Carlos' capable wife and mother to me. And she and Carlos would have been very happy.'

Alex contemplated that. 'Not the Renee we knew.'

'No.' Gran sighed and asked, 'How'd it go with the mechanics?'

I told her the Packard had checked out fine and the fender was repainted. 'Also, Gran, a friend got me into UBC's archives and I found some basic history about Carlos and quite abit about Professor Morgan.'

'Tell me.'

'It was September 1936 when Carlos registered into the UBC School of Engineering and was awarded his Master's degree the following June. No other information except he hadn't returned the keys to the science labs and kept his dorm room until September.'

'So, he and Renee could have been seeing each other until she and Mrs. Morgan left for the Baja.'

'Probably were.'

'What about the Professor?'

'He'd started giving classes in September, 1934 and continued giving those three courses in both spring and fall sessions until Sept, 1937. The record ended with a note: sabbatical granted.'

'If only we knew whether Carlos followed him to Vancouver because he needed Morgan's expertise for completing his invention, or because pre-war Europe was becoming an unsettled place to study.'

'We never will, Gran, and it doesn't matter' I licked the last of the cappuccino's foam. 'Did you learn anything about the Morgan's from Iona?'

'Like Carlos' mother and aunts, she liked the professor and disliked his wife, as did Carlos' mother and aunt. Alex, Iona mimicked Mrs. Morgan's high voice and British accent. "I am not complaining but aren't Mexican servants overly independent? I do miss England's efficient ones sometimes."'

I laughed and appreciated Iona's humour. 'Did you learn anything about Carlos' invention?'

'Only that it was going to manufactured by Rubin, which we know.'

'Damn!'

'But the interesting thing Iona did tell us was how the Professor's tweed blazer's pockets were always bulging with electrical parts. She described how he'd take out little long glass tubes, lined them up on a table and played train with her son. When Ana asked whether they looked like a glass saltshaker, Iona agreed.'

'Do you know if the Hernández hacienda is still there, Gran?

'Iona said there's about thirty homes there now, including three still owned by Hernández families.'

Gran paused. 'John wants to say hello. Wish you could see how elegant he looks, and he's smelling of aftershave, not horses.'

He laughed into the phone and said, 'That grandmother of yours gussies up very well, Alex. Tomorrow still departure day? How did the Packard make out?'

I told him fine and about the extra parts the mechanic insisted I take. 'He drives down the Baja most years. So, I'm as ready as I can be, John.' I added that I was following the route he'd recommended, taking Hwy 5 down past Seattle's airport, then angling to the old highway along the Pacific.'

'Well, Alex, have easy travels, and remember, I can be anywhere fast if you need me. Watch your back. Here's your grandmother again.'

'Alex, we've reservations for a late buffet lunch so best say good-bye now and have a wonderful time.

'Thanks, Gran. I'm looking forward to you joining me in La Paz, and please watch out for slithering snakes. Oh, and say hello to Winston for me.

CHAPTER THIRTY-ONE
- Sophia

The next day it was after midnight BC time when we arrived at Erin Lake. A long day and Shannon and I were meeting with Woiden this morning.

I felt I'd had about an hour sleep when John put coffee on my night table, gave me a hug and announced cheerily, 'I'm off, back tomorrow about six but if the horses load easily, I might be here be a bit earlier.'

'We'll be ready.' Shannon had agreed to overnight here.

After John left, I took my coffee and headed for the hot tub's screened deck off my bedroom. The warm water swishing over me refreshed me and I decided to start packing for Loreto as well as for the overnight at Winston's.

During our long layover in Chicago, I had phoned Shannon and she'd been blunt about her increasing apprehension. 'Soph, the detectives know so little about Cecil, they have to speculate about 'what if's? He would have been horrified.'

How could I help Shannon get through this black time? As I watched the banks of clouds building into a storm overhead, I knew it would happen eventually, especially if the murderer was identified, but it would take a long time for her to regain her vitality. I thought of Renee and how the person Iona had met was very different from the person I had known.

Shannon arrived at the Courthouse ahead of me and after parking by her SUV, I went down to the bench by the fountain. As we exchanged hugs, I discovered how much weight she's lost. The black circles under her eyes told me how exhausted she was but I asked, 'You doing okay?"

'Battered and bruised, just hanging in, I guess. And I don't have to ask about your days away, you're vibrant. Come on, let's go up to the waiting area because I want you to read something.'

The desk sergeant greeted us warmly, checked and reported that Detective Inspector Woiden would be with us in about ten minutes.

We sat down at the far end of the bench and Shannon took an official-looking envelope out of her handbag. 'The corporation's senior lawyer returned yesterday and gave me this. Skip the preamble and start about halfway down. And note the date, because the first time Cecil asked me to marry him was Christmas Eve 2005. I immediately declined and, as you know, have continued to do so.' She passed me the two pages of thick ivory paper.

January 11, 2006: 'In the event of my death, I bequeath seventy-five percent of my shareholdings in the Fischer Corporation to Dr. Shannon Saito ...

'Holy hell, Shannon! Did Cecil ask for your permission to do this?'

'No. After I refused his proposal, we talked about the past and its consequences for me. He did say all the right things and I'm sure he knew how tempted I was to change my mind. But all I said was that if and when I decided to marry him, we would find a judge, I would never be engaged to him again.'

'What did he reply?'

'That he'd have a judge lined up, in case. Three weeks later, he set these legalities up. Maybe I didn't know him as well as I think I did.'

For the first time since I've known him, I was very angry with Cecil.

'It infuriates and disappoints me, Soph, he was as selfish as Renee!'

'Read the next paragraph.'

After considering the options as outlined below, Dr. Saito is to inform the Fischer Corporation's Board of Directors and management team of her decision, and assist in facilitating the corporation's future ownership.

Option One: _Dr. Shannon Saito will continue to control all shares in my private corporation as its CEO and Chair, including acting in trust for the charities I have bequeathed with shares. At her discretion, all the current Board directors will be re-appointed or dismissed._

Option Two: _Dr. Shannon Saito will act as the temporary chair of the Board of Directors and, at her discretion, appoint a Manager to supervise all the corporation's operational systems. One year after the date of my demise, Dr. Saito had all rights to take my corporation into public and sell all her Fischer Corporation shares on the open market._

'Shit!'

I must have said that a bit too loud as the Staff Sergeant looked up and the couple beside us looked at the floor.

'Typical Cecil, isn't it?' she said dryly. 'Either way, he's left me his wealth, which I certainly didn't need and don't want.'

How could Cecil have been so arrogant? Hadn't he understood that wasn't ethical behaviour? What a load he dumped on the woman he professed to love because he needed an inheritor.

'Makes me more nervous about what the detectives will learn about the man I loved.'

'Understandable.' I was disappointed that he was like Renee, able to ignore or be indifferent about the potential effects on the other person.

'Shannon, does this complicate your own world?'

'I don't know but I do have to deal with it over the next year. What I'm hoping is that with Albert staying, we'll be able to hire the right person to take the corporation public.'

'You don't want to be involved?'

'Not at all, I like being a professor and software consultant.' She sighed, 'Soph, his leaving me his corporation's shares, and my son all his personal property, Cecil's treated me as if I were his widow. Now, these shares bind me to that damn man for at least a year!'

Unable to hold back any longer, I laughed and Shannon joined me. Everyone else waiting and the sergeant now looked at us and smiled.

Shannon wiped her eyes. 'I can hear what you're not saying, Soph. First Hito, and now, for the second time around, Cecil. How do I get myself into such complex relationships?'

'Hmmmm!' That was our long-standing code for "I'm not going to comment."

'Cop-out.'

'Yes!' I noticed Woiden waiting, wondered how long had he been listening?

'Good morning, Shannon and Mrs. Nord, how are you two? Let's go have some tea.'

I noticed he used her first name. Another hmmmm.

We stood up and once we were on the other side of the security door, Shannon said, 'Tea and some news, Detective? I hope you're almost finished interviewing all the lab staff. Find anyone suspicious yet? What we've agreed, Soph, is that someone hated him.'

I stopped leading the way down the long hall and turned to them. 'But isn't that forgetting something? Cecil may have done nothing, but the murderer wrongly perceived he had. In my mind, that's a very good possibility.' That had lessened some this morning around those legal documents, I don't like what he'd done.'

I hadn't been in the detective's office before, and his non-institutional decor increased my appreciation for this man.

A foot-tall quizzical grey ceramic cat gazed down from the top of the long wall of steel six-drawer file cabinets, and a tall silk plant was squeezed in the corner beside them. To my relief, the two large chairs in front of Woiden's desk had thick cushions. They were mocha leather, blended well with the oiled walnut desktop.

Woiden smiled. 'My office is not what you expected?'

'No,' I admitted and continued looking.

On his desk were a closed portable computer, a pen stand with note pad and a black phone with multi-buttons. On the wall behind it was a painting, a magnificent one.

'Your painting mesmerizes me, Detective.'

'Me, too. It's also special as the artist is my sister.'

I studied the large canvas of waves breaking against a narrow stone peninsula with an ancient Gary oak tree. Its broad and leafless branches spread wide and disappeared into the ocean's mist.

'Detective Woiden has often sat in that tree.'

'Well, in previous years. I've stopped climbing trees now as has my sister. But we still sit on the porch of our family's home and look at our sentinel over the Pacific.'

'Does she still live there?'

'A few months annually. She's like you, Mrs. Nord, travels extensively as she's a professional artist, renown for her trees. She always has a choice of whose tree to paint next. But both of us are unmarried so we still call Port Hardy our home, meet there whenever we can. Enough about me, I'll go get our tea.'

After he left, Shannon told me Woiden liked having a cup to hold when he was interviewing.

'Been here often?'

'This is the fifth time, Soph. We've gone over so much from the lab's history, its engineers, whom I don't know much about, to Cecil's inventions. Oh, and my overview as a board member of the corporation's stability and most profitable products.'

'You do know a lot about Cecil in some ways but must be frustrating to have big gaps in his history.'

'Very, what Woiden isn't comprehending is how little I know about Cecil's professional colleagues because they are hardware computer engineering specialists and mine are software. Sure, there's overlap once their inventions need software applications but not before.'

'I know what you're saying, Shannon. It's like me having little in common with a portrait photographer.'

'Exactly.' Shannon stood up and went behind Woiden's desk to study the oil. 'Isn't the layering of colours amazing?'

'Yes. What did you discuss the last time you were here?'

'We tried to create a historical timeline for Cecil after his university years.'

'How did that go?'

'It's very incomplete because I don't know and didn't stay in touch with any of my university friends. Went to Japan, married, had Yosh, and ignored everyone from those four years because I felt humiliated as well as betrayed. Cecil's lab partner was my closest girlfriend.'

'Oh, hell, Shannon! Does Woiden know that?'

'No. Think I need to tell him?'

'Yes.'

'It's all so long ago, Soph, so very vague. I've nothing to tell.'

I laughed softly and told her to remember pre-Renee's bequest, I hadn't pondered my childhood years for a very long time. 'Now, one memory seems to lead to another.

Woiden arrived with a tray holding a large brown teapot, cream, sugar and three patterned china cups.

I must have looked startled as he said, 'My mom taught me how to serve tea, no chipped mugs.' He poured three cups, added sugar to his as did Shannon.

'Okay, Dr. Saito, let's get back to the investigation. Have you thought of anyone we can add to the suspect list?' He sipped from his cup and added to me, 'What we're trying to identify, Mrs. Nord, is who Dr. Fischer would have let go behind him when his recliner was fully extended.'

'Other than me, I can't come up with anyone. I did consider whether he could have been having massages but I'm pretty sure not'

'Okay,' the detective said.

Shannon switched to sounding like a professor, her voice formal and firm. 'Cecil was very private, Detective. Even if I'd any inclinations to offer, he wouldn't have even let me massage him in his office. But, as we confirmed last time, many people knew when Cecil tilted his chair back - and the reality is, he did let someone go behind him.'

I nodded. 'Cecil probably told many people, John even knows he stretched out twice daily, mid-morning and mid-afternoon for twenty minutes with his head slightly lower than his feet.'

'Well, John isn't on the suspect list,' Woiden said dryly and opened his computer. 'Now, moving onto today's agenda. I have the updated coroner's report and it's very similar to the preliminary one. Dr. Fischer was very healthy, not a drug user or a heavy drinker. Death was caused by classic strangulation, though the pressure broke much more bone than usual and the coroner suspects that it was because of Dr. Fischer's prone position. The rope fibres in the wound have not yet been identified, and that research continues.'

'Did John phone you about his ranching friend's rope collection?' I asked.

'Yes and he's borrowing it for me. You three are going to his ranch tomorrow?' He looked at Shannon.

'Only overnight,' she said.

'Now, Mrs. Nord, a question for you.' Wooden finished his tea and his cup clinked as he put it on the saucer. 'How much did Cecil tell you about his earlier friends or relationships? Detective Moffatt has pointed out that other than Shannon, you and Albert seem to be Cecil's only connection with his past.'

'And I probably had a 20-year gap with no connection, no cards or phone contact except for what Lily told me during her very irregular calls. In fact, Cecil's phoning me to announce he'd moved to Thompson City startled me.

'Ah, Lily,' Woiden laughed. 'I had Detective Moffatt call her again last week and they had a long, convoluted conversation. So I tried calling her yesterday, hoping to find out about her parent's siblings or relatives. She efficiently put me in my place, told me she'd think about it and to please have Detective Moffatt call in two days.'

I laughed. 'Lily likes talking with Detective Moffatt?'

'Oh, yes, Mrs. Nord, he's chatted with her three times as she does know little bits about Cecil amidst her trivia. Moffatt has learned she's trying blue nail polish and her husband fired the person trying to teach him English again. But he's also learned that Cecil's baby was discharged to Karen's grandmother when he was unaware due to his severe injuries.'

He offered refills and sipped his cup again. 'Do either of you know about that?'

I shook my head and Shannon said, 'No, I didn't even know about the accident or that Karen died soon after giving birth. It must have been about ten years later when a university friend started working close to our home in Japan and we visited a couple of times before she left and went to Australia.' Shannon paused, then added, 'I isolated myself - Yosh was two months old before I even told my parents about my having married Hito.'

Woiden contemplated that. 'When you were engaged to Cecil, how much did you learn about Cecil's relatives?'

'Just that all his father's relatives, including a couple of brothers, disliked each other and didn't keep in touch. I did meet Lily once but she doesn't remember that. She was so young, living with a jerk of a guy Cecil disliked and waitressing long hours to pay the rent.'

Woiden typed into the computer for a few minutes. 'Mrs. Nord, can you compare Cecil as a youth to the man who returned to Erin Lake?'

'Other than his deep voice and his intense eyes, I wouldn't have recognized the man who returned. As a youth, he was so damn skinny and hunched over, wary. Who returned was a confident, gracious and good-looking adult.'

'Can you think of anyone here who would have been his enemy?

'Only his father, and that miserable coot was long dead. When John and I have speculated about suspects, we keep coming back to it having to be a financial partner or a wanna-be inventor. Except that doesn't make sense.'

Woiden looked at me, his eyes radiating his intelligence and patience. 'Because how would that person get behind the desk?'

'Yes,' I agreed, and flashbacked to Carlos and who could have put the machete in his back?

'Whoever strangled Cecil could have chosen a gun or even a knife. What John and I suspect is there's hate behind why Cecil was killed with a rope. Someone wanted to watch him die.'

Shannon nodded, blew her nose.

I continued, 'If a suspicious or unknown person had shown up at his office, Cecil would have pushed Security on his phone as he started raising his chair upright. As well, he would not have allowed many people into his office when he was stretched out in that chair, far too undignified.'

'Dr. Fischer was not holding the clicker to raise his chair, it was resting on his stomach,' Woiden said.'

'Cecil had to be strangled by someone he trusted,' Shannon added bluntly, sounding bereft.

My belly knotted, would she be left wondering, too?

'Albert's been working with Detective Moffatt and a forensic accountant trying to detail who was involved with the lab's development history and his contacts,' Woiden informed us. 'But as you know, Cecil liked secrecy, used codes. It's hard to follow who had approached him with an idea recently, let alone in his earlier years.'

'One more dead end,' Shannon said and notified him she would need a break soon.

'Okay, we're almost finished. Another ten minutes, okay?' She nodded.'

'Albert's made a good point about the missing vacuum tube,' Woiden continued. 'The time between Dr. Fischer's learning about Renee's artifacts and taking two tubes, and the date of his murder is far too short to be relevant.'

I didn't add Alex had told him that earlier, no point.

'Albert has also confirmed those particular tubes were very common, definitely not a key to some engineering invention, Mrs. Nord.

'I've seen this tool before,' I said. 'Demonstrates personal relationships, doesn't it, how the central persons connected to family and friends? Says a lot about Cecil that the last two rings are empty.'

Shannon sighed and agreed. 'Soph, if you and I did a profiler, although the family and intimate friends' rings would be similar to his, those last two blank rings wouldn't have enough room to list who also matters to us. And when I was organizing who to invite to your birthday, he said that I certainly wouldn't have to hire a hall for his friends.'

'So, is this accurate for Dr. Fischer?' Woiden flipped his unruly hair out of his eyes again.

'Yes, other than Albert and Andre, his friend and assistant who died skydiving, Cecil didn't want or let his colleagues become friends.'

I yawned noticeably. 'Sorry, Detective Woiden, but as you know, I returned from New York late yesterday.'

He jumped to his feet and apologized. 'We're done. Thank you both. Although it might not feel as though we've achieved much, we have.'

'Really?' Shannon sounded as weary as I was.

'Yes.'

'Why?'

'I've learned more about Dr. Fischer, which matters. We've established he was not juggling the books, that his corporation is clean and very efficiently organized for increased profitability annually. Now, as I listen to you two, I don't think he had a secret life.' He grinned, which took years off his lined face.

'So, you think the murderer has to be within the unknown wanna-be inventors?' Shannon probed.

'We don't know yet, Dr. Saito.'

'Are you making progress?' I asked bluntly.

'Frustratingly slow, Mrs. Nord, everything remains speculative, though we have eliminated many possibilities.'

He came around the desk to open the door and we
followed him down the hall. We exchanged brief good-byes
as the security door buzzed and opened.

CHAPTER THIRTY-TWO
- Sophia

The next morning, Shannon arrived in my driveway with John's stock truck right behind her. After she parked and put her overnight bag behind the truck's passenger seat, we mumbled good mornings to each other. I climbed up as she gave me a helpful push into the high seat and slid in beside me.

I shifted closer to John and patted his knee, then asked her, 'Sleep okay?'

'I did, Soph. And you?'

'Yes, I'm just fine,' I fibbed, wishing I could have slept all day. 'And glad you're finally coming with us to Winston's ranch, Shannon.'

'Me, too.' She yawned and requested, 'More heat? Though it's almost sun-up.'

I pulled my fleece tighter around me and increased the fan some, knowing there's only two options: too little heat or way too much.

As John turned on to the highway, he braked suddenly and we watched as a doe and two fawns scooted in front of us.

Shannon and I grinned at the little family and at each other. 'Finally, I am going to see where you've taken your most famous photos.'

I agreed as my black and white hoodoo posters that I regularly take at Winston's do sell in the thousands since I started releasing another six-photo series every November.

John said in his gravelly morning voice, 'Winston said this morning to tell you how much he's looking forward to your visit, Shannon.'

I queried, 'This morning?'

'We had a radio phone connection at five, Soph. He added more items to his 'bring-me' list and confirmed Shannon ate meat.'

'Hope you told him I love home-grown steak.'

I poked her. 'Probably won't get that because Winston's a gourmet cook along with being the most philosophical man I know.'

'Philosopher and chef, that's quite a combination. You two do remember I've only met this man once before? Briefly, we exchanged a few words about the setting sun.'

John laughed and assured Shannon, 'You'll like him, he's unique, eh, Soph? As well as being a horse whisperer, he likes reading complex books. Wrote a couple, too.'

I agreed 'unique' covered it.

'I regularly tell Winston, anyone who ranches up above the Fraser has to be both philosophical and have a large sense of humour,' John continued. 'I sure would never ranch that property.'

'Though you found it for him.'

'I did. Now, what did you two and Woiden discuss yesterday?'

'We answered so many questions about Cecil from various angles. He's another complex man.' Shannon described Woiden's relationship chart and not being able to add many friends to Cecil's. 'Seeing it and trying to fill in those empty circles was illuminating for me, and poignant. He had colleagues but, in many ways, he was like a hermit, didn't let many people come close. John, I've a question and I want a blunt answer, okay? Were you and Cecil close friends?'

John didn't hesitate. 'Compared to Winston and my most kindred friends, no. What Cecil and I had was more like being close cousins because of your and Sophie's relationship. Does that make sense?'

'Yes.'

In the silence that followed, I heard the horses squealing in the stock box and turned to check them through the back window. Winston's new stallion was restless about being confined, snorting and stomping around on his twelve inches of halter lead while the old mare was napping, very used to being transported, indifferent to the stallion's complaints

'Woiden keeps surprising me, he has a droll sense of humour.' Shannon said and told John about his being amused at Lily's preference for Moffatt.

'Yeah, he's a neat guy,' I agreed. 'Astute, usually low keyed, but finding Cecil's murderer is challenging his team, and I sensed they're not optimistic.'

Shannon agreed. 'To be honest, I'm little help and am shocked by how little I know about Cecil's past.'

I assured her that we all assume we know more than we actually do about some people in our lives. 'Look at me. How could I have lived seventy years of illusions about who I actually am?

'No, Soph, Renee's confessions are not about who you are, it's your heritage that's the illusion. You've been comfortably content with yourself ever since I met you. You know who you are, as I usually do with myself ... but not so much, right now.'

'Shannon, do you think the investigators have found any leads they aren't sharing?' John asked. 'What about that missing vacuum tube?'

'I don't know but suspect they haven't found any. It seems the murderer took the tube as no one else has it. The remaining one's been analyzed and it is a generic old electronic tube.'

'Somehow, because of the glass, Cecil thought the tubes came from England?' I had a flashback of him standing by the sliding door and holding one into the sun.

'Hard to comprehend Cecil being dead, isn't it?' I murmured after swallowing the lump in my throat.

'The big question is why is he dead?' John said.

'As it is Carlos,' I agreed.

'Well, my learning his roommate was somehow related to Tommy Flowers certainly makes me think Carlos' murder could be related to his invention.'

'Why?' I asked.

'Every computer engineer, whether hardware or software, knows how Flowers inventing the on-off switch is what enabled the British phone system to function, and we know that he was part of the team who invented Colussus. That was the world's first programmable electronic computer and not only did it help the Allies win the war, but its invention evolved into the next computer era.'

'So, Flowers being Carlos' roommate might mean he could have been a top echelon inventor?' I know I sounded as confused as I felt.

Shannon chuckled, 'I know, convoluted.'

'Yet it reminds me of how awed Cecil could be when he'd tried to explain to me what computers will be able to do,' I reply.

'Soph, that's it, what I haven't explained well to Woiden yet. Cecil loved the companionship of a computer and when we consider his circle of friends, we need to include his electronic ones.'

John passed a pick-up overloaded with bales of hay. 'That's true. Cecil's computer was like a horse can be to me, a companion.'

Shannon agreed.

I watched the white caps blowing on the long lake beside the highway and wished I could know more about my father and his inventions.

'Shannon, back to your own history. Did you go to Japan before Cecil had that car accident?'

'Yes, it apparently happened a couple of weeks after I had fled to Japan, the day after graduation. I wanted to be far away and Hito had offered to help any student find an internship there.'

'This was around being hurt by Cecil and your former friend?'

Shannon nodded and explained to Woiden and me that she'd found a boarding house near Hito's university before contacting him. He'd found her a computer software internship where she also taught the staff some English, and started inviting her out for dinners. Four months later, they married.'

'Do you think Cecil or your other fellow students know where you were?'

'No as I didn't even tell my parents, pretended I was touring with friends.'

I continued the story. 'Woiden told us today that they've learned Cecil was in hospital for five weeks, then disappeared until fourteen months later. He was employed by Albert's family's engineering company in London.'

'It's all so long ago, how relevant is it now?' John asked.

Shannon told him what Woiden said. 'Apparently some murderers plan his or her revenge for decades.'

I took a drink from my water bottle. 'Shannon, I was annoyed at Woiden's lack of understanding why having Yosh dominated your world.'

'Unmarried, no children,' Shannon laughed. 'I learned that because during an earlier session, I told him he had no concept of what being pregnant, then a new mother entailed, let alone in a foreign culture, and burst into tears. That stunned him. He kept apologizing, explaining why as he walked me to my van.'

John's voice full of compassion, 'Was that year very hard?'

'Next to now, it was my hardest time.' She blew her nose and paused, mulling what to say. 'Although I was a newly-qualified scientist, I was a spoiled only child and my knowledge about mothering, Soph, was about equivalent to Renee's when she was pregnant with you.'

I didn't know that - and Shannon doesn't know I was six months pregnant with Scott before I told Mother, Dad and Renee. I was in Toronto by then and when I found out I was pregnant, had married Scott's father. Although I'd barely known the word alcoholic, I certainly discovered what having an alcoholic husband meant.

I sighed to myself, wondering how the hurt from so many years ago can still seem sharp?

Shannon continued reminiscing about Japan. 'I had no women friends, no aunties, no girl friends. Hito was proud but taciturn about our son, and usually gone. I had no one to share the wonder of my baby with me.'

'What you don't know, Shannon, is I do understand. When I became a father, I learned my wife disliked mothering as compared to being a lawyer and we bounced our son around between sitters like he was a ball. Did it get better for you and Yosh?'

'Yes, when Yosh turned one, Hito's newly widowed mother claimed him as her grandson. We became part of a large ex- ended family who were very supportive.'

'Did you have much contact with your own family and friends?' I asked.

'No, I exchanged many letters and photos with my folks. I did bring Yosh home for a month when he was five and my folks delighted in him. Remember, there was no Internet back then.'

'Then didn't they both became ill at the same time and you and Yosh returned to Erin Lake? '

'Yes, but only partly because of my folks. As Hito's successes in the academic world increased, he was hardly home. I realized I didn't want Yosh to be raised to be only Japanese. I wanted him to have the freedoms of Erin Lake.'

John pulled into a rest stop. 'It's time to check the horses, ladies, and stretch my back.

'Good, I need a break.'

'Me, too. Okay if I jog ahead?' Shanon asked.

As I did a few knee bends, a woodpecker rat-a-tatted nearby, which reminded me of Alex's video of my photographs. Seeing many of those again reminded me of so many memories that had almost faded. I hoped again the vividness of Shannon's memory of finding Cecil will blur with time. After being with Woiden yesterday, I was a little more optimistic about he and his team finding Cecil's murderer. 'Soon,' I hoped, aware of how gut wrenching this waiting was for her.

I wondered again, who might Renee have become if Carlos' murderer had been identified and she hadn't had TB?

CHAPTER THIRTY-THREE
- Sophia

'Shannon, look down at the Fraser's boil,' John directed and eased the heavy truck onto the narrow bridge.

The wind roared as she opened the window and leaned out.

'Not much could escape from the fury of that whirlpool, could it? How far down is it?'

'About eighty feet,' John shouted.

When she rolled up the window, she asked, 'Where are we geographically?'

'Northwest of Vancouver and southeast of Thompson City. It's the massive trench between the Pacific Coastal Mountains and the Rockies,' John replied as we headed up the narrow road winding beside the steep sandstone cliffs.

'I love the Fraser's stark and isolated plateau county.'

'Do many people live here?'

'There is a considerable number of native bands whose peoples have resided here for centuries. Very few non-natives.'

'Is Winston native?'

I laughed. 'He's mixed heritage. John, will you tell Shannon about Winston's history? I never can keep it straight.'

'His father's grandmother was from this Fraser region, though she'd left the reserve and Winston has no claims to indigenous rights. But when he came here to visit twenty years ago he felt this geography was his home country. He hired me to find land with a potential for ranching.'

'What's Winston like?'

'Interesting, eccentric. He's a special friend. I helped him buy this land while cautioning a ranch here would be borderline financially, and very demanding to develop and operate. He complimented me on my honesty, and in the past twenty years has done what I never could have.

He has created a profitable spread.'

'Why couldn't have you?'

'This terrain's temperatures are too extreme for me, often minus thirty in the winter and over a hundred in the summer. And Winston's an innovator, needs challenges, many more than I could tolerate.'

I added I couldn't live here either. 'Shannon, this land's as complex as Winston. Wait until you see him, he looks like a caricature of a cowboy with his craggy face and handlebar moustache but the reality is he's also been a practicing psychologist and professor in Australia.'

'He's Australian?

'No,' I said. 'His father was a horseman from Saskatchewan with many ties to this area while his mother was a Danish poet whose father has come from Tennessee. I guess Winston's rather like these wind-carved hoodoos above us, Shannon. Many layers of yesteryears.'

John chuckled at my description. 'When he was thirteen, his folks died in a plane accident and his father's friend, a British horseman, became his guardian. He moved Winston to his horse ranch in Dorset, told him they would spend the summers on the ranch and suggested he go to a boarding school in a different country every year. Winston did that but I forget where he chose. Do you recall, Soph?'

'Copenhagen, London, Barcelona, Washington and Mexico City during his secondary schooling years, then he came to Vancouver and the University of British Columbia and did his master's in social psychology. After that, he moved to Australia until he inherited the ranch in Dorset. He went back and ran it for a year then decided England wasn't his ideal fit and sold it. Eventually he bought this massive acreage, what has become known as Headlands.'

'Has he been married?' Shannon asked.

John and I laughed. 'Once, and briefly, to Aleen, a stormy history professor from Glasgow who stayed at Headland's for about six months. When she returned to her Scottish home, Winston told John he was most relieved.'

'Neither of us met her but he's had two subsequent relationships and Soph and I liked both women. But one winter at Headlands was enough and neither stayed for a second.'

'We haven't told Shannon that Winston's a writer.

'Which might be why Winston likes the winters here.' John geared down and negotiated a steep hill before continuing. 'He's writing a book - the psychology of horse herds and how horses interact socially. He spends hours daily watching them'.

'How many horses does he have?' Shannon asked.

'Over two hundred head, about fifty quarter horses and the rest are mules,' John replied. 'The mules generate his main income, though his quarter horses are also in high demand. The offspring of this registered stallion snorting away behind us will sell for thousands.'

Shannon glanced through the rear window at the big black horse and the little mare. 'No wonder you and Winston are close friends, you're kindred, except you raise bulls as well as horses.'

I chuckled. 'It's the bulls that pay his bills, Shannon. John's horses are as much in demand as Winston's, but many of his are long-term residents as he doesn't like selling his beauties.'

'Soph, I sold five last year and already have three buyers lined up for 2008,' John sputtered. 'But you're right, I like keeping my horses and can charge big bucks for the bulls.'

The motor noise escalated as the truck worked to carry us uphill, making hearing each other hard. Once we were on a straight stretch, Shannon said, 'Cecil thought you were an astute business man, John.'

'Yes, he told me I could sharpen a pencil as efficiently as him and I told him I was honoured. His financial savvy was impressive.'

That reminded me of a question Woiden asked. 'Shannon, you shrugged when asked yesterday about who Cecil might have financed. Did someone come to mind? Wouldn't an inventor who's used to planning precisely be a prime suspect?'

'The core question remains, 'Why was Cecil murdered?' John agreed.

'I know,' she said, as we came around a curve and saw the large HEADLANDS in tall black metal letters strung between the two poles bordering the wide gate. In the distance, the sun reflected off a glass and log house framed by a palisade of stark cliffs.

'Here we are, ladies.' John parked the truck near the wide stairs and Winston came bounding down, opened the truck's passenger door and helped us down. He gave me a hug before sticking out his big hand to Shannon.

'Dr. Saito, Shannon, you are very welcome to my humble home and I am pleased to be meeting the woman behind the invitation to Soph's birthday party. I regretted not being able to attend.'

She shook his hand, told him that Alex and she certainly understood as he turned to me.

'Sophia, belated greetings and how is it you keep looking like you don't have birthdays?'

I told him he had a silver tongue and thanked him for the Himalayan birch tree he'd had delivered to me.

'Now, while John and I unload these horses, will you take Shannon up to the loft guest room? You and John are in the downstairs bedroom this time.' He hugged me before stepping up into the truck. 'Oh, and stir the stew and help yourselves to whatever - there's a cheese and olive tray in the fridge.'

Shannon laughed as she followed me into Winston's home. 'Humble, hey? Those wooden beams and the views through the tall windows are magnificent. '

I agreed as I led the way up the curved staircase and enjoyed Shannon's reaction to the circular room. She did as I had years ago, saw the four-foot skylight above the big bed and flopped down on the puffy white quilt.

'This time of year, the little dipper will be right above you.'

She lay there and sighed. 'Soph, this is the same feeling I have watching the sky from Cecil's studio. He would have loved us sleeping here. But enough.' She rolled off the bed, stretched and gave me a quick hug. 'Thanks for insisting I come. How about you go stir the stew and I'll be down after a shower?'

Sunshine glimmered on the hanging copper pots and pans in Winston's kitchen and reflected on the crystal wine glasses resting on the round table's burgundy cloth. The dining alcove was off the kitchen, floor to ceiling windows, divided from the kitchen by an indoor herb garden.

From the rich scent, I knew before I took the lid off, Winston had made me his beef bourguignon. He often does, when he hasn't made John's favorite moussaka. We're here a few times a year, me seeking just the right light on the hoodoos for my next poster series while John and Winston admire each other's horses.

Shannon will enjoy the food and the conversation, I thought, as I headed to our suite, wanting to get the dust off and feeling grubby in this heat. After, I took a loose yellow sundress from my knapsack and pulled it over my wet hair while I debated whether the back patio or the cooler living room. The soft chocolate couch there won, and I settled into it and enjoyed its panorama of galloping horses on the green pasture beyond the windows and the towering sandstone cliffs.

As usual when I'm sitting on this couch in Winston's great room, I could appreciate how he'd designed the ceilings. They go from soaring to regular, then English-pub beams leading into his little library alcove. Even that little alcove is unique as Winston used double-sided black shelves to act as dividers and shelve his massive book collection. Inside those walls of books is a narrow library table with his collection of dictionaries, a mocha-coloured calfskin recliner and a reading lamp that looks rather like a multi-branched tree.

The lamp of many options, John had named it after we'd

delivered it last November and Winston had proudly demonstrated its seven lighting features and where a coffee mug could sit.

He was as proud of that lamp as Cecil had been of his chair, I realized suddenly, but although there were similarities between the two men, their differences far outnumbered them. I mulled why and realized Cecil hadn't had Winston's self-humour and ingrained confidence He had been somehow vulnerable, whereas that word didn't fit Winston at all.

A strange thought, I accepted, and tried to figure out why. Had Cecil hidden deep secrets as well as having had a hard childhood? God, I hope not.

Yet how he was murdered - how my father had been slaughtered - created so many unanswerable questions.

Shannon came down the stairs in an emerald and blue caftan and I whistled.

'It's definitely not black, Soph,' she declared and sat down beside me. 'Cecil bought it.'

'It's gorgeous, suits you. I was just thinking about him - hard not to, isn't it? Now, would you like a gin and tonic? Or scotch, or what?'

'Water with ice, it's so hot and dry here. And I'll get it.'

'One for me, too.' I followed her into the kitchen, though we stopped to admire the five horses that were now staring at us from beyond the back porch. I asked her if she wanted to ride while she was here?

'Not really. I'm enjoying feeling clean and it's too hot. You?'

'Not at all,' I admitted. Shannon still has her mare and rode often but I don't anymore.

'That green grass tells me Winston's a guru at water systems.'

'Yes, he has built reservoirs that hold the spring melt and feed his gravity water system. That grass stays green, even in August.'

'Maximizing nature efficiently is what Cecil would say.' She turned towards me. 'Be honest, Soph, do you think they'll find his murderer?'

'I am so hoping they will,' and felt relieved when John and Winston called hello from the back door, because if I was being honest, each day that passed without meaningful leads make that seem more unlikely.

We joined them in the kitchen and I asked Winston, 'Living room or back deck?'

'Inside, Soph, the mosquitos will be biting soon and we're

going to have dessert by the fire-pit tonight. John, the lager's in the fridge, and will you put that cheese tray on the coffee table by the fireplace? Ladies?'

'A g & t, please,' Shannon requested and I agreed

'A tall one, with some lime?' he offered.

She took the glass Winston passed her moments later. 'Thank you, and for the special guest room where I'll be sleeping under the stars.'

'Know you're welcome here anytime, Shannon, even without these two,' Winston offered and swirled his scotch. 'And, lassie, I'm very sorry about your loss of Cecil. John's been telling me some about the investigation underway and it must be exhausting for you?'

'Yes.' She took a large drink and swallowed. 'It's hard, almost two weeks and not even one suspect. And the number of questions I can't answer keeps increasing.'

'A tough endurance,' Winston agreed and turned to me. 'What about the bequest Renee dumped on you, Sophie? As well as your new parentage? Did you have any suspicions before you read her letter?'

'None. Reading *I am your mother, and your father was a Mexican engineer* was inconceivable, nonsensical - at first, that is.

'How are you doing now?'

'I've a thin layer of compassion for Renee, Winston, but I'm dammed annoyed she's dead and not having to answer Alex's and my questions. But because of the documents and photos she left, I do believe Carlos was my father.

'And also murdered,' Winston shook his mane of greying black hair. 'Damn unfair way to tell you, though, Soph. Do you know, I'm not surprised you have Latin genes? Explains your innate graciousness and your classic cheek bones.'

He winked at me, leaned over his chair's wooden arm for his big basket full of rope strands and started straightening a number of them across his knees. 'Is having different birth parents upsetting for you?'

'Not at all, Winston, I'm far too old to care. But our having a different heritage does affect Alex's ALS genetic profiling, which seems to be more upsetting for me than him. But we've both agreed it is why it's wise to find out more about our unknown family. Did John tell you Alex and I are going to La Paz to research the Hernández clan?'

'Yes, but what he also reported with quite a whine in his voice was something about you going photographing snakes in caves?' Winston started plaiting rope and asked with mock horror, 'Snakes, Soph?

'Yes, and I'm excited to be the photographer recording them. Probably none of them have had their photo taken before.'

'Well, I'm with John. If you must, please do be cautious. Do you know the Baja has its own homebred vicious snakes and I've heard, quite a few imported species around its shipping.'

'Safety is my team's top priority.'

I knew Winston had lost a prize colt to a rattler's bite three years ago and was as anti-rattlesnake as John was.

'And Alex is driving his old Packard down, an adventure for him as he will be researching that ancient murder. Could be he might find details about unusual crimes in the universities' or Mexico City newspapers' archives.'

'Really?' I had assumed murders were common in Mexico and wouldn't get much news coverage.

'Alex might find hiring a researcher worthwhile as I suspect it will have been written about repetitively.'

'Why?

'Mysterious murders usually are, especially if there's a tie to someone like Rubin, a prominent manufacturer. And another thing I've been thinking about - the murderer had to be someone known to the dogs, Soph. You've lived in the Baja as I have and know there are always dogs and would have been seventy years ago.'

'Winston, I hadn't considered that,' John interjected as he stood up and leaned against a wall to stretch his back.

'Well, it still includes so many people outside the family,

like the professor and his wife. The dogs would have known them, perhaps not barked?'

'Maybe the professor's a suspect but I don't think his wife, Winston. Didn't we read somewhere that she was Renee's size?' Shannon said to me. 'The murderer had to be tall, what with the height of bed and Carlos on top of that.' She added unnecessarily, 'I've being considering how body shape and weight controls what's feasible.'

'Yes, it does,' I agreed, knowing that factor wasn't as relevant if strangling someone.

Shannon sniffled and blew her nose. 'Winston, what are the chances of the Forensics Unit identifying the rope from your samples?'

'Unknown. I have an extensive collection but locating what type of rope was used, and what was its usual use won't be easy.'

John added, 'When I consider how many hundreds of different applications there are for ropes, it is a challenge. Sailors, construction workers, gymnasts, loggers, farmers - all use rope and the weave and fibre content of rope varies with each different application. For instance, the ropes that work for securing boats differ extensively from the ropes Winston and I use as ranchers.'

'So taking Winston's samples over to Woiden is likely going to be another dead end?' I asked.

'Perhaps.'

'But worth a try by Forensics, as Woiden would say.' Shannon stood up and walked toward the front door. 'And changing the topic, what appeals to me now is a stroll before dinner. Anyone care to join me?'

'Me, I need to stretch out my back,' John said. 'Are you two coming?'

I declined, as did Winston.

After they left, he asked, 'Want to talk about how you're doing, Soph? You and Alex certainly didn't get the peaceful week you've been planning together. First, Renee's bequest, then Cecil's murder - and it is one of the most atrocious ones I've heard of, as was Carlos. I guess I'm glad you're off on a contract, even if it's photographing snakes.'

'Thanks, Winston. I'm okay, though somewhat exhausted. So little I can do for Shannon. The search for the murderer is muddying up her grief at losing Cecil and it's hard, confusing. She helped me so much when my son died.'

'Murder befouls as well as steals a life. Do you think there's hope the detectives will solve who killed Cecil? Losing someone in a vehicle accident or to a heart attack differs so much from one's mate being murdered. You can only wait to learn why as you keep comforting Shannon and praying Cecil was who you all thought he was. And, my dear, it being similar to what you're learning about Renee's world does have spill-off for you. Tell me about your reaction to Renee's bequest, learning about Carlos.

'Winston, my sympathy is shaded by her and my grandparents' dishonesty, what seems like needless secrecy.' I told him about Iona and my feeling how much knowing her earlier would have added to my years. 'Renee didn't ever give me and my son much, but others could have.'

'Of course,' he agreed.

'They kept my father a secret for my whole life, played pretend. Why?'

'Sophie, I know I would be furious, but what the hell can you do about it?'

'Nothing, it is what it is.' I looked over at the former psychologist and chuckled. 'Okay, I get it, it's okay for me to be as angry as I want with Renee.'

'Why not, Soph? It's you who was lied to about your truths.

'That does clarify it, thanks.' We watched three horses gallop by, their tails streaming behind them, and I wondered if talking about my loss was all I needed to do because I felt less weary. I live by the realities of my life, not by what have might been.

'Soph, what about Shannon? She's so bruised, yet I sense massive strength.'

'She has that. She and Yosh are as close as Alex and me plus she's brave with much self-humour. She'll come through this and be okay down the way. But, god Winston, I hope her and our memories of Cecil survive intact.

Winston finished plaiting his section of rope and lined up strands for the next one. 'That is the big if, isn't it?

'Well, I do know Shannon won't become like Renee - has no ability to be a martyr.'

'Martyr?'

'That's how I'm thinking about Renee's many decades after my father's life. We were raised within a narrow and judgmental community and I think that might have made it easier for her to become one, justify why she could keep her secrets.'

Winston guffawed and looked up from his plaiting. 'Dr. Sophie, you might have missed your calling, preferring photography over psychology. May I refresh your gin & tonic?

I laughed ruefully. 'You're as complex as that rope you're weaving, Winston. Thanks for listening because I do need to stop mulling all Renee's why's and why not's. It is pointless. And, yes, please, a light one.'

He got up and I passed him my glass.

When he returned, he asked, 'Tell me more about this lovely old lady in Boston who charmed you and John. Is she somehow related to Carlos?'

'She's a Hernández by marriage. That's what my last name would have been, if my father had lived. You would love Iona, Winston. Carlos was her nephew by marriage and she's Ana's grandmother and 88 now.'

'And just who is Ana?'

I explained she was also a sculptor and in partnership with Yosh. 'She was staying with Shannon when Cecil died and has become a close friend. What's strange is discovering she's also my and Alex distant relative because her father is Iona's son.'

'Will there be questions?' Winston joked. 'So somehow through Ana and Iona, you've already connected with your father's extended family?'

'Yes and I've learned a lot from Iona. She's also hoping to

arrange for Alex and I to meet Carlos' older sister, an ancient nun, who lives up in a mountain town not too far from La Paz.'

'That would be helpful.'

I glanced out the window. 'John and Shannon are almost here. Anything I can do to help with dinner?'

Winston put his rope basket away and when he smiled at me, I noticed how one side of his tidy moustache dips a little lower than the other. We'd never have been able to live with each other but it's lovely Winston's my dear friend, as he is John's.

'Salad's made. How about you warm the buns while I washup?'

Very early the next morning, Shannon and I sat on the front porch's steps and complained to each other about having to leave.

'I just want to stay and take photos for at least a week,' I lamented.

Shannon said that if she could stay, she'd stay in that bed, looking at stars and watching the sky's ever-changing shades of blue.

'We're almost finished, ladies. You ready?' John called, as he jumped down from the stock box where he and Winston had been securing the chests of rope samples.

I stood up, took a deep breath and stretched, savouring the soft tangy air. 'Smell that mountain sage, Shannon? It will be sweeter, come fall. How about coming back with us in later October?'

'Perhaps, Soph, thanks. And I will, sometime, but right now, my schedule is rather uncertain.'

'It is. And mine's overfull, I leave for Loreto in three days.

'Alex is still heading south tomorrow?'

'He is, we're having a phone visit tonight.'

'You nervous?'

'Not nearly as much now that Ana's travelling down at the same time as him,' I admitted as I had been feeling antsy about him being in a 1937 car and managing driving through rural

Mexico with almost no Spanish.

Shannon chuckled. 'He's right that having the Packard might help with the La Paz search. As John pointed out at dinner, every time Alex parks, someone will be reminiscing. Aren't cars the universal language of men?

'Ready,' John called as he climbed into the driver's seat.

We exchanged goodbyes with Winston as he boosted me, then Shannon into the stock truck. John honked three times as we drove down the long driveway and two eagles dropped down behind the Headlands sign to investigate.

We didn't talk much on the way home, listened to CD's and Shannon and I snoozed on and off.

As we started down the long hill down into Thompson City, he said, 'I'm going to drop off Winston's ropes for Woiden. The sooner Forensics has them, the better.'

He parked behind the Courthouse and loaded the two big display chests onto a dolly.

'My fingers are crossed too, Shannon. If they can identify the rope, it could be very helpful narrowing things down.'

'For sure,' she said pensively, then asked, 'What does Winston do with all the rope he makes?'

'Oh, it's all pre-sold. He has a waiting list for his piggin' strings and custom lariats.'

'Piggin' strings? What's that used for?'

'I think mainly by cowboys on the rodeo circuit and ranchers, of course. They're six-foot ropes that are used to tie a calf's feet together, once it's thrown down.'

Shannon looked at me and I shrugged. 'I've never seen one but what John told me was at a rodeo, after a competitor lassos a calf, he jumps off the horse, takes the calf down and uses a piggin' string to hobble the animal. The time that takes counts toward his or her total points.'

'Really?' I waited as she thought about that. 'But I don't think Cecil knew anyone within the rodeo circuit.'

I turned the Packard onto the freeway heading south, remembering Gran's good-bye.

'Adios, Alex, have fun and be safe as a travelling man.'

I was ready to be a travelling man. During our long phone call, Gran had tucked in much advice, twice mentioned that I was to watch my back and belongings and be careful not let the Packard overheat.

I'd flipped back at her, 'And you be real cautious around those damn snakes!'

What she didn't mention was the biggest issues. I don't know the language or appropriate Mexican customs or how to manage in tropical heat.

She didn't need to because we're aware of that. Though in earlier chats, she advised me to travel with other vehicles, make my stops in villages and plan ahead as the Baja highway frequently lacks shoulders and stopping isn't possible.

That one had startled me. How did people cope with having no place to stop? On top of that, Ana has told me that the many 18-wheelers travel fast and barely tolerate sharing the road.

When I'd returned from Erin Lake to Vancouver, around getting the fender repaired, I also had a heavy leather trucker's bag fastened onto the jump seat, and a second lock installed on the Packard's trunk as the 1937 factory installed one pops open with a screwdriver. Each time I park and get out, my old knapsack will be with me. I've fit it under the cooler on the passenger seat and it's bulging with my computer, toiletries including the mosquito spray, suntan lotion and first aid stuff, spare jeans and a shirt.

Plus my two files critical for this trip.

The red one has maps and all the legal documentation I

require to permit me and the Packard to be in Mexico. The blue one is considerably thicker and holds Renee's info and copies of all the portraits and photos she left. Plus, a notebook with emergency numbers for the US and Baja, duplicates of my I.D. and the list of motels where I'll be meeting Ana each evening.

She and I have discussed my do-not-do's and the Baja's complicated communication options at length. She was blunt about how inexperienced I am at understanding what it means not to have technology available.

"Don't count on having cell connections in most of the Baja," she'd warned and explained why. Tourist brochures and websites create illusions because they often include their future planning, not the lack of it now. "Cell services projected to be available in 2010 are often listed now."

When she'd added that fax is often available, I laughed and told her I hadn't used a fax machine for about three years.'

She'd replied with her sweet pixie smile, "Alex, it's not Canada. Mexico has both leading edge technologies and archaic ones. Or none."

My biggest challenge is my lack of Spanish, as Ana also bluntly pointed out. "But try! Even though yours is almost impossible to understand, by trying, you show respect. That matters."

She'd created a page of phonetically spelled emergency phrases for me but when I tried to say them, she'd shake her head and laugh.

'You do have un grande problemo, Alex.'

She'd bought the two translation dictionaries I'm carrying, one in my shirt pocket and the more comprehensive one in my knapsack. When I need assistance, she'd instructed, I am to point at the English print word and its translation, as well as smile, speak slowly and quietly.

'Most of we Mexicans are kind and will try to help but only if someone is polite to us.'

Well, doing that is easy whereas pronouncing Spanish isn't.

Gran's phone update last night on Woiden's lack of news about Cecil as well Iona's message that Mother Superior Luisa-Grace is now in Mexico City indefinitely around having eye surgery were both disappointing.

But hearing that Shannon has decided to stay an extra week in London after meeting Beth and Yosh and was going to take the fall semester off was good news.

The last message Gran had passed on was a reminder from John that he can be anywhere fast and that I am to call or have him contacted, if I need him. She'd laughed when passing his quip. 'Be aware of the cultural differences, ask questions cautiously and watch out for moose and critters.'

Those two do parent me - and I savour it.

When the flashing signs above the freeway advised me crossing the US border is taking 18 minutes currently, I thought about my next four days. Today I'm going to Portland, then tomorrow I'll not put many kilometers on as I want to wander through Oregon's little coastal towns and overnight beside the ocean somewhere. The next day, I'm looking forward to driving the narrow old California highway high above the Pacific and overnighting in San Francisco. Then it's back onto the freeways to the San Diego airport and picking up Ana. Early the following morning, we cross the Mexican border.

I reached for a jazz CD, paused and inserted the Learning Spanish one instead. Both Ana and Gran had advised, 'Practice and practice, say the syllables over and over, because to have anyone able to understand your Spanish, you need to learn the rhythms and how to accent a syllable correctly.'

My stumbling attempts so far are giving me a much greater appreciation of just how damn hard it is to learn a second language.

Gran hadn't hidden her relief when Ana decided to travel down to La Paz at the same time I was.

We won't be travelling together as Ana has to have her motorcycle on the road by dawn as she'll quit for the day before noon. I have to wait until full daylight to avoid hitting a black bull, cow, horse or goat on the highway. So, I'll be driving in the daytime and taking long lunches so my old car can be parked in shade over the midday heat.

When I told Gran that, she'd approved, then reminisced about 1978 and her first time driving down the Baja. Her old Volkswagen van boiled over regularly, and her projected six days of travel had taken her ten.

"So, Alex, don't expect to schedule your arrival times accurately. Even through the Baja highway has been much improved since then, those steep hills, hairpin curves, sandy detours around washed-out bridges, massive potholes and the animals on the road still can make your trip slow going."

When I mentioned our side trip in Tijuana to take pesos to Ana's pregnant cousin, Gran had been pleased. "It'll give you an ideal intro to Mexico as Ana's cousin will probably be living in a frontier-land village during the season."

'Frontier-land?'

"That's what Mexicans call the vast Tijuana border area," and had explained that many thousands of people lived there temporarily. "Agriculture workers come up for the seasonal work in the US, growing and harvesting crops. Big money as compared to what labourers could earn in Mexico."

'Ana's cousin's husband is one of them, Gran, because he works in the bean fields above San Diego.'

After we'd hung up, I recognized again how much I don't know about Mexico.

But if I'm lucky, I'll find out more about our Hernández relatives, particularly Carlos. What I had learned at the University of BC archives surprised Gran and I; Carlos was older than we'd projected, born on February 25, 1911, which made him ten years older than Renee and changed most of our earlier assumptions about timings of his education. He'd graduated with an Advanced Electrical Engineer Honours degree from UBC in June, 1937. What was likely rather than him going from London to Vancouver was he'd been working for Uncle Rubin before returning to school to take his graduate degree.

Which might also change why he was murdered. Could what looked like a crime of passion have been a cold-blooded killing around theft of whatever Carlos was inventing?

According to Shannon, what Detective Woiden asks repetitively is "who benefits?"

Maybe it had been the Professor? I didn't think he'd personally killed him but he could have been with a hired killer and able to keep the dogs quiet.

But as we read Renee's stuff, I'd been imaging he and Carlos liked each other, apparently having been together for so much of Carlos' schooling. So many unknowns!

I could almost hear Gran's voice. 'Alex, don't expect to learn much about Carlos because it *has* been seventy years.'

I pushed the gas pedal for the long straight stretch ahead and switched to thinking about Ana. Even though I theoretically don't want the complexity of a relationship, I can't wait to be with her again. I'm missing her smile, smelling her subtle perfume and watching how she moves.

Damn.

When I passed a sign stuck in the gravel beside the four-lane highway, GOOD LOCAL FOOD AT GOOD PRICES, I turned into the exit. I was starving.

CHAPTER THIRTY-SIX
- Alex

Ana had emailed me directions about where to park at the San Diego Airport and I pulled into that area twenty minutes before her flight was to land. I got out into the hot sunshine, leaned against the Packard and daydreamed as I enjoyed the sunshine and watched the planes touch down.

She startled me as she arrived from a different direction than I expected and touched my shoulder. 'Hi, Alex.'

'Hi, Ana.' She was gorgeous in a white and green summer dress, its skirt fluttering in the wind. I spread my arms, offered a hug.

She gave me a token one and after we climbed into the Packard, pointed, 'Go left at that far gate. Uncle's home is about twenty minutes south and there are many sharp turns.'

We're overnighting there and would leave very early to cross the US/Mexican border.

As we travelled, Ana explained she'd left her motorcycle there because she and her mother had decided Manuel needed to try riding again. He'd been a biker before, only stopped because of his wife's deteriorating health, but she was now in care and he was sad and lonely. 'Madre recently told me it worked, Alex. He's ridden mine often through the winter and is going to buy himself a bike.'

I was beginning to realize how connected Ana was to her extended family when she next explained that once we were in Tijuana, our first stop would be to her pregnant cousins' to deliver pesos.

Her Uncle Manuel was waiting on the porch of a little Spanish-style rancher overlooking the Pacific and I was startled by his appearance. He could be Gran's brother since his face shape, affable hazel eyes and smile were so like hers.

'He does look like Sophia and you, Alex, even though Uncle's from a different Hernández branch of the family than my father.'

When she introduced me, her uncle gave me a hug. 'Iona has phoned often so I feel as if I know you. Those are quite the wheels you've got. I haven't even seen a '37 Packard in years.'

He walked slowly around it and told his niece, 'Ana, this is as special as your bike. Come along an inspect it. You're sure you don't want to sell it to me?'

'No, I'm not selling my treasure.' She laughed and swatted his arm, as we followed Uncle through the cactus garden to the garage.

Ana's bike is a BMW 2005 K1200S, which, strangely, was what I'd almost bought before I had asked Gran for the wrecked Packard.

'Nice bike, Ana.'

'Nice understatement, Alex,' her uncle quipped.

'Thanks, I splurged and bought her after I sold my first major piece of sculpture. She's lovely to ride and good power,' she said modestly, knowing I knew she'd bought the top of the line.

This woman has layers upon tantalizing layers, I thought, and hoped to learn much more about her.

The evening with Manuel gave me more Hernández history as he and Iona chatted regularly, and Ana's family has been staying with he and his wife since she and her brother were toddlers. He told us after Uncle Rubin died in the late 1960's, the Mexico City factory was purchased by a major communications group. He didn't know anything about what Carlos might have been inventing, though knew he'd been murdered.

When we described Renee's bequest to him, he laughed and put a different twist on the story than Gran and I had even considered.

'The poor woman, Alex, just think about the dilemma she'd created for herself. She screwed up in not confiding to her daughter earlier; probably could never figure out if the time was right or how to do it. Then, she'd still wanted Sophia to know about her father and had all her precious bits to pass on. Assuming she was probably a procrastinator like me, that motivated her,' he chuckled ruefully. 'Ana, consider this fair warning, I might follow Renee's example, buy four blue containers for everything I can't throw out and leave them for you.'

She and I looked at each other, recognizing he wasn't joking.' I would welcome having them,' she said softly.

God, I realized for the first time, this getting old is a tough journey. And finally felt some compassion for Renee.

Later, after a leisurely dinner during which we talked about La Paz, I snuggled down in the guest bed, glad that by about six tomorrow, I'll finally be in Mexico.

The border traffic was already heavy when we pulled up to the long row of entry gates. When the custom guard waved at me to park, Ana signaled she would follow and pulled her bike in beside the Packard and we both went into the customs building. She helped me fill out the entry forms about how long I was staying and where. He added more official stamps and after I paid my pesos, issued my permission cards.

'There, you're legally here,' she said, fastening up her leathers. 'Now, our first stop is the garage where I'll leave my bike. Follow in the outside lane and if we get separated, I'll pull over and wait for you to catch up.'

She was easy to follow and how she handled her big bike impressed me. Once we turned into the gas station, she chatted briefly with the mechanic, locked up her bike and climbed into the Packard.

'Okay, Alex, use that exit, we're on the freeway for about five kilometers and we're about half an hour from Carmelita's.'

'Okay,' I agreed and asked, 'How long have you been riding, Ana?'

'Oh, quite a while; I got a 250 Kawasaki Enduro for my fourteenth birthday, but I'd been riding my brother's discards before that. Motorcycles are a family tradition as both my parents ride. We've had many holidays touring in the US and eastern Mexico.'

'Have you? Toured, that is.'

'Beth and I have, did about five thousand km wandering in Europe for a month after we ended up buying matching BMW's. That was in the summer of 2006. Haven't you seen Yosh's photos of us?'

'No, Ana, I haven't.' I didn't explain that was when Mom's ALS became worse and Lisa and my marriage began ending. I changed the subject. 'How big is Tijuana?'

'I think over a million and a half now - Alex, take that exit and be damn careful of the Packard's fenders! Turn right at the next corner, then immediately change lanes. We'll turn left at the school - and you'll have to wedge in. Then we go through the shopping area before heading up to the top of a long hill.'

'Goddamn!' I swore as a horn blasted and a delivery van shoved in front of the Packard.

We wound through the city's narrow and chaotic streets where loud mariachi music mixed with the stores' broadcasting their specials came in the car windows as did the smells of many spices mixed with diesel fumes and the rubber scent of burnt brakes.

I shouted at Ana, 'Tijuana is very different from Vallarta.'

'Went to a time-share there, did you? Is that the only time you've been in Mexico, Alex?'

'Yes. My former father-in-law gave us two weeks at an upscale resort in Nuevo Vallarta to celebrate our first anniversary.'

'Did you enjoy that city?'

'Well, to be blunt, at that point in Liza's and my marriage, we thoroughly enjoyed beach, booze and bed. Don't remember much else,' I admitted.

Ana chuckled. 'Well, Puerto Vallarta and Tijuana are two very different cities, though both are over a hundred years old, and both started as little beach towns. That's basically what Vallarta remains, though its growth and upscale options are amazing. Tijuana's become a massive crime pit along with

becoming a powerful and major Mexican city with many
amenities and cultural events ... Alex, watch the red pickup.'
We're taking the shortest route, but it does take us through
some seedy sections and on a rougher road. You okay with
that?'

'Of course.' I assured her that whatever worked for her was
fine with me. About ten minutes later, I was silently
questioning my words as the Packard bounced from pothole to
pothole up a dusty road lined with tin shacks and other
makeshift shelters.

When we finally crossed a short bridge, we were in a
different world, the streets lined with family homes with
bougainvillea growing up their high fences. I sighed with relief
as I followed the slow bus in front of me.

'Less than ten minutes to Carmelita's place,' Ana said.

I noticed a surprising number still seemed to be under
construction and asked her about that.

'This area is pretty typical for lower middle class and why
the houses are unfinished is because their owners can't get
mortgages, build a bit at a time. It's also usual to leave it a little
unfinished because no municipal taxes are charged until after
full completion.'

'That's why the rebar rods are sticking out of many roofs?'

'It is. Make a sharp left after the next curve.'

When I did, the Packard's tires bit into soft sand and dirt
and we headed straight up a long hill.

'Turn right at the top and we're there.'

We entered into a dense area filled with shacks, although
it didn't look like an unkempt shantytown. Most of the entry
stoops had cheery pots of peppers and tomatoes and some had
an older person dozing nearby in rocking chair.

Ana and I laughed when a pre-school child rode her
tricycle at the chickens in front of the Packard and waved at
us to follow. I eased along the laneways, barely moving. 'Must
be hundreds of people living here?'

'Sometimes, I think there's thousands, Alex, mainly
women, children and the families' old folks. Most of the men

are working across the border, doing construction work, picking fruit or harvesting vegetables. They come back here whenever they get either days off or laid off.'

'Their wives come and live here rather than staying in their usual villages or towns?'

'Yes, to provide their working men a home here because they work intensely during the growing and picking months. Most of the folks here are probably from Baja North but some are from Baja South. Carmelita and Joseph's home is in Guerrero Negro, just below the border between North and South Baja.'

'Quite a compromise for families to live up here?'

'Massive, but the wages are so much higher than in Mexico. After her baby arrives, Carmelita plans to stop coming and will start market gardening on their half acre. She's from the mainland, a distant relative of Madre's family.'

As they edged deeper into the crowded village, little children waved as did a number of women and very old men. On almost every second corner was a taco stand with three or four people gathered around a small table, talking and laughing over the blaring music.

Alex thought, no wonder Gran likes being in Mexico, it's vibrant. 'Do Mexican seniors usually live with family?'

'It's changing, but for now, almost always. They're valued within the households as they provide an extra pair of hands, help with the babies and children, and sometimes, are able to add some money.'

When they reached her cousin's, Ana requested he stay in the Packard before going into the tiny house. She quickly reappearing with a very pregnant woman with glowing black hair flowing down to her waist. She came around to Alex, offered her hand through the Packard's window and in English, insisted he come in.

'If your car's in the way, they'll honk.'

'Ten minutes only,' Ana agreed. 'We're overnighting on the other side of Ensenada and who knows what the traffic will be like?'

I followed then into the tiny and inviting home where a delicious smell was wafting from the pot on the small stove.

Ana pulled a thick envelope from her handbag. 'This is for the baby from Madre and me to celebrate your firstborn. How are you feeling?'

'Wonderful, Ana, though incredibly weary of being this size and now having very uncomfortable nights!' The gorgeous woman hugged Ana and murmured her thanks, then grinned at me. 'You señors never understand what making a baby entails, do you?'

'Nor do I,' Ana noted. 'Someday, I'll have bambinos but for now, I need to sculpt.'

Carmelita insisted we have ice tea and after we finished our glasses, passed over a small bag of mail and a full basket of figs to Ana. 'Will you drop off in Guerrero? And please eat the figs, too. How many days are you taking to drive down?'

'Four to La Paz. When will Joseph be back next, Carmelita?'

'In one week, and for only three days, then is away for two weeks. I suspect with your gift of pesos, Ana, he'll want me to take the bus home, and I will.'

'Going well for him?'

Carmelita's face shadowed. 'No, it's very hard because he's not with a good company this year. The good thing is it's making him rethink whether to keep doing this. His great-uncle bought a larger fishing boat, needs a helper. I want Joseph to do that, tell him with my veggies and free seafood and fish, he doesn't have to come here.'

'I'm glad.' Ana switched to Spanish to discuss how the pregnancy was going, then said, 'Okay, Alex, guess we better get moving.'

Carmelita patted my shoulder and opened her arms. I gave her a gentle hug around her amazingly big bulge. She startled me by wishing me good luck as I dig into the Hernández past, but to be very cautious asking questions about Carlos.

As I eased the car slowly back to the gate, I asked, 'Ana,

did you tell her about Carlos being murdered?'

'No,' and added that perhaps her mother had.

The trip to Ensenada was slow. I was following Ana through the stark hills and green crops growing beside the Pacific's tumbling whitecaps and puzzled the many enclosed oval rings floating not very far offshore before figuring out they were nets for fish farming.

In the flatter areas were conglomerations of little homes, haciendas and massive groves of palms or olive trees. Up in the steep sand hills, I could see the occasional large mansion amongst the cacti.

When Ana slowed and pointed to an exit sign, I gratefully followed her off the highway, ready for food and a stretch. She parked by an outdoor cafe and recommended tacos and key lime pie slices. Once we were seated, I asked, 'Ana, do many Mexicans speak English?'

'Some, many don't, though if a gringo is polite, they'll help figure out what's needed or find someone to interpret.' She grinned at me and asked, 'Finding Mexico different?'

'Realizing how different.'

'Well, Sophia's pointing out what's rude in Mexico is probably going to make sense now.'

'Oh, she stressed the little courtesies, explained how offensive Mexicans find people who don't even offer a token apology for their lack of Spanish.'

Ana stood up and agreed. 'She's right, Alex. Mexicans do value courtesy and respect. Which reminds me of one more thing. In the smaller communities, strangers are noticed, and very closely observed. If you're asked for details about where you're going, visit with the person and do tell him or her that your great-grandfather was an Hernández and you hope to find relatives of your family in La Paz.'

'Will do.'

'People will be approaching you, some because of the Packard, others curious about you. I think Mexicans enjoy casual social interchanges way more than Canadians and

Americans do, as long as the questions aren't intrusive, because we are also quite private.'

'Thanks, Ana.'

'Ready? Traffic is going to become dense as soon as we near Ensenada. Travel in the curb lane as much as possible and if I get cut off from you, pull over and park, I'll be back for you. Oh, and where we'll be stopping to buy your Mexican cell is on the far south side of town, past the Walmart.'

I climbed into the Packard, laughing to myself, because Ana had sounded like Mom teaching me manners when I was a kid. But I also recognized that without Ana's advice, I probably would have done my usual stand back and don't say much.

Like Cecil had. The unbidden thought surprised me but was true. Within our circle of family and friends, we enjoyed talking about just about anything, exchanged ideas easily without anyone getting riled up. What Cecil had told me not that long ago when we were talking about why I was going to do my Ph.D. around how communication abilities were changing was how our group conversations had been very hard for him to join in at first. He said he'd always been a yes-no guy as many engineers are.

I wondered, did that relate to his being dead? And did the detectives know that engineers were often terse communicators?

Had they been in Carlos' time, too? Though there probably wouldn't have been a detective in La Paz back then, probably only had a few town constables.

As I followed a car's length behind Ana's motorcycle, I thought again about the similarities between the two deaths. Each man was killed brutally and probably by someone he'd known. But the chances of knowing who that was decreased daily for Cecil, as they had for Carlos.

Ensenada's dense traffic necessitated Ana having to pull over and wait for me twice, but buying my cell phone went quickly as she had to take that over. The only English-speaking clerk was home sick.

'Thanks, Ana,' I said. 'Where to next and how can I repay you for being my travel guru?'

'Ten kilometers to go, Alex, and you can buy me dinner. But let me do the talking at the motel, your pronunciation isn't understandable.'

And I haven't played my Spanish tapes for three days, I accepted guiltily as I followed her.

When we reached the high walled beach motel, a guard asked Ana many questions before opening the gate for her and waved at me to follow. We drove to the office on the waterfront, filled in the paperwork and claimed our reservations.

Ana was in a top unit so before the clerk took her up to it, he unlocked my door and I entered a far more appealing room than I'd expected from its overnight rate. A big dramatic painting of a fiesta hung above the bed with a multicoloured spread and cushions. Across from it was a TV and a desk. I dropped my knapsack on the professional office chair and peered into the bathroom, was delighted to find a big, tiled shower. Within minutes I was under it.

By the time Ana arrived, I was sitting outside, snapping photos of the pink, yellow and purple sunset. She was in a swirly white dress and sure didn't look as if she'd been riding all day.

'Are you as hungry as I am, Alex?' She waved towards the shore. 'The cafe's down there, about half a block.'

As we climbed the broken stairs, I hoped the food was better than the repairs, and gasped with pleasure as I stepped through the door.

We were on a balcony high above the whitecaps, the sound of the ocean enhanced by the clicking of the palms' fronds in the wind and the railing was wrapped with twinkling lights. Ana chose a round table beside it, covered with a bright blue cloth and we settled into the comfortable leather and rattan chairs. I could hear a classical guitarist strumming but he was behind us, hidden by the many big pots of plants.

This is one of my favourite places,' Ana murmured, enjoying my obvious admiration.

'Already, it's mine, too,' I said. 'And perfect for my first night in the Baja, Ana. It even bumps the Six-Mile Lodge down a bit on my list.' I didn't add that even if I learn zilch about Carlos and our Hernández history, I suddenly knew I was supposed to make this journey. I haven't played nearly enough in my years so far and I intend to do considerably more. Perhaps, with Ana?

She shot that down after our feast of prawns and beer, and we'd strolled along the shore until we came to a bench and sat down to watch the tide roll in.
'Alex, you're already my dear friend and I know you're feeling the same vibes I am. But for right now, I have to be unavailable. I cannot risk any relationship with a man as it would probably lessen my ability to sculpt. When I finished Phoenix, I knew I need to take at least the next two years to keep honing my skills and be a focused sculptor.'
I murmured I understood as I tried to hide my disappointment and swallowed my silent 'Goddamn.'
Immediately I wondered what she meant? Did she mean she might be interested down the way? Or was she blowing me off? I didn't ask as I gently took her hand.
'Okay, Ana, let's keep on being good friends.'

Alex phoned last night but the connection had been terrible and I'm unsure whether he heard me. Hope he did, especially about the detectives being close to finding Cecil's murderer.

Just before he'd phoned, Shannon had called with Woiden's news. They were now searching for anyone connected to the lab and with a rodeo history.

'Rodeo? Really, Gran?'

I had explained that Winston's samples enabled Forensics to identify the rope and the killer had used a specialty rope used for controlling calves.

'One of Winston weaves?' he'd asked.

'Yes, it's called a piggin' string.' Our line had been crackling and we both recognized our call would be short.

'Woiden told Shannon that finding out who the murderer is may take a long time, but they will. She sounded so relieved.'

'Good.'

The line crackled again and our call ended but it was long enough for me to know Alex was okay and to share Woiden's report. I yawned deeply and accepted bed had won over the long soak I had planned. Even though I might not see a big bathtub again for a few weeks, I switched off the bedside lamp and slipped between the cool sheets.

I was overnighting in Vancouver as my flight for Mexico City departed at 7 am. By late tomorrow afternoon, I would be landing in Loreto and with Sammy and David. John was heading to Winston's again, this time to deliver two mules, and had dropped me off at the airport. When we'd arrived at Departures in a loaded stock truck, three porters rushed over and John pointed at the nearest one.

'The lady needs your help; photographers do not travel light.' He helped load my equipment and luggage, then wrapped me in his big arms and whispered, 'Have a good time, my Sophie.'

The smiling porter had asked, 'Check in, Ma'am?'

'Yes, please.' It would be so easy transferring in Vancouver with baggage checked all the way to Mexico. And I had valet service arranged for the transfer and customs in Mexico City and onto the Loreto flight.

Although my cameras come onboard with me in their custom case, the two tripods, battery storage box and light bars box go in the fragile baggage section. The agent knew me from my many such check-ins over the years and chatted as everything was sorted.

'Snakes? Well, Mrs. Nord, you certainly get around. Wouldn't suit me at all,' she'd assured me that all was now labeled and, fingers crossed, would be waiting for me in Mexico, then added snakes seemed more interesting than birds.

I crossed my fingers too, as without my equipment, our expedition would be hooped. Why we had been granted access to the caves was around documenting who lived in them in photographs.

To be honest, I accepted as I waited for sleep to come, I am a little antsy about being inside those caves. Most nervous about the tunnels that connect one cave to the next. They're bound to be damp, dark and smelly and wouldn't those same tunnels also have snakes travelling between caves?

I rolled over a few times, wishing the hotel pillows were not all too big before accepting that I needed a soothing bath and was soon wrapped in hot water. Baths are another thing Shannon and I share. It amuses us that we both like to read a full book in a bath, letting out cold water and adding hot. I hoped she was doing that, now that there was a glimmer of hope Cecil's murderer will eventually be identified. I wondered about Renee? Would she have admitted to being my mother if Carlos' death had facts instead of questions?

I sighed as I topped up the hot water and went back to mulling why I was about to board a cruiser on the Cortez and go hunting snakes.

Well, mainly because when Sammy invited me, I couldn't have refused.

Although now that I'm seventy, I won't be taking on many more physically challenging contracts, working with Sammy and David one more time appeals very much to me. And snakes fascinate me, especially when I watch their skin flow as they slither. Plus, snake photos are in high demand and who knows? Maybe I'll end up with a cover shot.

More than anything, snakes are a photographic challenge and I like that. There's scant information available about how to record snakes, but apparently listening is as critical as being visually observant as most snakes do make noise, either a soft hissing or the dry raspy sound of scales been rubbed together or the ominous rattle before a rattler strikes ...

I woke up in the tub, toweled myself off and climbed back into my rented bed.

The next day, my flights were uneventful but long, and I was very glad when my third plane landed at Loreto's airport. Sammy and David were there and after we exchanged greetings, they stowed my stuff in the rental van. They directed me to separate what was going to our hotel suite and what was going aboard the cruiser, which they then added to supplies to go aboard.

Sammy explained that our hotel suite was booked for the duration of our stay so we would leave the editing equipment and anything we didn't want on in our rooms.

'Good, because I do have excess luggage as I'm continuing on to meet Alex in La Paz.'

'We've had a glitch, Sophia,' David said. 'We have a replacement captain because the cruiser's owner broke his arm yesterday.'

'Not an ideal situation,' Sammy acknowledged ruefully.

I knew he'd done considerable research before choosing Mario and his cruiser because a capable, pleasant and cooperative captain/cook was critical for our expedition. But accidents happen.

'We also have added a fourth member to our team. Damien is the Mexican government's representative, a student biologist and our guide. Mind you, when we met him this afternoon, Sophie, he seemed about sixteen but he's actually ten years older and seems competent. He grew up in this area, knows the islands well.'

He turned the van into the hotel's long driveway and I sighed with delight. 'It's good to be back in the Baja.'

Floodlights illuminated the old mission hotel's gardens and three fountains and I contemplated a stroll through the fragrant flowers in the warm evening heat, but accepted bed appealed more than anything. When we return, I decided, as we would be here for three nights then.

When I gave the desk clerk my passport information, I greeted him in Spanish and he chatted away, warmly welcoming me and passing me a brown envelope. 'Señora Nord, two faxes have come for you.'

Our suite was welcoming with big spacious rooms, the rattan furniture's cushions covered in the traditional adobe red and cactus green materials and I would have happily toted off the three big decorator clay pots for Erin Lake.

Sammy pointed me to the bedroom facing the Sea of Cortez and David entered ahead of me to open the double doors to the deck, pointed to its lounge. 'Why don't you read your faxes here, Sophia, then join us? Would you like water, white wine or a margarita on the rocks?'

'Water now, please, and a glass of white wine after,' I requested as I settled in and chose to read Alex' fax first.

July 23/08 Punta Prieto, Baja
Dear Gran,
We're overnighting with Ana's relatives, Raoul Hernández and his family. Their hacienda is on the Pacific, not far from where we'll cross into Baja Sur. As well as being Ana's cousin, he's a sculptor, another one of her instructors over the years.
The family welcomed Ana with delight and me curiosity.

They have three young children who laughed when I tried to speak Spanish. The sweet little preschooler shook her head and danced, saying, 'No, Señor no.'

Despite that terrible connection with you a couple of nights ago, I think I heard most of what you said, though I'm unsure if I heard right. The suspect competes at rodeos? But it's good that the detectives actually have a tangible clue and might be closer to finding Cecil's killer.

This is long, my journal as well as a chat with you.

Our trip's going smoothly, Gran. The Packard likes these roads, hasn't overheated once and as you forecast, the Baja's scenery awes me plus travelling with Ana's a gift.

Last night, we stayed at the Mission in Cataviña and I wondered if you'd been here. It's a cultural lesson built in the middle of such interesting geography. I plan to return to explore all the fascinating rocks down the way.

When we'd arrived at the Mission, I was stunned as Ana expected me to be. I've never been anywhere before where the motorcycles are allowed to park inside, right beside its owner's room on the gleaming tile floors around a large indoor swimming pool. Her BMW's probably the most impressive one of the five already parked there. We met a Canadian couple also riding BMW's and joined them for dinner.

Their trip was fascinating to hear about as they are heading for Brazil.

The dinner choices were all Mexican recipes I haven't had before and my cactus heart salad with carnitas was delicious. And the old dining room with all its elegantly carved wood said something about those long-ago monks who lived here.

Our waiter filled us in on the monk who started the extensive cacti gardens over a hundred years ago. Gran, he collected plants and nurtured them for over seventy years. Ana laughed when I said I had no idea about Mexico's layers of history or the size of the country, it has 118 million residents now.

She gave me a new take, said, 'Neither have I about Canada, it's so complex, so few residents stretched out over that massive geography.'

Raoul's a gracious host and very interested in our search. He gave me a couple of names to contact in La Paz and projects they can help me find details about the Baja South Hernández's history, although he's part of the northern clan of Hernández.

I'll send another fax when I can, though I guess there's no rush as you'll be on your snake hunt. Take very good care of yourself, Gran, and I am looking forward to seeing your photos.

Say hi to Sammy and David.

Love, Alex

I felt as if we'd had a visit. His descriptions reminded me of my first trip down in the van, when I had headed out on my own. That was only months after Scott and Janet had married and two years before I became Alex's grandmother.

The second fax was in Shannon's hard-to-read writing and before starting, I stood up to stretch and watch the palms and plants blowing in the brisk breeze.

The palms were clacking as the sea's waves pounded against the breakwater and the moonlight danced on the whitecaps. I just knew I'll return here often, now somehow tied to my Mexican father. But I missed John and knew Erin Lake would remain my home.

I sat back down and picked up Shannon's fax again.

23-07-08
Dear Soph,
Woiden just called to tell me his team are searching for the woman very probably responsible for Cecil's death. Mary Howard is an installer of custom blinds and her company has the contract to replace all the window coverings at the lab.

She's been working on that since early May and the detectives are currently talking with all lab employees she may have had contact with during the past two months. So far, they've learned little as she'd only exchanged brief courtesies and her out-of-town employer knows little about her except she was an efficient installer and her pay cheques went to a box number. He reports she faxed in an emergency leave of absence notice the same day Cecil was killed. He hasn't heard from her since and her last pay cheque was just returned by the post office with the stamp: This addressee's mailbox was cancelled.

Soph, what Albert just learned from the lab maintenance department is Cecil's long blind wasn't working well. Do you remember that window? It fills most of the wall's length, right behind his desk and chair and it had repetitive problems. According to the maintenance invoicing, Mary Howard had been back to repair it numerous times and at no charge.

Cecil could have informed her of his meditation schedule around when not to come, Woiden suspects. And what is most significant evidence of her potential guilt is that she competes in rodeos.

Soph, he sounded optimistic, Woiden told me he believes they will find her and we'll learn why Cecil died.

I am missing him and spent time at his house today. It's still unreal that Cecil isn't coming home, but I'm apprehensive as well as relieved there's a suspect. We'll probably learn why she killed him.

I fly to London tomorrow and Yosh and Beth arrive from Greece the next morning. I can't wait to be with them, finally telling them about Cecil.

And, as you advised, I am staying for a week after they leave, have booked two shows and will go shopping for many new clothes, different from the ones Cecil helped me choose.

Wish you could be with me. Do watch out for wandering snakes, amiga. I'll fax from London.

Shannon xo

I joined Sammy and David in the suite's living room and was pleased to discover they had a fruit and cheese platter waiting.

'We decided a snack here would suit you better than the dining room,' David said as he took the white wine from the fridge. He was a small man as compared to Sammy and definitely the one in charge. Although he also had the same herpetologist credentials as his mate, he had excellent management and organizational skills and kept our projects flowing comfortably. 'Soph, we're to meet the cruiser's replacement captain and board at 8 am, so is breakfast at six okay for you?'

Sammy added, 'Damien will also meet us at the cruiser's moorage and I hope we'll be heading south by 9 am.'

'Six is fine. Are we starting at the farthest island in the marine reserve and working back to Loreto?' I asked, then popped a cracker heaping with spicy cream cheese into my mouth.

David passed me a napkin and answered. 'Yes, Mario and I spent many hours planning our route by phone and fax. He's been chartering in this area of the Cortez for over twenty years and he's an experienced diver, knows the islands, caves and waters well.'

'The replacement captain will be following Mario's itinerary and timelines. We're starting south and working back up to Loreto.'

'I would have preferred to have Mario behind the wheel, Sophia, but since he's chosen him to captain his cruiser, his credentials and experiences will be fine. Though I was surprised he's German and Mario warned me the cooking prob ably won't be all Mediterranean food,' David added ruefully.

Damn, I thought, not at all liking sausages and sauerkraut but as David's as fussy about his food as I am, I knew it would work out.

Sammy spread out a brochure with the cruiser's layout on the low table in front of me. 'Soph, the main salon looks roomy and I think we'll be comfortable there. The galley kitchen's off on the starboard with a long built-in table and a private bunk for the captain, though we'll share that bathroom as we're at the far end. Your bunkroom is at the bow end, very small, but with a mini-head, Sophie. A private corner for you as a week aboard a 50-footer with four men will probably be challenging at times.'

For sure, I agreed, but said, 'Thanks, Sammy, nice to have a door,' then yawned widely. 'Sorry, you two, my bed calls. Meet you in the dining room tomorrow at six.'

I discovered the dining room overlooked the Sea and as I walked in, wished I had a camera. The sun was above the Sea's horizon, creating a panorama of colour. Soft pinks, turquoises and purple-blues were melding with its yellow rays and I watched for a bit before walking across to join Sammy and David.

'Good morning.'

'Hey, you look great, I don't even have to ask if you slept well,' Sammy greeted me. Their table was by the open glass doors and I could smell the bacon as I slid into a chair.

Sammy poured me a glass of orange juice. 'Hungry?'

'Starving,' I agreed, gulped down the juice and pointed to the spread-out map. 'What's our journey going to be today?'

'We're going straight out to open water and we'll cruise down to this bottom island.' David put a finger on the map.' That's projected to take about six hours and we'll anchor between the island and mainland for tonight and, maybe tomorrow night, depending on what we find. Mario said this is a sheltered bay, calm and good for dropping the inflatable. We'll use it to come and go to the cruiser.'

Sammy added, 'The caves we're interested in are numerous in this area, both in the nearby islands and on the mainland. Our first site is the five connecting caves about here on the mainland, very close to the shore.'

'Damien will ensure we meet all the park compliances necessary and will do the paperwork required for each site,' David said. 'I was relieved to hear that because getting to do this project has required patience and tough negotiating.

'Even harder than the maze around our getting to photograph Tasmanian devils?' I teased him as he'd been furious to discover on that project that the bureaucratic paperwork was a maze and uncompleted.

'I've checked page by page and we're good to go.'

'Having Damien aboard will also ease the concerns of the marine park's wardens. They'll be checking regularly on us,' Sammy added.

'For what?' I asked as we headed for the buffet table.

'Our compliance to regulations like being inside the caves only between dawn to dusk and not removing even a seashell or rock,' David said as Sammy passed me a plate.

While we ate, Sammy explained the plans for tomorrow. 'Soph, the five caves we're interested in are across from our anchorage and we'll come and go to it. We won't stay within a cave system for more than two hours, and we'll take breaks out in the fresh air. Mario said the entrance into the mountain is only a short hike from the shoreline, though he was unable to map where,' Sammy explained.

Hike? I wondered nervously, how far? I'll be wearing waterproof cave boots, not hiking ones.

'You'll need help carrying your equipment. Will one extra person be enough?' David asked as he cut his strips of mango into smaller pieces,'

'I'll usually have one light bar, a tripod and two cameras so two people can handle easily, if you project reasonable landings from the zodiac to the shore?'

'Some are, Soph,' Sammy replied with a wide grin, fully understanding how landing onto a non-sandy shore in the usual 3-ft waves can be tricky with fragile equipment. Similarly, moving the light bars through the passages between caves will be challenging, especially if there's water on the pathway or a low ceiling.

'What neither of us has remembered to tell you is that Damien's also your assistant.' A bell chimed and the cook brought Sammy a heaping platter of the hot food he'd ordered. 'And you won't be carrying any equipment, Damien and I will, after we escort you to and from the zodiac.'

David shook his head at Sammy as he looked at the platter's selection. 'That's not following your doctor's orders.

Sammy ignored him. 'What we don't know is whether the caves have a diversity of snake species, which could mean we need fewer sites but, right now, until we know the density of snakes, we've unsure how many caves.'

I shivered slightly at a density of snakes. 'What are your photo priorities – do you want more full-length shots or close-ups?

The two of them laughed at me.

'Whatever you can get. Snakes don't pose.'

'Really, David,' and gave him the finger. "Haven't you pre-brooked their camera sessions? How will we find these elusive subjects I'm to photo?'

David gave me his slow smile. 'We don't know that either. No data is available for this area; we're the snake pioneers here. By the way, we retain all rights to the photos, though the agreements are to share all our data and photos with three Mexican universities and the Marine Park management.

Sammy added that a Guadalajara professor had recently sent him updated information about each of Mexico's known snake species. 'He projects we'll find many undocumented ones and after we do the first editing, he'll go over the photos, too, to help us confirm what actual species we've found.'

I nodded. Editing is my favourite stage, unveils what's in each photo. That's also when we decide which photos can be enhanced to publishing standards and if one of my shots is to magazine cover quality.

When we arrived at the wharf, the white cruiser's sleek lines appealed and I looked forward to being aboard again. Damien and I began to transfer my things and equipment to the tiny stateroom while the captain, David and Sammy had an intense conversation.

I hadn't been introduced yet, but he wasn't the casual team member I had expected. His tone of voice, officer-like white shirt and manicured hair reminded me of my late husband, and

I hoped this man wouldn't be as unpredictable.

I overheard David firmly confirming the chain of command. 'I'll be whom you report to and who answers any questions. Every morning, you and I will review our routes and the day's activities as well as the menu.'

The large man pulled himself upright and said that he'd expected to set the menus. 'I have added more potatoes, sausages and pork to the supplies as I cook hearty, simple meals,' he added as I joined them. 'Do any of you have dietary preferences?'

'We all do but I have the most,' David replied and winked at me. 'Captain Wagner, it's my pleasure to introduce you to our senior team leader and photographer, Mrs. Sophia Nord.'

Damn, sausages and pork, I thought as I stuck out my hand and wished Mario hadn't broken his leg.

'I am honoured.'

Damien stuck his head into the cabin. 'All's aboard and secured, David.

He nodded at the Captain. 'We are ready to cast lines and get underway.'

Our destination today is seventy kilometers south, an easy trip, if the squalls forecast stay light. I sniffed the salt air, glad I never was seasick, even in rough seas.

Within ten minutes, we were cutting though the aqua waves and I went to the upper deck's stern, sun hat tied securely and a digital camera ready. We'll encounter dolphins, sea lions or flying manta rays but I can only stay in this hot sun for about half an hour before moving to the shaded rear sundeck or airconditioned main cabin.

We reached our destination at three after an easy trip. Sammy requested Captain Wagner circle the island and parallel the mainland's shore at low speed and we learned the shore was much more rocky that expected, but accessible.

Sammy decided he was going to where the caves were this afternoon. 'Once we're anchored and can drop the zodiac, I'm going over to get an idea of the ground, in case it's foggy in the morning? Want to come?'

'Yes,' David, Damien and I agreed.

David and Damien lowered the 15-ft zodiac from its davit while I went and got our extra water bottles, food bag, camera and emergency kit that will be accompanying us whenever we're off the cruiser.

Sammy directed me to board from the swim grid and I settled on the middle plank seat, enjoyed the wind blowing ocean spray. The 25hp motor pushed the inflatable boat easily across to the shore. It was a mix of gravel, broken rock and some larger boulders, not ideal but better than many beaches I've been on. We pulled the zodiac up and secured it to a beached timber.

Sammy scanned the bottom of soaring mountains with his binoculars and after a few minutes, shouted over the wave noise, 'There's a narrow and tall slit down about three hundred feet, it might be an opening.'

We followed him with Damien carrying all my equipment except for the camera bag, and he echoed what I was hoping. 'Hope we'll be able to stand up to enter.' But that slit was a dead end as were the next two and Sammy returned to the first location to reexamine the numerous upright granite slabs there.

And disappeared.

'Sammy,' David shouted when his mate's head reappeared.

'Found it, it's only a dozen feet sideways from this keyhole entrance,' Sammy announced and beamed at us. 'But it's too late to stay here, feel that wind coming up.' He piled rocks onto a yellow cloth flag to mark the elusive gap. 'There, ready for morning.'

CHAPTER THIRTY-NINE
- Sophia

When we returned to the cruiser, we could smell cabbage cooking on top of the sweet sea air. David sniffed it and clambered out of the zodiac first.

'Okay, I'll bring the refreshments to the rear sundeck after I expand our menu.'

He was grinning when he returned with a large tray I helped him put on the low circular table.

'Am I going to have to eat cabbage?'

'No, that boiled stuff we're smelling will become the base for borsch, but I sure hope everyone likes coleslaw. He's made quantities, some with carrots, some with grated beet. Healthy.' He winked at me, aware I was thinking the snakes might not be the only thing smelling in the caves.

I found myself thinking about my father as we watched the sun move toward the horizon. How sad it was that he had such ashort life and sure that he would like to think of me here, using my talents and having a Mexican adventure.

I sighed and hoped it was going well for Alex and Ana, and that I would learn Cecil's murderer had been found when we returned to the hotel. Out here in a world with five people, we only had radio contact with the Mexican Coast Guard. As we ate our breaded pork chops, the sun set as it does in the tropics, light one moment, dark the next.

The winds had died down and we could hear a colony of sea lions bellowing at each other as we said an early goodnight and headed to our bunks.

I slept deeply and the sea was glassy the next morning when I went out on deck and viewed the mountain we would be inside of in a little while. Sammy summarized what he'd read last night over our toast, oatmeal and fruit.

'These five caves are documented briefly in a small 1953 scientific journal. At that time, all the tunnels were passable and three of the caves were noted to be large caverns. As well, the two naturalists saw considerable snakes but of what species is not included in their article.'

'I've known about these caves but I don't know anyone who's been in them,' Damien said.'

'David and I will go in first. From what little I saw last night, it's a narrow but high tunnel. Wait ten minutes, then follow.'

As we climbed out of the inflatable, we could see the yellow marker we'd left, about a football field away, easy traipsing, I judged.

Damien changed that with his request. 'Dr. Nord, please follow directly behind me.' He unfolded an aluminum walking stick and swished it in circles in the windswept sand and gravel, poking at the beige scrub bush growing nearby.

'It's hard to see a snake, scorpion or lizard in this bright sunlight until we've disturbed it. You're the most vulnerable because your short legs necessitate taking more steps. Watch for slither paths or tracks. Your boots are good, though.'

'David brought them from Australia, said the combination of canvas and rubber is designed to prevent cactus spines, snakes and other critters from gaining access. They feel comfortable, though are a little awkward for walking.

By the time we got to the entrance we could hear but not see Sammy in the tunnel. 'What do you think, David, are you another hundred feet in?'

The reply was muffled. 'At least but the floor's very uneven here, Sam. I'm coming back, we best rope up.'

When they joined us, both were beaming. 'It's a big cave in there from the echoing,' David speculated and dug into the supply bag. 'But we do need headlamps and ropes. Leave the equipment here and we'll all rope up and go in. I'll lead, then Sam and you, Sophia, with Damien following.'

I looked up at their faces and suspected mine would have the same combination of excitement and edginess. After all the months of planning, we're heading into the unknown through a narrow tunnel.

I was dressed in three layers of clothes as the temperatures between the outer air and cave would vary by many degrees.

'Are you excited, Dr. Nord?' Damien whispered. 'I am, still can't believe I'm lucky enough to be paid for being part of this. I start my third year of university in October and being here will provide me with all the data I need to finish my degree.'

I told him to call me Sophia and agreed as the darkness closed around us. We could no longer see the exit's light and our headlamps were making spooky shadows. I was glad we were roped together.

'Be cautious here, Soph,' Sammy said. 'Take little steps, there's three quite steep drops.'

After what seemed like an hour but was probably ten minutes, our headlamps illuminated the soaring ceiling in front of us. We heard various sounds and Sammy saw movement to the left, pointed and whispered, 'Most likely bats.'

'Bats?' I knew I'd squeaked when all three laughed and I patched in by asking, 'Will you be wanting photos of them?'

I told myself, of course there are bats in caves, and shivered. I'm easier with snakes than bats. The cave felt cold, the black air was damp and musky with a reeking noxious smell.

Damien had told us earlier, the more fetid the air, the more snakes. We turned off our headlamps and as my eyes adjusted to the deep darkness, I listened to the dripping water. My nervousness lessened as my elation grew. I was here and about to challenge all the photographic skills I've gained.

When Sammy and Damien returned with my equipment, I turned off my headlamp and David turned on a muted flashlight. I opened and stabilized the light bar, attached my digital with the fastest lens speed to the tripod. I held its remote in my right hand and slid the switch to on.

'Ready, team?'

'Go for it,' Sammy directed.

The bar of bright lights revealed an underground tapestry of colour. The nearest wall's ores and minerals reflected oranges, purples and greens vividly. In the far distance, I could see a shadowy conglomeration of rock formations.

This was a very big cave.

I pointed my camera at the rocky floor about twenty feet away to focus it and screeched softly as a partly coiled red diamond rattler was illuminated.

'!Vaya!' I heard Damien mutter.

I focused my lens on the diamond-patterned skin on the large snake and realized I was seeing movement, not up at the snake's triangular head but about midway between its head and tail. I stared at all the patterns I saw and figured out it was like wiggling painted sticks, little, short snakes. Babies!

'Watch,' I ordered and increased the lights' intensity, started shooting photo after photo.

The glare startled all of them and the mother reared up some as another baby rattler slid out of her oviduct.

I kept shooting, moving the tripod slightly to gain different angles as the newborn slithered towards its siblings. And saw the head of next baby appearing in the circular opening as I sucked in a deep breath and slowly let it out. I kept clicking.

'My god, Soph,' Sammy murmured. 'You've found a birthing mother! Amazing! Your first photos on this expedition are going to give you that cover shot.'

After I snapped two more sequence of shots, I shut off the light, sucked in another deep breath and agreed.

'Now, what?' I asked.

'Leave your equipment, I'll lead, and you hold onto David to go back down the tunnel. Go behind her, Damien.' Sammy took my elbow, passed me my headlamp. 'We'll give her privacy. She won't stay long after the arrival her last offspring. Although these rattlers give live birth, they do not mother.'

The sunshine was overwhelmingly bright when we exited. I closed my eyes to let them adjust, reached toward the sky and stretched my tight shoulders.

David laughed and Sammy joined in, gave him a brief hug.

'Unbelievable! I counted nine babies,' Damien said, his dark eyes glowing.

'I saw ten,' Sammy reported.

'Me, too, ten,' I agreed. 'I've so many good shots but I think the best one will be when the mother's head was up and close to her oviduct as the baby was about a third of the way out.'

'Do you know how very rare it is to see a birthing snake?' Sammy asked me and Damien.

'I didn't even know snakes had babies, I thought they laid eggs,' the young Mexican replied.

'Most do lay eggs, about two-thirds of the serpent species. But the other third, the rattlers, vipers, boas, garters, corn and coral snakes, to name some, reproduce by live birth.'

I smiled as I listened, elated to have captured a special phenomenon and decided that this is one of my most satisfying moments in a long career.

Sammy and David were on as much of a high as I was about the baby rattlers, and the pressure was off them as both herpetologists knew that this venture would be profitable from both a scientific prospective and from a financial one.

Our week continued as favourably as it started. We found a diversity of species as we moved to various moorages and eased our ways into many caves. We usually were able to set up near the entrance, didn't have to go deeper into the caves. And we were learning as we went. For instance, if a cave had a diversity of snake species, each one seemed to stay separate and, usually, in little clusters, easy to photograph. But when any of the snakes spooked, they moved so fast, it was hard to tell if any were coming towards us. Scary! I held my breath a few times, wishing I could be up a ladder - though, of course, snakes could climb ladders, too.

Most of them didn't flee from the lights as we'd expected. They stayed put and in a wide variety of poses. I snapped many shots of snakes draped out across rocks or slithering up a wall or curled up on an outcropping like a trophy display.

My new lights were impressive, I was getting clear shots with my long lens, able to see enough to zoom in on specific features. That mattered as it was each snake's skin markings that was critical for identification.

The days ran together as we moved from area to area and our routines became organized. Sammy and David went into each cave first and inspected for viability and safety. Damien and I followed with the equipment and set it up.

We had no incidents of rockslides or snake strikes and I never was uncomfortably close to a snake, but the noxious air was wearying, but the caves were worth it.

So far, we'd only had to crouch low in three tunnels which did make me feel anxious, but the caves at were worth it.

There was one day when a foot-long skinny snake slithered towards me as I was changing cameras on the tripod and Damien rushed over to a flip it far away with his stick.

'One of the fastest and most lethal, Soph,' David and Sammy agreed and complimented Damien on his eyesight. 'You've used up another of those nine lives of yours.'

Returning to the cruiser became a pleasure. We'd started profusely complimenting Captain Wagner about his food and it improved daily.

Though being around him continued to be eerie for me as he was so much like Waverley. As I watched him, I often found myself puzzling how I could have been married for almost twenty years to a man who couldn't relax.

I missed John more daily and was looking forward to showing him my baby rattler photos. One of his great pleasures is helping a mare birth her colt - and he likes all babies.

The weather continued to cooperate and we got a wealth of photos daily. Our captain was pleasantly adept at finding us sheltered bays. Even on the two nights we had dramatic storms with high winds, the cruiser's anchors held.

The second storm's noisy downpour went on and on and I

didn't sleep much. In the morning, we all agreed that the usual night sounds of manta rays jumping near the ship, seagulls and herons cawing overhead and the damn sea lions' loud playing and bellowing could be ignored, but the echoing of the driving rain on the hull disrupted sleep.

On our last night aboard, I had a swim before dinner and as I floated in the buoyant salt water, my thoughts meandered. I hoped there would be faxes from Shannon, who was now in London, Alex and Ana in La Paz and John. Cecil was often in my thoughts, and I hoped the murder investigation was going well, and that why he was murdered wouldn't change my caring about him,

With much time to ponder aboard, I've been mulling murderers.

Wondering if someone who can kill regrets, or even enjoys, stealing someone's life?

How abrupt being murdered is. Both Cecil and Carlos had been living one minute, gone the next. Perhaps because I started my career in pathology, I see the details of life versus death, know how unique each one of us is and how a body without breath is an inanimate object.

I rolled over, started a fast crawl and mourned for Cecil. How hard his youth had been and how he'd loved being the successful man he'd become. He'd become incredibly handsome, especially when he'd smiled, and I like teasing him about how his greying sideburns suited him. Although none of us had been sure he was ideal for our Shannon, what a massive loss for her.

What could have his relationship been with that drapery installer?

I sighed and rolled over on my back in the warm salty weather to watch a patrol of brown pelicans try to figure out what kind of sea creature I was, then resumed my fast crawl.

As was becoming usual when I thought about Cecil, I moved on to Carlos. This time, I wondered what the world I didn't get to grow up in would have been like. I think he would have enjoyed playing with me, teaching me as much as I have my young. I do like children and maybe that comes from my father along with these dark eyes and tight curls?

As I pulled myself up on the swim grid and took off my lifejacket, I felt cleansed somehow, even surer that Cecil hadn't been in a personal relationship with his killer, unless it was before he returned to Thompson City.

And I recognized more about how Renee's jumble of archives and artifacts had benefitted me. It was amazing to me that Alex and I were about to have time together in La Paz.

CHAPTER FORTY
- Sophia

The next morning, Captain Wagner edged the cruiser up against Loreto's long wharf to where a hotel employee was waiting with our rental van. After the shuffle of equipment and personal belongings, we bid Damien and Captain Wagner goodbye.

Damien gave me a shy hug and assured me he would be taking up my invitation to Erin Lake eventually. He also made sure I had his Mexican cell number, in case we needed help in La Paz. He told me he had many friends there and I was not to hesitate to call.

The Captain surprised us with his profuse goodbyes and thanks, telling the three of us what a privilege it had been to be part of our expedition. He asked if I would send him a few photos and I assured I was planning to do that. In fact, I'm also going to send him a lovely enlargement of a photo of him at the wheel.

The three of us settled into the van, sunburnt and weary, and more than ready for very long showers. I had managed on my narrow bunk, but I was looking forward to a much softer mattress with room to spread out.

As we went up the elevator, I opened the fax that had been waiting for me at the front desk from Alex, and glanced at its opening paragraph:

'Hi Gran, Looking forward to 2 pm Wed at the La Paz airport. I've much news, and a few surprises for you. It's been a good week. Hope it was for you, too!'

I decided I needed to shower before reading all its three pages and wondered about his surprises as I stood under the hot shower. Then, after toweling off, I climbed into the white sheets for a brief nap.

The church bells awoke me the next morning, and I bounced out of bed, feeling famished, and dressed in minutes. I grabbed Alex's fax and headed down to the buffet, found Sammy and David who were already eating.

'Hi, Sophia, glad you're here and we can get an early start on the editing. I was just telling David I think we have about one-third more images than initially projected. I agreed and the three of us grinned at each other, each aware it was only a week since our last breakfast together here, but what a week it had been.

I summarized Alex's fax for them as we ate, as they too were hoping that Cecil's murderer could be located soon. Alex wrote that Woiden had told John they were making progress. He also was pleased with how the research into Carlos was going and reported he'd hired a researcher at the university to check old newspapers as apparently that murder had been written about over the decades.

David and I complained about having overeaten while Sammy told us he'd ordered lunch sent up, headed into the suite and had a temporary editing studio set up within minutes. We were all excited as we could finally view the photos and needed to sort which ones would be published quickly. Sammy and David were heading back to Australia the day after tomorrow.

My flight didn't leave for La Paz until noon that day and I planned to shop for more cool cotton dresses. Loreto was already hot today, and I knew La Paz would be even more so.

On our second day, we finally wrapped up at 9:30 pm. All three of our computers were loaded with a wealth of publishable photos and the originals were on my hard drive and backed up on a data drive. We settled out on the deck in the evening breeze off the waves and toasted each other with a chilled glass of white wine.

Sammy and David were still having a fine time debating which photos could be sent to which scientific journal and I was jubilant at the overall quality of my photos: considering

which shots might be cover quality. The rattler and her
babies certainly were and seeing them onscreen awed us.

David grinned at me as he refilled our glasses. 'Sophie,
thanks, you are a photographer extraordinaire. We've a wealth
of rattlesnakes, rosy boas, shovel noses and a surprising
number of king snakes.'

'Plus a selection of some rare ones we hadn't even
expected to encounter,' Sammy agreed, raising his glass.

I toasted them back, declaring that this shoot was now our
most memorable one and asking for sheer devilment, 'What's
next?'

Personally, I was reassured that although I was now
seventy, this contract had been easy for me physically and my
acumen about lighting and camera choices had been right on.
And I'll be on taking on interesting contracts for some years
yet.

CHAPTER FORTY-ONE
- Alex

When the plane from Loreto settled onto the runway, we headed over to the Arrivals gate. John had a large SOPHIA sign to wave, I held the big bouquet of flowers Ana had picked out and she was cradling the ribbon-wrapped bottle of champagne.

Gran came through the swinging doors with the first group of passengers, saw us and burst into laughter as she threw herself at John. 'I'm so glad you're here. And very surprised.'

'Sophia, that yellow dress makes your tan glow, you look wonderful.'

Ana was, too. We were enjoying being together and her helping to search for Carlos' history was invaluable but, every day, I was more aware that her friendship wasn't all I wanted.

Gran greeted her, then turned to me and brushed my cheek. 'Alex, La Paz must agree with you, you're looking just fine.'

I bowed for the hell of it and passed over the bouquet.

'Gran, I've found my third home - I'm going to live in Vancouver, Erin Lake and La Paz.'

She grinned at me. 'All's okay?'

'It is. You'll like our sublet, a three-bedroom with a private sandy beach. Oh, and Shannon's long fax awaits you with news you'll welcome.'

We stowed Gran's luggage and photo equipment in the SUV John had rented. He'd arrived two days ago, and we'd set this up before I left Vancouver. He'd phoned and asked about his joining us, then booked his flight and told me to splurge on accommodation.

Plus, a second surprise for Gran was added after that. When Ana learned John was coming, she told her parents and invited them to join us in La Paz. She'd enticed her father by telling him that as Madre and Sophia would need much time together, he could entertain John by lining up some horse ranches they could visit.

He'd agreed enthusiastically and we would be in La Paz together for almost a week, then all of us were going up to El Triunfo and then take the mountain route down to their ranch.

I explained that to Gran around directing John where to turn. 'Ana's mother has invited the extended Hernández clan to a fiesta for us at El Triunfo and many are coming.'

Gran beamed.

'It will probably be a three-day one. Some of the family own casitas there and there's lots to rent in the neighbouring village of San Antonio,' Ana explained. 'The families who live down in the East Cape area are coming and the big extended one who have large pineapple orchards near Todos Santos.'

'Have you been up to El Triunfo before, Gran?

'No, but I know some about it and have intended to visit that famous mining area.'

'It's interesting,' Ana agreed 'Cooler up there, too, which is why some La Paz families have had summer sanctuaries up there for decades. They would live up there for months, away from the muggy heat and yellow fever. My folks' place was purchased when the mines closed in the 1920's and became Iona's, then she passed it on.'

'Alex, where's the next turn?'

As I leaned forward to direct him through the series of little residential streets to our villa, Ana asked Gran about her expedition and about whether the hoped-for photos of snakes had been achieved.

I heard the pleasure in Gran's voice and knew it had as she reported their successes had surpassed those hopes. 'I've some ready to show you, if I can connect to the villa's TV. Tell me more about the fiesta, Ana.'

'Oh, there'll be much food and cervezas, dancing and laughter. Many will be dress in authentic Mexican clothing and we'll gather in the park beside the old school.'

'Sounds fun, plus I want to take photos of El Triunfo's historical sites. Do you know if I have to arrange for any permissions, Ana?'

'I don't expect so. All the old mine management mansions and housing are occupied, some being used as store-fronts like the organ museum, so you can just ask. Do you know the famous El Triunfo smokestack?'

'I do. It was built by Gustav Eiffel before he built the Eiffel Tower in Paris, wasn't it?'

'Yes, and there's a big campaign going on to keep it in good repair, Sophia.'

During Ana and my dinners on our drive down to La Paz, she'd told me North and South Baja history and the story of El Truinfo. I was looking forward to having time to poke around in that area.

It had been a major silver mining area for about forty years and in 1910, about ten thousand people lived there. Ana knew it well as her family regularly stayed up there. She and her brother explored it, then when she became interested in sculpting, she'd begun scavenging for metal and rocks.

Now, she's recently inherited her mentor's cabin, high up in the mountains above the mining area. After the fiesta, she was going up to her Uncle's special place to pick up some of his sculpting tools and say her good-byes to him. She's suggested I come part way with her, stay in the mine administration area overnight and explore while she climbed up to the cabin, then we would take an old road down to tour East Cape on our way to her folk's ranch.

I had to agree, of course, wanting to be with her anywhere. Being 'just good friends' was getting tougher for me daily.

When John turned onto the road following the sea to our villa, I could stop navigating and said to Gran, 'Not much about Carlos yet. Ana and I have talked with numerous people but so far, we haven't gained many facts.'

Ana laughed and added, 'The Packard does work like a magnet, Sophia, and the local grape vine is working well. Alex is usually greeted by name wherever he parks. Tell her what one dear ancient lady claimed.'

'As soon as I parked outside a grocery store, she came over and stroked the hood ornament, then beckoned her teenage grandson over to interpret. He speaks English easily and asked me whether this had been Carlos Hernández' car. I agreed it was and got out the photos to show her. Gran, it turned out Carlos' family and her family were friends and he had taken her for a ride in the Packard when she was about eight.'

'I hope to meet her,' Gran requested.

'Of course, we'll do that,' Ana agreed. 'What I'm surprised about is how many very old people we've met. There are many in their nineties and some who either have surprisingly good memories or are creative story tellers. And although we haven't learned much about our Hernández family, we've learned considerable about La Paz back in Carlos' era.'

I explained how we'd been meeting a good variety of people. 'We're fishing for them, Gran. I park the Packard by the malecón, and Ana and I sit on a bench nearby, usually eating ice cream. For two reasons: she considers ice cream basic food, and her theory is it makes us appear friendly.'

She laughed and agreed. 'People do stop and talk with us, then Alex often shows them some of Renee's old photos. We've met a few elderly people who claim they knew them and visited at their hacienda, though their details are usually hazy. But one wizardly old man remembered Carlos being murdered and said he would bring someone to tell us more. He hasn't yet. Gran, maybe you should sit there with us tomorrow?'

'Of course,' she agreed and invited John, too. 'You can finally taste the wonderful limon ice cream.'

I continued, explaining what we learned about the land Carlos' family had owned. 'It's substantial, no wonder they could grow fruit on it. The old house got wiped out in a 1970's hurricane. Since then, thirty bungalows have been built on it.'

'I want to walk in that area, Alex.'

'It's special, I've had a few strolls around it,' and told her about the researcher we've hired. 'She's a fourth year Mexican history student who's optimistic about what she might find in the archives. She has also sent requests to various sources in Mexico City, both about Carlos's murder and about Rubin's factories.'

'Did you learn anything from the La Paz police?'

'They were kind but a hurricane in the 70's wiped out their old station, including all the policing records.'

Ana added one of the older constables who'd grown up in Mexico City thought that there were probably original copies of the murder report there but chances of accessing the info would be slim.

'That's another thing we've learned, Gran. Few archives within Mexico have switched to electronic recording and storage, most are still using paper and archive are stored in boxes. There are some plans for old archives to be digitized, but my guess is anything pre-1950's probably will never be as much of it is very fragile, the paper's crumbling.'

'Tell her what Caleda, the researcher, found,' Ana reminded me.

'She found a one-line mention of a Dr. Carlos Hernández's projected radio tube. Since her studies include what Mexico's exports were in the prewar years as well as during and after the WWII era, she's amazingly knowledgeable. What she suspects is Carlos' expertise, and perhaps the Professor's, was focused on radio innovation. Or, perhaps, television.'

'I'm overwhelmed at what you two have achieved,' Gran said as John cleared his throat and glanced into the back seat. 'Hey, you haven't told your grandmother what most fascinated me. Soph, do you know colour tv was invented in Mexico?'

'Cecil once told me that,' Gran said softly as John parked the Suburban beside a white wall covered in scarlet bougainvillea.

Ana hopped out and opened Gran's door. 'What I haven't told you yet is that my parents are here. We'll be meeting them for dinner.'

'Lovely.'

'And another thing, Madre's heard from Mother Superior

Luisa-Grace. If her eyes continue to heal as they are now, she hopes to be home in about two weeks.'

I led Gran through the patio entrance to our two-story villa and she smiled at me. 'This is a special place, thank you, you must let me chip in.'

'No, and John wanted to but it's my treat, Gran. Remember, I'm your financially-fixed-okay grandson.'

We stopped on the large patio and she looked at our private sandy beach and how a wide Nim tree was shading the cushioned lounges and told me, 'After a week with the guys on the cruiser and being in so many dark and stinky caves, I'm going to live out here.'

As I opened the glass patio door, high ceiling fans whirled above us in the great room and she added, 'Though maybe not. I like how they've furnished this, all white except for those vivid Mexican paintings. Now, where's John's and my room?'

'Down that hall, Gran, it's a suite. Here, take this,' I picked up Shannon's fax from an end table. 'It's lengthy and as her cover sheet directed, John, Ana and I have read it. Want to stretch out on your bed and I'll bring you some ice tea?'

CHAPTER FORTY-TWO
- Sophia

I almost choked on my first big gulp as I read Shannon's first sentence. Beth and Yosh wanted me to be the bride's matron of honour next February.

Alex passed me a tissue and laughed. 'Isn't it great they set the date? And I'm the best man. Shannon reported Beth again told her to prepare to be a grandmother as she's hoping for three children.' He nodded at the long fax and offered, 'May I read it aloud, I skimmed it too quickly earlier.'

'Please,' I agreed and sipped my iced tea.

Dear Sophie and all,

When I arrived at the B&B in London, Woiden's message was waiting for me. "Contact me ASAP, we have a very probable suspect."

But, before I tell you about Cecil's murderer, I'll share Yosh and Beth's grand news. Their wedding date is February 11, 2009 and Beth wants Ana, you and me to be her attendants and, of course, Alex's the best man. I told her you'd all accept.

Now for what has kept me weepy for the past two days. Cecil's murderer has confessed. She's been pursuing him for years because she claims he ruined her family. Woiden suspects that is not necessarily true but, Soph, I think it could be partially so. It's very sad.

Being with Beth and Yosh has helped me gain some perspective but Cecil's history has horrified me. Beth has firmly suggested I have to accept what I've been bracing myself for since I found him, why Cecil was killed.

I'm unsure what I think about it right now. I am now staying for another two weeks in London, as Beth says I'll sort that out better far away from home. Yosh pointed out that I've probably been sensing layers I didn't know about Cecil and that made me hesitant about marrying him.

But being my Yosh, he also bluntly told me to remember all the good things I know about Cecil and not to be judging him, because we are never going to know his side and his murderer might not have been honest about what that was.

That startled me. But I know he's right.

Although it appears Cecil wasn't who I thought he was, wanted him to be. To be honest, I guess I already knew that as he and I had disagreed a few times about what was ethical behavior and what wasn't. He could be hard, but he was also a caring man, a generous and respected employer for so many people, and so very caring to me.

Soph, I loved Cecil, but I am glad, relieved, we weren't married.

I'll tell you about his murderer after some more good news.

He and Beth are fine with inheriting, had already decided to eventually live at Erin Lake. When her contract ends Dec. 31, she'd decided to open a medical practice in Thompson City and they now are considering whether she could run it from Cecil's place. Yosh was already planning to build his studio at my place, now he'll build it next door at their place. Won't it be grand to have them as neighbours?

I finished my ice tea and Alex said he'd get me more as we were coming to the end of Shannon's fax. I nodded, knowing I would feel sad for both Cecil and Shannon from what she'd already written.

Back to what Woiden's told me, Soph, during the two long phone calls I've had with him.

The murderer is Lorraine Wellstone, a 47-yr-old woman who killed Cecil with a piggin' string.

She used to compete in rodeos and still attends some. Last year, she came to the Thompson City Rodeo and read in the newspaper about Cecil opening his new lab and saw the photographs of him. Reading about all his successes enraged her. She also had made a deathbed promise to her mother the year before to revenge her father.

In the same newspaper was an ad the blind company had inserted. She phoned them and was hired immediately as she had much experience as an installer. Her new employer had the contract to install new blinds throughout the older sections in the lab. She started measuring windows there and stalking Cecil as she schemed.

Woiden said she was located four days after the arrest warrant went out, and arrested as she tried to cross into the US from Saskatchewan. She was transferred to Thompson City and during her first interview with Woiden and Moffatt, admitted she'd killed Cecil.

Actually, Woiden told me, she bragged about it and it's usual for psychopaths to do that. She's proud of her meticulous planning and complex plotting of how to strangle Cecil. Stressed to them that because of her abilities with ropes, it was only natural for her to use one.

She also has lung cancer and expects it will get her soon and, fulfilling the deathbed promise she gave her mother motivated her to kill Cecil. Around that, she took that vacuum tube from Cecil's office and buried it on her mother's grave in Regina.

Now, I'll try and explain why I'm devastated about Cecil, Soph, but remember, this is only according to her.

When Lorraine was a child, her father, Stan Wellstone, was at university when Cecil and I went, though I barely remember him. I certainly didn't know he was working with Karen and Cecil in the lab, designing a medical device for diabetes.

Yes, designing the device that must be the primitive prototype of the one that made Cecil his fortune.

What Lorraine told Woiden and Moffatt is that after her father killed himself, her mother kept telling her it was her duty to someday kill Cecil.

Why is convoluted.

After graduation and when Cecil had healed from his injuries from the car accident, he and her father started working together.

Cecil supplied ten thousand dollars to set up a lab.

Her father was to do that while Cecil went to Europe to do the additional research they needed, but what her father did was stole the prototype and money, moved the family to Jamaica and changed his name.

When Cecil discovered that, he started searching Europe for Stan Wellstone but without success. He gave up many months later and moved to England to work for Albert's family's lab. But he continued searching and many years later, located him in Jamaica and confronted him. Wellstone was working as an engineer there, still had the undeveloped prototype. He gave it back to Cecil and apparently offered to repay the ten thousand.

His daughter claims Cecil refused to take the money and proceeded to methodically ruin her father's life. He disclosed his enemy's old identity and spread information throughout the electrical engineering community about Wellstone's being a druggie, thief and cheat at university.

Her father became a heavy drug user, got fired, went bankrupt and committed suicide. Left behind his bitter and sick wife and Lorraine, their young adult daughter who sought revenge all these decades later.

That window blind contract enabled her to replace Cecil's long blind and do something to it so she needed return to his office for repeated repairs. She said she learned about his stretching out in that chair. Killing him became easy, she bragged to Woiden and Moffatt because she's expert with her piggin' string.

Alex looked up and grinned. 'And this is your assurance that Shannon's okay,' as he passed me the last page.

INTERMISSION:
This fax is way too long!
More about how I am going forward soon.

Love, Shannon.

John came in with the pitcher of ice tea. 'Ana's left, we're to meet her and her parents at seven and, Soph, I'm to tell you she's wearing a long casual dress.' He filled our glasses. 'Unbelievable, isn't it? And we'll only ever know Cecil's murderer's story, not his.'

'True but ...'

'So you think Cecil could have maliciously bankrupt someone?' Alex asked.

I sipped before admitting, 'I guess I do. I think he'd have needed to revenge being betrayed. Remember, Cecil grew up plotting how he could payback his father's brutality to his mother, Lily and himself. I've always suspected that he did something to hurt the old man before he left home'

'We'll never know what happened back then or with Stan Wellstone but it's over now,' John said. 'Woiden called me the day before I was leaving. Lorraine Wellstone was killed.'

'What?' I sputtered.

'She attacked her cellmate in the exercise area with a rope made from blanket strips. The other prisoners piled onto her, suffocated her in the dirt.'

'My god, she died as brutally as she killed,' Alex said

John repeated, 'But it's over and that means no trial. I'm relieved Shannon doesn't have to endure that.'

I agreed, and welcomed the news for me, too.

CHAPTER FORTY-THREE
- Ana

I waited for Sophia, John and Alex on the old bench outside my family's favourite restaurant in La Paz. Madre had hustled Papa over here earlier to make sure everything was how she'd requested it. I was glad to be with them again and often amused.

My tiny Madre with her refined Mexico City upbringing and my large Papa, who looks as efficient as the owner of a massive ranch has to be, don't always agree. He can be overwhelmed at Madre's ongoing instructions.

But as Abuela's told me more than once, 'Ana, as much as I was hesitant whether Cilia could be right for my son, they are the perfect pair. Guillermo is very much like his father, Mexican to the core, and benefits from having a strong woman. He certainly chose one.'

As John parked the Suburban, I jumped up to open Sophia's door and Alex slid out of the back. Damn, he's more appealing in that burgundy shirt. Is he a strong man?

'Ana, my dear,' Sophia put her cheek to mine. 'You look magnificent.'

I was wearing a beaded aquamarine dress I had treated myself to in Barcelona. 'Madre loves me to gussy up,' I whispered to her as I ushered them into the wide hall where the maître d' gave us a small bow.

'Welcome, Señorita Ana and guests, I will escort you to Señora and Señor Hernández.

As we walked through the courtyard filled with palm trees, Sophia told me that she was so glad this La Paz restaurant was still here.

'Ana, it's a special place for me as I've been coming here since it first opened as a cantina thirty years ago.'

'The chief chef now is from Mexico City and the food's amazing.'

I felt glad to be Mexican when I walked in here, loved the ancient clay tiles of the floor and the bas relief hangings on the terazzo walls.

All the tables are divided by high plants and arranged under a wide palapa roof around the large and open garden courtyard and a fountain even larger than Cecil's. Their white cloths glowed in the soft light of many candles and the high-backed chairs are well-cushioned for comfortable slow dining.

Papa stood up to greet us and Sophia held out both hands. 'My heavens, the extra-large male version of Iona.'

We all laughed and I said, 'Isn't he almost a carbon copy of my grandmother, has her striking blue eyes, roman nose and fair skin? No one used to believe I was his daughter.'

Papa was in his heavily embroidered charro suit and I watched with delight as he gave Sophia a very deep Mexican bow. He radiates graciousness and authority.

As John does, I recognized, watching the two men shake hands and assess each other.

Madre and Sophia greeted each other with a hug while Alex and I smiled somewhat shyly at each other as he pulled out my chair, and sat next to me.

By the time we finished our appetizers, it was as if we'd all been close friends for many years. My parents seemed as appreciative of Sophia, John and Alex as I am. In fact, Madre, whom I sometimes swear has second sight, gave me a discreet wink before again smiling warmly at Alex.

Damn, the last thing I need is her declaring him suitable!

She was sitting beside Sophia and the two were chatting more than eating while Papa, John and Alex were agreeing a 1937 Packard is a treasure and after its restoration, Alex's would last for decades. Second to horses, Papa likes old cars.

My mouth watered as the waiter put my carnitas down in front of me and I smelled the tangy spices. Sophia turned to me. 'Celia has so much information about the extended Hernández family, Ana, and you didn't tell me that her grandfather's family lived near the Rubin Hernández estate?'

'I didn't know that.'

'Oh, yes,' Madre said. 'If Sophia had been raised there, our families probably would have been at the same social events. In fact, would you like me to ask my uncle about Rubin's factories and get a name for you, or Alex, to contact?'

He accepted enthusiastically and explained about the sale and how having the various names the factory operated under would be helpful.

Madre smiled warmly at him and I thought, if she was a cat, she would be licking her lips. As I am about to be thirty-one and she's told me she hopes for more grandchildren. I nod and am grateful my brother and Raquel have a little boy and baby girl because I'm unsure about actually having children. What Madre doesn't know and I won't tell her is that since creating Phoenix, sculpting has now replaced my longing for a baby. Creating big pieces is all encompassing and exhausting.

My mother values children above all, though she wraps warmth around all of us. She nurtures our vaqueros, their wives and children and often prefers to be with them rather than some of Papa's haughty guests who come to choose a stallion. Though she welcomes everyone to the ranch.

'Was it challenging for you when you moved to the Baja, Celia?' Sophia asked and I knew she was thinking about Iona and her story.

Papa overheard. 'Know that she only married me because she lusted for my horses and lands. Celia could outride me before we married and continues to do to this day.'

John's hearty laugh joined Papa's, attracting the five mariachi players who'd been making their way to the stage. They came over and surrounded our table, requested Madre to choose a song. She picked Las Simples Cosas, a complex song loved by talented musicians, and she knew it was my favorite one.

After the band moved onto the stage, we enjoyed their

music with our deserts and flaming coffees. When we stood to leave, they switched to a flamenco piece and my mischievous mother moved toward the stage and flipped her layers of gossamer black skirts at them.

'Like mother, like daughter?' Alex whispered in my ear and I gave him my most sultry smile and thought, I think he's got a lot of Carlos' genes.

Once we were down on the malecón, La Paz's very wide sidewalk with room for much street entertainment and many people, a family sitting on a white filigree metal bench facing the waves called that they were just leaving. Madre thanked them in her rapid Spanish and led Sophia and I over to the bench as the men strolled away.

Sophia murmured, 'Sitting by the Sea of Cortez at night is so very special. Even more so now that this is part of my heritage, too.'

'It is,' Madre agreed and told her it came with many relatives. 'I hope having the gathering of Hernández won't be overwhelming.'

'Not at all, I am delighted.'

We watched the few people still out on water boards and in kayaks, dark silhouettes gliding in the moonbeams on the waves and listened to the activity behind us. There was the usual mix of grandparents, proud parents and bambinos in carriages or toddlers riding plastic unicorns.

In Mexico, we like the nighttime and often come out of our homes for an ice cream cone and a walk before bed, then go to sleep listening to the parties and music.

Sophia spoke first. 'Do you know anything, Celia, about Marie, Carlos' and Mother Superior Luisa-Grace's younger sister?'

'Only what Luisa-Grace has told me. She still feels sad that she knows so little about Marie after she married and couldn't be with her little sister in her many times of need because of the war,' Madre said softly. 'The letter that Marie and her little daughter had died took three months to reach her.'

I thought of the sadness in all those letters from Marie to Renee, how short and hard her adult years had been.

Sophia told Madre how I had translated them and read aloud for us, asked if she would like copies?

Madre hesitated, thanked her and declined. 'No, I do not want to share them with Luisa-Grace, it would be unkind.'

Sophia nodded with understand as I asked Madre, 'Have you heard anything more from her?'

'She projects being home relatively soon and will fly into the San Jose del Cabo airport. We'll be taking her to the ranch for a few days before taking her home. She lives in an abbey quite near El Triunfo, and I'm to tell you she can't wait to meet Carlos' daughter and your grandson.'

I watched Sophia's slow smile and knew she was moved. From helping to sort Renee's bequest, I had figured out that she hadn't been blessed with the warmth I've had and continue to receive.

The men returned and as we walked back up the hill to our vehicles, Sophia asked if she and John could help them with the massive shop they were doing tomorrow. 'There's lots of room in the Suburban John's rented, maybe we could help transport the fiesta supplies up for you?'

'Please. In fact, a Suburban is exactly what we need for all the plants. And maybe you could take the beverages?' Papa said, then turned to me. 'Or are you and Alex riding up to El Triunfo with them, Ana?'

'No, we're taking my bike and the Packard because we're not coming back down to La Paz. I'm going up to Uncle's cabin for a night and Alex plans to explore the mining areas. Then we're going to tour East Cape on the way to the ranch.'

'A fine idea, Ana,' Papa said and added, 'Sophia, do you know we might have about fifty Hernández relatives at the fiesta? You'll have a feast of information about our family, a fine mix of fiction and fact.'

CHAPTER FORTY-FOUR
- Sophia

I headed over to the old one-room school being used for the fiesta and immediately started taking photos of the fiesta preparations.

Everywhere I looked, there was a special scene.

An ancient fiddler was sitting with two teenage musicians in the oak tree's shade, tuning up. I started with them, asking the elder's permission to take photos and he tucked his fiddle under his chin and posed. As I snapped away, they played me a tune, and I did a little jig to thank them.

The makeshift kitchen was a row of tables under a tent of tarps and when I went in, three women were laughing with Guillermo.

He was stirring a massive pot of something on a propane stove and complained to me, Celia had ordered him to help but, 'Sophia, my problemo is these women are trying to shoo me away.'

'Well, if your supervisors are okay with you leaving for a while, perhaps you could come with me. I've more questions about your family, the ranch and your relatives. You introducing me would be a help.'

The women listened patiently as I asked in my slow español whether I could take their helper. They answered with many jokes and soon Guillermo and I were sitting in chairs under an oak some distance from the musicians, who were now tuning up with gusto.

'Ask away, Sophia,'

'First, the serious stuff, what do you remember about your father? I know you were only ten when he died.'

'To this day, I awake from that nightmare, the bull's horn goring Papa. And the massive funeral when so many came and stayed for days, camping out or in the casa or bunkhouses.

'Tell me what you remember about the funeral.'

'Everyone was trying to comfort Madre. Ahh, Sophia, she was a magnificent woman then, as she is now, gives love easily to so many of us. Throughout that horrible day when we buried Papa up on the hill, Madre would find me and hug me, give me a clean handkerchief.'

I touched his elbow and shoved away my memories of the day of Scott's funeral, of my passing Alex a big white hankie.

'Can you describe Iona that day?'

'She was wearing a big black lace gown and wore a black veil. I remember watching her before the service, swearing as she tried to make her long red hair stay up under that veil. My little sister was only seven, like a tiny angel, dressed all in white and glued to Madre's side or in her lap.'

'Oh, Guillermo.'

'A hard day, and after, it was so tough without Papa. Looking back now, how my mother managed the ranch amazes me, even though the uncles and Papa's friends, often came to help with the big chores. Eventually, Madre found more employees to hire plus I grew quickly so was able to do more of the work.'

'Guillermo, did you meet Carlos?'

'No, I only know what I've been told about him, and about that Christmas shared with his family. I overheard Papa tell Madre that Carlos had been murdered and apparently I asked them what that meant.'

'When I visited Iona in Boston, she told Ana and me that she wished she knew more about Carlos' death, but she doesn't. She liked him and it pleases her that both Alex and I look like him.'

'Switching subjects here, Sophia, before we're interrupted, I want to ask whether you know about Madre and Uncle's friendship? He'd been coming to the ranch to do our welding and he adored her. About three years after Papa died, she had the welding shop built with a little apartment at the back and Uncle moved in there. He told us kids, usually a dozen or so

at the ranch, about a boss señora who had long flaming red hair
and chased away bad guys, rescued animals and people. He
always ended, "And she snorted some when she laughed." If
Madre happened to be there, she swatted him.'

'How wonderful.'

'It was. They laughed easily together.'

A youngster brought us ice tea which I chugged down
before I asked, 'You were ten in 1943, probably starting to
listen into the adults' conversations. Do remember anything
you overheard?'

Guillermo sipped from his paper cup as he thought about
it. 'Some family feud in La Paz, mixed in with the war stuff.
But as my friend's family were always feuding, it just seemed
usual.'

'What did you know about the War?'

'I thought it would never end and I could go and be a
soldier. But that was confusing because one of Papa's uncles
was for the Germans while the other one was for the English. I
didn't listen much because I found it too boring.'

'Boring?' I asked, surprised.

'I couldn't understand. It was only after Madre sent me to
school in Spain in 1947 that I learned much more, and that
was from a Spanish perspective.'

John and Celia joined us, he moving two chairs near us.
As she sat, I could see her multi-coloured full skirt and rose
blouse, 'Celia, you look like a fiesta.'

She told me I looked fine myself and I smiled, thinking of
how John had whistled after I put on this violet peasant dress,
and cheekily suggested I take it off for a while.

'Are we interrupting?' Celia asked. 'You two looked like
you were having a serious discussion, Guillermo.'

'Ahh, my dear, Sophia has me remembering way more than
I expected to about my younger years, though I can't recall
many details.'

'Remembering isn't your strong suit, my dear,' and winked
at me.'

I chuckled. 'One more question, Guillermo, did you know what happened within Carlos' family?'

He shook his head and Celia replied.

'I do know a little because of my visits with Mother Luisa-Grace. Every time we are together, she talks about her little sister and about how brilliant her brother Carlos was, how the three of them played together.'

I interrupted. 'Do you happen to know what Carlos was working on as an electrical engineer?'

'Only the very little Luisa-Grace has told me. He was creating something that would enable phones and radios to operate efficiently. Her memory is as sharp as Iona's, and she's equally worldly. Do you know she was a nursing sister on the battlefields in Italy?'

'Iona told me that. Celia, what has she said about Marie?'

'Not much, most are memories of her as a little child. When Luisa-Grace left to become a novitiate, Marie was eleven. She continues to mourn and pray for her, and for Marie's little daughter. She's told me about the feud that ripped apart her family and still contemplates why her Uncle Hector supported the Germans, as did Marie's bully of a husband. She confided that she remains unable to pray for either of them.'

Guillermo looked at his wife in wonder. 'You do know much more Hernández history than I do.'

'You know quite a bit, Guillermo,' I said and asked another question. 'What about La Paz, did your mother take you there?'

'No, after Papa died, our foreman drove the horses to the port.'

'Guillermo, tell Sophia about where Iona sent you.'

'After the war ended, Madre sent me to Spain to a Madrid academy that taught horse breeding in addition to the usual subjects.'

John sat up straighter in his chair. 'I want to hear more about that, Guillermo. I've a friend trying to start a school like that in our area.'

Celia winked at me as she interrupted the men. 'Guillermo, what do you remember about that radio-phone Carlos made for

Iona?'

'Only that Carlos and his friend from London installed it when Madre was pregnant with my sister.'

Phone? Did all those phones of Renee's connect to Carlos? I accepted we'll probably never know, then wondered if Guillermo might remember Marie? He would have been almost five when they spent that Christmas in La Paz with Carlos and Renee. 'Do you remember a lady with very yellow hair down her back playing with you.

'Oh, yes, I liked her very much and wanted to stay with her. I apparently got a smack on the bum because I wouldn't stop howling when Papa put me in the truck.'

Interesting that Renee had appealed to more than one of the Hernández men, I laughed to myself and asked yet another question. 'Do you recall anything about a big man with a beard who lived next door?'

'Yes, I do, he was a gigantic man with a white beard who made up funny rhymes for us, and he always had little glass tubes in his pocket that could make boxes talk. He made a train of them. I liked him but when he came over, they closed Carlos' workshop door and I wasn't allowed to knock or bother them.'

I was stunned, wanted to keep asking questions but guests were approaching us and I turned to Celia. 'Will everyone coming be a Hernández?'

'Oh, no, Sophia! There'll only be about forty of us and probably about a hundred guests who aren't relatives joining from the little villages, farms and ranches nearby.'

She smiled when I looked surprised at the number.

'Everyone's welcome to join into a fiesta being held in a former schoolyard. Many folks will stay over and party again tomorrow night. Guillermo and I are the official hosts for tonight but there's always plenty of food. In fact, we women usually send some of it home with bachelors.'

'No wonder you needed to buy so much food,' John laughed and added, 'You two bought twice as much as I do for my Christmas and New Year gatherings.'

'And, John, Guillermo has agreed to us coming up to British Columbia for the next one,' Celia announced. 'He wants to see your horses, and snow, and ride in a horse-drawn sleigh.'

'Good!' he beamed, then asked, 'Is that Ana's motorcycle I hear?' and admitted he's been getting a little concerned about whether the Packard had acted up.

We watched her park on the far side of the food tables and Alex pull in beside her. Quite a pair, though I've being sensing a coolness between them that wasn't there at Erin Lake.'

'Sophia, watch Ana,' Celia murmured, as her daughter pulled a red dress out of her saddlebag and put it on over her skimpy shirt. She then stepped out of her leather leggings, put them away and swirled to shake the wrinkles out of her very full skirt.

'She certainly doesn't believe in primping, does she?' her mother added ruefully as Alex joined Ana, looking handsome and very tall beside Ana's petite frame.

'They're quite a pair,' I murmured, thinking about how Alex looks now as compared to how tense he'd been during those last years with Liza.

'Do you know why they're ticked off at each other, Sophia? Ana's edgy, unusual for her.'

I shook my head and recognized, oh, have I met my match in Celia. She also reads body language like a book.

'Ah well, it will work out for them, or it won't.' She gave an elegant shrug and switched subjects. 'I haven't thanked you yet for your magnificent photos of Phoenix, you've captured her magic. Do you realize what an entity that stone woman has been for us since Ana started creating her?

'And now that we've seen your photos, we're astounded at our daughter's talent. Thank you and come along,' Guillermo directed, and waved toward the growing crowd. 'Celia, it's time to introduce our guests. Why don't you and Sophia greet Consuela's family and John and I'll go up the far side?'

Celia concurred and warned me that all the Hernández adults were anticipating visits so we would keep moving. She gestured to the group of people settling in their babies and old people. 'Consuela and Pablo are our family nearest the ranch. He and Guillermo have been buddies since boyhood and they have a massive market garden business outside of Santiago, about two hours from us. Actually, they have three farms in that area as when each of their two daughters married, the parents gave the newlyweds acreages.'

Ana and Alex joined us and Celia requested, 'Ana, after the introductions, will you get Gramps talking about the mines? It is interesting.'

The group welcomed us warmly and I noticed how many faces looked similar to Alex's and mine. It seemed a long time since I had held Carlos' portrait up to the mirror and compared it with our reflections but as Alex pointed out, it was only two months ago.

The Hernández genes are powerful, I decided as I took the smiling and drooling baby one young mother offered me. The little boy with black curls and laughing brown eyes looked so much like my Scott.

When we'd met everyone in Consuela's and Pablo's family except for an old man swathed in a thick and colourful poncho and slumped in a wheelchair, Ana led me and Alex over to him and put a hand on his cheek. 'Gramps?'

He beamed at her and wheezed, 'Awake now, Ana,' and extended a frail bony hand to me. I took it as I sat in the empty chair beside him.

'Gramps, remember the silver mines?' Ana asked loudly.

It was like she'd switched him on.

Celia whispered as she came up between Alex and me, 'Gramps is 102. He talks so slow, but I can translate.'

He straightened up a little. 'I be a silver miner when I be ten. And be very small, they made me squeeze into the cracks. It be very scary in a crack. But I grew too big so there become no jobs for me, no pesos for Madre, little food. Then I grow more and get to drive ore cars, many years. Silver all gone for very long time now. Only the giant still down by the tunnels.'

He drifted off to sleep and Celia completed the story for me.

'Mining at El Triunfo ended quite abruptly. When the price of silver dropped worldwide, the mines here closed, first one section, then another. Gramps was part of the crew who moved the rail tracks from one area to the other, so he was kept on until the last of the mining ended. It's a labyrinth underground, Guillermo says, but I've never gone down. I'm claustrophobic. I know Ana has, and more often and further than she pretended.'

Ana spread her arms wide and laughed. 'Could be, Madre.'

Celia gestured to the next group and the three of us followed her to meet more of the extended Hernández family. I asked permission from each group and snapped photos as we went, feeling somewhat stunned than I've gone from having only Alex as a relative to kinship with so many.

Each circle of friends and family were a delightful generational mix. Babies were being passed from lap to lap, festive-clad sisters and sisters-in-law chatted together around giving their children orders while the men laughed and sipped cervezas.

'It's like a pageant. Celia, thank you for arranging this.

An almost teenage boy came up to Alex, pointed at the Packard, then to the elder in a wheelchair not far from the old car and gestured for us to come. We walked over to the old woman wearing long dangling silver earrings and a bright red dress. She smiled graciously at us and started chatting away to her translator.

He turned and asked in precise schoolboy English, 'Was this Carlos' car?'

Alex had joined us and assured him and the old lady it had been and added that I was Carlos's daughter.

He translated that, listened for quite a while and told us, 'Auntie says when she was a child, Carlos took her and her brother for a ride. They went somewhere with a straight road and he drove them very fast, then they went slow again. She liked being inside the car.'

Alex nodded and asked if Auntie would like another ride. She declined but pointed to the boy, who smiled, nodded and was soon in the passenger seat. Which generated many children wanting rides and Alex spent much of his afternoon circling El Triunfo with a smiling passenger fastened in the seat beside him.

We ate and ate, then after a sunset of pinks, oranges and purples highlighted the steep mountain peaks west of us, the dancing began. The music became louder as more musicians joined in the impromptu orchestra.

Guillermo asked me to dance and as he whipped me around on the sandy old schoolyard, he told me that the musician making a clarinet soar was his close friend. He and his family lived by the sea near Los Barriles, not too far from the ranch, though he was often in New Orleans.

'He married a Hernández, Sophia, a wonderful piano player who's my second cousin. Or is it third? Anyway, they have six children, all amazing musicians.'

I wondered again if the Hernández genes carried extra creative ones and whether my talents with a camera came from Carlos' creative genes? Renee's side of my family didn't have any artists or musicians that I knew. Dad's only pastime was the radio or reading the newspapers and Mom was a wonderful baker, gifted many people with her cookies.

John and I danced like we had after the play in New York and I told him as we collapsed on our bed about 2 am, 'My feet are sore, isn't that grand?'

'He whispered, 'You were born to be dancing in the desert under a full moon.'

CHAPTER FORTY-FIVE
- Alex

I followed Ana's bike's dust up the winding road and sniffed again at the old car's new scent. It wasn't unpleasant but I couldn't figure out what it was until I remembered the little girl lathering herself with a lavender mosquito lotion. She must have spilled a little and had perfumed the Packard.

The families of the children thanked me for the rides but it had been a pleasure, as it probably had been for Carlos, too, seventy years ago.

Though it was a strange coincidence to be doing what he had done.

Winding around a sharp corner, I found Ana waiting but as soon as she saw me, she waved and sped off again.

Would she change her mind and let me go up to Uncle's cabin's area with her? Although I understood her wanting to be alone to say her goodbyes to him and wouldn't go all the way up, I could camp a mile or so from his place and sketch some mountains, greet the dawn.

We'd left early this morning after only about five hours of sleep but I felt great. Guillermo had made us chilaquiles and the three of us ate at the round table on the old casa's porch. We'd talked about the mines and how many tunnels there are to various levels and ore sites.

Ana had suggested, 'Papa, draw Alex an overview map,' and he got paper and pencil. As he drew a maze of lines, he told us he couldn't begin to count how many times he's been underground but only knew some areas well. Some areas smelled too bad to explore.

'Is it easy to get lost?' I asked.

'Yes and no. Not if you understand the track system.' He explained about the intersections of the narrow rail tracks as he drew them in and marked directions of the ore train's main line.

Then he'd folded up the map, passed it to me and told me to only go into the mine along the main tracks to the first intersection, no further.

I thanked him, agreed and put his drawing in my pants pocket.

Ana chuckled, 'Papa, that's exactly what you would tell Guill and me, except we could go to the third.

'And you pushed that sometimes, didn't you? Crawled into some side tunnels after Guill.

'I did but I was too scared to go far. And Madre had one rule I never broke. I never went underground without leaving a note with all our names, a description of where we were going and what time we went into the tunnels.'

Ana had asked her father about whether he believed the locals' myth that there was a colossal ghost in the tunnels.

Strangely, he didn't actually answer, and I felt Guillermo had hedged. 'I think some who claimed to have seen him have had too much mezcal'

Ana discreetly winked at me.

I'd ask her about that myth later, suddenly suspecting her father was one of those who had seen something.

Guillermo had switched back to discussing safety issues, told us about the sudden rockslides or how a tunnel had collapsed. Those scared me more than the ghost.

But if Ana let me go up the mountain with her, I wouldn't even be going down into the mines alone but with Guillermo, Gran and John. They were coming up tomorrow afternoon to go underground. Celia was too, but not going into the mine.

Gran wanted to take photos of the tracks and the old ore carts as well as the old village's crumbling buildings. After that, we would be in a convoy to head down the very old road to Los Barriles. We'd have dinner and then Gran and John were following Celia and Guillermo to the ranch and Ana and I were overnighting at her friend's hacienda.

The Packard hit a bump, my head mashed into the roof and

I started watching the deep ruts more carefully. The last thing I needed was to break the Packard's tie rod.

The countryside was as rough as the road and I found it ugly. Coarse gravel surrounded slag piles of chunky rocks and prickly, bushy ground cover. The cacti were increasingly sparses we went up hill and I suspected we were at a high altitude.

This is steep mountain country, very different from anywhere I've been previously. I'd asked Ana about the path up to Uncle's and she'd said its two miles wasn't too steep but rocky and the footing was a little treacherous.'

I eased the Packard around another sharp curve and caught a glimpse of my new sleeping bag in the rear view. Wondered again if Ana will agree to me climbing part way and camping out there?

I hoped so because I was concerned about her going alone. It was over a year since the old man had died and that path up might be not as in as good shape as she expects. She might also appreciate having some help bringing those tools back down.

During our dinners as we came down the Baja, Ana had told me stories about the man she called Uncle and one was about his cabin. Three men from the ranch had helped him take the timbers up the mountainside to the wide rock platform Uncle had discovered and gone through the legal process to claim. They helped him frame the cabin, ready for its future walls and put on a sturdy roof topped by tin. In the following years, Uncle had carried two-foot-square windows up in a box strapped to his back and built glass walls.

When Ana was twelve, Celia had allowed her to go up with her brother and Uncle. By then, the cabin was snug, an aerie.

Her voice had been reverent when she'd described watching the sun come up from her bunk through all the glass panes. She'd added how special it was to now be the cabin's owner.

How very different than my and Gran's reaction to Renee's stuff, I'd thought, envious of her and her Uncle's relationship.

She plans to keep and use his tools in their studio at the

ranch. I'm looking forward to seeing his sculptures, which she described as large miniatures, most with welded wires.

She also told me that him teaching her that technique was what had enabled her to wrap the wires around Phoenix. He'd taught her how to make those tricky welds and she'd said that when he'd seen her drawings of the massive woman-like sculpt she wanted to create, he'd told her that the student's talents had surpassed the teacher.

I sighed, accepting again that Ana loves being a professional sculptor and it satisfies her. She's like Gran, meticulous about her work and at ease with her increasing acclaim as an artist.

She's so very different than Liza. She'd often talked about her expertise but what I'd learned from client complaints was that she lacked some of the communications techniques they required.

Done is done, I reminded myself, wanting to stop with the comparisons.

When we danced last night, Ana and I were so in sync. I had kept a careful distance between us but when the mariachis began playing Cielito Lindo, Ana and other guests started singing and she'd nestled against me.

When I reached the ancient mine site, her bike was outside what must have been the administration building. I went inside the ancient adobe grey brick building and called, 'Ana.'

The building echoed, An-a, An-nn-a - much like the Fraser Canyon had echoed at me after the moose.

'Al - lex - lex,' came back and she appeared at the top of the stairs. 'Come on up.'

She led me down the long narrow hall. 'I think this room will be the best place for you to sleep, the roof's still solid in here. And being on the second floor, there's much less chance of snakes or scorpions crawling into your sleeping bag.'

I smiled at her, charmed by the three dusty fingerprints on her face.' Well, what I'm actually hoping is to sleep under the stars. May I hike up with you to somewhere near to Uncle's cabin and camp up there? I could help carry the tools down. I understand your wanting to be alone at the cabin, so I'll find a spot to stay and wait for you.'

Ana's black eyes flashed and she drew herself up about six inches, glared at me before responding.

'No. Thank you, Alex, but no! As I explained earlier, I want to be alone going to Uncle's cabin, she said, her tone icy. 'I'll see you back here about noon tomorrow.'

She turned on her hiking boots' heels and marched down the hall.

Oh, shit.

Women!

I recognized some wide chasm has just opened between us. I had overstepped.

But why the anger, the disappearance act. Why hadn't she just said that it wouldn't work?

That was sure the hell a different side of Ana than I expected.

It was similar to how Mom would have reacted. She'd always been very sure about what was right for her and would be angry if I didn't respect that. She raised me to ask myself, "Is what you want right for the other person as well as right for you?" and once she'd labeled a man as too pushy, she never went out with him again.

Obviously, my asking to hike part way up with Ana wasn't right for her. But why not just say that? Though she had told me what her needs, her wants, were. I guess I've screwed up, tried to impose my wants.

I clunked down the steps, needing to be outside and walking my anger off. We're both adults, for God's sake, and stomped down the road to the mine's entrance.

I looked into the wide hole with two sets of narrow tracks.

Back to plan A, I'll poke around in the mines.

I went back to get my flashlight and headlamp from the Packard and clipped the lamp's strap to my belt. It was about six feet and kept the flashlight retrievable, if I tripped.

Then flashbacked to the rope around Cecil's neck and how

the detectives learning about the piggin line led to the murderer. And about how Shannon was now having to accept Cecil had a dark side.

I guess we all do. She must be relieved she hadn't married him because no matter the circumstances, she sure the hell would never set out to bankrupt a family. Nor would I.

But I've blundered, lost Ana's trust. Will that make her permanently reject me?

I told myself to stop being an ass and park it!

Returning to the mine's entrance, I peered at the dark in front of me, hesitant. Pulled out Guillermo's map and as I studied it, wondered if wanted to go in. But why not? I could always turn back.

The first intersection was a good distance away and down at level two. but the slope's steepness would be moderate as it had been built for the ore trains' need to get back up, so I wouldn't have any difficulty returning.

I realized that creating those gradual slopes for the tracks was why the mines covered such a massive geography. I hadn't asked Guillermo how many levels, but as I wasn't going past two, it didn't matter. I switched the lamp fastened to my hat and started walking.

As the tunnel darkened and the entrance became a distant circle of light, my headlamp reflected off the rock walls and timber-beamed ceiling. I saw little glimmers of something in the light and turned on my powerful flashlight. In it, the walls and ceiling surrounding me glittered, probably with silver?

I shivered as it was becoming cold. Maybe I should have brought a vest? As the narrow-gauge tracks angled downwards, I no longer could see light from the entrance. I turned off my headlamp.

Spooky!

I switched it back on and thought, God, Ana, I wish so much you were here and I am so sorry for shading your memorial to Uncle.

CHAPTER FORTY-SIX
- Ana

By the time I had climbed up the narrow path to Uncle's, I was more sad than mad at Alex. Sad because he isn't the perceptive man I hoped he was. Why hadn't he understood why I needed to say good-bye to Uncle alone? And him presuming I needed him to carry down the tools because of his superior strength?

'I'm a sculptor, Alex, muscles on muscles,' I yelled, startling a flock of mountain chickadees. As the tiny birds fluttered away into the azure sky, I wondered if birds offend each other.

Yet perhaps I'd overreacted, again. Alex did say he'd stay nearby, and not intrude at all, and I did tell him I was bringing tools down but not that they'll easily fit into my knap-sack. Uncle's precious welding heads are light and his large set of Swiss diamond steel files weigh about ten pounds.

I guess I could have told him that before stomping off.

What was picking at me now was that I hadn't reminded him to leave a note before going underground.

Goddamn! No wonder I'm so hesitant about letting a man into my life, they've such complex egos. Though, I can almost smell Alex's subtle orange aftershave, feel his arms holding me as we danced last night.

'But I am not yet ready for another relationship!' I announced to the rock squirrel chattering at me. 'Might never be. Maybe I'll have a series of brief, uncomplicated relationships, but I don't want brief flings, never have accepted an overnight offer.'

I could almost hear Uncle's rumbling chuckle. "Well, my little amiga, perhaps you have a dilemma. How about parking it for a little while and concentrating on this rocky trail?"

I wiped a tear, remembering Uncle, and all the love and skills he gave me, as he had to Iona when they were special friends.

He'll be with me, especially each time I analyze where to place the chisel's point first.

'Thank you,' I whispered as I reached Uncle's bench overlooking the jagged mountains and sat down. He's taught me so much, but how to remove bits and pieces of a rock to let its image out was his biggest gift to me. I knew he wasn't too far away and I'll always be chatting with him as I work.'

This bench is where we sat and sipped hot chocolate as I learned how to look at rock. We always had a large chunk to study and we would look at the mountains' formations, speculate about how they would evolve.

This bench is where I began to be able to read stone.

Guess finding a rock's image is similar to what Sophia does. She said she finds the image she wants through her lens, and studies its relationship to the space around it and then takes many shots fast. That's how she captured my dancing lady's wires.

Phoenix would have pleased Uncle. Wish I could have shown him Sophia's photos of my welding. He'd have been pleased.

I stayed up very late, watching the stars and the moon's light creating shadows within the mountains' peaks. The peace Uncle loved up here flowed into me and I drifted, accepting my power and knowing whatever was to be between Alex and me would happen.

The next morning, I did some sketching sitting on the bench but mainly reminisced about Uncle's unconventional life. He had become a respected sculptor whose art is in many Mexican museums and private collections. But most of it is in his studio and home, or at Abuela's in Boston as well as my brother's and parents' homes.

As the sun rose higher and illuminated the mountains, turning shade into light, I was happy this now was my retreat and knew I would come back regularly: knew I'll never be alone here, Uncle's essence will live on.

When heat from the glowing yellowish-white globe became
uncomfortable, I went into the glass-walled cabin, wrapped
up his precious tools and put them in my backpack. As I slowly
wandered down the mountain, I let my mind return to Alex, all
yesterday's anger at him gone. I was embarrassed by my abrupt
departure, hadn't even had the courtesy of answering any
questions he might have had about going into the mine.

When I reached the Packard and my motorcycle, I called
Alex, ready to apologize.

I'd accepted that I do expect too much from men, and,
according to Madre, don't yet know how to give back enough.

Alex, I shouted.

No answer.

I went into the old administration building and called up the
stairs, then checked all the rooms. Nothing. Jogged around the
three blocks of crumbled mine buildings and over to the four
stone sheds that were still solidly intact.

Maybe he'd tripped and fallen in one of those, was unable
to hear me?

After I checked the last one and accepted he must be
underground, I started worrying. Is he in trouble? Or lost? Did
he go too far and it's taking him longer to make his way back?

Or has there been a cave-in and he's on the wrong side? Or,
worse case scenario, under fallen rock?

If only I hadn't stomped off without reminding him to leave
a note. Or had he and I missed it? I rushed back to the Packard,
checked it and my bike's saddlebags.

Nothing.

His big flashlight and safety helmet with light was gone.

What will I do? More, what can I do? I'm so nervous in
the underground's blackness and I've never been down alone.
I checked my cell phone to see the time and to confirm that
there's no service. It wasn't even noon.

My heart raced, knowing that our folks wouldn't arrive
until later afternoon. If I do go underground to search for
Alex, what if he comes out? Though that's not actually an

issue, I can leave him a note.

All my ifs overwhelmed me. I took three deep breaths and again analyzed my options.

There was really only one. Go underground.

That would be easier than just waiting and Alex might be injured, need help.

The only place I've been is called the Second as it's the second level of the mine. Although I've never gone down alone, I know how to get to that level's main intersection and have been quite a way past it, into that tunnel leading to the silver storage area. I can go and check that far.

Sound carries in a mine. If I call softly, we might be able to hear each other. Of course, shouting is taboo, too risky when underground, can start vibrations.

I debated whether to go in the entrance and decided to go down what my brother calls the spiral staircase. It's much faster than the main entrance and the way he and I have usually gone.

Hope I can be back before my parents and Sophia and John arrive.

Thank god they're coming!

I ripped a page out of my journal and wrote:

Monday - 11:45 am: Alex may be in trouble or lost in the mines.

Papa, I'm going down the shortcut, that spiral pathway that leads through the caves to the intersection, then to the silver storage cages. I will call him but don't worry, I remember, no shouting. And I won't go any further than that.

I'll come back up the same route, project being above ground by the time you arrive.

Much love to all, Ana

That message will work for Alex, too, in case he returns before I do. I weighted the paper down with my knapsack on the Packard's hood, then got the spare batteries from my saddle-bag, zipped them in a deep pocket in my leather jacket, put a bottle of water in another one and clipped my heavy

Baton flashlight onto my belt.

I took a deep breath, snapped up my riding helmet, glad I had bought the one with built-in light, and walked across the rubble to the burnt house and its thick rock fireplace. It towers forlornly in the midst of charred timbers and black charcoal, having once been in the centre of the mine manager's mansion.

At the back of it is a secret entrance to the mine.

When Guillermo, my brother, took me down for the first time, he'd taken me through a wide slit into the back of this chimney, showed me the tunnel's hidden entrance and asked, 'Are you sure you want to go down?'

'Of course,' I'd said, wishing I hadn't insisted earlier. He'd only agreed to take me after I crossed my heart that I would not tell Madre and Papa.

Guill stayed in front of me, guided me down some natural stairs and much slippery rock and some tight turns, murmuring reassuringly the whole time. I was terrified.

But a few years later, I took a boyfriend down because by then, Guill had grown too big to fit but he had met us at the intersection, then guided us to another area of the mine.

Even thinking about my big brother calmed me and I felt more confident, remembering why I was doing this.

Alex might need help.

I turned my helmet light up to high beam, told my knees to stop shaking, bent low and slipped through the slit between two big stones. Moments later, I was in the tunnel and as it widened, I straightened upright and started breathing again.

My light reflected off the walls of the slopping path through the rock, looked the same as it had when I was sixteen. Though it was even narrower than I remembered. I put a hand up on the rough rock sidewalls as I needed to control my speed going down the narrow corkscrew. After what seemed far too long a time, I was at where the high tunnel ended abruptly at a smooth rock face, and I could almost hear Guill whispering, "Ana, turn to the right."

When I did, my light reflected off the narrow split and I slipped through it into a high cavern, knew I was almost to the second level's intersection. That was the circle of rail spokes used by the miners to shift ore from the little ore cars that fit into the mining areas' tunnels into a larger ore car that went up to the surface.

The interchange was in the largest of a series of five caverns, beside the cave with the spiral staircase one. Off it were two inaccessible central caverns and the wide, relatively high ceiling tunnel where the rail tracks went to the locked iron barcages. That's where the mine's rocks with silver veins was stored until it was transported to the smelter.

As I checked for fallen rock and crawly critters in my lamp's light, I kept calling in a soft voice, 'Alex, Alex?'

And I listened, but the silence was as deep as the cold dark. I almost choked on the noxious smell, knew it hadn't been here when I had brought my boyfriend down when I was seventeen. What was causing it?

But my fear lessened some when I reached the intersection and I decided to call Alex at each exit to a mining tunnel. Then before I returned to the surface, I would go and check out the storage cages. I had to assume Alex would have followed the route Papa drew for him.

I swallowed the massive lump in my throat and blew air into my eyes, trying to prevent any tears, and had a big sniff and a 'Goddamn!'

If I hadn't been furious with Alex, I would have reminded him to take spare batteries and to leave a note about what time he went underground and what he was planning.

I reached the first tunnel opening into a mining area and although I knew he wouldn't have ventured into it, called, 'Alex, Alex?'

Nothing.

I unsnapped my long flashlight from my belt, breathing shallowly to not choke on that strange smell. Flashed it into the tunnel's blackness and on to the floor. I literally jumped when I saw footprints on an area of ground rock as fine as sand.

Many footprints, almost twice the size of my boots and smooth, no a sole pattern, had to be a moccasin.

Logically, I knew those could be from decades ago but when I squatted down beside them, I shivered. I was increasingly apprehensive but unsure about what. Time to check those storage cages and go back up. I was craving fresh air and to be away from that smell.

I was acutely aware of being alone.

Oddly, the rock path I was following seemed well used, shiny in my lights. I stopped, tensed up.

'Hell, silly,' I whispered, 'it's probably the old silver dust and it has been here since the mines closed, decades ago.

My boots have thick crepe sponge soles and I moved forward silently. But the back of my neck was twitching and the noxious smell increasingly strong.

Finally, my light saw upright bars ahead.

My heart pounded as I cautiously turned off my big flashlight and turned my headlamp down, huddled close to the wall, inching toward the first cage.

It was empty, about a 12 x 14 foot rock rectangle with its front wall sealed with one-inch round bars, set about six inches apart. I eased toward the second cage. Empty. Continued on, trying not to choke on the smell as I confirmed the third cage was empty. The fourth one was beyond the tunnel's sharp curve and my apprehension grew. And gasped, made myself not scream.

I found Alex.

Lying on a slab table. 'Oh, my God,' I moaned, 'Are you dead?

'Alex, Alex! You'll be okay. Wake up, Alex, please wake up, and prayed for a response.'

I grabbed onto a bar, concentrated on his chest. 'It's moving, he's alive.'

But it was pumping too fast, knew he was in shock as well as unconscious. I increased both my lights' intensity and focused on his head. It was tilted back, exposing his throat, and above his left eye, the bone was mashed.

Blood was still slowly dripping from it, clotting hasn't occurred, happened recently.

Who hit him, and with what?

Was he nearby, watching me?

I switched off the lights and as my eyes adjusted to the black, listened. I and could only hear Alex's raspy breathing.

I have to get into him soon, I decided and turned on my flashlight. I checked the area quickly before focusing the high beam on Alex's wound, then scanned every corner of the cage.

An occupied cage, because there was a large wooden chair behind Alex's head and some sort of floor bed in the corner.

I grabbed the large rusty lock on the crossbar in front of me and tried pulling on it, banging it against the cell's bars. Despite my pleading, the lock didn't release.

I gulped a sob and checked Alex again, shining the beam at his eyelids.

No reaction.

Whoever attacked him has the key and will have heard me. Is he waiting for me to come to the next cage? Or is he away elsewhere in the mines? Or even above ground?

If he is in the next cage, could I sneak up and mash his head? Find the key? Though the baton flashlight is heavy, built to be a weapon, there was no hope of sneaking up, I accepted.

But I needed to risk seeing what was down there. Maybe Alex had somehow wounded him? I had to go forward.

It seemed crazy but not checking would be even more so. I need that key!

I switched off both lights, put my back against the rock wall and inched forward, felt nauseated by the smell and my fear in the dark silence. After what seemed like forever, my hand encountered that cage's first thick round bar. I crunched down and turned my long flashlight to its dim setting.

'Holy god!' I shrieked and jumped to my feet.

Switched to high beam.

The scene in front of me was other-worldly, unbelievable.

I tried to absorb it, but it was like those awful Satan-will-get-you front pages in our family bible, like those abominations where angels and devils and snakes are intertwined - even looking at those coloured illustrations had terrified me as kid.

As what I was seeing did. And then I noticed the left hand hanging down and that all the fingers were missing.

I felt woozy, stuck my head between my knees and lamented, 'No way to get the key from him.'

After I straightened up, I tried to see the details more than the overall image, but it was like trying to make sense of a terrifying nightmare.

A massive snake was coiled up around a gigantic old man and an upright timber ceiling support. The thick snake had wrapped around his victim up to his armpits.

Suffocated him, I guessed, because above his widespread shoulders was a bluish face. It tilted bizarrely to the left and the wild maze of white hair hanging down almost to the snake's head was covering most of it.

I squatted, took three deep breaths despite the rancid air and analyzed this unreal scenario.

The snake's middle coils were as thick as a big man's thigh and covered by black patches on its silvery tan skin, rather like the pattern on a giraffe. The coils thinned as they wound up the giant's torso and its broad triangle head was facing toward the back of the cage.

But what I could clearly see was the machete buried between its eyes, the handle standing upright.

Oh, my god, I whimpered, suddenly realizing what else that snake meant. 'Did that snake bite Alex?'

The cage's door was open wide, but I didn't go in. I ran back to Alex, accepting I wouldn't be able to unlock the iron bar gate.

I watched his chest fluttering, saw that there was a wound on his leg and knew I needed to get past my panic and act fast.

Alex was alive but for how long? He had a severe head injury and possibly a snake-bite to his thigh. As I examined the metal bars, I asked myself, what will the doctors need to know?

Details about the snake for sure - it could be python or a boa constrictor? Or maybe a reticulated python? I've been brought up in a region with dangerous, big snakes and I'd also scanned Sophia's snake books at Erin Lake.

I remembered a large illustration similar to what I was looking at, a very large snake with dark irregular splotches on its skin. It had been Burmese python snake whose bite was dangerous but it coils to kill. As this one did, whatever species it was.

I keep testing the bars, hoping one of the bottom welds would not feel firm as I stared at Alex, and worried whether his breathing had become increasingly shallow? How the hell can I get to him?And remembered Uncle's diamond files in my knapsack.

I think they will cut iron.

'I'll be back soon,' I told Alex, longing to be beside him, helping him. 'You keep breathing, okay? Please, please, Alex, stay alive!

CHAPTER FORTY-SEVEN
- Ana

I raced through the junction, across the wide cave and slid through the entrance into the spiral tunnel, praying aloud, 'Stay alive, Alex, stay alive.'

Some skin peeled off my palms as I climbed up, supporting myself with the rough rock walls. And heard a faint whisper.

'Slower, Ana! Go slower.'

It must have been me muttering but it sounded like Uncle and I became cautious.

Finally, I could see some outside light far above me and I sped up again and slid through the exit. As I leaned against the old chimney to catch my breath, I wiped the blood from my hands on my jeans and sucked in the fresh air gratefully. But I could only smell snake.

The sunshine warmed me as did the old stones and I tried to figure out what to take back down. Gloves, for sure, I thought and recalled Alex listing to me what he'd brought. That had included syringes with antibiotics!

I opened the Packard's passenger door, dumped Alex's large daypack out on the seat and found the kit with six syringes and vials. I put them in my small hiking pack along with the zip lock bag of bandages, his travelling towel and three bottles of water.

I added to my earlier note:

2:07 pm - Alex's injured, head wound, perhaps has had a snake bite. He's unconscious, locked in the fourth cage and I hope to file out three bars to get to him. I'm going back down the spiral tunnel but, Papa, it's narrow, too tight for you and John. We'll need a stretcher.'

Jogging across to the chimney again, I prayed that parents and Sophia and John would arrive soon and was glad John had rented the Suburban. That would hold the stretcher.

Madre will know where to take him. I think Los Barriles is closer, but we'll probably go down to La Paz because it has the hospitals, the medical specialists. I wound down the spiral tunnel, my motorcycle gloves now protecting my hands.

'I'm almost back, Alex, I'm coming,' I murmured as I tried not to go too fast. 'You're going to live, going to be fine. We've got help coming soon, stay alive for me and for your Gran and John. Please, please, Alex, don't you dare die!'

I was almost down to the cavern when my headlamp started fading. I snarled at it, sat down on a natural step, turned on the baton flashlight and exchanged the two AA's in my helmet. The light was much brighter.

I kept humming, 'You'll be fine, Alex, you'll be fine' trying to block the images of that poor giant man and snake. When I reached the exit slit and went through the cavern, it was hard to ignore the vile air.

Alex was in exactly the same position, though his chest's compressions seemed slower, steadier. I talked to him as I inspected the lock's keyhole and tried Uncle's thinnest file in it, willing it to pop.

Nothing and I couldn't feel any movement inside. I took out a slightly larger file and tried to force the shackle open but with no room for leverage between bar and lock, it wasn't feasible.

The only option left was filing where the bar was welded. I knelt down and sawed fast until the file bit in, and started making back and forth saws, back and forth, back and forth.

Uncle's file started cutting in, ever so slowly.

Would I be able squeeze in when I got two out? Or would it need three? It was slow going as the file cut into the ancientiron and the wrong angle for my back.

I shuffled a little, trying to get more pressure on the file and kept talking to Alex, switched to seesaw singing,' Alex, come back, come back to me, come back,' in rhythm to my filing.

I wasn't even half through the first bar when Sophia called down the tunnel, 'Ana, I'm here!'

I stopped filing and stood up, tears dripping down my cheeks as I watched her run towards me. She pulled me into her arms and held me tight for a moment before we turned and studied Alex together.

'He's breathing well, isn't he?' She said, kneeling to pick up the file and started sawing. 'John and Guillermo are following the rail track in, bringing a makeshift stretcher. John wanted to come down the spiral with me but Guillermo forebade him to try.'

'He wouldn't have fit,' I sniffled, wiped my nose on my sleeve, got another file, knelt beside her and started on the next thick bar. 'Oh, Sophie, I'm so scared. And Alex might have a snake bite as well as a head injury.'

'That's what that godawful smell is, snake! I should have known, though I've never smelled anything as putrid as this.'

'It's dead as is the giant. You'll see.'

'Giant? And you think there's only one snake?' Sophia asked.

'My god, I don't know! There's a dead monster snake in the last cell. Might have bit Alex.'

'He's tough and healthy, Ana. Alex will survive. And if it had been a poisonous snake bite, he wouldn't be breathing,' she comforted me. 'We'll have him down to La Paz soon to a hospital your mother knows. It has a new neurological ward with good equipment and many specialists.

'He needs that, look at this head. We have to get to him above ground, Sophie.' I prayed that the specialists can help, that the injury hasn't damaged anything permanently as I sawed, frustrated that the smaller file wasn't cutting well.

'Ana, can you describe the snake for me?'

'It's a desert shade with blotchy brown patches and it's incredibly large. I think the old man it's coiled around was very old, he has long tangles of straw-like white hair.'

'From this smell, their arrival here isn't recent, they must have been living here for years.' She leaned back to straighten her back for a moment, then returned to filing. 'I'll phone Sammy and email photos. He'll be able to identify it.'

'Soph, in your thickest snake book, remember that full page Burmese python? This one looks like that.'

'What the hell would it be doing in the South Baja?

'They're from South America, Ana, though now a terrible scourge in Florida. Each female lays about two hundred eggs at a time so they're multiplying almost as fast as rats … but if it is, it's unlikely there's more than one snake in this mine. I suspect this one was the man's pet.'

I knew how worried she was about Alex from her rapid chatter.

We heard Papa's and John's voices.

'They're almost here,' I said unnecessarily.

'Yes, and soon Alex will have medical help,' Sophia's voice broke,

John came striding down the tunnel, 'How is he, Soph, Ana?'

'Badly hurt and we aren't through yet, these two bars are only partially filed,' I said.

'Great, that'll have weakened them. Your father's right behind me, bringing a sledgehammer and cutter, and I've got this heavy chain, we'll get you into him in no time.'

'We'll do it now, Ana,' Papa said as he stuck out a hand, pulled me up and gave me a hug.

John helped Sophia up and examined our file cuts. 'I think they'll break, Guillermo, let's try pulling, okay?'

Papa knelt and wrapped the chain twice around the first bar's cut and passed an end to John, then stood and faced the far tunnel wall.

'On three, pull, John.

They stood with shoulders touching, two giants themselves.

But not nearly as big as that poor old man the snake had squeezed to death, I thought.

When they leaned forward together, that first bar snapped.

'That was easy. Perhaps the welds will break even if the bars aren't filed?' John asked and moved the chain to the next one. Within minutes, they had four out and bent the long metal poles aside.

I went through the narrow opening with Sophia right behind me and started examining Alex, me shining light at his head injury and peering into that wound while she cut his bloody pant leg open with my belt knife.

'Major head wound, an open injury, can see cracked skull bone.'

Soph replied, 'His calf is badly swollen and the wound seems to be deep but the artery must be intact, there's minimal bleeding. Let's get those antibiotics into him, but first, I need to see this wound better, Ana.'

I shone my light directly into the long opening and she decided it was not a bite. 'The skin is cut, look at those smooth edges, probably not a snakebite. I think all snakebites are jagged.'

I unzipped my pocket and pulled the vials of antibiotics out as she asked, 'Where are the syringes, Ana? We need to zap him with all of them.'

She injected them into his thigh above the wound and put the empty vials into his chest pocket for the doctors. 'Okay, take him.'

I put the towel from Alex's pack onto his head. 'You two take the head, you and I will lift him on, John,' Papa ordered, and opened up the two iron pipes with Madre's big soft navy travelling blanket stretched out between them, lifted Alex with their massive hands onto it.'

'Now, Ana, are you okay staying with him while we have a look at that snake and old man?' Papa asked.

'Yes.'

'I'll take photos. Come on, John and Guillermo,' she said, loping down the tunnel. Let's not dawdle, we have to get Alex out of here!'

I could hear their voices clearly

'God, this smell,' Sophia complained. 'And that poor man! I can't believe what I'm seeing.'

'It's like a movie set,' John said.

'I've seen some sights in my day but never anything like this,' Papa added.' Soph, take many photos, I'm going back to Alex and Ana.'

He put an arm around my shoulder. 'Seeing that has made me think of those ancient drawings in that old bible of ours. Just looking at them used to terrify me when I was a child.'

'I thought of those awful pages, too, Papa. And I never want to inherit that bible,' I hiccuped a half-sob.

He pulled me into his arms and hugged me ever so gently.

The trip down to La Paz was a blur. Sophia had asked if I wanted to ride in the Suburban but admitted, 'You be with him, please, because I might go to sleep, I'm so very tired.'

Madre wrapped me in her thick shawl, insisted I drink a whole bottle of water before Papa lifted me onto the back seat of their truck.

'Rest, Ana,' he soothed. 'Soon, you'll be with your Alex in the hospital. He's going to heal and be fine again.'

As we bumped down that dusty road behind the Suburban, I kept thinking about what Sophia had said while the men had been securing Alex on the stretcher into the Suburban.

'Ana, while I was taking those photos and willing myself not to barf at the image and smell, I pretended I was talking to Shannon. Telling her I now understood how her seeing Cecil's tongue was not a memory that could be erased, and understanding how seeing this horror would stay with we four.'

I leaned against the truck's seat and sent messages to Alex, telling him how important he was to me, asking him to heal fast. And I tried not to worry about seeing his cracked skull.

CHAPTER FORTY-EIGHT
- Alex

The hospital smell hit me as I fought through a strange haze, trying to make my eyelids open. When they did, I saw Ana, her head resting on the white covers on my bed as she slept.

I reached toward her and discovered my hand had a needle taped to a winding snake-like tube going up a pole to a liquid-filled bag.

I've no idea what has happened to me but something sure has.

When I put a finger on Ana's head, she shouted, 'What?' Saw I was awake and walked around the bed to give me a gentle hug.

'All this after I told you to stay safe!' she admonished. 'Wait here while I get your grandmother.'

'Okay,' I agreed, delighted to find Ana here with me.

Nine days later, John parked the Suburban close to the villa's door and I slid out, feeling freed, despite the crutches and my temporarily limited abilities. The doctors had told me I was damn lucky to be alive and, apparently, still have all my cognizant abilities.

'Here, I'll get that door.'

Ana guided me into the entry hall and as I hopped by the long mirror, I saw our reflections in the long mirror.

She looked wonderful in a green sundress, and I looked like a caricature of an injured man. My splinted leg stuck out in front of me and the white gauze around the top half of my head was a startling contrast to the purple bruises below.

But both leg and head bandages would be coming off in six days. I had been poked and prodded often and my neurosurgeon and neurologist felt I had a good chance of healing without permanent damage. Though the neurologist had been firm about it being too soon to know if I have some residual brain damage. Apparently, ongoing assessments for a year are a necessity to trace the consequences from my severe head injury and concussion.

What remains unknown is what actually happened to me.

All I can currently remember is following narrow rail tracks into the mine through a tunnel to an ore car interchange. And hearing a thunderous shout, 'Carlos!'

I don't know any more than that.

Looking at Gran's photos of the coiled man and snake, we all assume it was the old giant who shouted and attacked me, mistaking me for Carlos. After, he'd driven the machete into the huge snake's eye before suffocating in its tightly wound coils.

And what I'm sure about is he'd killed Carlos. That's why seeing me must have been like an avenging ghost materializing after having haunted him for decades

Although he came close, I'm very lucky he didn't manage to kill me. My thigh's wound is a cut, not a bite, and there was some rust in it as there is in my head wound. The neurosurgeon was blunt, told me if the head blow had been half an inch over, I'd be dead.

I hobbled over to the couch and John and Ana helped me get my leg propped high. Celia and Guillermo arrived shortly after and joined into the fussing over me.

Being a patient isn't easy for me but having Ana with me, keeping track of my healing, more than makes up for it.

'Sophia, did you dig out that enlargement of Carlos?' Guillermo asked.

He pointed out at the hospital last night that he hasn't seen the package of family photos Gran made for me to bring to La Paz and told her he wanted to today.

'I'll get it.' On her return, she passed it to him, and Celia moved closer to view those photos from Renee's boxes, too.

'Dios mio, Alex! You're the spitting image of your great-grandfather.'

'I guess in the giant's muted miner's light, you were his nightmare,' Celia said. 'The avenging angel finally coming for him - that poor ancient man must have been terrified.'

'Poor ancient giant? What about me?' I whined.

'Poor young Alex, too' she smiled at me before turning to Sophia. 'Do you think he's who murdered Carlos? I do.'

'Me, too,' she and John agreed together.

'I do,' Guillermo added and told us that he'd phoned his mother to tell her what has happened, hoping that Iona would know something about the massive man. 'All she remembers is hearing the myth about the mine's giant ghost years ago but never gave it any credence. Now, she is quite sure the giant is Matias.'

'Who's Matias?' John asked.

'Madre can't recall much about him, though he was there that Christmas we spent in La Paz with Renee. She told me he was Carlos's mother's nephew, so his first cousin. He'd fallen from a stool as a toddler and that had badly damaged his brain. Iona thinks that Christmas, he was about seventeen and abnormally big. She was nervous about him because Matias wanted to play with me and my toys but had no idea of his own strength.'

Celia added, 'I talked with Iona the day after Guillermo had and she'd remembered an incident where Matias had snuck up behind Renee and tried to pick up her long blond curls. She'd screamed and he'd been made to stay in his room for a couple of days. Iona pointed out that Carlos, apparently Matias' special friend, had yelled at him. As well, Renee had taken Carlos away from Matias, changed their relationship,

'I've been talking with Iona, too,' Gran said as she refilled our ice teas. 'She's sure Mother Superior Luisa-Grace knows about Matias.'

'Do you agree?' Ana asked her mother. 'How is Luisa-Grace doing after her setback?'

'I phoned yesterday and her eyes are improving again. She

is still unsure about when Guillermo and I can pick her up, hopes it will be next Saturday.'

'Tell them what she said about the giant,' Guillermo interrupted.

'I was about to,' his wife said wryly. 'After I told her about Alex's injuries, I asked the wily old dear, 'What do you know about the old giant and the humungous snake in the mine?'

'Well, what, Madre?' Ana prompted her mother.

'Patience, my daughter,' Celia said and we all laughed, aware that once a child, always a child.

Ana was sitting at the end of couch, having rearranged my injured leg on two cushions. I smiled at her, jubilant that she cares.

'She did what Mother Superior's do so very well,' Celia sighed. 'She made me wait for over a minute on the line before announcing yes, she did know some about the giant. She told me she has much to confess and wants all of us together to hear the story about Matias and her. Suggested we could come to the ranch when she flies into Cabo and she will tell us.

'Will that work for you, Celia?' Gran asked. 'I can't wait to meet this grand old authoritarian.'

She'll know much about Carlos, maybe even what he'd invented. I think she's about three years older than him so perhaps she'll know what he was inventing.'

'When might she be able to come home?' I asked.

'She has a visit with the ophthalmologist in three days, Alex, then will know if she can fly into San Josè Del Cabo a week from today.'

'By then, I will be out of these bandages and allowed to travel. Can finally get to the ranch'

'Me, too,' John gave Guillermo a thumbs up and added, 'Might even buy a stallion.'

'I'm looking forward to being there, too, though I don't intend to buy a horse,' Gran laughed as she rejoined us, carrying her MacBook, 'Now, an interesting email's just arrived from the Mexico City herpetologist.'

Gran had phoned Sammy while I was in surgery, and he'd immediately contacted the Mexico City professor who'd help arrange our Loreto project.

He had taken over and figured out how to get the snake and man out of the cave. He declared the snake was invaluable to the university as a lab specimen and with the cooperation of a number of Mexican authorities, arranged for the military to assist removing the two corpses from the mine to the university. Three days after attacking Alex, the old man and his snake were taken to the University of Mexico's pathology lab.

A La Paz Police constable had become the Baja's official representative in the complex process, and he'd invited Guillermo and John up to meet the herpetologist at the mine. The rescue and transfer of the coiled snake and man had become a Navy practice exercise.

After, John and Guillermo came to the hospital and described to Ana and me how the herpetologist arrived in a large Mexican Navy helicopter with eight sailors on board to facilitate the removal. It had taken over two hours for them to get the awkwardly shaped remains aboard, John told us.

'They had seen Sophia's photos and had been most concerned about transporting such bulk through the two tunnels. But what turned out to be their biggest challenge was that cage door. They had to cut the wall out.'

'And the helicopter had to be fumigated and the sailors' uniforms replaced,' he added.

Gran told us Dr. Martinez, the herpetologist, told her once the snake and timber were separated from the old man, he'd been blessed by a priest and given a private Catholic burial.

He also reported that he and Sammy had decided the snake reacted to the smell of Alex's blood. The giant's fingers had been found in its mouth and they had some residue, probably from when he moved me to the slab table from wherever he injured me. Then when he went near the snake, it reacted to the blood as it smelled like fresh food to him.'

'So, Gran,' I asked, trying to wiggle my splint and leg into a more comfortable position. 'Anything else in your email from Dr. Martinez?'

She grinned at me and read:

To short talk, Mrs. Nord, here is the preliminary report on the Burmese python: A female, length of 5.8 meters which is 19.3 feet. The machete in her right eye caused death. The debris found on the python's teeth and in its mouth included considerable flesh and a portion of human hand with the three fingers attached.

Gran stopped and sipped her ice tea. 'Next is the summary of the giant, labeled Pathology Report of the python's male victim.'

This very large man died from a python's coiling around his body. After the air was squeezed from his lungs, he suffocated.

He is in his ninth decade, though his organs are surprisingly healthy, do not show the usual deterioration experienced by that age.

His brain had sustained an early childhood injury causing permanent damage and would have prohibited normal development.

As well as being suffocated, he had suffered two snakebites: one into his upper interior thigh, which though acutely painful, would not have killed him immediately. The second bite removed some of his left hand's outer posterior flesh and all finger digits.

'That's it,' Gran said. 'Perhaps you want to frame a copy of this report, Alex? Surviving two Goliaths is a memorable event.'

I thanked her and declined.

CHAPTER FORTY-NINE
- Ana

Mother Superior Luisa-Grace was in her black robes, wearing a white wimple around her wrinkled and peaceful face, with a pirate patch covering her left eye. She and Sophia were sitting beside each other on a love seat, too far away for me to listen in to the intense conversation they appeared to be having.

I was across the big room, pretending to be dozing in Papa's big soft chair and amused to be watching Carlos' older sister and his daughter. They were as alike as two peas in a pod, even though one was aged and bent and the other still vibrant.

When Sophia, John and Alex had arrived from La Paz this morning, Luisa-Grace welcomed them enthusiastically, requested she and Sophia have a visit before she had to go for her nap before the family gathering later. Her one eye twinkled, 'I'll nap until about 4 pm so let's meet in the great hall then and I will share Matias' history?' She'd added we'd need something to drink as it was a complex and lengthy story. 'And sad for more than only Matias as I will include some of the details about our La Paz Hernández' downhill saga.'

It was over an hour before we were to gather so I snuggled deeper in my chair, enjoying its slight whiff of Papa's pipe, and thinking about all my hours in this special room.

Madre has redecorated it since my previous visit home and I like its new rattan furniture with sage, brick and bright pumpkin orange cushions. The ambience somehow suits my three sculptures Madre is currently displaying, along with two of Uncle's. She is the keeper of most of my sculptures I am not ready to sell and changes what's she's displaying quite often.

Alex hobbled in on his crutches and peered down at me,

trying to decide if I was asleep or pretending. He grinned when I whispered, 'Don't those two look as much alike as you do to Carlos?'

He nodded, motioned towards the porch and we went outside.

'She's a gift for Gran. And I find it eerie to see how Gran will look in fifteen years.'

'Emphasizes how young seventy is, doesn't it? Alex, would you like to go up to Uncle's studio? I'll get the side-by-side ATV and promise to drive very slowly.'

'A slow ride will be appreciated, I'm sore from the drive down.'

'I'll be back with your chariot,' and jogged up the hill to the long garage with all the ranch's work vehicles.

As usual, the surrounding sounds affirmed I was home. I could hear the blacksmith pounding in the smithy, the chorus of moos from the cattle on the hillside, a cowboy in the nearest barn enthusiastically singing off-key and two little children bellowing at each other over something.

Although Abuela's home in Boston is mine, too, it's secondary compared with here. This is where my roots are.

I angled the ATV slowly down the hill and tried to see our hacienda through Sophia's eyes. She'd been charmed when they arrived and declared she wanted photos of everything. She'd requested my folks' permission and pleased Madre by asking if she would pose by the bougainvillea beside her new gazebo.

Over lunch, what we'd mainly talked about was how interesting the three of them had found our miles of fields on their slow drive into the ranch. John had found it similar to his and Winston's ranches but added, 'Your cacti is much more interesting than our sage.'

Guillermo laughed, 'And we don't want that weed. Apparently our combination of cacti is unusual as within one area we have the spiky round barrels, spreading ocotillo and majestic cardons. And did you notice that wherever there is some water, groves of palms are growing?

He'd explained the ranch's total land base was now over double what its 1905 original acreage was and offered, 'Want to go riding after lunch, John? I want to show you the horse herds.'

John had immediately agreed and Papa grinned, said he had a special young stallion for him to ride.

As I told Gran and Alex later, he was certainly honouring John because Papa doesn't let anyone ride his second horse except Guill.

When I pulled the ATV up to the porch, Alex maneuvered the three steps, put his crutches in the back box and swung in beside me, firmly declining my offer to get him a cushion.

I took the smoothest path up the hill that I could find and parked close to Uncle's home's front door. It faces uphill, away from the ranch, its view all horizon and sky. What Uncle saw from his studio was such a contrast to what he saw from his other windows, all overlooking the ranch.

He and Papa had designed and built this place when Uncle turned sixty. And according to Madre, the year after Abuela had passed all the ranch's management over to my parents and moved to Boston. She'd enrolled in art school, resuming what she'd been doing when she married my grandfather and had then decided to buy a house in Boston.

Uncle's house isn't large but it's full of light and its high wood block ceiling is unique as are the stark white naked walls. What dominates his room is his many intricate sculptures. They are displayed on various pedestals and shelves, most with room to walk around and view from various angles. And there are also three of mine, much larger than all Uncles sculptures. Two tall, odd people are resting on the floor and a third, my first one, is on a table in front of the window wall.

As we entered, the sun was coming in from the west and highlighting his and my work.

'Wow,' Alex said softly.

'Dramatic, isn't it? Uncle had massive talent. I'm amazed each time by how many techniques he excelled at, Alex. Look how he integrated welded wire into his most of work.'

Alex nodded and moved carefully about on his crutches, studied each piece. He stood in front of my three and I came over as he studied them. 'Ana, now I know how you could create Phoenix. Uncle's work and yours mesmerized me. Look at the light bouncing off that one.'

I murmured my thanks.

'My love, do you know how awed I am by your work?' he continued softly. 'And I do understand how much of your energy and strength goes into bringing your creative concepts to life. I appreciate that and always will.'

'Do you really understand how much of me sculpting takes, Alex?'

'Yes, my little darling, I do.' He dropped his crutches, opened his arms and I stepped in, nestled against his hard body.

'Ana, I need you to know whenever you're ready to let me share your world, I'll be waiting. When I came out of that fog after surgery and found you asleep on my bed, I knew. I want to be yours. What I offer is forever.'

We held each other in that sunlight for a long time and I felt a different peace than I've ever known before. I searched for words and whispered, 'Okay, me, too I want you, Alex.'

At five, there were seven of us gathered in the living room around the Mother Superior. She was sitting on a carved wood, high-backed armchair, bolstered by many cushions, her tiny black boots resting on a padded footstool.

Gran and John were on the love seat across from her, Madre, Papa and Guill, my brother who is so like Papa, were on the long couch. His wife and children, my dear little niece and nephew, are away for two weeks and he confided to me how lost he feels without them.

I was in the soft chair again and Alex was on a hard dining room chair beside me, his cast resting on a stack of cushions and his hand near mine on my chair's wide arm. His fingers brushed against my skin and heat waves flooded within me. He smiled and discreetly winked.

The Mother Superior raised her hands and gave us her murmured blessings before asking, 'Is everyone comfortable and ready? Because Matias' story is long and very convoluted. Please do interrupt, ask me questions as you think of them, or stop me when you need a break.'

'We will,' Celia assured her. 'But, my dear, if you become weary, we can continue tomorrow.'

'Thank you but I hope I can finish now. To start, I'll tell you about my and Matias' relationship. Know that I have regrets about it and wish I could have made our poor relative's life easier, provided more comforts and companionship for him. Though also know, that in many ways, I think Matias' years suited him, gave him a freedom and an unusual companion that a care home certainly couldn't have provided.'

Her voice's strength and her choice of words have such cohesiveness for someone who is ninety-five, I thought and hoped I have many of her genes.

'So how did it evolve that Matias ended up spending many years living with a giant snake in an abandoned mine?' she asked, summarizing for us and proceeding to answer, giving us both the how's and the why's.

Our first shock was learning that Professor Morgan was Matias' father. But when Luisa-Grace explained how Carlos' mother's youngest sister had gone to London as a student, met Ryker Morgan and married him, it all started to make sense to me.

The Professor became part of a Mexican family who gave him the rights and caring they provided to each member of their extended family. Carlos had been so much more than Morgan's student, he was also his responsibility, his nephew-by-marriage.

After the Morgan's had Matias in London, they started bringing him to La Paz each summer. The child charmed all of us and became ten-year-old Carlos's special little friend.

'When Matias was almost four,' Luisa-Grace's voice

slowed, 'the cherished lad climbed up on a stool and fell down nearby stairs. After a year of London doctors and hospitals, the diagnosis was he couldn't fully recover and the devastated family moved permanently to La Paz.'

She paused, gave us time to absorb what a tragedy had happened. 'The professor was only there for summers as he continued to teach in London, so Madre invited Matias and his mother to live with our family.'

She paused to sip her glass of water. 'Carlos, little Marie and myself treated our cousin as if our baby. When Matias was seven, his mother died and his father came less often from London, though remained part of the family. Then Carlos was sent to London to school and the professor began mentoring him, and started coming to La Paz for the summers again to be with Matias. That pleased Madre until he married and brought that crazy English missionary woman.'

Sophia's sigh echoed throughout the big room and John took her hand.

'Yes, Renee's missionary,' Luisa-Grace said to her. 'I was a novitiate by then and never met her, but Madre wrote me over the following years about her schemes. I can tell you the one that amused her the most was her plan to build a home for unwed mothers in La Paz.

'Now, I'm jumping us forward to when Matias killed Carlos. By then, I was a nursing sister in Rome, and it took months after the murder before I even heard about it, as the international mail system had collapsed.'

She pondered for a moment. 'This is difficult. What Papa's letter told me as compared to what I suspected years later are very different.'

'In what way?' Madre asked.

'He wrote that Carlos had been murdered by an unknown man but when I was eventually able to have a visit with him, I suspected that my father knew it was Matias who had killed Carlos. I am equally sure that Madre, Marie and Renee never knew that.'

'That does make sense,' I said slowly. 'Matias had full

access to Carlos' bedroom and of course the dogs wouldn't
have barked.'

'Yes, Ana, but it wasn't until 1948, when the Church's
authorities sent me back to La Paz to serve as the senior
nursing sister for the Abby's nuns, that I learned that.'

'By then, Madre and Marie had been dead for years and
strangers had bought our big home. Papa had remarried and
moved to Mexico City. He wrote and requested I be allowed
to meet with him on his next trip, citing to the priest
supervising the nuns, 'important family matters.' And I finally
had a long visit with my father.'

Luisa-Grace sipped again, sat up straighter and smiled at
us. 'I am going to share a little aside about me, and my beliefs
as they were partly why I could do so little for Matias. In my
youth, I thought serving God meant signing on for a life of service but I didn't know that meant many years where priests had
control of all my hours. Now, in my precious old age, I'm fully
in charge of all my hours without consultation. And it is a joy.'

Gran snorted to hide her laughter behind her hands.

'Back to our poor giant, the one thing I've forgotten to tell
you is he apparently grew that large by something stimulated
inside his brain by his childhood accident. Plus, Professor
Morgan was a very large man.'

She returned to summarizing her visit with her father. He
had arranged with the priest that she could now be responsible
for Matias as a duty she owed her mother, though he would
supply some funds annually.

'To my surprise, I learned Matias was already working in
the market gardens attached to my cathedral community and
had been since Carlos' death.'

'I had actually seen the poor monstrous man before that
but had not realized he was my cousin. He lived in one of the
garden sheds and was supervised by the friar he worked for,
a gentle and generous man. I began visiting them monthly
and learned how valued the two of them were for the
amazing amount of work they did. And that Matias' pet
snake was allowed to be nearby in a canvas bag.

'Snake?' Papa asked. 'Not the snake?'

'No, Guillermo, he had that one for quite a few years, then it was killed by a dog. Matias became so morose that the good friar went to the market and bought him another one. I think Matias had three or four snakes as his companions in his shed over the years.'

'Did he know you were his relative?' my brother asked.

'No, though he would smile at me, which changed his quite ferocious expression immensely,' she replied. 'I grew to know Matias as much as anyone could. He'd developed a lisp, was difficult to understand and was only comfortable with the friar.

She explained that in the massive complex around the cathedral, there was enough support and food for him and he was okay. 'So when I was sent to open a medical mission down in Chiapas, then in Veracruz, he continued to garden, supervised by the aging friar and lived with a snake.'

On her return, she learned that the friar was ill and everything was about to change for Matias. The new priest-administrator was about to contract out the market gardens and the shed Matias lived in for decades was to be ripped down.'

Madre asked how Matias ended up in the mine, aware Luisa-Grace's voice was giving out.

'Indirectly, Matias ended up there because of Uncle.'

'Really?' Papa sounded more than surprised.

'Through Iona, I managed to contact her and she told Uncle I needed help with Matias. He came to La Paz and took over, arranged for him to be cared for and work for a farming couple in El Triunfo. Matias had a new little shed at the bottom of the large garden and still had a pet snake.'

Sophia asked, 'Do you know what year Matias moved? Are you getting too weary? We could finish in themorning.'

'It was 1987 and I am almost done. Tomorrow, I want to talk about happy things, hear all about your photographic career and have Ana tell me about her grand sculpting.'

'Sounds wonderful,' Sophia and I said in unison, and Alex patted my shoulder.

Luisa-Grace became brisk as she continued, told us how

they moved Matias. 'But it didn't work out as we'd expected. Apparently, Matias and his snake feared the people's many dogs and he started taking his snake up to the mine. Within weeks, he moved into one of the stone sheds there. Uncle arranged for the family to take him wood and basic supplies, beans, rice, dried goat and firewood for his cooking stove, and set up the ongoing financial payments to them. He sent a note to me about twelve years ago that the food they delivered was always gone, but Matias had moved down into the mine because of a cold winter and they never saw him. And that he had arranged for ongoing funding for the El Triunfo family. I have to admit I never even wondered about Matias after that.'

'How could he have fed that gigantic snake?' Guill asked.

'Apparently when he first moved to the family's shed, one of the sons taught Matias how to snare and there were always many rabbits, so he had fresh meat for himself and his snake.'

'So he lived independently for the rest of his life,' John summarized, standing up to stretch his back against a wall. 'As you say, he had freedom.'

Luisa-Grace smiled at John. 'Exactly. And a companion.'

Alex picked up his crutches and went over to her. 'That poor old man, he might have had many years left if I hadn't strolled down those tracks.'

The Mother-Superior slid out of her chair and gave Alex a hug. 'God is in charge, not us. Matias has now gone to his rest and I have the privilege of hugging my dear Carlos' grandson and meeting my brother's daughter.' She waved at Sophia to come over.

'Hold my hands and let's send our blessings to Renee. Although in my opinion, she didn't treat you fairly, Sophia, but through her bequest, she is the catalyst who has brought us together, enabled a reunion of the La Paz Hernández family.'

I watched Madre join them, put her arm around the little nun's shoulder and take charge.

'Thank you, Luisa-Grace, you've answered many of our questions. Now it's time for your eyedrops. And perhaps a nap before dinner?'

CHAPTER FIFTY
- Sophia

We returned to La Paz the next day around Alex's doctor's appointments and I had been pleased to see he and Ana snuggled together in the back seat.

Now after an amazing day, John and I had tucked in early.

'A grand evening,' I murmured as I snuggled into his hairy back, enjoying how the hairs tickled my cheek. 'Are you as content as I am, John?

'I am, m'dear. And glad we'll be going back to the ranch for a week before going home.'

'Me, too.'

''Though I have been lying here thinking about why Matias murdered Carlos. Why?'

'We'll never know but I've wondered if when Renee screamed over him touching her hair, he decided she was an evil angel? He might have thought he was protecting Carlos?'

'From Renee?'

'No, from evil, John, perhaps he'd decided that Renee was an evil angel. Who knows what his realities were? But we assume that his seeing Alex and thinking he was seeing Carlos terrified him and he struck, needing to again kill the avenging angel. Remember, he was raised in an atmosphere of good or evil, devils and angels.'

'Really, Soph?'

'Perhaps, John,' aware I was as unsure as him. What I was sure about was it was over. Alex is healing and I know how my father died.'

'What about Renee?

'She did what she thought was best for me. Who knows? Perhaps in those times, she was right. My grandparents gave me a loving and stable home and their lie became the reality.' I mused aloud as I massaged his lumbar area, knowing he's never without pain, but like all old cowboys, manages his aches without complaining. 'But, damn, John, how I wish she could have admitted she was my mother and shared her stories with me.'

'Well, you know some of it now,' he murmured soothingly. 'Is that enough?'

Suddenly, I knew what's enough. It's time for us, time for me to stop thinking and saying, I have a home at Erin Lake and John has a ranch. Our reality is he and I have two homes and we'll switch back and forth between them as convenient.

I started to ask if that would suit him and heard his snoring begin. I snuggled closer and thought, tomorrow.

I drifted and watched the moon rays reflecting on the sheers across the open door to our private deck and hoped they were also illuminating Ana's and Alex's bed. They were at the apartment she'd sublet, expecting to use it this winter and her studio at the ranch.

When they'd returned from the doctor, they'd told John and me they would be marrying down the way. We were delighted.

And when we took them out to dinner to celebrate, they proudly filled us in on how it would all work out. They plan to fly back and forth between Vancouver and La Paz regularly and wherever they are, Alex will be working on his doctorate as Ana sculpts.

I pulled the quilt up and laughed to myself, glad to be feeling happy for him again.

When we'd left the cafe, Alex had given me a long hug and whispered, 'She wants me, Gran, and I don't have any doubts, I want her. Oh, do I want her.' He winked and limped after Ana.

I rolled over and started stroking John's back, thinking Ana's a lucky woman. I'm pretty sure my grandson inherited my sensual Latin genes.

The End

Lynne Nicol
for her fiction books

Lynne Stonier-Newman
for her non-fiction books

Author's Note:

Latin Legacy is my first book to be published under my birth name, Lynne Nicol. Why did I switch? Stonier-Newman is too long for a mystery cover. From now on, I will use Lynne Nicol for my future fictional books and continue to use Lynne Stonier-Newman for my non-fiction writings and history books.

Published under Lynne Stonier-Newman:
BC history: PETER O'REILLY - The Rise of a Reluctant Immigrant;
THE LAWMAN - Adventures of a Frontier Diplomat;
POLICING A PIONEER PROVINCE - The BC Provincial Police 1858 - 1850 (UBC Non fiction book of 1991 runner-up)

Audiobook: The Whys of Women. Poetry and short fiction stories; Canadian-Eh?; A Smorgasbord of Short Stories and Poems.

www.ingramcontent.com/pod-product-compliance
Lightning Source LLC
Chambersburg PA
CBHW032117310726

48972CB00001B/257